Praise for MATTHEW HUGHES

"A tremendous amount of fun."

George R R Martin

"An actuary's dull life is interrupted when he accidently summons a demon. The premise is bold, thought-provoking, and original. [Hughes] utilizes strong imagery, detailed descriptions, and a relatable protagonist to show human nature in the hottest spotlight."

Tangent Online

"Matt Hughes's boldness is admirable."

The New York Review of Science Fiction

"Hughes continues to carve out a unique place for himself in the fantasy-mystery realm. A droll narrative voice, dry humor and an alternate universe that's accessible without explicit exposition make this a winner."

Publishers Weekly

"Matthew Hughes is the best-kept secret in science fiction."

Robert J Sawyer

"If you're an admirer of the science fantasies of Jack Vance, it's hard not to feel affection for the Archonate stories of Matthew Hughes... Hughes has strengths of his own to draw upon: his own considerable wit, and a flair for reified metaphysics surpassing anything conceived by Vance."

Nick Gevers, Locus

BY THE SAME AUTHOR

Tales of Henghis Hapthorn
The Spiral Labyrinth
Hespira

Fools Errant
Downshift
Fool Me Twice
Black Brillion
Wolverine: Lifeblood (as Hugh Matthews)
The Commons
Template
The Other

MATTHEW HUGHES

TO HELL AND BACK
The Damned Busters

**ANGRY
ROBOT**

ANGRY ROBOT

A member of the Osprey Group
Midland House, West Way
Botley, Oxford
OX2 0HP
UK

www.angryrobotbooks.com
Holy industrial action!

An Angry Robot paperback original 2011
1

A catalogue record for this book is available
from the British Library.

UK ISBN: 978-0-85766-102-9
EBook ISBN: 978-0-85766-104-3

Set in Meridien by THL Design.

Printed in the UK by CPI Mackays, Chatham, ME5 8TD.

To Pete and Coralyn Steel,
and Lou Anders,
for making it possible.

ONE

The demon's sudden appearance, along with a puff of malodorous smoke and a short-lived burst of flame, took Chesney Arnstruther by surprise.

He recovered quickly, however. The existence of demons had been thoroughly covered during his youthful education, which from the ages of five through fourteen, had included three hours of Sunday school – taught without pussyfooting by his mother, a leading member of the congregation. The minions of Hell had also often figured in the sermons of the Reverend Erwin P. Baumgarten, their pastor, who had fallen under the spell of the Book of Revelation even before he had attended Rock of Ages Bible College.

In adolescence, Chesney had drifted away from old-time religion. His was a rigorously logical mind that could not abide the contradictions and absurdities in scripture. He found a more reliable truth in the elegant architectures of mathematics.

But though he had long since given up thinking about demons, he was still able to recognize one when it flashed into existence right before his eyes. The brief pyrotechnics attendant on the fiend's sudden manifestation scorched the top of the young man's almost-finished poker table, so that his first reaction was a surge of indignation at the ruination of the green felt surface, which he had almost finished tacking into place.

Chesney said, "Get the blue bling blithers off my table!"

The demon, which resembled a huge toad that had been tinkered with to give it oversized, clawed hands, spread its lipless mouth to reveal a smile full of dagger-like fangs. "You invite me to depart the pentagram?" it said, in a voice like bones cracking.

"What?" said Chesney. An instinct for self-preservation now reasserted itself, overcoming the shock of the fiend's arrival and the still-throbbing pain from his hammered thumb. "No, I'm not inviting you to anything, except to go back where you came from!"

"To hear is to obey," said the demon. "Just sign here and here, initial there." It had produced a roll of parchment and used the tip of a claw to mark three places with an X.

The young man glanced at the document. His first thought was that its author must have learned penmanship from a seismograph; the letters were all spiky, scrawled across the page with ferocious violence. His second thought, when he managed to decipher some of the content, he expressed out loud: "No way I'm signing that! You'd get my soul!"

"That is the standard arrangement. You summon one of us, we do your bidding, you render up your insignificance."

"My what?"

"It's the technical term, where I come from."

"I don't care if it's the word of the week," said Chesney. "My soul is not an insignificance to me. I'm not signing."

"Then I can't do your bidding."

"I don't have any bidding for you to do. I just want you to go back to 'where you come from.'"

"That sounds like bidding to me," said the demon.

"Well, it's not," said Chesney, sucking away the blood that was still welling from beneath the nail of his left thumb and gesturing with the hammer he held in his right hand. "It's a rejection of the entire concept of bidding. Especially if the bidding costs me my soul."

The demon looked annoyed. Chesney did not find it a happy sight, but he stood his ground. "Now, go away."

"I can't," said the toad. "You summoned me. I'm here until I've done whatever it is you need doing. Even if it takes overtime – for which, you ought to know, I get nothing extra – so sign the agreement and let's get to work." A ripple passed over its warty skin. "It's cold up here."

"I didn't summon you," said Chesney. "It's some kind of mistake."

The demon slitted its yellow eyes. "All right," it said, "let's go over this. This is your pentagram I'm standing on, right? And" – its nostril slits widened as it took a deep sniff – "that's your blood there, deposited by your hand sinister? And you did say, *'Hodey-odey shalaam-a-shamash woh-wanga kee-yai'* didn't you?"

"Oh," said Chesney, "now I get it. I can explain."

It all began with Letitia Arnstruther, Chesney's mother who raised him singlehandedly from an early age after Wagner Arnstruther, his father, departed for parts unknown with a waitress he met at a truck stop. A devout woman, Letitia could not abide rough manners, and she especially frowned on coarse language, in both of which her husband abounded. Indeed, her son had often wondered – though he'd never had the courage to ask – what strange concatenation of events must have occurred to unite his parents, even temporarily, in matrimony. He did not wonder why his mother made no attempt to find

Wagner Arnstruther and invite him to repair their broken home.

Yet one thing was clear to him as he grew from childhood to manhood: even the mildest profanity would net him cold looks, even colder suppers, and downright chilly silences, the punishment sometimes stretching through an entire week and beyond. Therefore, as a defense, whenever Chesney felt the need to express himself in strong language, he taught himself to substitute strings of nonsense syllables. The habit, deeply ingrained at an early age, had endured long after he left home – and the Reverend Baumgarten's congregation – to attend college in another state.

It was in college that Chesney fell in love with numbers. He was especially enamored of the sheer decorum of the interrelationships that numbers can form with each other; they became his fascination. Though he lacked the creativity to pursue a career as a theoretical mathematician, and the inclination to teach high school math, his degree led to his taking a position as a junior actuary at Paxton Life and Casualty, a mid-sized Midwest insurance company. He spent his days calculating the risk of death or injuries for tiny slices numerically carved from the US demographic spectrum. His evenings were mostly given over to his second love, also discovered after departing from his mother's sphere of influence: comix and graphic novels, especially those that featured oddly talented individuals who fought crime on a freelance basis.

A life of crunching numbers suited Chesney's unusual personality, which had been studied by experts from the age of four through ten. He was severely introverted, but that was not uncommon among actuaries, who were not expected to be the life of any party. Most of the men in his department – and it seemed that the actuary profession attracted *only* men – had grown up almost as friendless as he had. Five of them, however, had made it a habit to get together at each other's homes to play small-stakes poker every other Saturday evening. Chesney was asked to join when one of the five had dropped out because he was leaving town, and it turned out no one else in the department was willing to spend time with the remaining four.

Poker became another of Chesney's limited set of loves. Oddly, though, he did not apply to the game the same standards of logic and mathematical rigor that governed other sectors of his life. Chesney never applied his math skills when he played poker. He bet high on weak cards and stayed in for pots he had no realistic chance of taking; for him, winning wasn't the point – what counted was the sense of being in the game, the heady rush of risk and possibility that he couldn't get if he folded early. This characteristic endeared him to the other players, all of whom played strictly by the numbers and who thus regularly went home as the beneficiaries of a transfer of wealth from Chesney's wallet to theirs.

The game's venue rotated among the players, and after a couple of months, Chesney was told that he was expected to host the next get-together. He went home and examined his premises with an unhappy eye. He had a cramped studio condo in a downtown high-rise, with a Murphy bed that pulled down from the wall. The place had a kitchen nook, the wall between it and the rest of the single room being pierced by a pass-through that had a countertop and two stools. Otherwise, Chesney's domestic arrangements consisted of a couch fronted by a coffee table, and a chair and matching table made of extruded plastic out on the postage stamp-sized balcony.

There was nowhere to sit and play poker, even if two of the five sat on the end of the Murphy bed. Chesney went trolling through furniture store sites on the internet, and soon settled on five folding chairs that could be stacked in the downstairs storage space when not in use. But for a decent-sized poker table, he sought in vain. They were all, apparently, made to accommodate seven players, and the designers must have assumed that most of those players would be of significant girth. There was no way Chesney could fit such a table and chairs into his small living space, even with the bed up, without hauling the couch and coffee table down to the locker.

That seemed a burdensome chore. Instead, he rallied his minor skills as a craftsman – he had taken one term of woodwork shop in high school – and resolved to make his own playing surface. It would have only five sides, there being only five in the group, and with some judicious trimming it would seat them all comfortably.

Chesney had asked the lumber yard to cut the three-quarter-inch plywood top to size and had bought ready-made legs from the store's do-it-yourself department. Along with a drill, a multi-tip screwdriver, a sheet of green felt and a box of tacks, he felt ready to tackle the project. He already had a hammer, having found one when he moved into the apartment.

"So you see," he told the demon, "I was tapping in a tack. I hit my thumb hard enough to make it bleed. I shook my hand and some blood hit the table. At the same time, I swore – the way *I* swear – and the next moment, there you were." He paused to suck the last droplets of blood from his thumb. "It was just a mistake."

The demon gave him a look that was almost as cold as one of his mother's worst. "You expect me to go back and tell that to my supervisor?"

"It's the truth."

"Where I come from, truth is not a highly prized commodity."

"Well, I don't know what else I can tell you," Chesney said. "I didn't summon you."

"Yes, you did. Or I wouldn't be here."

Chesney tried to explain. "It's like when a tree falls in the forest—"

"Yeah, because somebody chopped it down."

"Let me finish. If it falls and nobody hears it, it doesn't make a sound."

The demon twisted its face in incomprehension. It was quite a twist. "The guy who chopped it down is deaf?"

"Never mind. That's not the right example, anyway." He thought for a moment then said, "It has to be with intent. I may have inadvertently said the words that summoned you, but I was not summoning you when I said them. The mere sounds don't matter. There has to be the intent behind them."

"Intent?" said the demon. "That's your angle?"

"It's not an angle. It's an explanation." He sought for a different word and one appeared in his mind. "No, intent is the wrong word. It's about *will*. I did not will you to come, therefore I'm not bound to accept the offer."

"So you're definitely not signing the agreement?"

"Definitely."

The demon spread huge hands like a giant, toothy toad that intends to take no responsibility for whatever comes next. "Okay," it said. "But let me tell you, this is not over."

And with a second puff of stinking, yellowy smoke and a sharp lick of red flame, it was gone.

"So what are you, some kind of wise guy?"

The question broke Chesney's immersion in the graphic novel – *Champions of Justice* – he had been reading. It hadn't been just the question, though; there had also been the sudden whiff of sulfur and the gravelly quality of the voice, which sounded as if it had come out of the mouth of a tyrannosaurus with laryngitis. He looked up to see, standing on the other end of the bench in the downtown minipark where he ate his lunch on sunny days, another demon.

This one had the head of a weasel that had been refitted to sport a pair of canine fangs of sabertooth caliber, and coal-black eyes the size of saucers. It was about the height of a small boy, but its body was a miniature version of a pot-bellied, heavy-shouldered thug in a pinstriped suit with wide lapels and a ridiculously small tie. It wore two-toned shoes of patent leather with the insteps covered by pieces of strapped-on cloth – *spats*, Chesney thought they were called, though he'd never seen them in real life, and only on the Penguin in *Batman* comix – and its stubby, hairy-backed fingers flourished a half-smoked cigar as it waited for an answer to its question.

"I beg your pardon?"

"We don't do pardons, mack," said the apparition. "That's the other outfit's racket."

"The other outfit?"

The demon poked one thumb upwards. Chesney noticed that its thumbnail was chewed down to the quick.

"Ah," he said, nodding. "I assume you're here about the mistake?"

"We also don't make no mistakes. So we need to clear this little thing up, see? Real quick-like. Twenty-three skidoo."

"Why do you talk like that?" Chesney said.

"Like what? Last time I was up this way all youse mugs talked like this."

"We've moved on. So should you. I'm not interested."

The demon moved closer, put one hand on Chesney's shoulder. He could feel the heat of it through his suit jacket and shirt. "We can make you a real sweet deal, pal."

"No."

"You ain't heard the offer yet. It's a doozie."

"You mean, 'an offer I can't refuse?'"

The demon's weasel lips drew back in what Chesney's hoped was a smile. "Hey, I like that," it said. "I can use that."

"Leave me alone or I'll call..." He had been going to say, "a cop," but he saw from the creature's expression that the threat carried no weight, so he switched the ending to, "a priest."

The humped shoulders shrugged. "That don't cut no mustard with me, mack. I'll just ankle outta here and come back when you're alone."

Chesney sighed. "All right make your offer, but the answer's still going to be no."

But even before he could get the last words out, the park disappeared and he was standing in a room about the size of his condo, the walls lined with metal doors of various sizes, each with a number and a slot for a key. "Where am I?" he said.

"Swiss bank," said the demon. "Get a load of this." It tapped one of the large doors down at floor level, and the panel popped silently open. A metal box slid out onto the floor, and the demon flipped up its hinged top. Inside were bound stacks of high-denomination bills, leather jewelry cases and at least two full-sized ingots of pure gold.

"All mine, I suppose?" said Chesney.

"And that's just for starters."

"Won't the owner mind?"

"Where he's going, they don't take cash."

"No, thanks."

The huge weasel eyes narrowed. "Okey-doke. Then how 'bout this?"

They were in a dimly lit room. After a moment's disorientation, Chesney realized it was a bedroom – no, he corrected himself, a boudoir. The demon did something and the sourceless light strengthened. The room was big; it would have had to be to accommodate the vast, circular bed, strewn with silk covered pillows and red satin sheets, on which reposed a buxom blonde, her eyes closed and lips parted in blissful slumber. She was not wearing much, and what little she did have on did nothing to detract from the strong impression she created. Chesney's lifetime exposure to unbridled pulchritude – outside of rented porn – was less than scant; he found himself staring, and had to drag his gaze away.

"Whadda ya say now?" said the demon, its weaselish eyebrows bobbing suggestively.

"No," said Chesney, though the single syllable seemed to catch on something in the back of his throat.

"Oh, picky, huh?"

The blonde was replaced by an even more buxom brunette. She stretched in her sleep, rearranging and simultaneously revealing elements of her anatomy in a way that caused the actuary to emit a small, involuntary sound. But then he said, "No."

"We got a full selection," said the demon and Chesney was looking at a redhead who would have stopped Titian dead on the bridges of Renaissance Venice.

"No!"

The demon cocked its weasel head at him and moved a finger. The redhead was replaced by a muscular young man whose nudity revealed prodigious personal qualities.

"Certainly not!" said Chesney. "You're wasting your time." He glanced at his watch. "And mine."

"Keep your hair on," said the demon. "I'll get a bead on you yet." Immediately, the boudoir was gone and they were standing in an office that struck Chesney as somehow familiar. Then he saw the seal woven into the rug and registered the room's oval shape. "Howzabout it?" said the weasel boy.

"You've got to be kidding," Chesney said.

"You'd be surprised."

"Who? Which one?"

"*Ones*," said the demon. "But I ain't saying nothing more. We don't rat."

"Take me back."

The demon studied him. "Look, mack," it said, "we've done moolah, molls and moxie. What else is there?" His brows drew down and his huge eyes narrowed. The cigar stub poked at Chesney. "Say, you ain't one of then eggheads who wanna *know* everything? Like, you really *are* some kinda wise guy?"

"No."

"I mean, we make that happen for you. It's just, you don't see it too often, you know?"

"I don't want anything. Just leave me alone." He blinked and found them both back on the park bench. The demon brought its outsized eyes closer to Chesney and in the center of each black circle he saw a small red flame kindle and grow.

"Listen, bud, you wanna take the deal," it said. "You're making a lotta trouble for a lotta guys you don't wanna make no trouble for."

Chesney stuck out his small chin. "I'm not making trouble for anybody," he said. "This is your mistake."

The demon growled and it cocked one stubby fist while saying, "Smart guy, why I oughta..." But when the man on the bench did not flinch, the creature clasped its hands together and put on as conciliatory expression as a be-fanged weasel could contrive. "Listen, mack," it said, "I'm just a yob doing a job. I got a dozen demons to supervise and we're busy, see? Everybody's working double shifts and we don't got no time to monkey around. So, take the deal or take the consequences."

"You don't get it," said Chesney.

"What? What is it I don't get?"

Chesney interlaced his fingers over his small pot belly, thought for a moment, then said, "It never really made sense to me, the whole Heaven or Hell thing." – the demon winced and said, "Hey, lay off the H-word," – but the man continued, "Numbers made sense. But now you show up and make it abundantly clear that the game is played pretty much the way Pastor Baumgarten preached to us, all those Sundays I was growing up."

"Ah, you don't want to listen to those holy Joes," said the fiend.

"Yeah, I think I do. You see, I make a deal with you, I get a few years of fun down here, assuming the fine print doesn't let you renege early. Then, bang, I'm spending eternity dining on hot coals. The alternative is I turn you down now and wind up with forever in paradise." Chesney spread his hands. "I mean, do the math. It's a no-brainer."

"Most people we deal with, they don't see it that way," the demon said.

"I'm an actuary. It's my job to play the percentages."

Now the demon actually looked worried. "Listen," it said, "you don't know the whole score. I'm trying to keep a lid on this thing, but you don't play ball, she could blow. I mean, sky-high, you get me?"

"No," said Chesney. "And *you* won't be getting *me*. What did they used to say, last time you were here? 'Take a powder?' 'Amscray?' 'Agitate the gravel?' Take your pick."

He went back to *Champions of Justice*. When he heard the clap of air as the fiend disappeared, he glanced at his watch and was pleased to see that no real time had elapsed. He wanted to finish the current chapter before his lunch break was up. It featured his favorite comix hero, a mild-mannered, bespectacled UPS courier who battled drug cartels and international terrorists in the bowels of a dysfunctional metropolis. The brown-clad crime fighter was about to turn the tables on a cabal of ninja-trained mujahideen. "Go, Driver, go," Chesney breathed.

It was Saturday and he was getting ready for tonight's poker game. He had bought taco chips and salsa and more beer than the little refrigerator could hold. The table was set up and looked great, once he cleaned off the blood with a little club soda. Chesney went downstairs to the storage locker and came back with his arms clasped around the five folding chairs. Nudging open the apartment door that he had left ajar, he was surprised to see a little blonde girl in a pinafore and white ankle socks standing beside the table.

"Are you lost?" he said.

"I just got one question," said the little girl. Actually, Chesney realized there could be some debate as to exactly who was doing the talking, since the voice asking the question came not from the girl but from the fanged mouth of the ruby-red snake that uncoiled itself where a tongue would have been if this had really been a little blonde girl instead of another demon.

He put down the chairs. "What?"

"Just tell me, are you ready to go all the way on this?" said the snake, in a voice that would have suited a little girl, provided she was also a fiend from Hell.

"Yes, I am," Chesney said. "I didn't give much thought to my soul before you guys started demanding it. Now I figure it's worth hanging onto."

The snake went back where it came from and the demon crossed its arms and looked up at him in a way that let the man know he was being weighed up. Chesney noticed that pinned to one of the pinafore's straps was a large button with a design on it: a pair of crossed pitchforks against a background of leaping flames. Underneath were the letters *IBFDT*.

"What's the button?" Chesney said, but the demon didn't answer. It finished its examination of him, then nodded as if in confirmation of something it had been mentally chewing on for quite a while, and disappeared. When nothing further happened, Chesney unfolded the chairs and put them around the table. He had just finished positioning the last seat when the phone rang.

"It's Clay," said the voice on the other end. Clay was not the best poker player of the five but he was the one who made the least secret of how much he enjoyed raking in a pot after Chesney had stayed in far too long.

"We're all set here," Chesney told him.

"I'm not playing tonight," Clay said.

"Why not?"

"I dunno, I was getting ready to come, but suddenly I just don't feel the urge."

"We need you," Chesney said. "Four's not enough."

But Clay said, "Sorry," – although he didn't sound it – and hung up.

Chesney folded up one of the chairs and leaned it against the wall. The phone rang again; it was Ron, the one who had originally invited Chesney into the game. "I'm not coming," he said.

Like Clay, he wasn't sick or jammed up in any way. "You don't feel the urge?" Chesney asked.

"Yeah. I don't feel much like doing anything."

Chesney folded another chair. He'd never played three-handed poker, but he doubted it would be as much fun. Within ten minutes, he didn't have even that diminished enjoyment to look forward to: Jason and Matt both called and canceled.

Saddened, Chesney gathered up the folding chairs and took them down to storage then followed with the disassembled table. He came back upstairs to the refrigerator crammed with beer and the bags of taco chips on the countertop, opened one of each and sat on the couch. Normally, taco chips and beer were one of his favorite snacks, especially when the former were dipped in fiery salsa, which he had also bought in larger than normal quantities. But now, after he had taken the first edge off the hunger and thirst he had built up moving furniture around, he found that he had lost any appetite. He scrunched up the top of the bag, put the lid back on the salsa jar and poured the last half of the beer down the sink.

What do I do now, he asked himself? No answer came. He thought about going out and renting a DVD, as he often did on a weekend night – sometimes even getting a straight-out porn flick. But the prospect had no appeal tonight. He'd really been looking forward to poker; it offered the only moments in his well ordered existence when he felt the excitement of uncertainty.

Finally, he put on his coat and set off to walk the six blocks to the comix store. He knew the release dates of all his favorite titles, and a new *Freedom Five* should be on the rack by now. He made his way along the sidewalk at his usual gait, shoulders indrawn, hands in pockets, focused on the concrete before him. It wasn't terribly dangerous to make eye-contact in this neighborhood – he could quote the statistics for random, stranger-on-stranger street crime – but there was no reward to compensate even for the minimal risk. Nobody would welcome his gaze.

He had gone about a block when something about the background noise level penetrated his lonely thoughts. He raised his eyes from the sidewalk and looked around. He lived in a part of the downtown that tended to liven up on Saturday nights. This block had two old-fashioned bars and a night club that drew twenty-somethings who liked to dance in a trance engendered by a combination of vodka, strobe lights and more decibels than were good for their chances of not needing hearing aids before they were out of their fifties.

Evening was settling in and the street should have been filled with cars, the bars with drinkers and the night club doorway with bouncers selecting from a lineup of the future deaf. The thump of the club's bass kickers ought to have been underlying the tenor honk of horns – parking was a competitive sport hereabouts – with the treble laughter of girls-in-groups topping off a layered cacophony that was the regular Saturday night soundscape.

But the street was quiet: only a couple of cars moving sedately past empty parking spots; the club's sound system silent; no squeals from clutches of girls because there were no girls. The sidewalks – and, when he looked through the neon-signed windows, the bars, too – were practically empty.

Something big on TV tonight he wondered? Is that why the guys aren't coming to play poker? It would not have been the first time he had missed some major node in the mass culture. The people at work had stopped asking him which singer he planned to vote for on *American Idol*; he would just look at them with a puzzled expression and shrug.

He pushed at his unresponsive brain, trying to recall if he'd heard anything. Some pneumatic teenage girl singer was coming to town as part of a major-cities tour; he'd overheard a couple of the office clerks talking about how their daughters were planning to get tickets the moment the internet box office site came online. Last time, the concert had sold out in under a minute.

But the ticket sale, even if it was happening right now, would only account for the absence of teenage girls on the street; they'd all be hunched over their home computers, index fingers poised to click their mouse buttons. Instead, the entire block was almost deserted. And now Chesney let his gaze go farther, down the next block and the one after; he turned to look back the way he had come, and it was all the same – the sidewalks and pavement virtually empty.

Maybe it's something big, he thought. An attack? He decided to forget about the *Freedom Five* and hurried back to his apartment. But when he flipped on the cable news channel, all he saw was a female anchor telling him about some vote in Congress that had not turned out the way it had been expected to.

The image cut to a reporter standing outside the rotunda of the Senate who was saying that a spending bill laden with earmarks had failed to receive a single affirmative vote. Even the senators who had amended the legislation to shoehorn in their pet projects had inexplicably voted nay. Chesney listened for a while, but found it hard to take much interest. He was about to switch to another channel when something about the reporter's demeanor registered: normally, this commentator spoke with an air of forced gravitas, as if the truly important part of any story was not what had happened or why, but the fact that he, the reporter, was deigning to take notice of it; but now he was reciting his notes from a piece of paper as if he were ticking off a shopping list.

Strange, thought Chesney. The remote report ended and the anchorwoman came back on. It was only as he was looking at her that another oddity clicked into focus for him. The Senate correspondent's tie had been askew and his hair had not been perfectly combed. And now he saw that the anchor, too, was less than perfectly coiffed and made-up. She looked less polished – quite ordinary, Chesney thought – and her presentation lacked that quality of being ever so pleased with herself that was standard for people in her line of work. Instead she rested her jaw line on an upturned palm and her elbow on the desk, and read from the unseen teleprompter without much interest.

By coincidence, the next item was about the upcoming concert tour of the teenage girl singer. The anchor reported that tickets had been expected to sell out almost immediately, but that since the box office opened an hour ago, only a few hundred tickets had been sold – and those appeared to have gone to indulgent parents and grandparents buying them as presents.

Now the image cut to breaking news: a would-be suicide bomber in Islamabad, Pakistan, had been about blow herself up in front of a police station. Instead, she had removed the explosive vest she wore under her voluminous black robe and given herself up to a group of policemen loitering around the entrance. And the officers, instead of hustling her inside for a painful interrogation, had sat down with her on the front steps. As the camera panned over them they seemed to be having a restrained discussion, with much rueful head shaking and nods of mutual, though somewhat sad, agreement.

Chesney clicked through a few more cable news channels, ending on a live show that featured a curmudgeonly commentator who liked to bring on guests with whose politics or world views he disagreed, then browbeat the invitee with insults and invective. He saw the pundit sitting slumped in his chair, a bearded professor in the guest spot, both of them shrugging and conversing in mild tones. The usually choleric host was saying, "Of course, it doesn't really matter much one way or the other, does it?"

The academic nodded in bland agreement and said, "No, not really."

Chesney switched off. Something was out of the ordinary, though he could not yet put his finger on just what it was. Maybe some new virus going around, he thought. Maybe we've all got the flu.

He switched to the entertainment channels, found a sitcom that he had enjoyed from time to time. It was about a dysfunctional family. None of the characters got along, and a lot of dialogue consisted of one or another of them scoring points off the others with sarcastic putdowns – some of them scathing, and many of them more than a little risqué. In the past, some of the sallies and verbal duels had caused Chesney to squirt cola out of his nose; but tonight's episode seemed like a constant barrage of unnecessary cruelty. In the five minutes before he turned it off, he didn't laugh at a single gag, although the studio audience that had been there for the taping was driven into paroxysm of mirth as the grossly overweight young male lead went into a sustained rant about his chain-smoking mother-in-law's sexual history.

Chesney switched off the TV. The silence in the apartment seemed suddenly profound: no horns or engine noises rising from the street; no stereos blaring from any of the neighbors; no arguments, either, although Saturday night was prime time for the several unhappily married couples in the block to bring their week's disappointments to each other's attention, with the paper-thin walls letting all the neighbors share in those domestic dramas.

He was puzzled. He thought again about going to the comix shop, but the vicarious thrill he got from following the adventures of the *Freedom Five* did not lure him tonight. After a moment's thought, he decided that he was feeling let down by the collapse of his first shot at hosting the guys for poker. Or maybe it was the flu.

He felt his forehead, found no fever. He sat on his couch for a long while, trying to think of something he wanted to do. But nothing came, and finally he pulled down the bed and lay on top of the covers until he fell asleep.

TWO

Sunday mornings invariably began with a call from Chesney's mother, urging him to turn on his television and tune in to whichever one of the religious programs had most filled her with enthusiasm. Most often, it was *The New Tabernacle of the Air*, fronted by the Reverend William Lee Hardacre. He was broad-shouldered, tall, and fiftyish, with silver hair that looked as if it had been poured into a mold and let to set overnight. He wore tailor-made suits with western-style piping on the lapels and a big gold and diamond ring that flashed as brightly as his piercing blue eyes whenever he raised his hands to call down divine blessings – or, more often, wrath – on some celebrity whose behavior had caught his attention over the preceding week.

Reverend Billy Lee, as he was known to the throngs who loved him, had started out in life as a lawyer, specializing in labor-management mediation. Well into a successful legal career, he caught the fiction bug and began penning a series of bestselling novels set in the world of corporate law. Then, somewhere in the middle of his seventh blockbuster, he experienced some kind of spiritual epiphany. He gave up both his legal practice and his literary output to enter a seminary. When he emerged from his religious studies – it was never clear whether or not he had obtained the doctorate in theology he had sought – he launched *The New Tabernacle of the Air*.

As a television preacher, the Reverend Billy Lee did not fit the mold. He had no choir, no guests, no books to flog, no "prayer requests" backed up by a phone bank of telemarketers cadging donations from the faithful. Instead he sold commercial time to charitable foundations and businesses that could demonstrate a commitment to ethical standards.

The show opened with Hardacre at a desk, commenting on news items from the past week. His analysis was always sharp and often insightful, especially when it came to spotting hypocrisy among the famous and powerful. The final ten minutes would see the preacher single out one particular celebrity – a movie star, a politician, a professional athlete, a pundit – for what a *Time* magazine profile of Hardacre once called "a precise and comprehensive flaying."

Like a prosecutor summing up for the jury, the preacher would detail the excesses and egotisms of his weekly target then invite his legions of viewers to write to the object of his censure – he always had their actual mailing addresses to pass along – and express their views. Letitia Arnstruther never failed to take the reverend up on that invitation. She spent most Sunday afternoons at her writing desk, pen scratching over lilac-colored stationery, composing missives full of pointedly phrased descriptions of the eternal fate that awaited them if they failed to change their ways: "Your bowels will roast on eternal coals, your eyeballs will boil in their sockets, your parched and swollen tongue will protrude as you beg for one droplet of soothing moisture – and beg in vain."

Her concluding paragraph always expressed a sincere hope that the sinner would turn from his iniquities, and thus avoid the wrath she had so lovingly detailed. She liked to read her best passages over the phone to Chesney, and urged him to join her in the campaign to rid the world of whatever evil the Reverend Billy Lee had unleashed her and her fellow devotees against.

But today, the phone had not rung in Chesney's studio apartment. Grateful to be left alone, he got up late and ate a bowl of corn flakes while rereading a standalone issue of *The Driver*, the one where the hero foils a plot to kidnap a billionaire's beautiful daughter to force the magnate into financing the presidential election campaign of a man who was a member of a secret terrorist organization. But though he had always enjoyed the comix artist's striking images, especially the way the amply endowed kidnap victim was rendered, this time the tale failed to capture him.

Before he knew it, he had tidied up the nook and washed and put away his bowl, spoon and coffee cup. Normally, he made a point of leaving them in the sink. Sunday was his day to be sloppy and lazy, which he knew was a reaction against all those Sundays when he was growing up: his mother always made him tidy his room to a military standard of neatness before they went off to their first church service of the day. She'd also made him wear a tie.

He wiped out the sink until the stainless steel shone, surprised that he did not feel even a twinge of disaffection for the task. Drying his hands, he looked around to see if there were any other chores that needed doing and a moment later he was tidying the bedclothes and pushing the bed up into the wall.

Still the phone hadn't rung. He wondered if something might have happened to his mother, though that seemed as unlikely as if "something might have happened" to the Himalayas. Letitia Arnstruther was the kind of person who happened to others. She herself was as unaffected by the doings of others as Mount Everest was by the tiny, gasping creatures that crept up to its ice-capped peak. Except, Chesney admitted, when it came to sins committed by persons of note – especially what she always referred to as the "sins of the flesh," by which she did not mean gluttony.

The few Sundays when she hadn't called had coincided with an exceptionally enrapturing performance by one of her favorite television preachers. He found the TV remote and flicked on the channel that carried *The New Tabernacle of the Air*, which went out live in this time zone.

He caught the Reverend Billy Lee in mid-fulmination: "Lust and fornication, brothers and sisters! Sodom and Gomorrah! The fleshpots of Egypt, the Whore of Babylon! But I say unto you that these are as nothing compared to the recent conduct of the celebrated TeShawn 'Bad Boy' Bougaineville."

Chesney was vaguely aware of having heard of the person in question. He thought Bougaineville might have been the football player who had shot up his girlfriend's Lexus when her behavior had failed to satisfy him. Chesney remembered the man saying, "*Bleep*, I done give the dumb *bleep* the *bleep*in' ride inna firs' place."

Chesney muted the sound. The preacher was in full cry, his helmet of silver hair shining in the carefully positioned lights so that it formed a halo above his earnest face. His eyes flashed, his capped teeth gleamed, his square jaw jutted as he bit off each phrase, while a trickle of sweat descended from one temple. He could imagine his mother seated on the overstuffed sofa, knees locked and hands clasped, leaning forward, with a flush of pink in her cheeks. TeShawn would be getting a memorable letter from Letitia Arnstruther.

That'll be it, he thought. But then something odd: across the bottom of the screen came a crawl. Chesney watched the words go by. *The program scheduled for this time period is not available. We present a repeat performance of last week's* New Tabernacle of the Air. *We are sorry for the inconvenience.*

Chesney clicked the remote. Live coverage of a football game was scheduled to begin just about now. He found a pre-game interview with a young man described as the NFL's most highly paid wide receiver and realized it was none other than TeShawn Bougaineville. But instead of talking trash, the player was tearfully confessing to a long-standing fondness for cocaine and fast women. The sports reporter interviewing him was in tears. "How awful for you," he blubbered and the expression of sympathy made TeShawn break down and sob.

"What the hepty-doo-dah's going on?" Chesney said. He switched channels again and saw the Sunday public affairs show, *In Contention*. But the three regular panelists were not shouting each other down or trading insults. Instead, they didn't have much to say about anything, and what they did say seemed to Chesney to lack all conviction.

He shut off the TV and went out. It was a mild day and he headed for the park, a wide belt of greenery that paralleled both banks of a slow-moving river. It was usually a lively place when the weather cooperated: couples necking on the grass slopes, skateboarders daring each other to try potentially neck-snapping stunts on the step-seats of the concrete amphitheater where local theater groups put on plays; older folks walking in pairs and shaking their canes at in-line skaters who whizzed past them on the asphalt paths.

But today it was quiet, only a couple of solitary pedestrians staring into the river's muddy flow, a woman sitting on one of the steps of the amphitheater, her chin in her hands. Chesney made his way past the Civil War memorial, heading by habit toward the basketball court where a food cart sold hot dogs. He always bought a steaming hot chili dog smothered in fried onions and ate it on one of the nearby benches, keeping an eye out for any young women who might come jogging past in their form-fitting pants and halters. For the past few months, he had been keeping a special watch for the reappearance of one young woman in particular.

It had been on the first really warm Sunday in the late spring. Chesney had been sitting here and choking down a foot-long when he had noticed a truly spectacular pair of spandex-covered breasts come bouncing long the path. It was four or five seconds before he raised his eyes to the face above the twin objects of his attention, and it was only then that he realized that he knew her. The number of young and beautiful women that the actuary knew socially could have been counted on the fingers of Captain Hook's left hand, but he had actually spent several minutes in the company of the one who was then trotting, with a lithe and lissome grace, in his general direction.

Her name was Poppy. She was twenty-four and blonde, and the possessor of a heart-shaped face that contained the most arresting pair of deep blue eyes Chesney had ever had turned upon him. Their single previous encounter had been an opportunity for the young man to make a good impression: she had approached the left-side elevator in the lobby of Chesney's building just as the doors were closing. He was already in the car and had reached out a hand and caused the doors to part again. She had given him a smile that he would have considered fair compensation if the doors had bitten off his hand and added a blithe, "Why, thank you, kind sir!" in a playful theatrical tone.

Chesney had swallowed and almost managed to ask her what floor she wanted. But while he was still forming the words in his mind and wondering if he could voice them in a breezy manner to match hers, she had reached past him, the sleeve of her silk blouse touching his wrist while a gentle waft of some exquisite scent tantalized his nose. The effect was paralyzing and before it passed, she had pressed the button herself. She was going to the top of the building, the tenth floor, where Chesney had never been. "Up on ten," was the rarefied zone where the lions of the company roamed – vice-presidents and senior vice-presidents and the pride of the pride: president, chief executive officer *and* chairman of the board, silver-maned Warren Theophilus Paxton, himself.

The elevator began to rise. She looked at him, he quickly turned his eyes up to the row of illuminated numbers above the doors and, at that moment, the car jerked to an unexpected stop.

"We're stuck," she said.

"Um," Chesney managed, then added a look of what he hoped was reassuring fortitude in the face of danger.

"Can you do something?" she said. "I don't want to be late for Daddy's birthday."

There was a button to push in case of emergency. Chesney pushed it. Somewhere, a bell clanged and kept on clanging until he released the button. Next to the controls was a steel panel with the outline of a telephone on it. He opened the panel and found a phone handset. He put the phone to his ear and heard nothing, but a moment later a woman's voice told him he had reached the automated response service of the company that installed and serviced the elevator. "Please hold," she said. "Someone will be right with you."

Chesney could talk to women on the phone. "We're stuck," he said. He could actually talk to women in person, if they weren't young and attractive. He could even talk to the young and attractive ones, so long as it wasn't face to face, and provided they gave him time to construct a sentence.

The woman on the phone said nothing in reply to his remark. After a moment, she repeated the exact words she had spoken before, and he realized he was hearing a computer-generated response. Then there was a click and a man with a sing-song Indian accent said his name was Gary and how could he help? In the background, Chesney could hear other Indian voices.

"We're stuck," Chesney said again. He could hear a rattle of keys on a computer keyboard at the other end of the line, then Gary said, "You are in elevator number one?"

"The left one," Chesney said. "I don't know its number."

"There is no cause for alarm," the Indian said, and somewhere near him a woman with the same accent spoke the exact same words with the same cheerful intonation. "We have alerted the" – there was a pause, then Gary went on – "Muncie Fire Department. They are on their way. Remain calm."

"But," Chesney said, "We're not in Muncie. We're not even in Indiana. We're in–"

"Just a minute," said Gary. Chesney heard a click, then the phone joined an electronic version of *Raindrops Keep Falling on my Head* that was already in progress. He heard several bars of it, then the woman's voice he had first heard interrupted the music to tell him that his call was important to them and that he should remain on the line rather than hang up and call again.

Through all this, the young woman was leaning against the elevator's back wall, her arms crossed over her chest and her chin tucked down. The polished toe of one patent leather pump tapped up and down. When she heard the faint tinny music coming from the phone at Chesney's ear she rocked forward and one hand made a circular gesture that said, "We need to move this along." Aloud she said, "Look, we can't be more than a foot off the ground. Couldn't you just pry open the door and we'll get out?"

"Um," said Chesney. He looked at the phone in his hand as if it might convey some useful information, but it had moved on to the next song in its repertoire: an electronic version of *The Sunny Side of the Street*.

Chesney had long known that his few successes in life had been confined to areas that he thought of as being filled with distinct pools of light. The pools represented those relatively narrow areas where he knew he had solid, certain footing – areas like mathematics and the arcane details of the often-complex alternate universes captured in comix. But these oases of illumination were hedged around by great swathes of murk and darkness, huge lightless plains of dimly-lit terrain that were full of unseen pits into which he could blindly stumble. One of the darkest corners was that part of human existence that involved conversing with an attractive woman. If only more such women – or, in Chesney's actual experience, *any* such women – had ever engaged him on the topics on which he was expert, he might have built up sufficient confidence to explore the dark savannas. But they hadn't, and so he hadn't.

As *The Sunny Side of the Street* came to its underplayed final bars, the young woman made an exasperated noise somewhere deep in her perfectly formed throat and reached down to slip off one shoe. She forced the end of one stiletto-thin heel into the crack between the elevator doors, creating a gap large enough to insert her fingertips. Then she looked at Chesney and said, "Hang that up and help me."

He did, and together they pried the doors apart. As she had said, they were no more than a foot above the lobby floor. She stepped down and, with a single backward glance that dismissed him forever, she entered the next elevator. Chesney descended from the stuck car and watched the doors close. Behind him, the phone struck up *The Girl That I Marry*.

Later, Chesney told his co-workers an edited version of the incident, in which he had taken the initiative in prying open the doors. He also told them of some fairly witty remarks he had passed during the experience, which had calmed the young woman's initial fears and even made her laugh. One of the other actuaries asked for a closer description of the rescued maiden and when told about the small mole below the corner of one cornflower-blue eye, had said, "That was Poppy."

"Yes," said Chesney, "I think that was what she said her name was. I was a little busy telling off those idiots from the call center in Bombay." But when he saw how the others in the group reacted to the name, he said, "What?"

"Poppy," repeated the one who had identified her. "As in Poppy Paxton. As in W.T. Paxton. As in…" – the man pointed a thumb at the ceiling – "God."

Then, two Sundays after the elevator incident, Chesney had seen Poppy Paxton jogging toward him along the path that led past the hot dog stand. She didn't notice him. But it occurred to him, as she ran past and away, that if she tripped and fell, he could be right there to help her, could get some ice from the chili dog vendor's soft drink compartment so soothe her ankle – of course, it would be just a minor sprain – and perhaps she would sit with him on the bench until she felt well enough to walk. They would talk, and he would say wise and interesting things, and she would nod and say, "I never thought of it like that. What an intelligent observation." And then...

But Poppy Paxton never jogged past Chesney's bench again, even though he had sat there every Sunday since, sometimes eating three chili dogs over the course of the morning, which meant he had heartburn most of the afternoon. And today not only did Poppy not come, but none of the other jiggling bosoms passed by either. After a single bite of the hot dog, he set it down on the bench and let it go cold. The man who sold them was closing up his cart. Now he pushed it slowly toward the parking lot.

"What's going on?" Chesney said, aloud.

"You talking to us?" said a voice behind him.

He turned. The speaker was one of a group of young men, in their teens and early twenties, whom he had sometimes seen playing ball on the single-basket court. They were tough guys, wearing clothes that showed their muscles and their gold chains, two of them with red bandanas tied around their shaven heads. Usually, they swore a lot and played loud rap music from a boom box. Sometimes they shouted at Chesney when he went past, words that he only partially heard and always pretended that he didn't, walking by with his eyes averted.

"No," he said, trying to keep a tremor out of his voice.

"Oh," said the one who had spoken, olive skinned with a sparse mustache, a chain tattoo encircling his neck, "that's okay. My mistake." They walked away, and Chesney noticed that none of them moved with their customary macho swagger.

"What," he said again, "is going on?"

• • • •

Monday morning, the stock market went *phut*. At least, that was how the cable news reporter put it in the report that ran while Chesney was eating his cornflakes.

"No one can remember a day like it," the man said, standing in the middle of an empty trading floor. "It's now two hours since the New York Stock Exchange's opening bell, and most brokers and traders haven't shown up for work. The only trades that are being made are by automatic computer programs and some charitable foundations. Otherwise, this place is dead. Nobody's interested in making money."

The bus ride to work was eerily placid. No one jostled for first place in the line, and Chesney even saw a teenager get up to offer an old lady a seat. The traffic was sedate; the taxis were actually yielding right of way, and nobody ran a red light.

At the office, he had barely settled behind his desk when he was interrupted by Ron and Clay. They came into his cubicle, wanting his point of view on a discussion they were having on whether their work was morally defensible.

"I think it's ethically neutral," Clay said. "We're only calculating risk factors for different demographics, so that policies can be designed that balance risk and reward for the company."

"Yes," said Ron, "but the side effect of that process is to identify some groups that will be denied any coverage at all."

They both turned to Chesney and said, together, "What do you think?"

It was not a question the actuary had ever considered, but he did so now. "I'd want to think about it," he said. "Evaluating people based on categories of risk can be seen as extending from a recognition that fundamentally, life is not fair."

"I agree," said Clay.

"On the other hand," Chesney continued, following the logic, "just because life is not fair, does that mean we can reinforce the unfairness? Life, after all, is not a moral being, capable of making ethical choices. But we are."

"That's the way I see it," said Ron.

"On the other, other hand, if we don't work out the risk factors, the insurance business can't function. Ultimately, nobody gets insured, and that can't be good." He paused. "It's tricky."

Clay said, "Maybe we could calculate the net benefit-to-misery ratio inherent in the way the industry works now against the same ratio if there was no insurance for anybody."

"But how can we be sure that benefit and misery cancel each other out?" said Ron. "Maybe an ounce of misery is worth a pound of happiness."

"And then there's the moral obligation we have to our employer to earn our salaries," Chesney put in.

"But if we're part of an immoral enterprise, our obligation is to quit," Ron countered. "'First, do no harm,' as the Hippocratic Oath says."

"Isn't it odd that these issues have never come up before?" Chesney said.

"Well," said Clay, "we've always been too busy."

"We ought to be busy now, shouldn't we?"

"Not if we've been part of a fundamentally immoral system," said Ron.

"Or amoral," said Clay.

"But for moral beings, can anything be amoral?"

And around and around the discussion went.

At noon, tired and hungry after a hard morning's debate, Chesney went out to the park bench to eat his lunch. He chewed his sandwich without much appetite, wondering if it was proper for him to eat his fill when hundreds of millions of people around the world were malnourished. On the other hand, he couldn't do much about the problem if he was underfed. "Not that I have been doing anything about it," he said to himself. "Maybe I should."

His eye fell on the headline of a tabloid newspaper that someone had left on the bench: *"Conscience Bug" Spreads.* Chesney picked it up and read the story. A scientist from the National Centers for Disease Control was speculating that there might be a viral vector for the wave of morality that was sweeping the world. *Something seems to have disabled our "selfishness circuits,"* the report read. *Greed, anger, lust, gluttony – indeed, all of what used to be called the 'seven deadly sins' – have suddenly stopped affecting our conduct.*

It's as if, after having spent all our lives with a devil and an angel on each shoulder, none of our devils are showing up for work.

"You are causing me a great deal of trouble," said a genteel voice. Chesney lowered the paper and saw a dapper, bearded man – *no*, he corrected himself, a dapper, bearded *gentleman* – sitting on the other end of the bench, his hands folded over the head of a black walking stick.

"I beg your pardon?" he said.

"That is something I am not often inclined to give," said the stranger. "And certainly not to you, after all that you have done."

There was something familiar about the face and voice. It took Chesney a moment to make the connection, then he had it: the man was the spitting image of the actor who had played Kris Kringle in one of Chesney's favorite movies from his childhood: the original 1930s version of *Miracle on 34th Street*. He had the white beard and the snowy hair, though his eyes did not twinkle as he regarded Chesney with an animosity that seemed to struggle with amused contempt.

"You're not another demon, are you?" the actuary said. "I've told you–"

"Not another demon, no," the other interrupted, "though I am the one they all work for." And now any vestige of amusement went away. "Or at least they did until you came blundering along."

"I don't understand."

The dapper gentleman pointed a finger at the newspaper Chesney still held in both hands. The words *none of our devils are showing up for work* floated free of the page and rose until they hovered in front of Chesney's eyes, where they enlarged until they were six inches high. Then they burst into yellow and orange flames that died down to inky smoke that dissipated in a nonexistent wind, causing a sooty detritus to sift down onto the actuary's thighs.

"You," said Satan, "you ridiculous little man, have singlehandedly caused Hell to go on strike."

The way Lucifer explained it to Chesney, it all made actuarial sense. It was basically a problem of numbers and demographics. Hell, like Heaven, was an autocracy. His Satanic Majesty ruled, aided by his inner circle of fallen angels who, before the Fall, had held high ranks within the angelic hierarchy: Thrones and Dominions, Powers and Principalities. Now they were Dukes and Princes of the Abyss, and below them were the legions of demons who had been mere rank-and-file rebel angels and archangels before they had all tumbled down to the black iron shores of the Tartarus, the lake of fire. To these foot soldiers fell the tasks of punishing and tormenting the human dead who earned eternal damnation, and of tempting the living toward modes of conduct that would eventually bring them across the stygian divide and into the waiting furnaces and pitchforks.

In the early years, it had been enjoyable work. The tormentors had fallen to it with a spirit of inventiveness that had created some wonderfully ironic punishments: Sisyphus and his rolling rock; Tantalus and his disappearing food and drink; Nero and the out-of-tune orchestra that ceaselessly played his most beloved compositions. The tempters, meanwhile, relied on a combination of their incessant whisperings in humanity's collective ear, coupled with the spirit of human inventiveness, to generate a constant stream of new customers.

But, as the ages wore on, Hell's success provided for its own undoing. There were, after all, only so many demons. The constantly accelerating intake of the newly damned could not be matched by any increase in the legions of Hell. This imbalance began to cause difficulties.

Back in the days when humankind numbered only a few hundred million, the average demon assigned to the punitive battalions was charged with "making it hot" for only a few hundred of the condemned. Now the world's population was heading for seven billion, and a great many of them – still urged on by the corps of tempters, still full of creativity when it came to finding new ways to transgress – were crowding through the gates of Hell, abandoning all hope along the way. The Pit was infinitely expandable, but, in that subterranean depression, a fixed number of overworked demons were having to deal with an exponentially increasing quota of the damned. Their productivity had reached its limit, yet the demand for *more, more, more* never ceased. The fiends were fed up.

Over the past century, to this volatile dynamic had been added the first labor organizers whose misdeeds had come back to haunt them as they departed the mortal coil. Of course, the true saints of unionism did not find themselves consigned to the travails of Hell. But from its inception, the labor movement had attracted the same range of opportunists and self-servers as would any activity that offered the unscrupulous an avenue toward power and self-enrichment. So, although no Joe Hills were to be found in any of the nine circles, the Jimmy Hoffas were amply represented.

The rabble rousers saw a familiar scenario: their tormentors were overworked and underappreciated. And the fact that there were not enough demons to keep every damned soul in constant misery gave the condemned organizers the leisure to recognize a familiar opportunity. Before long, some of them had talked their way off the treadmills of red-hot iron and arranged to take up residence in the less dreadful infernal *arrondisements*. From there they began to advise their erstwhile tormentors on tactics and strategy.

Not long after, the first delegation from the newly formed Infernal Brotherhood of Fiends, Demons and Tempters approached the Dark Throne to propose that His Satanic Majesty enter into discussions on matters of mutual interest. These initial approaches were not well received; indeed, the demons that carried the messages to the feet of the Adversary were summarily blasted to fragments, but being eternal, they eventually reconstituted themselves and came back for another try.

Meanwhile, the fundamental problem was not being solved. Hell was becoming increasingly dysfunctional. As an experiment, management tried assigning some above-ground tempters to the punishment function. But this meant giving the heavenly opposition too great an opportunity, of which they took full advantage. The collapse of the Soviet evil empire was a significant setback for the infernal agenda, and the temporarily reassigned tempters were sent back upstairs.

Meanwhile, as a stopgap, Hell's management and its workers negotiated their first contract. This, however, was a field of expertise in which management excelled, and the final terms were not much of an improvement for the members of the IBFDT. But it was a start, the Brotherhood's advisors counseled, a base to build on. All that was needed now, they said, was for management to breach the contract. Then the whole infernal work force would come out on strike, and they wouldn't go back until they had a deal they could all live with.

And then, into this delicately poised situation, this powder keg awaiting only a spark, stepped Chesney Arnstruther. The toad-like demon that answered his unintentional summons had been called away from its regular duties, pouring molten gold down the throats of misers. According to the contract, it should have been excused from its tormenting quota while it was engaged in getting Chesney's signature on the standard soul-purchase contract and carrying out whatever that contract required. When it returned without the contract, its supervisor told it that it still had to fill all the misers with gold – and there were plenty of misers.

The demon had balked. Its supervisor, the fanged weasel that talked as if it was channeling every bad impression of Edward G. Robinson, had tried to straighten the matter out by getting Chesney to accept the contract. By the time it returned, having failed to resolve the issue with the intransigent actuary, the toad demon had already gone to its IBFDT shop steward, the little girl with the snake-tongue, and the ranked dominoes had begun to quiver.

In Hell, a contract is a contract. The supervisor had no choice but to demand that the toad demon fulfill its quota; the shop steward countered that the IBFDT member had been exempted from its quota when it was called away. The supervisor argued that the toad demon had not brought back a signed contract, so no exemption could apply.

There was no clause in the agreement between Hell and the IBFDT that covered the anomaly. Supervisor and shop steward stared at each other for a long moment, then the latter had stepped upstairs into Chesney's apartment to ask him the pregnant question: "Just tell me, are you ready to go all the way on this?"

When Chesney had said, "Yes, I am," the dominoes began to topple.

"Now you understand," said Satan.

Chesney shook his head, not in denial but from the still resonating impact of all the information that the Devil had caused to appear instantly in his consciousness. The knowledge itself was difficult enough to absorb, but its transmission into his brain had been accompanied by graphic images of the afterlife's dark side that would have given Hieronymous Bosch the collywobbles.

"Now let me show you a few things," said Lucifer.

"You've shown me enough already," said Chesney, but his view was not accepted. A surprisingly cool hand took charge of his arm and a moment later they were somewhere else. It was somewhere high, the actuary quickly realized, like a great precipice, but the perspective was odd. Then it came to him: "'All the kingdoms of the world,'" he quoted. "This is where you brought—"

"If you dare to speak the name," said Satan, "I'll kick you over the edge." He shook his shoulders as if throwing off a cramp. "Besides, it didn't happen the way you heard it."

"You're saying the Bible got it wrong?"

"What would be the point of offering Himself dominion over all the kingdoms of the world, when He was the one who created them, and besides, he already had Heaven?"

"Then why is it in the book?"

"Who knows why He does what He does? I never did. Maybe it's because He turned the job over to a gaggle of ghostwriters, all of whom had their own little agendas and political points to make. I don't think *He's* ever read it, or it would make more sense."

"But–"

The Devil raised one tapered finger. "'But' is another word it is not wise to throw at me. In any case, I did not bring you here for a literary debate. Look out there."

Chesney looked, and it seemed to him that whatever he looked at somehow enlarged and deepened until he was transported into a fully rounded scene. He found himself standing in a factory that made computers, but its assembly line robots were stilled, its employees absent, its huge dust-free space, full of nothing but inaction and silence.

"No greed," said the Devil. "No one ordering the goods, because no one wants to make a profit by selling them. And even if they did, no one wants to make wages by manufacturing them."

An instant later, they were back in the high place. "Look," said the Archfiend again, and Chesney felt himself drawn into another setting: the nightclub down the street from his studio, all its booths empty, its lights extinguished, the dance floor deserted, the ranked bottles behind the bar growing dusty.

"No lust. No young men strutting to impress the young women, no young women letting themselves be impressed."

And then a four-star restaurant, chairs piled on tables stripped of their cloths, grills and ovens cold, coolers full of meats and vegetables turning dry and drab.

"I get it," Chesney said. "No gluttony. And you can show me how nobody's trying to keep up with the Joneses because the envy's turned off, and the leisure industry's flat on its butt because people aren't feeling slothful. And fashion's dead because there's no vanity."

The restaurant disappeared and they were back on the high place.

"And what were you going to show me for anger? Some guy sitting in a cave twiddling his beard?"

"You want to see anger?" the Devil began, but then he made a visible effort to restrain himself. "I'm showing you," he said after taking a deep breath, "that what I do is woven into the warp and weft of the world. You have undone one of the fundamental fastenings of existence."

"No," said Chesney, "all I did was hit my thumb and not use profanity. All the rest of it came from your side of the house."

Lucifer didn't look much like Kris Kringle now. The illusion shattered completely and Chesney was again sitting on the park bench, but now he faced a lean, dark-haired personage with precisely planed features and a tiny, pointed beard. When he flexed his long-fingered hands, as if he would have liked to strangle the actuary, a faint whiff of sulfur stirred the air.

"We can make you a special offer," the Devil said. "No fine print, no surprises. Anything you want. President. Movie star. Richest man in the world, Bill Gates for your butler, the Queen of England as your maid."

"But in the end," said Chesney, "you'd take my soul."

"That is the customary arrangement."

"But I'm not the customary customer, am I?"

The Devil's brows drew to a vee. The air around them somehow darkened. "This must be resolved," he said.

"Fine," said Chesney. "I accept your arguments, the warp and the weft, the necessity of sin. I'm still not prepared to give up my soul just to plug a hole in Hell's collective agreement."

The answer was a growl and a grinding of teeth.

"I sympathize," said Chesney, "I mean, I really do. But can't you cut a deal with your employees?"

Lucifer sighed. "They're being very hard-headed."

Chesney thought about it. "Maybe you could promote some of the worst sinners to be assistant tormentors."

"I've thought of that. But it goes against the rules. The worse people are up here, the worse they have to suffer once I get hold of them."

"Can't you change the rules?"

"Not that one. I didn't make it."

Back in Sunday school, it had always seemed odd to Chesney that the really bad sinners – like Hitler or Attila the Hun – got punished when they got to Hell. If Hell was really in favor of sinning, the people who were best at it ought to have been welcomed with parades. He'd offered that thought once to his mother. It had not been welcomed.

Chesney came up with a new idea. "How about promoting the least sinful?"

"We've tried that," the Devil said. "They're not very good at it. They lack verve."

"Maybe a shorter work week?"

"We're already running into backlogs."

The actuary shook his head. "Then I got nothing," he said.

"If you accepted the deal," Satan said, "I could arrange for you to live a very long time."

"No matter how long it was, eternity will always be a lot longer."

"Yes," said Lucifer, "and it's growing longer still while we sit here getting nowhere."

"I appreciate," said Chesney, "that you're not 'making it hot for me' up here."

"Again," was the answer, delivered in a tone that

suggested immense anger barely under constraint, "I don't make the rules."

The odor of sulfur sharpened and then Chesney was alone on the bench.

THREE

Just as Chesney had been able to recover from his surprise when the first demon had interrupted his table-building, he was not totally gobsmacked to find himself in his present unique circumstances. He had always felt, in the innermost corner of his being where he felt things that he told no one else about, that he was destined for some sort of great achievement. The fact that his life so far had offered him few avenues of approach to his expected destiny had not totally discouraged him. Nor had the fact that the only time he had ever mentioned this feeling to anyone – his mother, when he was ten – she had strongly discouraged him from holding his breath in anticipation.

Despite the lowball cards life had generally dealt him, Chesney never abandoned his belief. He nourished it in secret, first by reading and rereading the biblical tales of other disregarded young men who had risen to greatness: Joseph and his triumphs in Egypt and David the sling-swinging shepherd boy who had risen to take Saul's throne. After he left home and discovered that there were other sources of inspiration, he further fueled his hopes in the exploits of Malc Turner, who developed his powers as The Driver after handling a mysterious package misdirected from a parallel dimension.

Ever since his encounter with the toad-demon, Chesney had been nurturing an unvoiced hope that all of this was building toward the realization of some greater plan – and that he might be its keystone. It occurred to him now, as he made his way back to the office, that his desire to make some singular mark in the world must be pure; the demon that tempted him to commit the sin of pride was walking a picket line somewhere in Hell. That realization led him to another: if he usually had a tempter, he must also have an operative from the other side of the dichotomy.

He stopped before the gap in the hedge that hemmed in the little park. "Hello," he said, tentatively. "Are you there?"

No answer came.

"I'm talking to you," he tried again, "my guardian angel. Or at least the one who normally works to counter the demon assigned to tempt me."

Still no answer.

"I know you must be there. And you don't have much to do right now. I could really use some advice."

A small voice spoke reluctantly in his ear. "We're not normally supposed to be audible," it said.

Chesney looked around but there was no one in sight. "These aren't normal conditions, are they?"

"True."

"So what would you advise me to do?"

The voice said, "Hmm." After a long moment, it said, "We're also not really very good at advising. No real training, you see. Basically, we're here to counter the temptations. Ours is a reactive role."

"You mean, whatever my tempter says I should do, you say I shouldn't?"

"And vice versa."

"It doesn't sound as if you put a lot of thought into it."

"I don't suppose we're meant to," the voice said. "Thinking is not encouraged. That's what got Luci—" The voice censored itself. "I mean that's what got you-know-who into all his... difficulties. We just do the divine will."

Chesney said, "Still, you have to be more experienced at this sort of thing than I am."

"I'd really have to ask someone senior. I can't tread too heavily, you understand. Free will, again."

"But I'm freely asking you for advice. You must have heard what the Devil said."

"Oh, yes. I must say it was strange to see him again. Must be donkey's years. I suppose he's tied up most of the time in administration, you know. That's what thinking gets you, I suppose."

"Back to my situation," said Chesney. "What's the right thing for me to do?"

"Oh, no," said the voice, "no, no, no. I really couldn't say. The most I'm authorized to do is to encourage you to consult your conscience."

"I thought you *were* my conscience."

"No. You got one when you got free will."

"Well, what about *your* conscience? What does it say?"

"Don't have one," said the voice. "No need. No free will."

"Angels have no free will?"

"Thank goodness, no. I think... you-know-who was the only one of us who ever had it, and look at how much trouble it caused him and those he talked into following him. No, you can keep that free will stuff. Most of you fall afoul of it. That's why Hell is so overworked. No, we just do Himself's bidding, no questions asked."

"All right," said Chesney, "what *is* His bidding?"

"Hmm," said the voice. "He hasn't said anything to me."

"Could you ask Him?"

Another pause. "We're only supposed to run errands when He sends us. I don't know if I'm authorized."

"You said you could ask someone senior?"

"Oh, yes. I could ask a Throne, maybe even a Dominion."

"Then would you please do so, and get back to me?"

"If they say I can."

Chesney thought for a moment, then said, "It sounds as if you have quite a lot of bureaucracy on your side."

"We do like things tidy," said the voice.

The office was empty when Chesney returned from lunch. It had been empty all morning. He had felt a slight obligation to come in, born of a sense of duty to the employer, but now that he thought about it he realized that it was more a matter of following his normal routine. He had never been one of life's wild cards, he knew, but now he had to face the fact that he had become pretty much entirely a creature of habit.

He had disposed of the last few items in his electronic in-basket before going out for lunch. Now he switched off his PC and sat gazing at the blank monitor. Consult your conscience, his guardian angel had said. For many years, indeed until quite recently, his conscience had always spoken to him in terse and querulous tones: it was the voice, internalized in his infancy, of Letitia Arnstruther.

"I should go and see her," he said to the empty room. And, first tidying his desk, he rose to do so.

He waited far longer than usual for a bus. When one finally arrived, he took a closer than usual look at the driver, wondering if the man was driven to come to work by a sense of duty or, like himself, by sheer force of habit. In the inert expression on the driver's bland face, he recognized the look of another prisoner of routine.

He was the only passenger on the bus as it carried him through virtually empty streets, taking the bridge out of downtown and heading for the suburbs. It was an express service, and normally Chesney took it as far as the major intersection where the Buy-Buy mall and a brand-name outlet center faced each other across several lanes of traffic. There he would transfer to a local route for the remaining eight blocks to his mother's house.

But when he had stood at the connecting point for twenty minutes, his transfer slip in hand, and no local bus came, he set off to walk the rest of the way. The first two blocks, passing the parking lots of the mall and outlet center, were an eerie experience. Usually, the vast stretches of asphalt were jam-packed with cars, SUVs and minivans. The most recent comers would cruise the white-painted lanes, watching for someone pushing a loaded shopping cart toward a vehicle then creeping slowly along at their heels, to be ready to pounce on the ephemeral treasure of a vacant slot. Sometimes when the person being followed arrived at their vehicle, it was only to transfer goods from cart to trunk before heading back to the stores for yet more consuming. When that happened, the driver, who had been waiting for the parking space engaged in loud horn-honking and inventive cursing.

But today the lots stretched lone and level, empty of all but a few plastic shopping bags skirling and whirling in the errant breeze. The stores stood unlit and empty, and the roads that were normally thick with comers and goers were bare of traffic.

As he walked along, Chesney became aware of a rising tide of guilt within him. The soundless, unpeopled streets, as he left the commercial zone and entered the residential neighborhood in which he had grown up, were now not just strange – they were an unspoken reproach to him, personally. Because, after what the Devil had told him, it was beginning to sink in that all of this silence and inactivity was the doing, intentional or not, of Chesney Arnstruther.

The dawning awareness brought a question to the front of his mind: was good the mere absence of evil? On the basis of what he was seeing and experiencing, he wasn't at all sure such a case could be made. He now lived in a world that was demonstrably shorn of evil, the forces of iniquity having packed up their tools and booked off work, but he could not bring himself to say that this new world was good. It was more accurately summed up by a word that he had recently come across in a newspaper article on neologisms that were making their way into updated dictionaries.

"*Meh*," said Chesney. "That's what it is. Not good, not bad, just meh." He walked on another block and found himself passing the property he had always called "the wedding cake" house. As far back as he could remember, the owners of the small rancher set far back on the large lot had filled the sizable space between house and street with all manner of carefully tended plant life. The ground sloped down from the house to the street, the incline being divided into several terraces, each of which was held in place by its own retainer wall of whitewashed brick or stone.

A minority of the plants in the garden had their roots in the earth, the beds ringed with whitened stones. But most of them were in pots large or small or in between. Some of the containers were simple truncated cones, others were ornate urns that might have blended in with the decor of a Persian satrap, and still others combined size with fanciful shapes: hollowed-out swans, back-arching salmon, old-time sailing ships, reclining mermaids. They crowded every square foot of space, except for the walkways, and every one of them shone a gleaming white.

And from every white enclosure spilled a riot of color: iris blue, poppy red, daffodil yellow, pansy purple, carnation pink, and shades and blossoms that Chesney – no flower aficionado – could not have named. And, always, dawn to dusk, along the layers of the wedding cake one or both of the owners would be – moving, weeding, spraying, tending – a man and woman identically thin, wispy haired, stooped of shoulder and bent of knees, both with hands so gnarled that they more closely resembled roots than any human member.

Always... but not today. The white terraces stood as empty as the streets. The wide window at the front of the house that overlooked the garden was blind, dark drapes closed. And, as Chesney stopped on the sidewalk and looked at the familiar floral display, he saw such as he had never seen in this place before – a dead leaf, curled dryly from a stem; a blossom past its perfection, shedding petals like a sad metaphor; and most unthinkable of all, the first yellowy-green sprout of a weed bumptiously rising out of the pristine soil of a flower bed.

Why don't they come out and tend the garden? he asked himself. It was not a question he put gladly to himself, because ever since the interview with Satan, he knew the answer. The old couple's obsession with their garden had not sprung just from a love of its quirky beauty. It had also stemmed from pride, and pride was a sin, and sin was on strike.

And that was Chesney's... He had been going to use the word *fault* in the privacy of his mind. But he realized that he wasn't prepared to go that far. At least not yet. But it is definitely *my* doing, he told himself. He had to shoulder some of the responsibility, and therefore some of the blame. But how much? He didn't know. And, not knowing, he couldn't judge how much effort his share would obligate him to put out to rectify the situation.

As he walked along, he wrestled with the math, but that normally reliable calculator couldn't come to grips with the ratios. There weren't enough solid digits to feed into the equations. There were too many unknowns, too many variables. He needed certainty. And thus he hurried his pace. Because, when it came to delineating fault, for cutting through a tangle of who did what and how and to whom, to reveal the core of culpability, Chesney knew of one incisive, discriminating mind that could pierce the darkness like the brilliant beam of a lighthouse in an old-time cartoon.

One and a half blocks later, he turned off the sidewalk and onto the front walk of the house where that intelligence had reigned, constantly sorting moral wheat from chaff – and finding far more of the latter than the former – for as long as Chesney could remember.

He stepped up onto the porch, knocked as he turned the big brass doorknob, and called, "Mother, it's me."

He stepped into the dark-paneled hallway and was immediately wrapped in the house's familiar odor of ancient furniture polish and lavender potpourri. No answer had come to his announcement, and he spoke a little louder: "Mother?"

"In here," came her voice and he opened the heavy glass-paned door that led into the parlor – perish the thought that he should ever refer to it as a "living room" – and stepped into the space that he most associated with his mother. The scene was as always: the old-fashioned overstuffed furniture, inherited with the house and still dappled with doilies on arms and backs, the wide sweep of a curved-legged coffee table covered in envelopes, writing paper, sheets of postage stamps, and a ceramic object with a roller that dipped into a shallow reservoir that could be filled with water, the use of which saved Letitia

Arnstruther the literally distasteful chore of licking stamps and envelopes.

And she herself was where she most often was when she occupied the parlor. She sat at the antique writing desk, a relic of the age when Victorian ladies communicated with each other and the world through scented note paper and fine penmanship. Mrs Arnstruther's handwriting would have come up to those long-ago ladies' exacting standards, though the characters of the persons to whom she wrote would have raised many a refined eyebrow.

For, in the years since Chesney had left his mother's house, thus ceasing to be the chief focus of her days, her primary occupation had become the composition of perfectly scathing letters that she sent to individuals who had come to her attention through programs like that of the Reverend Billy Lee Hardacre. The recipients of her views – most of them politicians, movie stars, musicians, journalists, authors and academics – would receive Letitia Arnstruther's unsparing assessments of themselves and their activities, along with her earnest recommendations as to how they could improve their lives by changing their activities or their opinions. Should they choose not to take her well-meaning advice, she offered them detailed descriptions of the eternal fates that surely awaited the recipients of her advice, which for all their elegant phrasing, made for harrowing reading.

So imaginative were her renditions of the sufferings of the damned that, in another life, she might have won renown as an author of fictions meant to chill the blood and shiver the spine. But fiction was far from Mrs Arnstruther's mind as she described the impalings, amputations, roastings, piercings, gougings and rough penetrations into intimate parts that awaited her correspondents. To her, these torments were as real as breakfast. And her contemplation of their visitation upon the recipients of her missives, far from causing her chills or shivers, always brought a rosy glow to her rounded countenance. She enjoyed her work.

But now Chesney found her seated at her writing desk, a two-page letter unfinished before her, her fountain pen – she had never liked ballpoints, far less the modern felt-tips – idle in her plump fingers. Her cheek rested against her upturned palm, and the eyes she turned toward her son lacked their customary glint. "There you are," she said, as always, though without even a tinge of the usual accusatory tone that allowed Chesney to add in his own mind the unspoken completion of the phrase: *and about time, too*.

"Mother," he said, "are you all right?"

The answer was a sigh. "I suppose," she said. "But somehow I seem to lack my usual energy." She gestured at the paper before her. "I was trying to write a letter to that young woman who gyrates on the television, but..." – she sought for the words – "it just won't come to me." She put down the pen and leaned back in her brocaded chair, letting her hands fall to her lap. "I feel so... listless."

"Mother, come sit with me," Chesney said. He took her hands and drew her over to the sofa. "I need your advice."

Normally, such an admission would have had Letitia Arnstruther immediately firing on all cylinders. She gave off advice the way pinwheels gave off sparks. But, as she sat at one end of the overstuffed chesterfield, she remained subdued, and startled her son by answering, "I don't know if I'm any good at advising anyone today. I just don't seem to have much mental energy."

"I know, mother. And I even know why," said Chesney. And not much more than a minute later, so did Letitia Arnstruther. He had to admit that she took it well. He had been wondering how others would react, but his mother at least absorbed the information with no more than a show of genuine surprise, followed by a welling up of concern for him.

"My poor Chesney," she said, "what an awful burden you have to bear."

He was taken aback. He could not recall ever hearing his mother express sympathy. Even when she was patching up his boyhood cuts and scrapes, she was more given to issuing instructions on how to avoid their happening again. But he had no time to dwell on the past, so he told her: "I don't know what to do."

"Well," she said, blinking, "you must do what's right."

"That's the problem I've been wrestling with. It couldn't be right to take the deal the Devil has offered me – that would be siding with evil. Not to mention damning my immortal soul. But it's not just about me. While Hell is on strike, nobody's doing any sinning anywhere in the world. If I give in, I would be responsible for all the evil that would follow once Hell goes back to work."

"So you shouldn't give in."

"But the whole world has come to a stop," Chesney said. "It turns out that sinning is what makes the world go round. With sin turned off, nobody's motivated to do anything, except for those who keep on out of habit or a sense of obligation. Why even you…" He broke off when he saw her look of consternation.

"Me?" Her expression took on an introspective cast. After a moment, her eyes widened and went to the piles of stationery and stamps on the coffee table then on to take in the writing desk. "Oh," she said. "Oh, my."

"I'm sorry, mother," he said.

"Pride," she said, as if to herself, then, "no, it's more out of envy. Now, why did I never see that?"

"I'm sorry," he said again, "very sorry."

He saw her pull herself together. "Well," she said, "first

of all, you have nothing to be sorry for. You meant no harm. You're trying to make good come out of it."

"But I don't know how."

"And why would you? You're an actuary, not a philosopher." She seemed to have recovered some of her old energy. She reached for a spiral-bound notebook on the coffee table, flicked through its pages until she found what she was looking for. "Here it is," she said and reached for the cordless phone on an end table. She punched in a long-distance number and waited for an answer. But when it came, her brows briefly drew down and she clicked the phone off and put it back on its pedestal. "Voice mail," she said, rising from the sofa. "That won't do. We'll have to go see him."

"Who?" said Chesney.

"A man who has experience in these matters," she said.

"Who?" Chesney said again, rising to follow her. She was already through the door to the hallway and her voice came back to him over the rattle of car keys that always hung from a hook in the entrance hall.

"The Reverend Billy Lee Hardacre."

Letitia Arnstruther had not only inherited a house and furniture when her widower father, a lifelong district attorney, passed on. She had inherited his beautifully maintained mid-Sixties vintage Dodge De Soto sedan, with leather seats and hardwood dashboard. She rarely drove the huge car, finding parking a difficult chore, but now she wheeled it sedately through the near empty streets toward the interstate. Her white-gloved hands gripped the wheel at two and ten o'clock and she kept the speedometer needle just below the speed limit.

"I'm not sure about this," Chesney said, not for the first time, sitting on the passenger side of the Dodge's wide bench seat.

"But *I* am, dear," said his mother. "No one knows more about Heaven and Hell than the Reverend Billy Lee. He's made a study of it."

"But I'm not sure we should be bothering him."

She did not take her eyes off the road. "He's a minister of the gospel. How could it bother him to help someone in spiritual trouble?"

Chesney pictured Hardacre's face as he normally saw it, formed into an image of stern condemnation, eyes lit with what seemed a less than holy light as he foretold the doom and damnation that were the wages of the sinners he singled out for examination. "Well, maybe," he said.

The Reverend Billy Lee's home was in a rural community an hour and a half's drive south of the city. As one of the *New Tabernacle of the Air's* Saints Circle – those who wrote more than a hundred letters a year – Letitia Arnstruther had three times been invited to social functions in a marquee set up on the long, manicured lawn. As far as either Chesney or his mother knew, no one had ever been invited inside the mansion itself, where the reverend presumably wrestled with Satan and always came out on top.

The estate was enclosed by a redbrick wall broken by two white marble pillars from which hung a tall pair of black iron gates, the vertical bars of which bore the sunburst-and-crucifix logo of the *New Tabernacle of the Air*. Letitia lowered her window and spoke into a grill mounted on the pillar that supported the left gate. Chesney could not hear the answer – the voice was indistinct – but after a moment the barrier swung silently open. They followed the long drive of crushed white stone and parked on a wide apron in front of the doors of a multi-car garage. The sounds of the DeSoto's doors closing and their footsteps on the pristine gravel were loud in the silence that hung over the place.

"I'm still not sure…" Chesney said.

"You don't have to be, dear," his mother said. "I'll be sure for both of us."

They ascended broad steps up to a pillared portico. There was an old-fashioned bell pull instead of a button. The woman gave it a solid tug. From inside, Chesney heard the sound of mellow chimes, but the door remained closed. Letitia yanked the cord again, harder and longer.

"I'm coming," said a voice from within. A moment later, the door opened. A medium-sized, balding man in faded jeans and a gray tee-shirt stretched over a definite paunch looked up at them. "What can I do for you?"

"We'd like to see Reverend Billy Lee," said Chesney's mother.

"You are seeing him," said the man.

"I don't like to contradict," said Letitia, "but I've met Reverend Hardacre—"

"And I don't look like him," the man finished for her. "Well, I'm afraid this is what he looks like without the girdle, the padding in the shoulders, the lifts in the cowboy boots and the two-thousand dollar hairpiece." He held up one hand and Chesney saw the flash of his diamond-studded, heavy gold ring. "This is part of the act, too, but I can't get it off. Too many steak and lobster dinners, I reckon."

He peered up at the woman through washed-out hazel eyes and continued, "I don't have my contacts in, but I think I recognize you. Letitia Arnstruther?" When Chesney's mother confirmed the identification, Hardacre said, "You're the one who writes those awful letters. Sometimes I get copies from the lawyers of people I've sicced you all onto. They're practically pornographic. I used to not know whether to laugh or wince. Of course, now I know." He winced.

Chesney saw that his mother was not taking the Reverend Billy Lee's unembroidered revelations well. He thought he had better change the agenda. "Mr Hardacre," he said, "I'm Chesney Arnstruther."

Hardacre looked him up and down. "You're not the husband?"

"The son. We need to talk to you."

The preacher shook his mostly hairless head. "I don't think I'm any use to anybody right now, son," he said. "If I ever was any use before, which is a matter for debate."

"That," said Chesney, "is what we need to talk to you about."

Hardacre led them to a sitting room that could only be described as baronial: a vast stone-flagged floor covered in a handful of plush Persian carpets, any one of which would have more than handled the needs of Letitia Arnstruther's parlor; a high, domed ceiling from which descended a chandelier of black iron with gilded scrollwork; one wide wall pierced by tall, mullioned windows flanked by drapes of heavy, dark velvet; a fireplace in which a ox could roast, and above it a life-sized oil painting of the Reverend Billy Lee in a pose reminiscent of Charlton Heston's Moses preparing to part the Red Sea. Concealed lighting bathed the portrait in a glow that ensured that the image would be the first thing to which a visitor's gaze would be drawn.

Before the fireplace was a conversational grouping of massive armchairs upholstered in ox-blood red leather. Chesney thought they were designed to impress rather than to offer a comfortable seat, but he hadn't come for a relaxing chat. "My mother," he said, perched on the edge of the seat and regarding the preacher across yards of red and purple carpet, "thinks you may be able to help us with the…" – he sought for an appropriate word – "situation we all find ourselves in."

"What… situation?" Hardacre said.

"I've accidentally caused Hell to go on strike."

The reverend's face did not at first register any emotion. After a moment, Chesney saw the man's brows rise and fall, while his lips half-pursed then turned down at the corners in a frown of concentration. Finally, his eyes widened and his mouth half opened, the index finger of his right hand stirred the air in front of him then thrust forward to point at Chesney. "Ah," he said, nodding. "So that's it."

Chesney felt a ripple of relief pass through him. He exhaled, and only then realized he had been holding his breath while waiting for the man's response. He had been expecting to have to argue his case, but instead found himself in the position of the character in a mystery who provides the sleuth with the one clue that illuminates all the others.

"I've been puzzling over it ever since yesterday," Hardacre said.

"I would have thought you'd have been praying over it," Letitia said.

The Reverend's eyes couldn't twinkle without the blue contacts and the carefully focused lights of his television studio, but he managed a pretty good version of his down-home smile. "Not much point in that, ma'am," he said. "We kind of have an agreement: I don't bother Him, and He lets me get on with things in my own way."

"So you're not really a man of faith?" she said. Chesney heard nothing in her tone but innocent wonder. On any other day, the words would have been freighted with scorn and anger, but no power was stoking his mother's fires.

"That's a complicated question," the preacher said, pausing as if to consider it. Then Chesney saw him put the matter aside as he continued, "but it seems your son has a more pressing conundrum for us to deal with. So why don't you tell me how you got yourself – and all of us, I guess – into this fix?"

So Chesney told him, starting with the poker night and working his way up to the encounter with Satan in the park. Hardacre listened, interrupting here and there to pose a small question. When the tale was told, he bowed his head, steepled his fingers and touched them to his lips, a gesture not of prayer but of concentration. After a long silence, he looked up and said, "I think your mother has indeed brought you to the right man." He paused and quirked his lips, then said, "Ordinarily, I would say that with a genuinely overweening pride, but I now understand why the fellow who supplies me with that emotion isn't on the job.

"Even so," he continued, rubbing his palms briskly together, "no reason why we shouldn't get down to work."

"What can we do?" Chesney asked.

"Well," said the reverend, "it's been a long time since I've handled one, but first we're going to bring all the sides to the table and see if we can get a bargaining session."

"I will not," said Satan.

"You gotta," said the red snake protruding from the little blonde girl's mouth. "We've given all we've got. Management has got to cut us some slack."

"I do not manage Hell," said the Archfiend. "I *reign* over it. I will not yield."

The little girl folded her arms across her pinafore. Satan examined the ceiling, as if he found it far more interesting than the fuming demon across the table.

"All right," said the Reverend Billy Lee Hardacre, "I think that's enough for our initial session. Now I'd like to suspend negotiations while I explore some opportunities for finding common ground. Then we'll meet again. Shall we say one hour?"

"You gotta be kidding," said the IBFDT president.

"Pointless," said the Devil.

"Not so," said Hardacre. "I believe I see a way out of this seeming impasse."

The demon used a scatological term to express contempt and disbelief. Satan only turned his stygian gaze upon the mediator and lifted one thin eyebrow to convey the same sentiment.

"You'll just have to trust me," said Hardacre.

"Why should we?" said the Devil.

The preacher rose and ordered the papers he had spread before him on the table. "Because," he said, "I know something you don't."

Chesney and his mother had spent the bargaining session in a butler's pantry next to the big dining room that Hardacre had designated as the site for the encounter. The mediator had left the door slightly ajar and they had listened in. Now as he came through from the meeting, Chesney said, "That didn't seem to go well."

"It always starts like that," Hardacre said. "If it didn't, they wouldn't need a mediator." He had dressed for the occasion: one of his carefully tailored suits, hand-tooled western boots, the silver-haired toupée.

"What did you mean," Letitia asked, "when you said you knew something they didn't?"

"Ah," said Hardacre. He laid the thick sheaf of pages he'd been carrying down on a side table. "That will take some explaining. And first I need to talk to someone else." He looked at Chesney. "You said that your guardian angel was going to seek advice from someone higher up the ladder?"

"Yes, but I haven't heard back. I got the impression it didn't want to deal with me."

The preacher nodded. "I'm sure it didn't. But we can't allow them that option." He addressed the air. "Time to show yourself. We need to talk."

Nothing happened. Hardacre sighed. "I can solve this, but you have to buy in." He waited. "Otherwise, it all stops, and He'll never know how it ends." When he said, "He," Hardacre pointed a finger upwards.

A soft chime sounded, an achingly beautiful note that hung in the air, and a tall, fine-featured man with hair as blond and fine as corn silk, dressed in an impossibly white suit, was suddenly standing before them. "What do you mean?"

Hardacre had his own question: "Throne or Dominion?"

"Throne," said the angel. "Now, what did you mean?"

"I mean," said Hardacre, "that He's written Himself into a corner. When that happens, it's up to the characters to save the story."

Chesney thought it was probably the first time the angel's perfectly smooth brow had ever had to wrinkle. "I beg your pardon?" it said.

"I'll explain," said Hardacre, "over lunch."

"I'll be glad," Hardacre said, serving out plain bologna sandwiches and glasses of water, "when we get this settled. I miss gluttony."

The angel did not partake but joined the three mortals in the dining room. "You were going to explain," it said.

Hardacre chewed his sandwich without enjoyment and swallowed. "It all goes back to when I was writing my seventh novel," he said. "I got stuck halfway through. I'd started out knowing what the story was about, but the further I got into it, the more the characters took on a life of their own. They developed in ways I hadn't anticipated. After a while, I couldn't see how I could make them do what the story said they ought to do."

"I believe that's not an uncommon situation," the angel said. "Don't authors sometimes find that the characters take over the story?"

"Indeed. And a wise writer follows where they lead. Characters make stories. The writer creates them then puts them down in an arena called the blank page and lets them go at each other, full rip. They have to go at each other because they are really just bundles of attributes – characteristics – that guarantee they're going to collide with each other. So you get conflict, and out of that conflict comes story. A good writer trusts his characters enough to let them be who they are. You let them do what they do, because what they do is who they are. The author is never on surer ground than when his characters are doing what their natures demand they do – like I said, full rip, putting it all on the line.

"So when I got blocked, writing that novel, I just sat back and let my characters decide where they wanted to go. Away they went, and together we made a different book from the one I had set out to write. That made me realize that it's not the writer's story; it's the *characters'* story, and the author is just writing it for them."

"Very witty," said the angel, "but what does it have to do with the situation?"

"The experience," Hardacre said, "taught me that you can not only learn by reading books. Sometimes you can learn by writing one. And that's when I had my revelation, the one that made me give up law and literature, and go after a degree in theology."

Chesney chewed his almost tasteless sandwich and listened to the preacher offer his argument. The more he saw of Hardacre, the more he saw how the man took over the situation, the less the actuary could maintain his belief that he was the central figure in this story. He found himself thinking that perhaps it was time to accept that he would always be an outsider, one who watched from the sidelines as more determined people pushed and elbowed each other, or stroked and pulled together.

Yes, he had started something when he accidentally called up a demon, but it now looked as if he would not be the one to finish what he started. Listening to Hardacre expound to a high-ranking member of the heavenly hierarchy, he thought, I guess he's the hero of all this. I'm just the character who gets the ball rolling, so that somebody like the Reverend Billy Lee can step in and play the leading role. He looked at his mother, whose eyes were locked on the preacher, even though there was an actual angel right there in the room, and wondered if any woman would ever take that much interest in him.

"But you never actually received a degree in theology, did you?" said the angel. Chesney saw that the news came as a surprise to his mother.

"No," Hardacre admitted, "my doctoral thesis was not accepted." He paused for effect. "But I'll bet it would have to be accepted now."

Again the angel looked perplexed. But Hardacre had turned to Chesney now. "You're an actuary. You work out the odds of this or that event happening to this or that segment of the population."

"Yes."

"Have you ever noticed that the guy upstairs has often dealt to us from a stacked deck?"

"What do you mean?" Chesney said.

"Take Adam and Eve," Hardacre said. "He sends two innocents out into a garden where an evil intelligence is plotting to destroy them. Does He warn them about the snake?"

Chesney shook his head.

"Or consider Cain and Abel. Cain's a farmer. Abel's a shepherd. They both work hard, bring Him their best offerings – and Cain probably had to work harder to grow crops. All Abel had to do was follow a bunch of sheep around. But He blesses Abel's offering and disses Cain's."

"But when Cain kills Abel," Chesney said, "God doesn't punish him. He sends him off to find a wife and even puts a mark on his forehead to warn people to leave him alone."

"Exactly," said Hardacre. "Did God not consider murder – and of a brother, mind you – not a punishable offense? And when Cain asks, 'Am I my brother's keeper?' he gets no answer. Seems like a straightforward question of ethics, but God's apparently stumped for an answer."

The angel opened its mouth to speak, but Hardacre kept right on. "And then there's poor old Job. His life gets caught up in a bet between God and the Devil. His wives and kids are killed, his goods are destroyed, he gets covered in boils, and when he complains he gets told to mind his own business."

"It wasn't quite like that," said the angel.

Hardacre waved the objection away. "And there's other stuff. There are two different creation stories in Genesis. And there's the story of Noah and the Flood. He doesn't like the way His creation is going, so He erases the whole thing and starts all over. Who does that?" The question was rhetorical; Hardacre immediately supplied the answer: "Writers do that."

"What is all this leading to?" said the angel.

Hardacre put up a hand in a way that asked that the question be deferred. "One more thing. The most important clue of them all: I kept noticing all the books."

"Books?" Chesney said.

"He's always encouraging us to write books. The Torah, the Gospels, the Koran, the Rig Veda, the Book of Mormon, lots more. Even when virtually everybody was illiterate, he was inspiring people to produce books."

"He wants you to remember what was important," said the angel.

If Hardacre's tempter had been on the job, Chesney thought, he would have nudged the preacher into at least a prideful snort. Instead, Hardacre just said, "I don't think so."

"You question?" said the angel.

"Yes, because that's what we're supposed to do." He appealed to Chesney. "If He wanted us to read a book, why didn't He just write one and have it delivered to us at birth? Why not just put the information into our heads" – he looked at the Throne – "the way he did with you? Why all the different versions, contradicting each other? And all written by us?"

"I assume you have an answer?" said the angel.

"I do," said the preacher. "But when I defended it as my doctoral dissertation, I got shouted at." He came back to Chesney. "But all the different books are a collective clue. They're what literary critics call a recurring motif."

"But what does the clue tell us?" Chesney said.

"The obvious," said Hardacre. "All of this," – he gestured broadly to include all creation – "is His book. And He's writing it to learn something."

"He is what He is," said the angel. "What does He have to learn?"

Hardacre turned to the heavenly visitor and gave him a gentle smile. "Morality, of course."

"To quote you," said the angel, "'I don't think so.'"

"You don't think at all," said Hardacre. "You were created, ready-made and perfect, to already know everything you need to know. What He needs you to know. You immortals – all of you, including the ones down below – are not characters in this story. The thing about characters is that they *change*. You don't change. You're just fixed factors, background actors, like weather or gravity.

"That's why we have free will and you don't. *We're* the ones who have to think. We have to work it out, move the story forward, make it come right in the end." He spread his hands. "The question is: what is 'right' in the end? What's the point of all this?"

Chesney's mother spoke. "To earn salvation."

The preacher shook his head. "But we wouldn't need salvation if He hadn't given us free will and sicced the Devil on us. And why would He keep changing the rules? For a long time we were damned if we ate pork and lobster, or wore cloth made of two different fabrics – then all at once we weren't. It used to be we could have lots of wives and concubines, then we could only have one, then He changed his mind again and told Mohammed he could have four. For a long time, 'an eye for an eye' was the acceptable standard, then suddenly it's 'forgive them their trespasses.'

"Besides, if He knows which of us is going to end up in Hell before He creates us, then isn't He at least partly to blame for creating the ones who are going to fail?"

Chesney made the connection. "You're saying He doesn't know what's going to happen."

Hardacre poked a finger in his direction. "Aha."

"But what about all those people who end up down there?" said Chesney. "God lets them fail and suffer so that He can learn something?"

"You can't make a story without some conflict," the preacher said. "Conflict means some people have to suffer. They can't all win. He's not writing a *Care Bears* episode."

"But that's cruel," said Letitia.

"It's the price we pay. And that He pays, too. Because He's partly responsible for our screw-ups."

"It's still cruel."

"Yes," said Hardacre, "but it's not real. *We're* not real. And when the story is all told, when He writes 'The End' at the bottom of the last page, then all this will wrap up. No more Hell, no more Heaven, no more angels, devils, saints or sinners. The story's done. It will be as if we never were."

"Then what happens to us all?" Chesney said.

"We go back where we came from."

"But where's that?"

Hardacre tapped his temple. "Where do any characters come from?"

"You're saying," the angel said, "that we are all characters in a book He is writing, and when it is finished, we will all be reabsorbed into Him?"

"You have a problem with that?" Hardacre said. "What did *you* think would happen in the end?"

"The world would end and all would be judged. The good ones of you will live in Heaven; the bad will go to Hell. You have read the Book of Revelation?"

"Oh, yes, just as I have read Zarathustra's writings and the Norse sagas," said the preacher. "The seminary had a good library. They're like the two Adam and Eve stories – early drafts. Since then, the story's moved on."

"It's a remarkable theory," said the angel. "But I'm not surprised that the seminary rejected it."

"Angels are never surprised," said Hardacre. "How could you be when you know everything you need to know? Just as you won't be surprised when my theory turns out to be correct."

"You believe you'll prove it?"

"In about an hour," said Hardacre. "When we resume negotiations."

The angel seemed genuinely curious. "How?"

But Hardacre only held up a finger while his other hand fed a baloney sandwich into his mouth.

"What is that doing here?" said Satan. For all Hell's reputation as a hot place, the look he gave the Throne could have frozen a bonfire.

"He's part of the solution," said Reverend Billy Lee Hardacre.

"No," said the angel, "I am not. I have no authority to intervene in this situation."

"You will have," Hardacre said. "Now, if we can all sit down, I'd like to put a proposal on the table."

They sat, though the Devil turned his head so that he did not have to look at the Throne. His sharp-pointed fingernails drummed impatiently on the polished wood.

"I've asked Chesney Arnstruther to be present because he is obviously part of the situation," Hardacre said.

"Very well," said Satan.

"Fine by me," said the snake-tongued little blonde girl.

"And Chesney's mother is here, well, mainly because she's his mother."

The Devil made a gesture of irritation but offered no objection. The IBFDT president shrugged its pinafore straps.

"Now, as I understand it," Hardacre said, "this dispute grows out of two roots: one, the number of sinners to be punished in Hell has grown exponentially and will continue to increase, putting limits on your work force's ability to maintain productivity; two, the arrival of labor organizers has introduced the concept of collective action."

Hearing no contradictions, he went on, "Shall I assume that under no circumstances would you countenance

doing less tempting, thus leading to a decrease in the intake of sinners?"

"That would not be acceptable,' said the Devil.

"That means we cannot address supply, therefore we
must deal with productivity. I have a suggestion for that:
down among your... population, in addition to labor organizers, you're bound to have a few public relations
consultants."

"Quite a few," said the Archfiend. "It's a field that re-
wards amoral inventiveness."

Hardacre said, "I suggest you pluck a few out of the
furnace and get them to advise you on the concept of
'opinion leaders.' Briefly explained, they are those individuals within any community who are not officially
recognized leaders but whose actions and views carry
more weight with their neighbors than do the deeds and
words of the bulk of the population. Public relations
practitioners have developed reliable techniques for
identifying them. If you concentrate your tempters on
opinion leaders, you can pay less attention to those who
follow their lead."

Satan stroked his pointed beard. "That would free up
tempters to join the punishment corps?"

"Exactly." Hardacre turned to the IBFDT president.
"Would you have any problem with a reallocation of the
work force?"

"Would seniority transpose from one corps to the
other?" the demon said. Hardacre looked to the Devil,
who thought a moment, then nodded. "Then we would
have no problem," the demon said.

"But your proposal would give an advantage to... the
other side," said the Archfiend, with a hate-filled glance
at the senior angel. "They already have superiority of
numbers."

The Throne said nothing, but a tiny smile moved the corners of its perfect lips. Satan growled.

Hardacre spoke before the rancor could escalate. "Suppose that the other side withdrew some of its effort, concentrating more on the same opinion leaders, easing up on humanity's rank and file?"

The angel gently stirred the air with two elegant fingers. "We would not do that."

"You would, and you will," said Hardacre, "if my theory is right."

"What theory?" said the Devil and the IBFDT president.

"He thinks," said the angel, "that we are all characters in a book that Himself is writing."

The demon vibrated its snake-tongue against its little-girl lips, making a unique sound of scornful disbelief. The Devil made a small sound and rolled his coal-black eyes.

"If I'm right," said Hardacre, "we'll know fairly soon."

"How?" said all three of the non-mortals at once.

"We'll know because the solution that you" – he nodded to the angel – "just found completely unacceptable will suddenly become completely acceptable. Just as there once was a hard shell over the earth called the firmament, and then there wasn't. Just as it was once possible to build a tower or put up a ladder that would reach from earth to Heaven, and then it wasn't."

"I don't remember the firmament, and the Tower of Babel is just a myth," said the angel.

"Because there's no need for you to remember," said Hardacre. "But the firmament and the tower, the sun that could be stopped in the sky, they were as real as this room. Then they were revised out of subsequent drafts. He keeps rewriting back chapters as he goes forward. I used to do that myself."

"How could you know this if we don't?" said Satan.

"Characters know what they need to know. That's how the internal dynamics of story-making work."

The Devil gave the mediator a hard look. Chesney admired the way Hardacre stood up under the power of that stare. "I find your idea offensive," Satan said, "not to mention ridiculous."

"If I'm wrong, we all just sit here and the story comes to a dead stop. If I'm right, we make a deal and move on."

They sat. The only sound in the room was the staccato drumming of Satan's fingers on the table top. Chesney noticed that the wood was becoming gouged and scorched.

After a while, Reverend Billy Lee said, to no one in particular, "When you find you've written yourself into a corner, the thing to do is: remove a wall."

They waited. The Devil's drumming grew more impatient. Smoke rose from beneath his fingertips. He opened his mouth to speak.

And the Throne said, "We accept."

Satan cast his heavenly adversary a suspicious glance. "Didn't you say the proposal was unacceptable?"

"Did I?" said the angel. "I don't recall."

The Devil blinked and his expression took on an inward cast, as if he had just lost the train of his thought. "What just happened?"

"I think we got a deal," the IBFDT president said.

Billy Lee Hardacre said nothing. But Chesney had never seen a man look so happy.

"But you cannot tell anyone," said the angel.

It seemed to Chesney that Hardacre was about to argue. Then he saw a sequence of thoughts cross the preacher's face, the last one being acceptance. "Yes, that's fair," he said.

"And you," the angel said to Satan, "may not tempt him to tell." Satan's brows clouded, and the room suddenly smelled of sulfur, but the angel went on implacably, "or the deal's off."

The Devil's lips drew down in a grim frown. For a long moment, the issue hung in the balance. Then he said, "Not acceptable."

"Of course," said the Throne. "It's your pride. Your damnable pride."

"As it always was," said the Archfiend, "and always will be."

Hardacre spoke. "Perhaps if the instigator of the crisis offered an apology."

Satan raised an eyebrow. "An abject apology?"

"But he is blameless," said the Throne.

"All the better," said the Hardacre.

Satan considered it. "The idea does have an appeal," he said. "He will have to bow down to me."

"But not serve you," said Hardacre.

Satan made a motion that dismissed the point as being of no significance. "And in front of all my subjects. We'll give everybody an hour off."

"Us, too," said the demon.

"Except for necessary crowd control," Satan shot back.

"Agreed. We'll use the reassigned tempters."

Hardacre looked around the table. "Then I think we can call this dispute settled," he said.

"Like flip-flonkin' flickafack, you can."

They all looked at Chesney. If he could have, he would have regarded himself with equal surprise. The words had come out of him before he had known they were there. And now he heard himself continue, "It's not fair. I have nothing to apologize for."

His mother had been regarding Hardacre with a gaze that looked to Chesney like pure adoration. Now she turned to her son and put a gentle hand on his arm.

"There is, my dear," she said, "a precedent."

"Are you saying you won't do it?" Hardacre said. "There's a lot riding on this."

Chesney's reaction had been an unthinking rejection of the injustice. Now he thought about it while Heaven and Hell waited to hear what he would say. And then an idea came to him. More than an idea, it was a revelation.

Maybe, he said to himself, I am the hero of the story after all. Aloud, he said, "I will do it," – he even paused for effect – "on one condition."

Hell, even on a temporary visit, was a deeply unpleasant experience. The heat made Chesney's skin ache, the air was caustic in his lungs, and the sights and sounds brought up surges of horror and pity from inner depths that the young man had not known he possessed. Still, he bore up under the pressure and when the time came he spoke, clearly and loudly, the words of the formal apology as they had been negotiated by Billy Lee Hardacre and His Satanic Majesty, that being the formal title by which Chesney was required to address the recipient of his apology. Then he made a deep bow and held it until he heard a small grunt of satisfaction from HSM.

The event took place on a narrow promontory of naked rock that arched out over an enormous pit, into which the entire population of the underworld had been crammed. Demons lashed and prodded them into serried ranks that stretched far beyond Chesney's powers of vision to penetrate the foul and filthy air. When Chesney straightened from his bow, he saw the final phrases of his apology – "and do most humbly beg Your Satanic Majesty to overlook the inconvenience and impudence of my unpardonable conduct" – as huge letters of fire slowly fading above the pit. After his little grunt, the Devil made no response other than to wave the matter away as if the whole business were of not the slightest consequence.

The IBFDT president then stepped up and signed an ornately decorated and sealed document. Satan did likewise. The ruby-red snake protruding from the demon's little-girl's mouth then shouted, with a surprisingly stentorian volume for such a small serpent, "We've settled. Everybody back to work."

FOUR

A moment later, Chesney found himself back in his studio apartment. The electronic calendar on the countertop between the main room and the kitchen nook said that it was the same day on which he had first summoned up the toad-demon. The calendar's clock function ticked over to the second just after he had smashed his thumb with the hammer. As with the firmament and the Tower of Babel, the days when Hell had gone on strike had been written over and thus they never were.

Chesney's thumb hurt and bled, but he suppressed the urge to utter anything more than a heartfelt groan. Nor did he shake the wounded digit, spraying blood on his unfinished poker table. Instead he popped it into his mouth and sucked it.

"Isn't that a pretty sight?" said a gravel-scratchy voice. Chesney turned to see the diminutive, weasel-headed supervisor in the Al Capone suit, regarding him with disgust. "A thumb-sucker, yet."

Chesney extended the hurt thumb. "Heal it."

The fiend shrugged.

"Xaphan, I command you," Chesney said – they had now been formally introduced – "heal my thumb."

Xaphan rolled its weasel eyes then gestured brusquely. Immediately, the pain left Chesney's thumb, the swollen redness disappeared and the split flesh from which his blood had flowed was whole again.

"Good," said the young man. "Now let's get to work. We don't have much time before the guys come over for poker."

The demon consulted a gold pocket watch chained to its vest. "I can give you one hour, fifty-nine minutes, five seconds. And no banking any unused time."

"I know the terms of the deal," said Chesney. "So in the future, don't waste time reminding me." He rubbed his hands. "Now, first thing is, I'm going to need a costume. It has to be bulletproof, knifeproof, fireproof, acidproof... " – he thought for a moment – "well let's just make it generally proof against anything that could harm me."

"You gonna want a cape?" Xaphan said.

The young man shook his head. Malc Turner, aka The Driver, didn't wear a cape. "But I'm thinking I should have some kind of utility belt to hold all the doodads I'll need."

"What kind of doodads?"

"Doodads that let me climb walls and see through doors, that kind of thing. We'll work it out later."

"You ain't gonna need no doodads," said the demon. "Anything you need to do, I'll make it happen."

"What if I need super speed?"

"I can do that."

"The strength of ten men?"

"Yep."

"See through walls?"

The half-sized fiend waved its hand and the wall between Chesney's apartment and the neighbors' became transparent. The neighbors themselves, a couple who had recently immigrated from Mumbai looked up from their couch in some startlement.

"Transparent for me," said Chesney, "not for everybody." Xaphan moved his hand again and now the Indian couple were looking at each other with a *did-you-see-that?* expression. "Can you make them forget that happened?" the young man said.

"Sure."

The man was getting up and approaching the wall, one hand gingerly extended.

"Then do it!"

Now the neighbor was standing in his living room, looking at his outreached hand with a puzzled look on his face. His wife said, "Sanjit? What are you doing?"

Chesney said, "Make it opaque again." The demon shrugged and the wall reappeared. "Is there anything you can't do for me?" the young man said.

"Can't remake the whole universe," said Xaphan, counting on its stubby fingers, "can't do nuttin' that's outside the deal, can't do nuttin' that conflicts wid some other mug's deal." Now it wagged one of its little digits. "Hell don't fight Hell. That's about it."

"Okay," said Chesney, "now back to business. First, I need a good name."

"Howzabout 'The Bozo?'"

"Enough of your sass," Chesney said. "I'm thinking, maybe, 'The Actionary.' How's that sound?"

The demon rolled its oversize eyes. "Like some punk thinks he's top of the world."

"Listen," said Chesney, "a deal's a deal. You're my 'condition' and your boss agreed to it. I get you two hours out of every twenty-four, you come when I call you, and together we fight crime and bad guys."

The fiend put its hands in its pockets and scuffed its spatted shoes against the carpet. "I don't like this. I don't like you."

"You don't have to. Back to the costume. I've always liked Batman's colors, blue and gray, good for lurking in the shadows, but I want a big capital 'A' on my chest."

Xaphan muttered something that Chesney didn't catch. He ignored it and continued. "And gloves – no, gauntlets, that's the word – and boots to match. And it's all got to fold up small enough to fit into a pouch I can carry in my pocket, for when I have to go into action on short notice."

"Just say, 'Xaphan, costume,' an' I'll put it on ya pronto."

"Really?"

The demon sniffed. "We're Hell," it said, "we don't monkey around." It looked Chesney up and down. "You're kinda scrawny. You want me to bulk ya up a little? I could give ya a cleft chin and a little curl of hair down over your forehead, howzzabout that?"

Chesney was tempted; then he realized that wasn't supposed to happen. "Hey," he said, "part of our deal is you don't tempt me."

The demon shot its cuffs and hitched its shoulders. The motion was familiar to Chesney but it took a moment for him to recognize the source: old black-and-white movies starring Jimmy Cagney. Now the demon lifted its weasel chin and the Cagneyesque resemblance was unmistakable. "Yeah, okay," it said, "a deal's a deal."

Chesney said, "I'll need a mask so I can keep my identity secret. A half-mask, like The Driver's, covering me from the forehead down to the end of my nose."

"What else you want? Maybe a fortress of solitude? A glass airplane?"

Chesney ignored the sarcasm. "No, but I'll need a bigger apartment."

Xaphan flicked its hands in opposite directions. The inner walls of the studio blew outwards. Chesney saw his startled Indian neighbors sitting dazed amid billowing clouds of drywall plaster. "Undo that," he said, and when the walls instantly went back in place, "and from now on you only do what I directly order you to do."

The demon sulked.

"At least until we've worked the bugs out," Chesney said.

"Bugs?" the demon said. "That's a good one, coming from you."

"'Bugs' hasn't meant 'crazy' for, I dunno, fifty, sixty years," Chesney said. "You should get a software update."

"You don't like how I talk?"

"To tell you the truth, not so much."

"Well," Xaphan said, "so's your old man."

"Can't you talk properly?"

The demon looked reflective for a moment, then it said, "Here's how I done it the time before last." It shimmered and suddenly Chesney was seeing a fanged weasel head emerging from a stained shirt with frills on its front and huge puffy sleeves. Its head was wrapped in a colorful bandana and its legs in coarse leggings that disappeared into scuffed calf-high boots. A sash that separated shirt from leggings had a broad-bladed sword thrust through it. The sabertooth fangs opened and Xaphan shouted, "Avast, ye hog-swivin' mutton-thumper, a pox on yer jibber-jabber and fetch me a flagon o' best rum!"

"I only understood half of that," Chesney said. "Go back to the way you were."

The gangster version of Xaphan shimmered back into view. "Say," it said, "ya got any rum around here? I remember I kinda developed a taste for that stuff."

"No."

"Maybe we could go out for some?"

"No," the young man said. "Now where were we? We've done costume." He snapped his fingers. "I know, tell me where some really bad guys hide out."

"Oh, swell," said the demon. "You just slay me. You sure you're ready?"

"I want to try my hand, learn by doing."

"Okay. You want me to just put you somewhere?"

"What about a vehicle, like the Batmobile?"

"You live in an apartment house," Xaphan said. "You wanna park some kinda fancy flivver down there onna street? This is how you keep your identity under wraps?"

The young man reluctantly abandoned the dream of peeling through the city on a whine of turbo-charged horsepower. Batman had needed a mansion built over a secret cave. Besides, Malc Turner got by with a standard-issue UPS truck. "You're right," he said, "how about you just get me where I need to go."

"Now you're cookin' wid gas," said the demon, with a saber-toothed smile. It raised a hand.

"Wait a minute," Chesney said. He was learning how to read his assistant's weasel face – or maybe it was just that a weasel-faced demon couldn't help but look as if he was planning to pull a fast one. "No getting me there stark naked, or sending me skidding into a room on my ass, or–"

"Yeah, yeah, I get ya. Don't need no list."

"So where were we?" Chesney said again.

"Costume. Plus you wanted a bigger apartment."

"Yes. Make it happen, but nobody gets hurt, and nobody loses out–"

"Yeah, yeah. I got it." The fiend moved a hand and they were standing in a larger room, better furnished. From the view out of the window Chesney recognized that they were in the same building but on a higher floor.

"What happened?" he said.

"This place suddenly became vacant," Xaphan said, immediately raising a hand to forestall Chesney's reaction.

"The guy who was here hit the number in the state lottery. Now he's lit out for Florida or someplace."

Chesney felt the sudden chill that had filled his innards fade away. "That was pretty nice of you," he said, "helping the guy out like that."

The weasel eyebrows wriggled. "I don't do nice. He's the kinda mug who's gonna blow through the five mil in coupla years. Then he's bumming nickels to buy a bottle of rotgut."

"Oh." Chesney wasn't sure how to respond. The demon smoothed it out for him by saying, "What the guy does with the dough, that's up to him, see? Not your say, so not your problem. Besides," – it ostentatiously fished out its pocket watch – "we're eating up the day, here."

"Right," said the actuary. Outside the window, the afternoon had turned to evening. Dark clouds were forming over the skyline. On one of his new apartment's walls hung a full-length mirror and now Chesney saw that the demon had dressed him in the costume he had specified. The young man ran a gauntleted hand down his chest, over the big, gray capital "A" set against a circle of blue flames, then down to his belly. He noticed that his chest and shoulders were wider than they had been, and the close-fitting cloth revealed an abdomen that was both flatter and bumpier than the real thing. He was going to order Xaphan to undo the improvements, but then he experienced a rare-for-him second thought: he looked better like this, and image was important in the superhero business.

"Good job," he said. "So, a spectacular crime, we foil it, make a splash. What have you got?"

"I dunno," said his assistant. "Maybe you oughta start out small, pinch some punk shoplifter or–"

"No! You only get one chance to make a first impression. I want to do this right."

The demon pursed its narrow black lips in thought, then held up a stubby index finger. "Got it! A kidnapping. Beautiful young heiress. How's that sound?"

"Perfect!"

"And a bonus," Xaphan said. "You already know her."

"I know an heiress?"

The demon moved a finger upward as if flicking an invisible switch. Immediately an image glowed in the air for a moment before it evaporated: heart-shaped face, blonde hair, blue eyes, a tiny mole on one cheek.

Chesney took a sharp inward breath and let it all go as he said, "Poppy Paxton!"

"That's the one. They're gonna snatch her from outside the Peabody Museum in…" – Xaphan consulted its time-piece again – "about thirty seconds."

Chesney was finding it difficult to get his breathing under control. An invisible hand seemed to be compressing and releasing his diaphragm so that he breathed in and out in short bursts. "We… gotta go!" he managed.

"Say the word," Xaphan said.

"I just did!"

"Oh. Yeah. Okay."

"No, wait! The guys are coming for poker!"

"You want me to cancel it?"

Chesney started to say, "Sure," but he was learning caution. "No tricks?"

"They'll get a call from you sayin' you're sick."

"Okay."

"Done."

"Let's roll."

The living room disappeared. Chesney had an impression of a half-lit place filled with rushing winds beneath a torn sky, then almost immediately he was somewhere else: a sidewalk in a part of the city where the buildings were large and built of stone in a style that would have made Julius Caesar feel right at home. Across the street was the city hall, with its dome and fluted pillars. Next to it was the stained brick fortress that housed Police Central. And that meant that right behind him was the Peabody, where Chesney used to go and stare at the dinosaurs twenty years before.

He turned and saw the three flights of wide granite steps separated by two landings; they led up to the grand brass and glass doors beneath an art deco frieze that was supposed to show the march of time. One of the doors was just swinging wide on its great hinges; framed in a spill of golden light from within was the figure of a young woman in slacks and a cashmere coat. Behind her came a heavyset man in a business suit and topcoat.

The streetlights were just flickering on as the young woman stepped lightly down the first flight of steps, the man behind her coming with a slower, more ponderous tread, now pausing to light a cigar. Chesney recognized them both, though he had only seen Warren Theophilus Paxton once before, when the Chairman, as he was invariably referred to around PL&C, had briefly stopped by the third-floor Christmas party to grunt something that might have been "Seasons greetings," before being whisked away in his limousine to somewhere he would rather be.

Poppy Paxton now crossed the landing between the top and middle flights of steps and began to descend the latter. Her father seemed to be moving even more slowly, and Chesney thought he looked like a man with much weighing on his mind. Neither was paying any attention to the oddly costumed person standing near the bottom of the steps, beside the rectangular plinth that supported one of the bigger-than-life-size bronze lions that flanked the staircase.

"Can they see me?" Chesney whispered to Xaphan.

"Not yet," said the demon. "Figured you'd want to kinda make an entrance. Me, they ain't gonna see at all. Also, you say anyt'ing to me, nobody else hears it."

By now, the young woman was descending the lowest flight, her hair bouncing as she tripped lightly down the steps. At that moment, a black Cadillac Escalade slid almost silently to a stop at the curb. A sliding door on the near side opened and two men in dark clothing jumped out. They were big men but they moved quickly, without hesitation. One held a length of rope; the other had a cloth bag with a drawstring.

"I need speed and strength!" said Chesney.

"You got 'em!" said the demon.

"Okay!" Suddenly the young man felt lightfooted as the arches of his feet developed more spring. The scene before seemed to slow down, the men from the Escalade moving in slow motion. "Let's do it!" he said.

He was aware of a flash of bright light from somewhere above and behind him, lighting up the faces of the two men who were inching their way across the sidewalk. With exaggerated slowness, the men turned toward him, shock slowly taking charge of their expressions. He went at them Driver-style, his gauntleted right fist planting a solid uppercut into the solar plexus of the one with the bag while the heel of his left hand connected with the stubbled chin of the rope man.

Both blows were effective. Chesney thought his punching ability must approximate that of two Mike Tysons in their prime. He found it even more satisfying than he had anticipated. The first villain bent double with a *whoosh* of escaping air; the second man back-pedaled rapidly across the sidewalk and fell into the back of the Escalade.

A third man had been getting out of the vehicle's front passenger-side door as Chesney had gone into action. He now grabbed his bent-over accomplice by the rear of the gasping man's belt and spun him, then let him go tumbling through the gaping side door. Immediately, the third man stooped, snatched up the cloth bag his accomplice had dropped, then jumped in after the two casualties, yelling "Go, go!" and yanking the sliding door shut as the vehicle sped away in a squeal of tires and a stink of hot rubber.

Chesney's first thought was to give pursuit and he turned to give an order to his assistant. But instead of a fanged weasel his gaze fell, for the second time in his life, upon the wide eyes of the most beautiful woman he had ever seen at close range. His throat began to constrict.

The demon was sitting on the plinth, between the paws of the lion. "Xaphan…" Chesney said, under his breath. It was a call for help.

"Our deal," the demon said, "only covers crimefightin' remember? It don't say nuttin' about puttin' the moves on frails." It now gave the young man its widest, toothiest, and therefore least appealing, smile. "You're on yer own, mack."

Chesney swallowed and focused again on Poppy. His super-speed had departed so she was moving at a normal rate as she tilted her head to one side to regard him with an expression that was two parts amusement to one of *You've got to be kidding*.

"What," she said, "was all that about?"

"Um," said Chesney. He swallowed again, then rallied his forces. "Those men," he said.

"Yes?" she said. Her mouth opened and her hand made an encouraging gesture, like someone urging a stammerer to reach for the next syllable.

By now the older Paxton was hurrying down the steps, cigar clamped between his teeth. Chesney had to speak fast. He threw himself into the challenge, the way Malc Turner would. "They were going to kidnap you."

Now Poppy's face showed consternation. She looked up the street to where the van had long since disappeared. "What?"

"One had a rope, the other had a bag to put over your head."

"I didn't see any rope, or any bag," she said, looking him up and down now. "There was this flash of light and then... well, I don't know what I saw. I was still blinded by the–"

At this point, her father arrived and took charge, one arm moving his daughter back and to the side while he squared up to Chesney. "What's the meaning of this?" he said. He gave the costumed man the same head-to-toe scrutiny. "Who are you?" he said. "Hell, *what* are you?"

Chesney looked to Xaphan again, saw the demon's pin-striped shoulders move up and down in a shrug while it pretended to examine its nails. But the young man had read enough issues of *The Driver* to know that Malc Turner was frequently misunderstood by people he tried to help, though he also knew that a hero didn't let civilians set the agenda. "I'm the guy who just saved your daughter from kidnappers," he said.

Paxton removed the cigar from his mouth and stepped closer, pushing out a pugnacious chin. The older man was angry, Chesney could plainly see, but he was shoving his anger down and out of the way while his mind worked. Chesney had the impression Paxton was the kind of man who put thought before action and right now he was deciding how he would handle this.

"Daddy," Poppy said, "let's go. I–"

"In a minute," Paxton told her, though his eyes never left Chesney's masked face. "You're saying you foiled a kidnapping."

"I did."

"How did you know that was what was happening?"

"I... I can't tell you that."

"Why not?"

"Because you wouldn't believe me?" The truth was that the fine print in Chesney's agreement with Xaphan's boss prevented him from telling anyone that he had made a pact, however benign, with the Devil. Satan had insisted on that clause; this wasn't a deal he wanted noised around.

Paxton drew in some smoke, the cigar's lit end smoldering under Chesney's nose, then blew it out of the side of his mouth. "I wouldn't, huh?"

"Daddy," Poppy said again. Her father raised the hand that held the cigar in a gesture meant to shush her, but she went on to say, "The police."

And now the older man stepped back and looked past Chesney. A voice from behind the actuary said, "Everything all right here?"

Chesney turned. A man with a thin face and a thick mustache, dressed in a wrinkled, off-the-rack suit, was standing where the kidnappers' van had stopped. A uniformed patrolman was trotting across the street behind him. The plainclothes cop flipped open an ID wallet that held a gold-colored badge and a card with his picture on it. "Lieutenant Denby," he said, "Major Crimes Squad." He gave Chesney the same top-to-bottom inspection that the young man was coming to recognize would be the universal response to first encounters, at least until he had established himself in the community. "And you are?"

Chesney opened his mouth but before he could speak, W.T. Paxton eased him aside in much the way he had done earlier with his daughter and said, "He's with me, Lieutenant."

Denby's eyebrows climbed his wrinkled forehead. "Is he? And who are you?"

"Paxton, of Paxton Life and Casualty." When he saw that those six words had not kindled the right response in the policeman, he hooked a thumb over his shoulder at the museum and added, "Honorary chairman of the Peabody."

Denby's eyes had gone back to Chesney. "What's the 'A' for?" he said.

"Actionary," Chesney said, then with some emphasis, "I'm The Actionary."

But Paxton wasn't finished. He stepped past Chesney and drew the policeman's attention back to him, and when he had it, he said, "And a member of the Twenty."

The last remark registered with the detective. He gave Paxton the kind of look an intelligent man gives to a large dog that might bite. "I see," he said. Then Chesney saw a connection get made in Denby's mind. He looked from one man to the other then pointed a finger at Paxton. "Insurance," he said, then swung the digit toward Chesney. "Actionary." He looked toward Poppy and his eyebrows climbed again as he turned the finger pointing into a palm-up inquiry. "And you're...?"

"My daughter," said Paxton.

The plainclothes man had to move up onto the sidewalk just then as a long, sleek limousine pulled up to the curb. A uniformed driver got out and put on a hat, hurrying around to open the rear door.

"Where've you been, Harris?" Paxton snapped. "You're late."

"Sorry, sir. A car pulled right across the road in front of me. For a moment, I thought it might be a hijack attempt."

Paxton grunted. "Get in," he said. Poppy moved past him and took a seat in the back of the limo. It was a moment before Chesney realized that the reason the older man was standing beside the open door was because the instruction had included him as well.

"I have to go," he said.

"Nonsense!" Paxton said. "We need to talk."

Chesney very much wanted to return to his apartment and discuss what had happened with his assistant. The plan had not gone as he had foreseen. If anything, he had been too effective. The kidnapping was foiled before anyone except the kidnappers knew what was happening. He glanced toward the demon, still sitting between the paws of the bronze lion. Xaphan returned him as bland a smile as a saber-toothed weasel could manage.

"Get in!" Paxton said again. Chesney abandoned his plan of stepping around the nearest corner and being whisked away by his helper. He had a feeling that Lieutenant Denby might keep an eye on him, and a sudden disappearance would be hard to explain. Besides, the limo contained Poppy Paxton, and after all, he had just rescued her from kidnapping – and from who knew what other indignities the men in black might have inflicted upon her.

He climbed in. Moments later he was seated in the limo's rear-facing seat, with two sets of Paxton eyes on him. He noted that the father's were that palest shade of blue that writers called "icy," and there was nothing warm in the gaze that their owner turned on him. Poppy's were warmer, even if the only sentiment he could read in her gaze was curiosity – and not the good kind, the kind of curiosity that might lead to a closer relationship; it was more in the "just-how-weird-is-this-guy?" vein that Chesney remembered from the few times in high school or college when he had summoned up the courage to talk to a girl. The same scent that had rendered him helpless in the elevator at their previous encounter grew warm in the enclosed space of the car.

"So," said W.T. Paxton as the driver got into the front

and the car took them smoothly away from the two policemen, "what's with the get-up?"

Chesney looked past father and daughter and out the rear window of the limousine. There was a wing-shaped antenna mounted on the trunk, with a grinning weasel-faced demon sitting on it.

He took a deep breath, let it out, said, "I'm a crime-fighter."

That, at least, caught Poppy's attention, although he saw that the jury was still out on her assessment of his weirdness quotient. But she let her father carry the conversation forward.

"Really?" Paxton said. "And how's that working out for you?"

It was a good question, Chesney thought. And the answer had to be: not the way I'd expected. He had definitely foiled an attempt to kidnap Poppy Paxton. When the moment for action had come, he had done it all just right – in fact, just the way The Driver would have. He could still feel the sense of power and purpose as he had driven his fist into the first man's breadbasket and pushed his accomplice back into the van. In that moment, for the first time Chesney could remember, he had felt completely real – the hero of the story.

But ten seconds later, it had all been over. He'd been standing on a sidewalk, with people looking at him as if he'd just grown an extra head. And one of those people was the one person in the world he would have most liked to make a good impression on, the person who was now looking at him with an expression that said he was taking too long to answer her father's question.

He found it was easier to talk in her presence if he didn't look directly at her. "I'd say," he said, "that the results are mixed."

Paxton nodded in a way that said he took the answer as an understatement. "How long have you been at it?"

"This was my first... operation."

"And you just happened to be there when those guys tried to snatch my daughter?"

"I had... information."

"A tip-off?"

"You could call it that. I have a reliable source." Chesney thought about that for a moment, then added, "Semi-reliable."

Paxton was giving him a probing look. "So you know who the kidnappers were?"

"No." He made a mental note to ask Xaphan.

"You didn't say anything to the police," Paxton said.

If the conversation had been happening on the top floor of the Paxton Life and Casualty Building, Chesney realized, in a boss-to-underling mode, he would have felt intimidated by the older man. But there was something about being in his costume that made all the difference. He was a crimefighter talking to a civilian; indeed, he was talking to a man who ought to be grateful to The Actionary who had just prevented his daughter from being kidnapped. He was in a zone of pure light as he met Paxton's gaze and said, "Neither did you."

That response earned him a different look from the older man. For a long moment there was no sound in the soundproofed vehicle as Paxton regarded Chesney as if the young man was an investment under evaluation. He felt himself being weighed and judged – and not just by W.T., because into the silence came a small sound voiced by the woman, a sound that told the actuary that the answer he had given her father had caused him to rise a rung or two on the ladder of Poppy Paxton's opinion. He found he could turn and look into her own considering gaze.

The mask helps, he thought. Wish I'd thought of it years ago.

As if she could read his thoughts, she reached across the space between them as if to lift the mask. "Do I know you?" she said.

He did not pull back. He'd arranged with Xaphan that the mask could not be removed by any force but Chesney's own hand. Malc Turner was always having to keep bad guys – and his female admirers – from trying to peek under his half-mask. He felt the coolness of the tip of her red-tinted fingernail as it touched his cheek. The touch sent a shock through him, but he remained still. "It doesn't come off unless I want it to."

She made the same wordless sound again. "Some other time, maybe." Chesney had seen women smile that way at men, mostly in movies, never at him. For a moment he found it hard to breathe.

Then her father broke the spell. "Settle down," he told his daughter, "I've got business to talk with this fellow."

"What business?" Chesney said, glad of the opportunity to focus on something other than Poppy's paralyzing smile.

Paxton's cigar had gone out. He relit it with the limo's gold-plated lighter. "You're like one of those guys in the movies," he said. "You can climb walls and swing through windows?"

"Yes." Chesney hadn't tested those abilities yet, but they were in the specifications.

"And you can throw a punch. I saw what you did to those guys back there."

Chesney nodded. "I have the strength of several men."

Poppy made a different noise this time. Chesney knew he had gone up another couple of rungs.

"I'm not going to ask you how you got this way."

"Good. I couldn't tell you anyway."

Paxton was thoughtful for a moment, then said, "Can you fly?"

"No. I can jump pretty far." He hadn't tested it, but he was sure."

"Vision, hearing?"

"Well beyond the norm."

"Through walls?"

"If necessary."

Paxton sat back and puffed on the panatella. "But your information is not perfect. Semi-reliable source, you said."

"Yes."

"Which could be a problem."

"I'm just getting started," Chesney said. "I plan to develop a research and information capacity." He looked at Xaphan, got another shrug. "It might take time, but I'll get there. I'm good at working things out. Very good."

Paxton examined the smoldering tip of his cigar, tapped some ashes on the carpeted floor between them. His bottom teeth scraped at his upper lip while he worked out something of his own. "Tell you what," he said after a moment, "I've already got a research and information capacity. I run an insurance company."

"I see," said Chesney.

"How about I put my company's resources at your disposal? We develop crime statistics, intelligence, maybe even some surveillance capabilities. You take the data and run with it."

Chesney thought about it. It was an interesting proposal. Better than that, it was precisely what he needed to augment what he could get from his unreliable assistant. But he had one question. "Why?"

Paxton made an expansive gesture with his cigar hand. "Same reason I endowed the Peabody with a new wing. I'm a philanthropist."

Nothing had ever filtered down from the top floor to Chesney's department to support that statement. But he knew it was possible. Many people compartmentalized their lives, doing things in the world of business that they would never do to a neighbor. The richer you were, the better you could compartmentalize. "You want to help me fight crime?" he said.

"Why not? It would be good for business. My claims department pays out a fortune each year to victims of crime – property and violence. Plus, as you saw this evening, even I and my family can fall prey to the criminal element."

"I don't see myself as a glorified claims adjuster."

That got him another sharp look from the older man. "You know the insurance business?" And before Chesney could answer, Paxton said, "Yeah, how come 'The Actionary?' I know a few actuaries, and, believe me, you don't remind me of any of them."

Chesney looked away. He'd thought "Actionary" was a good pun; it had an "action sound" to it. But experience had told him that he never looked so lame as when he had to explain one of his puns. Then inspiration struck: In the first issue of *The Driver*, Malc Turner had been asked for the origin of his hero name. And Chesney remembered his answer: "Captain America was already taken."

That won him a little snort from Poppy Paxton, but it was the good kind of laugh – another rung ascended. Her father was taking a thoughtful drag on his cigar, a man making up his mind; and now he nodded and said, "Okay, we won't ask each other too many questions." He flicked more ash on the carpet. "But what about the offer?"

"I want to think about it," Chesney said.

Paxton reached into a vest pocket, pulled out a slim gold case and extracted an oblong of heavy, creamy card stock. His name was embossed in heavy black letters, a phone number and email address below. "When you're done thinking, get in touch," he said.

The young man took the card, slipped it into a pouch on his belt. "I will."

"I've already set up a research group," Paxton said. "When you're ready to work with me, it will be ready to work with you."

"You're very sure of yourself," Chesney said.

"You don't get to be me by wallowing in self-doubt," the older man said. "The world belongs to people who get up in the morning and *do something*. Now, is there someplace we can drop you?" Paxton said.

His daughter added: "A secret cave, or do you have a lonely eyrie?"

Chesney looked at her, but there was no mockery in the smile she gave him. "Anywhere will do," he said and a rush of happiness went through him, because he'd been able to look her in the eye and speak without losing control of his organs of articulation.

Moments later, he was standing on a sidewalk in the Stoney Bellereve neighborhood, watching the limousine pull away. Through the back window, he could see the back of W.T. Paxton's massive head, and the face of Poppy as she threw him a farewell smile. No girl had ever before smiled at Chesney Arnstruther in a way that said, "I'm looking forward to seeing you again," and he was savoring the moment.

It was not, however, the kind of moment his assistant wanted to prolong. The demon tugged at Chesney's arm, his other hand prominently displaying his chained pocket watch. "Pursuant to our agreement," Xaphan said, formally, "I got to clue you in to the fact that our two hours is just about up."

Chesney came back to the world. "Right," he said. He

looked up and down the street, saw a few cars and no pedestrians. "Can anybody see us right now?" he said.

The demon tucked his watch away. "There was a guy looking out an upstairs window cross the street when you got out of the limo, which I gotta say was a real doozie. Cars come a long way since last time I was here."

"Is he looking now?"

"Nah. His attention got attracted somewheres else."

Chesney could hear a smoke alarm shrieking from nearby. "He doesn't get hurt, right?"

"Just his dinner's kinda spoiled," Xaphan said. "He'll get over it."

"Then let's go—" He interrupted himself as a thought occurred. "Wait," he said, "can you get me into that special research group W.T. was talking about?"

"Does it got to do wid crimefightin'?"

"Well, yeah. It's doin' research on crime." He thought the fiend was looking for a way to deny the request, so he added, "And it would mean you wouldn't have to do so much."

Xaphan nodded. "I guess so. Okay, it's fixed."

"Then let's go home."

They were in the place of rushing winds. Thunder banged close by, then they were back in Chesney's living room.

"What is that place?" he said.

"You don't need to know," his assistant said, "so I ain't gonna tell ya."

Their agreement was that Chesney could call upon the demon's services for a total of two hours between one midnight and another. Xaphan's working time did not need to be scheduled in advance; he was always on call. "I'll summon you sometime tomorrow after work," he said, "unless something comes up."

The demon made a noncommittal sound and shrugged his shoulders. Then where he had been there was nothing but a dissipating puff of yellow vapor. Chesney went to open a window.

A half hour before the end of the working day on Monday afternoon, Chesney was summoned to the tenth floor. The receptionist at the entrance to the executive suite directed him down a hallway to an unmarked door. He knocked and the voice that told him to enter was a familiar one. It belonged to Arthur Entwistle, who had been Chesney's supervisor until a few weeks ago, when there had been a mysterious shake-up in the actuarial ranks of Paxton Life and Casualty. Several of the most experienced number crunchers had left the third floor. The word that circulated through the building was that they had been assigned to some special project and sworn to secrecy. Chesney's boss had been picked to supervise the hush-hush group.

Entwistle was thin on top and thick in the middle, and used to encourage the younger actuaries to call him "the Chief." Somewhere along the line, someone had changed that to "Sitting Bull." The "Sitting" part of the nickname referred to the section head's fondness for his executive swivel chair, while "Bull" was shortened from an eight-letter word.

Chesney and Entwistle had never gotten along. The supervisor wanted the young men under him to regard him as a father figure. He was big on back-patting and arm-around-the-shoulder moments, accompanied by "man's man" inquiries as to their love lives and weekend antics. These were not overtures to which Chesney could adequately respond, and Sitting Bull soon developed a distaste for the young man. Even though Chesney was the most gifted number cruncher on the third floor, Entwistle had not chosen him to join the special group.

So the expression that Sitting Bull wore when Chesney came through his door that morning was mixed. "Arn-struther," he said, "we're moving you upstairs. You're joining C Group."

Chesney looked around him. Entwistle's was a half-glassed corner of a larger space with floor-to-ceiling windows that had once been a conference room for senior executives. Through the glass he could see a half a dozen work stations, each with an actuary bowed over a mouse or keyboard, eyes on a monitor. "What will I do?" he said.

"Meta-analysis," Sitting Bull said.

Chesney saw no empty desks. "Has somebody got sick? Or..." He didn't want to finish the question, in case it turned out that Xaphan had made room for him in the section by creating a permanent vacancy, Hell-style.

"No, no," said Sitting Bull, and again Chesney saw a conflicted set of emotions in the man's face. "I'll tell you straight out, I wouldn't have picked you for this job, Chesney. You're not a good team player. You're a team of one, if I ever saw one."

Chesney shrugged and nodded to acknowledge a life-long truth.

"But," the supervisor went on, "Seth Baccala was looking over the quarterly reports, specifically the productivity scores for the third floor. Did you know you're the most productive actuary in the group?"

Chesney shrugged again. He never made comparisons. He thought that was probably part of not being a good team player.

"Baccala asked why you hadn't been brought in when C Group was ramping up. You know what I told him?"

"That I'm not a good team player?"

"Exactly. What I didn't tell him was that you can some-times be a smart-ass." Sitting Bull rolled his eyes. "This meta-analysis you're going to be working on is a personal priority of W.T.'s. I gave it to Ron to work on first, but W.T. was not happy with what he produced. So you're going to be taking over that project."

"All right," said Chesney. What he was thinking was that Xaphan had come through without doing any harm. Perhaps their relationship would smooth out as it developed, though he was pretty sure that the demon was not much of a team player either. In fact, his impression of Hell was that it consisted of tens of thousands of teams-of-one.

"We'll see what happens once you're finished with the job. Maybe you can stay up here."

"I'd like that, I think."

"And nobody's going to ask you to be a good team player. We both know that's not you."

"Yes."

"Okay. They're putting a workstation in for you over in the corner," Entwistle said. "Go and get yourself settled in."

There was a connecting door between the chief's corner space and the rest of the long room. Chesney went through it and saw that a man in a gray coverall was laying down a pad of hard plastic while another was wheeling in a desk with a chair on top of it. As soon as the desk was set up, an unkempt young man from the IT department arrived to equip it with a phone, tower computer and monitor. While Chesney watched, he connected the equipment by fiber-optic cables to a central LAN router.

The workstation's position gave Chesney a view through one of the high windows that had flooded the former boardroom with light and probably given the PL&C directors a sense of being masters of all they surveyed. Now the glass was covered in a semi-transparent film that colored everything outside in shades of bronze and removed all fine detail from the cityscape. That didn't matter to Chesney. When he worked, he *worked*. His eyes would lock onto the figures on his monitor and the rest of the world would have needed to exert itself considerably – perhaps a rain of fiery meteorites or a hundred-foot high tsunami – to call his attention away. He examined the computer they had issued him. It was a high-end system, better than the equipment he'd worked on downstairs. The IT nerd, a shaggy-haired young man in a tee-shirt that celebrated a feature-length Japanese anime production, was connecting a cable.

"No wireless?" Chesney said.

The IT tech looked up, shook his hair. "All hard-wired."

"Security?"

"Up the wazoo." He pointed at a plastic box mounted high on one wall. "And your cell phone won't get a signal. Landlines only. With encryption scramblers."

"Serious," said Chesney.

"Old W.T.'s got some kind of major bug up his–" The IT tech was interrupted by the emphatic clearing of a throat. He turned and went pale, then found something he had to do right away in another part of the building.

Chesney turned his head and discovered that the throat in question was a familiar one. It led directly up to the firm chin of Poppy Paxton, an item of her anatomy that was now elevated along with her nose, down which she regarded Chesney in an imperious manner.

"You are not paid," she said, "to pass judgments on my father."

Chesney blinked, swallowed, blinked again. The confidence that had begun to fill him during the ride in the limousine now seemed to leak out of a tap that had apparently opened in one of his feet. He imagined it pooling around his loafers, melting the carpeted floor so that he would sink through it and disappear like a jungle explorer in a pool of quicksand.

He realized it was necessary for him to say something that would salvage the situation, but the only utterance that was available was not up to the task. "Um," he said.

The syllable triggered a memory in Poppy Paxton. "You're the one from the elevator!" she said. Her perfectly arched eyebrows climbed to a previously unreached altitude. "Oh, no. You won't do. This," – her hand took in the concentrated quiet that filled the big room – "demands the best of the best!" She looked around with the same expression she would have presented to an upmarket store of which the sales clerks had failed to meet her standards, looking for a manager to whom she intended to give firm instructions for the permanent removal of Chesney Arnstruther, preferably accompanied by a kick in the seat of the pants that would confirm for him that he was not welcome to return.

Last night, in the guise of The Actionary, he had scaled several rungs in the ladder of Poppy Paxton's esteem and had breathed the rarefied air of the high ground. At this moment, he wanted nothing more than to repeat the experience in his mundane identity. He had never wanted to prowl with the lions here on ten, but now he did, if it meant he would have the chance to see her, up close, again and again. He summoned up every remaining ounce of his confidence; more than that, he actually reversed its flow out of his loafers. The quicksand drained and dried beneath him. "I am," he said, "good with numbers."

She turned her gaze back on him, eyes wide in mock surprise. "It speaks!" she said.

Chesney looked down at the desk, but he was surprised to hear his own voice say, with some force, "I'm damn good with numbers!"

"They talk to you, do they?"

He looked up, right into the coolness of her blue eyes. "They sing to me," he said. It was a line he'd heard in some movie or TV show, and he delivered it the way he remembered the actor doing it.

Now her eyebrows came down and got together for a reassessment of the odd creature before her. She tapped the tip of her tongue against the back of her top front teeth, then she said, "And what's the name of the tune?"

All at once the actuary realized that he was on the brink of a new experience. For here he was, talking to an attractive woman, which meant he was in territory that should have been dangerously dark; but the subject of their conversation was that which stood beneath Chesney's brightest sun: numbers. He was in a pool of light.

He imagined that his remote ancestors must have felt like this when they stepped out of the Paleolithic forest and into the vast possibilities of the grassy veldt. So when he said, "They sing to me," and she said, "And what's the name of the tune?" a feeling like helium bubbles effervesced through his torso and the scene was suffused with a sublime clarity. He held Poppy's gaze and let a moment of expectation slip by before he answered her. "Order," he said, "and predictability."

He could see he was definitely back on the esteem ladder. She tucked her chin down and regarded him from under knitted brows. "All right," she said, "what's the property crime rate in the city?"

More joy. He had been researching the subject even before his encounter with demonic entities. "The whole city?" he said, "or specific neighborhoods?"

Her expression said, *Oh, so you came to play?* while her voice said, "Best and worst."

He didn't have to think. "Best is Bellereve – 103.4 incidents per one hundred thousand residents; worst is

Franklintown – 814.9 per hundred thousand. Trend line is about the same for both: three per cent increase per year over the past seven years."

As he'd been speaking, she had taken out a Blackberry PDA and begun tapping its keys. After a moment she looked up in surprise. "That's right," she said.

It seemed she was waiting for him to respond. It was time to be casual. He knew that from sad experience. Intensity was the mood-killer. "It's kind of a hobby of mine," he said.

"You're a crime freak? You own a police monitor?"

From the way she asked the questions, it didn't sound to Chesney as if "Yes" would be the right answer, even though he had, in fact, just acquired a monitor; he thought it could help him in his new career. "Just the numbers," he said.

"Oh," she said. "Well, good." She seemed to be casting about for something more to say until she settled on: "Keep up the good work."

Behind her, Chesney now saw Sitting Bull come out of his cubicle, throw a troubled glance at the combination of the poor team player and the boss's daughter, then exit through a door at the end of the room. He went out and came back almost immediately, followed by a smoothly groomed man of about thirty in a closely tailored suit of conservative cut. Sitting Bull led the newcomer to where Chesney and Poppy stood.

"This is him," the chief said, indicating the actuary, "Chesney Arnstruther." He did not bother to perform the reverse introduction; everyone at Paxton Life and Casualty knew Seth Baccala, the boss's right hand. Around the third-floor water cooler, Baccala had been known as "W.T.'s baby strangler." It had not been suggested that the executive assistant had ever strangled any babies, just that if W.T. ever need that job done, Seth Baccala was the one who'd do it.

Baccala had a soft voice, the kind that's often developed by people who have no doubt that whatever comes out of their mouths is going to be listened to. "You missed the original briefing," he said, "and I've got a meeting in five minutes. So I'll summarize for now and we'll go into it in more detail tomorrow. Besides, W.T. himself will want to meet you.

"This is a special section denoted to developing an in-depth understanding of crime and crime-related matters in our city. Eventually, the focus will expand to cover the whole state."

"Why?" Chesney said. The interruption caused a reaction in Sitting Bull as if he had unexpectedly touched a live electric cattle fence, and his hands came halfway up as if he wanted to clamp one of them on the back of Chesney's neck and the other over the actuary's mouth.

But Baccala went on speaking as if he hadn't heard. "Everything that happens here is strictly confidential. You don't talk about it outside this room, and inside the room you talk about your work only as much as is necessary to carry out your responsibilities. In other words, no water-cooler chat, no gossip. Is that understood?"

"Yes."

"Arthur, here, will give you a nondisclosure agreement to sign. You will notice that the penalties for breaching the agreement are stringent. Please have no doubt that they will, if necessary, be imposed, in full and in detail."

"All right," Chesney said. He had had very few conversations about his work, having met very few people who thirsted for knowledge as to what the life of an actuary might entail.

"On the other hand," Baccala said, with a smile that despite its meagerness still seemed forced, "you have been bumped a pay grade and your parking space will be moved closer to the main door."

"I don't have a parking space," Chesney said.

"Why not?"

"I don't have a car." His attempts to learn to drive had been thwarted by his tendency to focus excessively on particular details of the process rather than on the overall aim of guiding a vehicle safely through streets full of other moving vehicles. His instructors could not rely on his being able to grasp that adjusting the side mirror to the precisely correct angle was more important than noting the color of the traffic lights at an upcoming intersection.

Seth Baccala took the information in stride. "Then Arthur will get you a bus pass, on the company."

"Thank you."

"Your first assignment is to perform a meta-analysis on a particular aspect of the relationship between certain crimes and media coverage. Arthur, would you get... Chesney, was it?"

"Yes," Chesney said.

"Would you get Chesney started?"

"Yes, sir."

Throughout the conversation, Chesney had been distracted by Poppy's presence. He knew that this encounter was coming to an end and he wanted it to close on a note that would sustain the good impression he believed he had made. He looked at her instead of at either of the two men as he said, "I'll do my best."

The look she gave him was encouraging. He could have added that he always did his best, explaining – as the consultants' report had explained to his mother back in grade school – that "the child has, in a sense, only an on/off switch, not a rheostat. He is completely engaged by the things that interest him, sometimes to a degree that resembles obsessive compulsive disorder, though his is not a case of actual OCD; conversely, he finds it very difficult to concentrate on things that do not attract his interest. He will need strategies to moderate the former and overcome the latter."

One of those strategies had involved learning not to tell people whatever was on his mind. Chesney used that strategy now to suppress the urge to explain himself. From the smiles that appeared on the others's faces – Poppy's seemed to be encouraging – he knew that reticence was once again the right choice.

FIVE

"What about a bank robbery?" Chesney said.

The demon ostentatiously showed the costumed crime-fighter his old-fashioned timepiece. "It's eight-fifteen at night, mack. They're all closed."

"Nobody tunneling into a vault?"

"No."

"A jewel heist?"

"Nope."

"Raid on a priceless art collection? A fur storage facility?"

"Nuh uh," said Xaphan. "Besides, I don't see classy dames wearing fur coats no more. How come?"

"It's a long story," Chesney said. "Let's pay attention to the business at hand."

The demon shrugged. "You're the boss."

Chesney thought his assistant's statement lacked conviction, but he did not want to let himself be distracted. "So there are no major crimes planned for this evening?"

"Not around here."

"Where would we have to go?"

Xaphan blinked and looked thoughtful for a moment. "Big horse shipment coming inta Frisco on a freighter.

Triple murder in Atlanta – that's a gang thing. Warehouse getting torched in Chicago. Guy who got fired from the post office in Waco is gonna shoot up the place, but he's not too handy with a gat, so it's nuttin' but flesh wounds. That's about it. The rest is pretty much routine."

"You mean muggings, kids stealing cars, burglars hauling away somebody's TV set."

"Yeah. So whadda ya say, wanna call it a night?"

Chesney fixed the demon with a hard look, but it returned his stare with the bland expression of a large, fanged weasel that lacked any vestige of a conscience. "What aren't you telling me?" he said.

"A lot of stuff," Xaphan said, ticking off the items on his stubby fingers. "The correct time in Belgium, your third grade teacher's favorite brand of breakfast cereal, how long it takes to boil an egg halfway up Mount Everest, what happened to that kid who wet the bed at Bible camp, who's gonna win the World Series–"

"Enough!" said Chesney. "I get it."

"Do ya?" said the demon. "Do ya really?"

"What are you saying?"

Xaphan sniffed, shot the cuffs of its shirt out from under those of its suit jacket, then hitched its shoulders under the pinstriped cloth. Chesney was sure now that he'd seen Jimmy Cagney do that same move in old gangster films. But the demon was answering his question. "Lemme level with ya, mack. I gotta help you do this cockamamie crime-fighter thing, you're all dressed up like Halloween, with your little mask that don't come off. But I don't got to fill you in on how the world works. That you get to find out for yourself."

"All right," Chesney said. "No need to rub it in."

"I'm a demon," Xaphan said, "we always rub it in." But it sniffed again, cocked its head to one side and said,

"Lemme ask you something. You wanna fight crime, but you don't know where to find it. Why don't you take that Paxton guy up on his offer? You know the info's legit 'cause you're workin' some of it up."

Chesney looked at himself in the mirror. They'd made some further modifications to his outfit – widened the shoulders, put a few more flames around the big "A." It was really shaping up. "I'm thinking about it."

"What's got ya worried?"

"Who says I'm worried?"

"Guy offers to help you do what you always wanted to do, you give him the cold shoulder. Gotta be a reason."

"Maybe there is. I don't have to tell you everything either."

"Maybe you just don't like him horning in on your action."

Chesney said nothing, brushed a nonexistent speck of dust off the big "A" on his chest.

Demons always rubbed it in. "Or maybe you're a little scared of that dollymop daughter of his."

The young man was stung. "I did all right with Poppy! Even," – he gestured at the mask – "without this."

A weasel shouldn't have as much lower lip as the demon now used to show its skepticism. "Oh, yeah," it said, "she's waitin by the phone, expectin' your call."

"Knock it off!" Chesney said. "Let's go fight some crime."

The demon spread its hands. "Sure. Whattaya got in mind?"

"Well, you say there's nothing big going down tonight. How about something small, but public?"

"You wanna break up a bar fight? There's one starting just after ten-thirty."

"No."

"Got a purse snatching, about five minutes."

Chesney sighed. "Really, is that it? The crime statistics

show a high incidence of violent offenses this time of the evening."

"Most of that's mom-and-pop stuff," Xaphan said. "Guy comes home from work, he's feeling sour cause his boss chewed him out. He has a coupla beers, gives the wife a smack cause she's raggin' on him about how he never takes her anyplace."

"There's got to be something."

"The purse snatching is public. At least it's in the park. Poor little old lady."

"I guess," Chesney said.

"I'm just kiddin' ya," said the demon. "It's actually a young cutie."

"Oh, well. Then, I suppose."

"Tell you what I can do," said Xaphan. "There's some reporters going to cover the mayor's speech tonight. I could fix it so that you do your party trick right where they can see."

"Reporters?" said Chesney. "You mean a television news crew?"

"Yeah, they got those cameras go on their shoulders. Me, I liked them old-time shutterbugs, the flash powder popping off. Smelled like… home."

The idea appealed to Chesney. But something told him to use one of his therapist-imbued strategies. He wasn't yet sure that Xaphan had his best interests at heart. "No, maybe not," he said. "I'm still new to this. Let's wait until I get the bumps smoothed out before we bring in the media."

"You say so," said the fiend.

"But we'll stop the mugging. And let's do it like before, so I just appear out of nowhere, with the flash of light."

"You got it."

There came the rush of dark winds again. Chesney had time to think that he ought to ask Xaphan again where they went when they went "inbetween," then there was no time for anything but the action of the moment.

They were in the park near the amphitheater and the basketball courts. The asphalt walkway was a band of darkness, the streetlights throwing scattered pools of light. A young woman wearing a worn topcoat over some kind of light blue uniform dress – maybe a hotel maid's or a nurse's aide's – was walking as swiftly as tired feet could manage at the end of a long day, her arms pulled straight down and her shoulders bent by the weight of two well-filled plastic shopping bags. Her purse was slung by its strap from one shoulder to the opposite hip, across her body, just the way the anti-theft posters on public transportation advised.

She was nearing the basketball court, where several young men were watching two of their number play one-on-one against each other. The woman saw them before they saw her. She quickened her pace, her eyes averted, though from his vantage point Chesney could see that she was watching them from the corner of her eye.

Now she caught their attention. The one who had just jinked around his opponent and sunk a basket with a leap and a high, looping motion of one arm saw her first. He recaptured the ball then paused, bouncing it in a slow rhythm, waist-high. The others turned to follow his gaze, and for a long moment, the bouncing ball and the walking woman were the only things moving in the park. Chesney was reminded of a nature show he had seen on TV: a trio of young cheetahs had caught sight of a limping gazelle. The cats' heads had moved in unison, slowly forward, exactly as the young men's did now.

The one with the ball stopped the bouncing. With a gentle flick of two hands he tossed it to the smallest and youngest of the gang, and gave a sideways toss of his head. The youth caught the ball and looked as if he wanted to argue with the leader, but then he ducked his head turned and loped away in the direction the woman had come from.

Taking the ball home, Chesney thought. His big brother doesn't want him in on this.

Now the group split. Four of them turned and loped off in the same direction in which the woman was heading, toward a place where the asphalt path was flanked by tall bushes. The other three watched the target go by, then ambled along after her.

"Night vision," Chesney said. His assistant obliged by sharpening his eyesight so that the twilight murk became the equivalent of a sunny afternoon. The streetlights were almost painfully bright, but The Actionary's eyes were on the shadows thrown by the bushes on the path ahead of the woman. The four who had gone ahead had positioned themselves there. One of them was bouncing on his heels, another reflexively spreading and closing his fingers, while the other two stood with hands in pockets, heads and shoulders craned forwards.

The young woman had not seen where the four went, but she was aware of the trio coming up behind her. As she neared the bushes, she looked back over her shoulder. The three sped up their pace now. They were looking right at her.

Chesney was reminded of a scene from another nature documentary: the lion that walked openly toward the herd of zebras and wildebeest, scaring them and making them run toward where the rest of the pride waited to pounce. "Get ready," he said to Xaphan. "Give me the flash when I say 'Now.' And maybe throw in some kind of sound effect."

"Like what?"

"I dunno. How about a clap of thunder?"

"Thunder? Yeah, sure. You got it."

"Good," said Chesney. Then a thought intruded. His contract with the Devil contained a clause that said Xaphan could do him no harm, by acts of commission or omission, arising from any interpretation of his instructions. But that protection was not extended to bystanders. "Not enough to deafen anybody," he now added. "Or give them a heart attack. Just enough to scare them."

The demon did its Cagney hitch and sniff again. "If you say so."

"I do say so." Chesney had been continuing to watch the scene in the park as they spoke, and he had been silently and invisibly moving toward where the path passed between the bushes. So had the woman with the shopping bags. She had been trying to walk faster, despite her burdens, but abruptly she stopped. She must have seen the nervous movements of the heel bouncer or finger flexer in the shadows ahead.

Now she set down the grocery bags and tugged at her purse to bring it around to her front. She flipped open its closing flap and dug around inside, coming out with a silver cell phone. With his enhanced vision, Chesney saw her face lit by the glow of the phone as she slid its top into the activating position. She tapped three times on the keyboard and raised the phone to her ear. Her other hand continued to root around in the purse.

Now the four lurking behind the bushes came into view, blocking the path. Chesney was pleased to discover that his mind was bathing this situation in one of his pools of light. He had no uncertainties about what was happening here. They were supposed to wait until she was almost upon them, he thought. Then they jump out, startle her, and while she's not sure what to do the three behind come and take her purse.

But it wasn't working according to plan. The young woman stood her ground, talking into the cell phone. Her other hand came out of the purse holding a stubby black canister, finger poised above a raised red button on its top. She pointed the pepper spray toward the four in an unmistakable manner.

Chesney was now trotting toward the woman, angling from the side as she turned toward the four in front and the three behind, the arm that held the canister of pepper spray swinging to match the direction of her gaze.

But the gang of young men was not fazed by the threat of the spray or the possibility that a police car was on the way. They outnumbered her seven to one, and Chesney thought they had done this kind of thing before. The young man who had held the basketball – Chesney could now see that it was the thin-mustached one with the chain neck tattoo who had spoken to him when Hell was on strike – flicked up his head in a signal. The four in front moved closer, spreading across the path, while the other three spread and crept forward.

They were going to form a circle around their victim, taunt and tease her until she was off balance. Chesney had been on the receiving end of that kind of treatment throughout his school years. Then one would dash in and cut the strap of her purse and run off with it. The Actionary's enhanced vision showed him the flash of a straight razor half concealed in the palm of the chain-tattooed gangsta.

They closed the circle. The woman was talking into the phone, but there was no sound of sirens in the distance. If there were other pedestrians in the park, they were not coming to her assistance. The young men moved in, laughing and catcalling, one after another of them dashing forward to touch their prey, as if in a game of tag, then leaping back as she threatened with the pepper spray. Chesney saw the one with the razor, angling around to be at her back, biding his time. The blade now slid free of his palms and flashed a reflection of streetlight.

Chesney was moving steadily forward, his eyes on the razor and the man who held it. He was only a few feet from the circle of cruel laughter. "Ready, Xaphan," he said.

"Yep."

The woman was facing two of the gangstas, firing a liquid line of chemical at them as they danced back. The razor wielder was behind her. Now he darted forward, eyes on the strap that ran from her shoulder to her waist, his blade extended and his other hand ready to seize the purse when it fell free.

Chesney was just behind the two in front of her, his arms outstretched and his hands reaching to slam their heads together. A second later, his fingertips touched their bristle-cuts.

"Now!"

The flash came again from behind him, and the clap of thunder seemed to loosen his bones. Still, he recovered immediately and brought his hands together, his arms superpowered like Hercules in the old movies. The two hoodlums' heads banged into each other with a gratifying *crack!* and both of them dropped like suits that have slid from their hangers. Chain-tattoo was caught by the flash and thunder just as he was reaching with both hands to cut the purse loose. With his optimized vision, Chesney saw the pupils of the man's dark eyes contract to pinpoints in the sudden glare, then widen with shock as the costumed figure of The Actionary appeared before him.

The young woman was equally startled by the sound-and-light show. Her mouth opened in a small, perfect circle and she stumbled backwards and a little to one side, giving Chesney a clear shot at the man with the razor. He was the leader, and he was the one to seize and hold for the police.

The crimefighter reached for the flinching purse-snatcher, the words "Citizen's arrest!" ready on his lips. But before his strength-augmented hands could grasp the razor man's wrist and disarm him, blinding agony struck Chesney's eyes and his sinuses suddenly became a tiny corner of Hell.

"Xaphan!" he screamed, floundering backwards, his gauntleted hands clawing at the stinking, burning liquid that coated his mask and, worse, his eyes and unprotected nostrils.

"What?" said the demon.

"Fix this!" Chesney choked. His nose was streaming now, his eyes flooding with tears, and still the burning sensation went on and on – it actually seemed to be increasing its intensity.

"Fix what?" said Xaphan.

"Blind! Can't breathe!" Chesney said. He was bent over, fighting the urge to retch.

"Oh, okay."

An instant later, his eyes were clear, his nasal passages too, the pain a fading memory. He straightened up and found himself alone on the asphalt path. He looked around, saw the gangstas, moving toward the basketball court, as fast as they could go while supporting two of their number who were barely able to walk. When Chesney looked in the opposite direction, he saw the young woman, shoulders again hunched by the burdens of her shopping bags, walking at quick-step toward the park gates.

For a moment, Chesney was frozen by indecision. What would The Driver do in a case like this? Not that he recalled Malc Turner ever being maced by a victim he was trying to rescue from muggers. But still, Chesney thought, The Driver always gave priority to a victim's needs, even if it meant letting a perpetrator escape, at least temporarily. He ran after the woman.

"Ma'am! Stop!" he called as he gained on her. She did just that, putting down her bags and turning to present him with a view of the spray canister's nozzle. Chesney skidded to a stop, gauntleted hands raised in self-defense. "I just want to make sure you're all right!"

"Stay away from me!" the woman said. "I already called 911!"

"I mean you no harm," Chesney said. "I saved you from those muggers."

She looked him up and down. He supposed it was the kind of inspection he would have to get used to. Then she drew his attention to the spray canister by waving it threateningly. "Stay away from me!" she said again, this time adding, "Nutjob!" Then she stooped to retrieve the bags, the pepper spray never leaving her hand. She turned and headed for the gates.

Chesney followed, though at a safe distance. "I really did save you from the muggers. The flash and the big bang, that was me."

She slowed then paused, turning to face him. The bags were still in her hands, but one of those hands also held the spray. Chesney stopped, hands up, as before. He tried a smile.

She cocked her head to one side to inspect, just as Poppy Paxton had done. He supposed he'd have to get used to that, too; not everyone would be as familiar with the concept of a costumed crimefighter as a devoted reader of the *Freedom Five*.

"That big light, the noise," she said, "that was you?"

"One of my little tricks."

She considered this for a moment. "I guess it worked," she said. "They ran off. I still got my purse."

"So you're okay?"

"I'm fine."

"Well," Chesney said, "that's good."

"How about you? I thought I got you with the pepper spray. I know I got somebody."

"I'm fine." Chesney moved one hand in a *no big deal* gesture. "I shook it off."

She put down the bags and looked at the canister, still clutched in one hand. "You're not supposed to be able to do that. What's the use of mace if you can just shake it off?"

"I'm not... an ordinary target," Chesney said.

She looked him up and down again. "I suppose not."

The conversation seemed to have come to a halt. She looked at him in a way that said, "So are we done here?" and Chesney found he was experiencing a familiar situation: a one-on-one encounter with an attractive woman – he could see now that she had small, fine features, the kind of face more likely to be called cute than beautiful, but her eyes under straight-cut mouse-brown bangs were large and full of intelligence. And now he realized that he had seen her before: she was one of the semi-regulars who jogged past the bench by the hot dog vendor's cart; he realized, with some embarrassment, that whenever she had gone by he had mostly been looking several inches below her face.

"So," she said, after the silence had stretched on a couple more seconds, "are we done here?"

"If you're okay," Chesney said. He wanted to prolong the occasion, but none of the conversational gambits he remembered from books on how to win women's favors would apply to this situation.

"Fine," she said again. "Thank you." She turned to leave, but stopped and turned back again. "If you don't have another mugging to go to," she said, "you could help me with these bags."

He came forward and took one of the bags. When he reached for the other, she said, "You don't have to carry them both."

"It's no bother," he said. "I'm pretty strong." With the costume's assistance, he showed her how he could lift each bag with one finger.

"Boy," she said, "look at you. Come on." She set off toward the gates again, and he walked beside her.

He had taken her 'look at you' remark for a compliment and smiled, but now as they proceeded in silence he realized she might have intended a small put-down. "I wouldn't want you to think I'm some big show-off," he said.

They were passing beneath a tree the branches of which overhung the path. She addressed her answer to the leaves above. "Thunder and lightning and he shakes off a faceful of mace, but he doesn't want to show off."

"I just meant–"

"It's all right." She turned to look at him. "My name," she said, "is Melda. Short for Imelda, which was my grandmother's name but I don't like it. Melda McCann."

"Pleased to meet you, Melda McCann."

"And?" she said after a moment.

Chesney had been running her name through the echo chamber in his head and deciding that he liked it. It took him a second to respond to her question. "And what?"

"And what's your name?" she said, pronouncing each word slowly.

"Oh," he said, then, "um. My identity has to be secret."

They were now at the park gates. She looked up at them as she had at the branches before, and said, "Of course it does. Or people would be phoning him up at all hours, wanting help with muggers, or getting kittens out of trees." She turned her face to him. "So what," she said, "do I call you?"

"The Actionary," he said.

"That's what the big 'A' is for?"

"Yes."

"Actionary," she said, as if trying it out. "Yeah, it's got a ring. So you're an action kind of guy?" she accompanied the question by making her hands into fists and shadow-boxing the air.

"When I'm crimefighting," said Chesney.

"And when you're not?"

"I have a regular job."

"Doing what?"

"I can't tell you exactly."

"Secret identity?"

"Uh huh."

"But it's a respectable job?"

The question seemed to be important to her. Chesney said, "I can tell you I work in an office. On a computer. A lot of it involves numbers."

"Hoo boy," she said. "Strong and intelligent. This could be my lucky day. Unless he lives with his mother." She had been addressing a sign that stuck out from a clothing store across from the park. They had crossed the empty street during a break in traffic and were moving along the sidewalk. A few passersby gave Chesney the eye, and he heard some low-voiced comments from people as they walked on. He decided to pay them no attention.

"So do you?" Melda McCann said, in a pointed tone.

"Do I what?"

"Live with your mother?"

"No."

"Or with anybody of the female persuasion?"

"I live alone," Chesney said. Then he thought he should add an explanation. He didn't want her to think of him as the kind of guy who couldn't get a girl, even though so far that was the truth. "It's part of the lifestyle."

She stopped. Once more she gave him that head-to-toe examination and he saw her face settle into lines of resignation. "The lifestyle," she said, as if that explained it all. "So you're gay."

"No!"

She put out both hands, palms up as if she was lifting something, in a gesture directed toward his costume. "You're not gay?"

"I'm not even particularly happy," Chesney said. He'd heard the line in some movie and was proud of himself for now being able not only to remember it, but for delivering it deadpan, just as Paul Giamatti had – or was it Bill Murray?

And she laughed. It was the best laugh he'd ever gotten from a woman: a short, sharp explosion of honest mirth and genuine appreciation for his line. He knew right away that he was going to want to hear that sound again. The laugh became a smile – and it was a smile that Chesney liked as much as the laugh – then she nodded and said, "Okay. This is me."

She was pointing with a thumb over her shoulder toward a porchless front door set in the ground floor of a brick-faced building. It took Chesney a moment to grasp her meaning, because he was still basking in the laugh and the smile. Meanwhile, she was unlocking the door then turning back to him and holding out both hands for the groceries. He passed them to her and she put them inside the front door.

"So," she said.

"So."

"You'll have places to go, other maidens to rescue."

"There is something I have to do."

"Okay," she said. There was a silence, then she said, very clearly, "Melda McCann."

"Melda McCann," he repeated.

"I'm in the book." She looked at his costume again. "I'm thinking you're not."

"No."

"But you'll call me." And when he didn't answer, she said, "Right?"

No girl had ever asked Chesney to call her. There seemed to be only one possible answer. "Yes."

"Good. Don't make me come looking for you." To that, she added another of those moment-brightening smiles.

"Okay," Chesney said, "I guess I should–" At that point he had to stop speaking because she had moved toward him, raised herself up on her toes – he was a little taller than she was – and lightly touched her lips to his.

For Chesney Arnstruther, who could count on his fingers the number of times he had been kissed by a girl and still have room for most of the Seven Dwarves, it was a totally unexpected and tender occasion; it was thus even more unfortunate that the sweetness of the kiss was followed immediately by the sourness of Melda's expression as her face scrunched up in pain and she pawed with both sets of fingertips at her lips, between bouts of spitting and exclamations of "Ow!" and "Jeez!"

"Xaphan!" Chesney said. "Fix that!"

"What?" The demon appeared beside him, blandly looking around like a weasel without a clue.

"Nothing I do can hurt innocent people! It's in the contract!"

"Yeah, yeah." The demon waved a hand and Melda stopped spitting and pawing.

"I'm sorry about that," Chesney said.

She blew out a long breath. "You and me both." She licked her lips. "But, hey, it was my pepper spray. And it seems to be all gone now."

None of the books of tips on how to conduct an inter-genderal conversation had covered moments like this. Chesney thought he might say something about how at least it had been a memorable first kiss, but he had learned from experience that things that sounded fine in his head often had a different-than-expected effect when he said them out loud – especially when the re-mark was uttered in the presence of an attractive girl. So he said nothing.

"Well," Melda said, "at least we're not going to forget our first kiss."

Now it was Chesney's turn to laugh, and if Melda thought it was from appreciation for her wit rather than out of pure relief, it made no difference. "You're absolutely right," he said.

She looked at him and said, slowly, "Melda–"

"McCann," he finished for her. "And I will call you."

"Soon."

"Soon."

She turned to go in, then looked back. "Are you going to disappear in another burst of thunder and lightning or do you want me to call you a cab?"

"Just don't watch," he said.

"Okay." She went in and closed the door.

There was an alley a few paces away. Chesney stepped into it and said, "Xaphan, home."

"That didn't work out so well," said Chesney. "Again."

The weasel-faced demon contrived an expression of in-nocent bafflement. "Whadda ya mean? You jumped them strong-arm guys. Biff! Pow! Saved the dame's pocketbook. You're a hero. You even got smooched."

"I'm a hero who got pepper-sprayed. The costume was supposed to protect me."

"It protects you where it covers you. You could run a locomotive into your keister, you wouldn't even get a bruise."

"You're saying that because the mask has holes for me to see and breathe, a guy could kill me with a pointed stick?"

The demon considered the proposition. "He'd have to be pretty fast. You got speed like greased lightning."

"I can't work unless I'm fully protected," Chesney said. "That was the spirit of our agreement."

"Don't talk to me about spirit," said Xaphan. "I *am* spirit."

"You're evading the issue."

The demon sighed. "All right, I'll make a note. Fully protected."

"You're still evading the issue."

"Now what?"

"What I said before: that didn't work out so well. Again. The key word here is 'again.'" Again Xaphan went for baffled innocence, but Chesney wasn't in the mood to play along. "Listen," he said, "I'm an actuary. Which means I look for patterns of events. And I'm a good actuary, which means if there's a pattern there, I'm going to find it."

The demon looked down at its shoes, up at the ceiling, anywhere but at Chesney. After a moment's wait, the young man pursued his point. "Twice I go out to stop a crime that you tell me is going to happen, twice I rescue a young woman, twice things don't go quite the way I wanted them to."

Xaphan struck an argumentative pose. "What *I* said: you smacked the bad guys, you rescued the dames."

"Why does it have to involve young women?"

"What? You already got too many frails in your life?"

"Stop dodging," Chesney said. "I want to know what's going on. Why am I being steered?"

"Who says you are?"

"I do. I want to know if I'm being fitted into somebody else's plans."

"Everybody's part of somebody else's plan, mack. That's how the game is played."

"So I *am* being steered. And who's doing the steering?"

The demon blew out its furry cheeks. "Well, who do ya think?" it said.

They had been arguing in the living room of Chesney's new apartment. Now the young man sank into the new reclining chair he had bought to be the centerpiece of the room. "I need to think about this," he said. "You're dismissed." But when his assistant shrugged and gave him a brief ironic "bye-bye" crimping of its blunt fingers, Chesney said, "No, wait! Tell me one thing, and make sure it's the truth: W.T. Paxton – is he really sincere about fighting crime?"

"Yeah," said Xaphan, "he really means it."

"No ulterior motive?"

"Like what?"

"You're being evasive again. Does he want to use me for some secret purpose?"

"You mean, like, does he want to rule the world?"

"No," said Chesney, dismissively, but then caught himself. Demons were perfectly capable of making the truth sound like a lie. "Does he, in fact, want to rule the world?"

"No," said Xaphan, "he don't wanna rule the world."

"What does he want from me?"

Another shrug of the pinstriped shoulders. "He wants you to help clean up crime in the city. And he wants to get the credit for it."

"Why?"

The weasel eyes turned toward the ceiling. "I don't think I gotta tell you that. It's got nuttin' to do wid your deal."

"But does he want to use me to do something bad?"

"Nah. The lug's kinda stuck on himself, if you get me, but he ain't tryin' ta pull a fast one on ya. That tale he told ya is the straight goods."

"That's the truth?"

"I ain't allowed to lie to ya."

"But is it the whole truth?"

"No, it ain't the whole truth," the demon said with a roll of its oversized eyes. "The whole truth of anything is the whole truth of everything. Cause, as you one of youse guys once memorably said, everything is connected to everything else. But it's enough truth to be getting along with." It popped open its big pocket watch. "Speaking of which, it's time I was anklin along. Your two hours is about up."

Chesney wasn't completely satisfied, but he was becoming more and more certain that Hell did not deal in complete satisfaction. "All right. But I'm going to be thinking about things," he said. "I'll call you."

He had scarcely spoken the last word before he found himself watching a puff of vapor blowing away. He got up and went to the side table that supported his cordless phone. W.T. Paxton's card lay on the polished surface. Chesney picked up the handset and pressed the six button three times. Whenever he did that before dialing, his call would be untraceable and unrecordable. It would not even be noticed by Homeland Security's supercomputers.

Chesney heard the hiss that told him his cloaking power was engaged. It sounded less like static and more like a nest of snakes. He hesitated. The situation did not feel as if it were bathed in a pool of light. But after a moment he punched in the numbers on the embossed card.

Almost immediately, a firm voice spoke in his ear. "Who is this?"

Chesney hung up without speaking.

SIX

The special crime-statistics section on the tenth floor was under the nominal leadership of Arthur "Sitting Bull" Entwistle. But it was clear to Chesney – and to anyone else with an elementary grasp of group dynamics – that the man who was really in charge of what was now being called C Group was Seth Baccala. Still, it was a source of great pride to Sitting Bull that he was reporting almost directly to the head of the company, something that only those of vice-president rank would normally do. It was thus also a cause for stark terror for Entwistle, since there were no insulating layers between himself and a man who, if things did not go well, could ruin him with a word.

The chief's half-glassed office was positioned just outside the almost-always closed door of Baccala's office, but Sitting Bull spent little time behind it. Instead he prowled the long room, peering over the shoulders of the actuaries as they worked, or perching on the corners of one or another's desk, to voice some variation on: "So... how are you coming along?"

Chesney found himself alternating between pity for the overstressed drone and irritation at being constantly interrupted at his work. He performed a mental statistical analysis and determined that he felt sorry for Entwistle eighty-three percent of the time, and annoyed almost seventeen percent; that was because there were six desks, the corners of which the chief could perch on, and he distributed the weight of his buttocks among them fairly equally. One sixth of the time, or nearly seventeen percent, he was looming over Chesney, emitting a fug of spiced deodorant being overpowered by anxiety-sweat.

By ten-fifteen on the second day of Chesney's membership in C Group, Sitting Bull had eased himself onto a corner of Chesney's desk for the first time that morning. "How's it going?" he said, and the young man could smell the metallic tang of fear beneath the minty sweetness of the antacids Entwistle constantly chewed to settle a nervous stomach.

"Fine," said Chesney, without looking up from the screen. Ron had made a good start on the meta-analysis – at least he had assembled and graphed the obvious components. But the work needed further refinement, and Chesney could already see the directions in which he would deepen and expand the analysis.

"Good, good," the chief said. He'd been leaning with one hand on Chesney's desk blotter, the better to peer at the material showing on the young man's monitor. Now he straightened, and the actuary saw that Entwistle had left an almost perfect palm-print on the absorbent surface. The chief saw it, too, and rubbed his palms together to dry them, an activity that sent more of his underarm odor wafting Chesney's way.

"This is big stuff," Entwistle said, his balding head sinking into his shoulders in a habitual motion that reminded Chesney of a puppy accustomed to swats from a rolled-up newspaper. "Big stuff, indeed."

"I know," said Chesney. "I heard what W.T. said."

At five minutes past nine that morning, the door to Baccala's office had opened and W.T.'s factotum had put his perfectly groomed head into C Group's space. The overhead light had gleamed off his buffed and manicured nails as he used two fingers to beckon Chesney and Sitting Bull into his office. But their journey had not ended there; as they came through the door, the executive assistant had gone before them to a leather-covered portal in the opposite wall. This he opened, revealing an inner door covered in a polished hardwood veneer on which he discreetly knocked.

Chesney had heard no response, but Baccala's ears must have been attuned to the right frequency, for he pushed open the barrier and, with a brusque yet elegant motion of his hand, invited the two men to tread upon the most select turf that the Paxton Building had to offer: the inner sanctum of PL&C's lion of lions, the personal office of Warren Theophilus Paxton, himself.

They trouped in. Chesney saw Entwistle nearly stumble as he adjusted to walking on the thick pile of the golden carpet. Or perhaps the chief had felt a momentary impulse to take off his shoes when stepping onto holy ground. It was a big office, Chesney thought. In fact, Paxton's was the kind of big office that other big offices aspire to be.

Seth Baccala eased off to one side of the room and took a prim seat on a brocaded couch that, Chesney saw, also held the shapely form of Poppy Paxton. He sneaked a look in her direction, which brought him one of those looks that cheerleaders used to shoot his way back in high school if he ever had the temerity to stare at them across a lunchroom.

But now Warren Theophilus Paxton was commanding his attention. The chairman, chief executive officer and single largest shareholder of Paxton Life and Casualty was seated behind a desk made of several different kinds of wood, all of them at their most polished and gleaming. The top looked large enough for a small aircraft to land on in an emergency. W.T. had not turned his face toward them as they entered, apparently engrossed in reading a file, but when Chesney and Entwistle stood before him he closed the folder and set it down in the center of the expanse before him. Then he lifted his stern countenance toward them and Chesney thought that the CEO's silver mane seemed even more leonine than it had in the limo; he wondered if the lighting in the office had been designed to suggest a halo around the great man's head. Probably, he thought. Whatever demon from the tempters corps was hovering around the man's ear must be a specialist in encouraging the sin of pride. If Hell ever issued a series of posters exemplifying the seven deadly sins, Paxton could have modeled for vanity.

The meeting was short. "Chesney, isn't it?" Paxton said.

Chesney admitted that it was.

"I just wanted to take a moment to welcome you to C Group," W.T. said.

"Thank you," said Chesney, then realized that the boss had been about to say something else and that he had interrupted him.

W.T. had been thrown off his stride, but only for a moment. "You're welcome," he said, then paused as if to gather himself together. His next utterance had the ring of a practiced set of remarks. Chesney had the strong impression that he was hearing, word for word, exactly what the other members of C Group had been told when the special section was first set up, two weeks before.

"In the next little while," Paxton said, "we're going to do something good together." He raised a finger to correct himself. "No, not just good. We're going to do something *great* together. We're going to make a difference, a real difference, a *big* difference."

He paused to make sure that Chesney understood the magnitude of the difference he was talking about. The young man was pretty sure he wasn't expected to respond verbally. The voice W.T. most liked to hear, especially in his inner sanctum, was his own. The actuary nodded.

Paxton accepted the nod as if it were not just a sign of comprehension but of shared commitment. "Yes, indeed. We're going to take on crime in our city, in our state. We're going to hunt down criminals and stop them dead in their tracks." And we're going to do it" – he tapped one silvery temple – "by using our heads, our skills, our expertise."

His next rhetorical gesture was of a pink fist repetitively smacking into an even pinker palm, both reflected in the polished surface of the desk. "We're going to be the most significant crimefighting force to ever come down the pike. We're going to be the brains behind law enforcement, giving our overworked police the backup they need but just don't have time to provide to the front-line officer themselves."

He paused again and looked at Chesney. The young man nodded again, but he was not sure that the gesture registered on the CEO. Paxton's gaze had lost focus, as if he were looking out over a wider audience than an actuary and his supervisor. "We must, each one of us, do our best work. And in return, as we wrestle crime to the ground in our city and in our great state, we will have the satisfaction of knowing that when the call came, it was we who answered, it was we who stood up, it was we who made a difference."

He flashed Chesney and Entwistle a smile, the kind that expects a smile in return, and the young man did his best to be complicit. He sneaked a glance at the section chief;

Entwistle was attempting a sincere beam of his own, but being in the presence of power left him capable of achieving only a rictus of amiable terror. Fortunately, the man was relieved of the intolerable strain of being in the presence of greatness by Seth Baccala, who now rose from the couch and indicated that, having been motivated, Chesney should now follow him back into his office, which stood between Paxton's grand space and C Group's room. Poppy came too, closing the door to her father's office and leaning against it. Chesney and Sitting Bull were waved to two chairs before Baccala's desk.

Now the real briefing took place, conducted by the executive assistant in purest technocrat. Speaking from notes on a single piece of paper on his desk, he laid out the section's objectives: a real-time computer model of criminal behaviors in the city, testable against experimental changes and capable of evolving over time. They would not only identify overall trends and characteristics of crime, but would narrow the focus to individual criminal elements and data clumps.

Chesney's interrupted. "What's a data clump, in this context?"

The answer did not come from Seth Baccala. "A gang," said a rough-edged voice. Chesney turned and saw, leaning half through the door that led to C Group's space, the plainclothes detective who had appeared on the scene after the thwarted kidnap of Poppy Paxton. The man was wearing the same wrinkled suit and the same look that careworn practitioners of any complex and ancient art apply to suggestions by neophytes-come-lately that there might be a new and better way to get the job done.

Baccala showed no irritation at the interruption. "This is Lieutenant Denby of the Major Crimes Squad," he said. "He will be C Group's liaison with police headquarters."

Denby came into the room and gave Chesney and Entwistle the kind of quick and unappreciative inspection a reform-school teacher might give to a new language arts class. From the way he hunched his shoulders and chewed the inside of one lip, Chesney deduced that the detective had neither sought out his new assignment nor caught it and clutched it gladly to his chest when it was tossed his way.

"A gang," Denby said again, "as in a collection of anywhere from a dozen to several hundred assorted thugs and sociopaths, who just might have more firepower than some countries' armies. A bunch of hard-assed gangbangers who would as soon blow your brains out as tell you the time of day, and maybe sooner. A posse of plug-uglies who will take your 'data clumps' and shove them up your–"

"Thank you, Lieutenant," said Baccala. "We've been expecting you." To the others he said, "Despite the lieutenant's lack of enthusiasm, this project has the full support of Mayor Greeley and Police Commissioner Hanshaw."

Denby made a noise somewhere in the back of his throat that, although not a word, yet eloquently conveyed his lack of regard for the public servants in question. He moved his tongue around his teeth as if he was dealing with an unexpected foul taste in his mouth.

"Also the full support," Baccala went on, "of the Chief of Police, who has personally assigned the Lieutenant to be our contact point within the department." He turned to Denby, who was now sitting on a corner of Baccala's spacious and uncluttered desk, tapping the end of a pencil against his knee, giving the activity his complete concentration. "Have you anything to add that would be useful at this point in time?"

Denby stopped tapping and looked up at Baccala, then at each of the others in turn. "Crimefighting," he said, "is no job for amateurs. Good police work comes out of instinct coupled with experience. Some of your little group might have the right instinct. None of you have the experience."

He looked at them again, but this time his gaze stopped when he came to Chesney. "You got something to say, Sherlock?"

Chesney's instinct was to hold his tongue. But he was aware of Poppy Paxton's presence somewhere out of his line of sight. And besides, crimefighting was one of the areas that, to Chesney, were bathed in clear light. "I think," he said, "that crime is one of those fields in which the gifted amateur can sometimes make a valuable contribution."

Denby's response was to allow his mouth to hang open in a silent "Oh" that eventually became audible and was followed by, "You're going to be a lot of fun, aren't you?"

"That's enough," said Baccala. "Arthur," he said to Entwistle, handing the section chief his one page of notes, "would you conclude Chesney's briefing while the lieutenant and I have a private word?"

Sitting Bull was on his feet even before the executive assistant had finished speaking, accepting the paper with two hands as if it were an object of great worth. Denby slumped into the chair Chesney rose from, ran a hand over his face as if to wipe away fatigue and presented W.T.'s assistant with an expression of eager attention that for a moment turned him into a mocking version of Sitting Bull.

Poppy followed Chesney and Entwistle as they returned to the main room, but left the door to Baccala's office partly ajar. When the actuary and his supervisor were seated in the latter's small corner space, Sitting Bull went through the points on the paper Baccala had given him. But over the chief's nasal drone, Chesney could not help hearing some of the high points of an exchange between the two men that included the phrases, "if you ever hope to make captain – or even collect a pension" and "useless exercise dreamed up by one of the Mayor's drinking buddies." Then Baccala's phone buzzed and a moment later he said, "Right away, W.T."

The detective came back into the C Group working area wearing an expression that convinced Chesney it would not be a good time to discuss gifted amateurism. Besides, his attention was commanded by Sitting Bull and he realized that the supervisor was saying "Arnstruther!" in a tone that meant that he had just said it moments before and that it had not had the desired effect.

"Yes, chief?"

"Are you with us?"

"Yes, chief."

"Are you clear on all of this?" Entwistle gestured with the page of notes.

"Yes, chief. We're creating a comprehensive, detailed, and evolving model of criminality in the city which can later be extrapolated to cover the state."

"And?"

"And it's a secret?"

"Exactly," said Sitting Bull. "All data is proprietary information not to be divulged outside this room. Now if that's clear, you can get back to your meta-analysis."

Chesney rose to leave. But because of the way the doors to Baccala's office and to the rest of C Group were placed, he found that he would have to squeeze past Poppy to exit. Her attention was on the argument coming from Baccala's office, where Denby was not going down without a fight. Chesney found himself reluctant to ask her to move. He turned back to Sitting Bull. "I never did get an answer to my first question," he said.

Entwistle looked up. "What question?"

"Why are we doing a meta-analysis that focuses so strongly on the media dimension? What's the point of that?"

"The point?" echoed Sitting Bull, "What's the point?" as if the answer were obvious. Then he looked at the piece of paper Seth Baccala had given him, but finding no clues, he looked to Poppy, but she had switched her attention away from the row in Baccala's office to what was going on in Entwistle's and now she was looking at the chief as if she, too, wanted to hear the answer to Chesney's question.

Sitting Bull's gaze went back to the paper and his head began to recede into his shoulders again, putting Chesney once more in mind of a puppy that had never had a good experience with a rolled-up newspaper. "I mean," the young man said, "I don't see a two-way correlation between media coverage and crime. The media covers crime because people are interested, but criminals don't generally commit crimes just to get on TV or in the papers. It seems like an unnecessary adjunct to the model. So why are we doing it?"

Again, it was Lieutenant Denby who provided the answer. The policeman had finished with Seth Baccala and had heard Chesney's question as he came out of the executive assistant's office. "It's because they want to know which crimes get the full treatment from cable news and the tabloids," the detective said. "Which, as any cop could tell them," – he glanced toward Poppy – "is any case involving a blonde, middle-class-or-above, young woman who goes missing under circumstances that suggest kidnapping or murder. Especially, serial murder."

Poppy spoke up now. "And why, Lieutenant, would my father and his associates be interested in that?"

Denby cocked his head to one side and showed her a gee-I-don't-know face. "Hard to say, miss," he said. "Maybe they're worried about something."

It had been on the tip of Chesney's tongue to say,

"Maybe because you were almost kidnapped the other night," but he caught the words before they could tumble out over his bottom lip and swallowed them.

Denby, however, had a policeman's eye for detail. He had noticed. "Was the gifted amateur going to give us the benefit of his insight?" he said.

"No," Chesney said.

Sitting Bull said, "Back to work." He made a shooing gesture intended to move Chesney toward the door. Poppy moved out of his path and the young man made to leave, but Denby put out a hand and stopped him.

"Wait a minute," the detective said.

"What?" said Entwistle.

"Looks like," Denby said, "I'm stuck with this assignment. I was coming in here to talk to you" – he looked pointedly at Sitting Bull – "about how we go about... liaising." He pronounced the word as three separate syllables. "But I've just made up my mind. I want him." He tapped Chesney's shoulder.

"He's not..." Entwistle sought for the right word, couldn't find it, and settled on, "a good choice."

"Sure he is," said the policeman. "He at least asks the right questions." He gave Chesney a sideways look. "Even if he has an unjustified faith in 'gifted amateurs.'"

"I'm to be your liaison, Lieutenant," Sitting Bull said. His head had come halfway out from its hiding place between his shoulders.

"I think the lieutenant's made a good choice," said Poppy. To the policeman, she said, indicating Chesney, "Did you know that he also sings?"

Chesney raised a corrective finger, but, "Um," was as far as he could go in contradicting the young woman who was offering him a smile he was pretty sure was not one hundred percent well intended.

"No," said Poppy, "that's right – he doesn't sing, but he does get sung to."

Chesney let it go. Entwistle was looking at Poppy, his head falling back into its former hiding place. "All right," he said to Denby, "you can have him."

After lunch Chesney finished working up the parameters for a meta-analysis of media coverage of major crimes in the city, by state and region. It was interesting work, much more so than what he had been working on the day before: calculating the percentage of middle-aged single men who would sustain death or serious injury after slipping in the shower. He had been able to work out a formula that closely correlated height and weight with likelihood of a shower-related accident. The overweight and taller-than-average were, as he had expected, the most likely to sustain damage. Oddly, though, men who were in the top percentile as to height but way below the mean in the weight department were also susceptible. He suspected it had to do with having to reach so far down to retrieve the soap after dropping it.

Denby had disappeared after the briefing. But an hour into the afternoon's work, the phone rang on Sitting Bull's desk. Through the open door to the half-glassed office, Chesney heard the chief's old-fashioned standard phone greeting – "Mr Entwistle on the line!" – then a few seconds later, "Arnstruther! Lieutenant Denby wants you."

Chesney looked at the phone on his desk. No light was blinking. Then he noticed that Entwistle had hung up. The chief was making one-handed shooing motions at him. "You're to go to Police Central. Take a cab." He rooted in his desk and came up with a white chit with blue printing on it. "Blue Line has the company account."

Twenty minutes later, Chesney entered the city's expansive police headquarters, a 1930s-vintage citadel to law and order built of red brick with pale sandstone facings that had been darkened by two decades of coal soot before the city switched over to oil in the fifties and later to natural gas. The walls of the high-ceilinged foyer were lined with narrow but soaring art deco arches topped by brass torches from which an indirect glow gave the place an air of brooding gloom beneath and a dome of soft light above. A uniformed patrolman took him up to Denby's office, the same size and half-glassed design as Entwistle's, where the lieutenant sat behind a desk piled high with files and folders. The detective waved the actuary to a chair then spent several seconds just staring at him. Finally, Denby said, "Have we met?"

The question took Chesney by surprise. "I don't think so."

Denby put a hand over his left eye and stared at Chesney again. "Right brain," he said after a moment. "Better than the other side at pattern recognition. Sees through the left eye." Chesney said nothing, maintaining as neutral an expression as he could manage. After another long silence. the detective uncovered his right eye and said, "Are you the guy?"

"The guy?"

"The guy in the blue and gray suit. With a mask."

"No," said Chesney. He added a laugh.

Denby gave him a sideways look and continued, "The suit coulda been padded. Besides, I never forget a chin."

Chesney was pretty sure that "No," wasn't going to be any more convincing as a reply to this observation than it had been to Denby's last one. So he said nothing.

The detective let the silence lengthen. Then he said, "No, you're not the guy. He had... presence. You're just... here." He let another silence measure itself out. Finally, he said, "So, just what are they planning?"

"Who?"

"Greeley and Hanshaw and Paxton. And the rest of the Twenty, for all I know."

Chesney knew who the mayor and the police commissioner and his own boss were. But not the "Twenty," whoever they were. But he recalled now that W.T. had used the term on the night when The Actionary had foiled Poppy's kidnapping. "What's the Twenty?" he said.

That won him a boy-you're-good look from Denby. But when the detective realized the actuary really wanted an answer to his question, he said, "Where you been, boy? You live in a cave?"

"I just crunch numbers."

"Huh," said Denby, and took a moment to order his thoughts. "The Twenty is what you call the group that runs this city. Not the Mayor's Office, not the City Council – although the Mayor is usually a member, and even some of the councilors – but the guys with juice. Juice – if they don't have that in the particular cave where you crunch your numbers – is power. Political power. And more-than-political power."

"What, exactly," said Chesney, "is more-than-political power?"

"It's where juice comes from." Denby made a gesture that involved his index and middle fingertips rubbing against his thumb. "It's called money. Mucho money. So mucho that you can call up a politician and tell him how high to jump. Or make an inconvenient drunk driving charge get lost in the DA's in-basket."

"That's not right," Chesney said.

"No," said the policeman, "it isn't." He waited to see if Chesney would say anything more, but when nothing was forthcoming, Denby leaned back in his chair and made a tent of his fingers and studied them as if they were objects of compelling interest. "It goes back seventy, maybe eighty years," he continued, "to Prohibition times, when the gangs used their money to buy political protection. The old money in town didn't care for a bunch of stubble-chin thugs cutting in on their dance partners, so they set up a committee of the twenty wealthiest men, pooled their resources, and reminded the mayor and council of the old rule of politics: you dance with the one that brung ya.

"They hired their own goons, ex-soldiers and former Pinkerton men, to outmuscle the mob locally. Then they used their clout in Congress to help get Prohibition repealed. That put an end to the immediate problem. But just to make sure nothing like that ever cropped up again, the Twenty became a permanent club. There's actually about fifty of them now, but they still call themselves by the same old name."

The detective leaned across the desk. "So if you're thinking of getting mixed up in Twenty business, my advice is: don't. Guys like you, they're just the grease that keeps the gears spinning smoothly."

"And guys like you?" said Chesney.

"Guys like me..." Denby sat back again and folded his hands on the desk, "guys like me can see a line. We don't cross it, we're okay. Guys like you, you never know where the line is until it rears up and bites you in the ass."

"That's some line," Chesney said.

"Yeah, and it's some bite."

The conversation seemed to have come to a pause. Chesney shifted in his chair and said, "You wanted to see me."

"Yeah," said Denby, "and now I have. You can go."

"I've got work to do," the actuary said. "Why did you call me all the way over here?"

"To see," said the detective, "if you would come."

Chesney stood up. The man's attitude annoyed him. But at the same time, it seemed they were going to be the contact points between C Group and the police department. And Denby obviously knew more about the city and how it worked – how it *really* worked – than he did. Clearly, there were elements of crimefighting that were not easily reducible to numbers. He kept his voice neutral as he said, "This liaison thing, how do we make it work?"

Denby looked up at him and matched his tone. "Your group needs something from the department, you call me."

"And you arrange it."

"That seems to be the size of it."

"All right," said Chesney, leaning over the desk and offering his hand, "I look forward to working with you."

Denby looked at the hand, then up at the young man's face. "I was right," he said, "you are good."

Back at the office, Chesney set up a mathematical model of typical crime-related coverage in newspapers and cable news: types of stories and the column inches or minutes of airtime they commanded. He soon saw that Denby's rule-of-thumb prediction was right; when a middle-class girl or young woman went missing under circumstances that indicated foul play, the media rode the story hard and long. If the victim was blonde and if she was snatched in one of the "heartland" states, the model's indices all climbed. A story that climaxed in a successful ransom pay-off or the discovery of a corpse went off the charts.

He inputted the numbers onto the computer and had the system prepare a series of core graphs, then turned his attention to spin-offs from the mainstream stories. He tracked the waxing and waning of different kinds of reportage and commentary as the story went through its stages, and the roles played by the archetypal figures in the drama: police, relatives, neighbors, lawyers, commentators, politicians, the ghouls who flocked to wherever the cameras were rolling, and the average person-in-the-street who followed the story and was interviewed for a reaction.

Chesney found himself engrossed in the work, far more than he had ever been down on the third floor. He wrote up his interim findings in a couple of pages of analysis, but let the graphs and his mathematical model mostly speak for themselves. When he pushed the button to send the report along the secure link to Sitting Bull's electronic inbox and straightened up in his chair to work the kinks out of his neck and shoulders, he realized that he was alone in the office. The rest of C Group had gone. He looked at the clock in the corner of his monitor and discovered that it was nearly six.

He stood up, rotating his head, then his shoulders, then crossed the big room to a large free-standing armoire, left over from the time the space was Paxton Life and Casualty's formal boardroom and the directors had used the cupboard to hang up their coats and hats. Chesney had worn a light topcoat to work – the onset of fall had begun to put a nip in the morning and evening air – and he opened the door to retrieve it. As he was putting it on, he heard sounds of movement from Seth Baccala's office and the factotum's voice saying, "Let me make sure we're alone."

The actuary didn't hear an answer, but it occurred to him that the person Baccala was speaking to might be Poppy Paxton. Anything that concerned her interested him – especially if she was having conversations with Baccala that required privacy – although he also dreaded what he might find out. None of the images that flashed unbidden through his mind gave him any comfort.

Even so, he gave in to the impulse as soon as it formed, and stepped into the armoire, pulling the door closed after him. A moment later, he heard Baccala's voice say, "All clear." Then the lights in the big room went out.

Chesney inched open the cupboard door, and saw that C Group's space was still empty. A crack of dim light limned the edge of the door into Baccala's room; it had been left ajar. He crept out of the cupboard and crossed to put his eye to the crack.

The assistant's office was empty, its lights turned off, but the door to W.T. Paxton's palatial lair was half open, throwing an angled oblong of light onto Baccala's carpet. From within, Chesney could hear the tinkle of ice dropping into crystal glasses, then the gurgle of liquid being poured. Baccala was saying something, but the actuary could not make out the words. Chesney was drawn into and across the vacant room until he stood behind the half-open door. He felt both a compulsion and a sense of disgust with himself, as if he were one of those creeps who prowl around lovers' lanes, eavesdropping on the parked couples.

I should go, he thought to himself, even as he edged a little closer to the gap in the door, the better to hear.

"I still think the original plan is the one to go with," Baccala was saying.

The voice that answered was not Poppy's, but that of her father. "No."

"I've seen the preliminary meta-analysis of the media implications. I'm sure the final numbers will bear me out."

"This is not just about numbers," Paxton said.

By nature, Chesney was no snoop and he would have silently left the two men alone with what sounded like a business discussion, except that it was clear to him that the business they were discussing concerned him – at least to the extent that they were talking about an analysis he was performing. Then Paxton's next remark got his full attention.

"The guy in the outfit," W.T. said, "my instinct tells me he could be a game changer."

Baccala's response must have been nonverbal, because the actuary didn't hear anything but the gentle chime of ice against crystal. And it must have contradicted Paxton's assertion, because now the older man pressed his point. "You didn't see the guy in action. He came out of nowhere and he put down Blowdell's pros like they were boy scouts. Three seconds, no more, and it was all over."

"But who is he?" Baccala said. "*What* is he? What's his angle, what does he want?"

"You're saying we don't know enough about him." Chesney heard another clink of ice, then a thump as the glass was set down on a table. W.T. had just drained his whiskey. "I agree. That's why I've invited him around. That's why we'll use Blowdell to get a line on him."

"We don't need some kind of wild card in the middle of this," Baccala said.

"Agreed. But you didn't see the guy. If we get him in our corner…"

"That's *if*. But what if he remains a wild card?"

Chesney heard an overtone of reluctance in W.T. Paxton's voice. "Then Blowdell… takes him off the table. Now, tell Ballanger we're coming down."

Chesney moved silently across Baccala's office to the C Group space, hiding in the dark as Baccala came into his office. He heard the assistant pick up the phone and speak into it. The actuary went out into the hallway and around a corner to the elevators. He pushed the button and waited. He wasn't concerned about being found by Paxton and Baccala. They would take the private express elevator that went nonstop to the basement parking garage and the chauffeured limousine.

The elevator chimed and the doors opened. As soon as Chesney was inside, he said, "Xaphan. To me."

The fanged weasel in the wide-lapeled pinstripe looked up at him. A faint odor of sulfur rose to Chesney's nostrils. "What's up?"

"Do you know what W.T. Paxton and Seth Baccala are planning?"

"No."

"Find out."

"No can do."

The young man was taken aback. "You have to obey my orders. That's the deal."

"Only as far as this crimefighting hoopdedoo-hah goes. Anything else, you got to make a separate deal." It waggled its eyebrows suggestively. "Under the usual terms."

"You're saying you can't tell me what Paxton and Baccala are up to because they're not planning a crime?" He told the demon what Paxton had said about someone called Blowdell taking Chesney "off the table." That had sounded as if it had some criminal overtones.

"Maybe," was his assistant's answer, "but even so, I can't give you no dope about it."

"Why not?"

The weasel faced looked thoughtful, then Xaphan said, "Cause what the guy said is the straight goods. You're a wild card, see. You muscled into things that don't concern you, other people's games which were already on the table." The demon hitched its shoulders. "That don't give you – whatta they call it? – Blanche Carter, you can do whatever you want and I gotta help."

"Carte blanche," Chesney corrected him.

"Huh?" said Xaphan. "I dunno. I never met the skirt."

"You're telling me that there are situations – criminal situations – that you can't help me with."

The demon pointed its cigar stub up at Chesney. "You got it."

The young man thought about it and didn't take long to make the connection. "'Games that were already on the table,'" he quoted. "You mean situations where Hell is already engaged."

"You wanna put it that way, yeah. That includes situations it looks like we might get into."

"Baccala and Paxton, or one of them, is in league with the Devil."

"I never said that."

"Then they're not?"

"I never said that, neither."

"Well, just what *are* you saying?"

The demon gave him a surprisingly wry look for a saucer-eyed weasel. "As little as possible."

Chesney thought some more. "What *can* you tell me?"

"Think back," said Xaphan, "to what I just said."

"'As little as possible?'"

"Now you're in the picture."

Chesney sighed. "So I can't go up against anyone who's got serious backing from your boss?"

The demon held up both palms. "You know the way we work. Contracts are sacred. Guy makes a deal with us, we don't make a deal with some other bozo that's gonna break the first guy's contract."

"Ah," said Chesney, thinking it through, "so does that mean I'm covered, too?" The demon looked away. "Well, does it?"

"You didn't hear it from me."

"No," said Chesney, "I didn't." He was going to have to think about this some more. A lot more. "Hey," he said, "is this elevator stuck?"

The car gave a slight lurch. "Nah," Xaphan said, "I kinda figured you'd want to keep this little chinwag just between us."

The elevator stopped at the fifth floor and a tired-looking man with a briefcase got on, tugging his collar straight to settle his overcoat onto his bowed shoulders. As the door closed, he sniffed the sulfurous air in the car and gave Chesney a dirty look. "Never," he said, "eat the chili special in the cafeteria."

Downstairs, Chesney went out through the lobby doors and followed the sidewalk until he came to a store whose lights were out. He stepped into the recessed doorway and told Xaphan to take him home.

"Is this about crimefightin'?"

"Home is where I plan my operations, so yes." A moment passed in the place of winds then he was shrugging off his coat in his living room, saying, "How do I find out what Paxton is up to?"

The demon had apparently grown tired of having to look up at the young man. It levitated until they were seeing eye-to-eye. "Why don't you ask him?" it said.

"I will." Chesney went to the phone and punched in the three-sixes prefix then dialed the number on Paxton's card. The same voice answered as the night before. "I see nothing on call display. Who is this?"

Chesney took a moment to settle himself, then said, "We met outside the museum."

"I've been waiting for you to call."

Chesney heard a note of self-satisfaction in the remark. "It doesn't mean I'm taking your offer," he said.

"Was it you who called last night?"

"Yes."

"So you're unsure," Paxton said. "Well, let me tell you what I've been doing. I've established a research facility, just as I said."

Chesney could not resist saying, "I know. C Group. Reporting to you through Seth Baccala."

There was a silence on the line, then, "How did you know that?"

Chesney was enjoying this. He remembered a line from a Malc Turner graphic novel. "I make it my business to know what I need to know."

Paxton gave a thoughtful "Huh," and let another silence stretch itself down the phone connection before saying, "Okay, I suppose I have to respect that. But we need to meet."

"I may be there later tonight," Chesney said. "If not, I'll call you tomorrow."

"Come to the side door on Polk Street. Baccala will let you in."

"I'll find my own way in. And it's just you and me. Leave him out of it."

"No," said Paxton, "anything we do, he's going to be a part of. He needs to be in the loop."

Chesney conceded. "But I deal with you," he added.

"My daughter may also have a role to play."

"I can live with that." Chesney hung up without saying goodbye. His mother would have scolded him for poor manners, but it seemed the kind of thing a crimefighter would do. He turned to the demon, its spatted shoes still hovering three feet above the carpet. "I need to see the Reverend Billy Lee."

Xaphan made a face, which – considering the normal set of its features – was highly effective in communicating its displeasure at the young man's suggestion. "That guy gives me the heebie-jeebies," it said.

"Let's go," Chesney said.

"Is it crime-related?" the demon said, angling for a loophole.

"It's crime-related. I need his advice on whether I should work with Paxton," – he fixed his assistant with a meaningful look – "since you're not being completely helpful."

"You want I should bring him here, or you want to go where he is?"

Chesney did not want to appear in a flash of lightning if Hardacre was taping a television program in front of three hundred people. "Is he out in public?" he said.

"He's at home," said Xaphan, "in his study."

"Then let's go to him. But no thunder and lightning. And put me just outside the room. I don't want to scare him."

Instantly they were in the winds and darkness. Then they were in the great entrance hall of Billy Lee Hardacre's mansion. The space was dimly lit, but from beneath the heavy wooden door came a golden light. Chesney raised his hand to knock.

"Uh-oh," said the demon.

The young man paused. "What?"

"I'll see ya when the coast is clear." And without a further word the fiend disappeared.

Chesney knocked. From within he heard a chair scrape and voices. Then the door opened and Chesney saw two things that surprised him – one a little, the other a lot: the minor surprise was that behind the preacher, standing by the desk, was the angel that had negotiated for the heavenly side to settle the strike in Hell: but the thing that caused Chesney's eyes to widen was the other figure in the room, seated in a chair in the corner. There was only one thing the young man could have said. So he said it: "Mother! What are you doing here?"

The angel had departed, Hardacre having said, "We need to talk to the boy." Chesney was seated in an armchair, one of three arranged in a conversation group in the corner where his mother sat, still wearing the prim smile with which she had greeted her son. The young man was suffering an attack of cognitive dissonance the like of which had not struck him since he had weathered adolescence.

He knew that he had a tendency to divide up the world into distinct categories, with clear boundaries drawn between them. Some of that tendency came from "the way his brain was wired," as the consultants had put it, all those years ago; but a not inconsiderable part of the way he thought was a result of his mother's strenuous efforts to inculcate in her odd son a rigid sense of morality. So Chesney knew that cohabitation without benefit of matrimony belonged in the category of things that were irrevocably forbidden. He knew that because his mother had spared no pains in making it a cardinal point on his moral compass. Now he had found that his mother was not only "living in sin" – the term she had always used – but was doing so when she was still "married in the sight of God" – the phrase that occurred whenever she dismissed the concept of divorce – to Chesney's long-absent father. Adultery, he shouldn't have had to remind her, was one of the activities proscribed in the ten commandments themselves. It was a major, full-weight, no-nitpicking *sin*, and she was committing it.

He was about to acquaint her with these facts when his mother, her face pink – though, Chesney soon realized, not from embarrassment – spoke before he could. "You can lower that finger and close your mouth," she said. "I will not hear a word from you about my relationship with Billy Lee."

"Mother–" Chesney nonetheless began, but Letitia Arnstruther raised her own index finger, and Chesney had to face the fact that when it came to raising a forbidding digit, his own efforts were but a wan and sickly imitation of the original that now quivered before his face. And though his words, when he formed them in his mind, might seem as short and sharp as one of the belt-buckle daggers he had seen advertised in the backs of old comic books, they were no more than paper airplanes thrown at the prow of a battleship when they went up against Letitia Arnstruther.

She now spoke over his inchoate objection, as she had done on many a previous occasion, to set the agenda for their present encounter. "We are married in the sight of God, and will be in the sight of the state as soon as we have time to get the license. You forget that Billy Lee is an ordained minister. He has the power to marry people, including himself to me."

"But you're married already!"

Now Chesney saw something he had never seen nor ever expected to: the pinkness of Letitia Arnstruther's cheeks was overpowered by actual, blushing red. "Oh, yes," she said. "About that...I was motivated by a desire to cause you no embarrassment. You had, after all, enough problems to be getting on with."

"What are you saying, mother?"

She looked down at her hands, folded in her lap. "The fact is, Chesney, your father and I were never actually married. I was below the legal age to wed – it was twenty-one in those days – and your grandfather would not give consent." She shrugged delicately. "Just as well, I suppose. Wagner was not really good husband material. And he would have been a terrible father."

She dusted her plump palms together in a gesture with which Chesney was long familiar. The matter was now closed. If Chesney was ever to know how he came to exist, he would not be hearing it from Letitia Arnstruther. "Now," she said, "why are you here?"

Hardacre had been hovering by the desk, his attention ostensibly on the papers scattered there. Now he came to take the third chair. "Yes," he said, "what have you come to see us about, son?"

Chesney examined his feelings. He was not at all sure he wanted this man to call him "son," and he was entirely sure he would not be calling Bill Lee Hardacre "father" or any variation of it. On the other hand, he was used to letting his mother decide complex issues – her world was apparently one pool of light after another – and so he decided to move on to the matter that had brought him here. As he made that decision, a motion caught his eye: Xaphan appeared, reclining along the top of a bookcase that held copies, in various sizes and languages, of Hardacres bestselling novels. His fanged jaw was propped up by an upturned palm, while the other hand tapped invisible ash from the end of his cigar. His weasel face somehow expressed deep amusement at Chesney's discomfort.

"I've got a problem," the young man said.

"Poor dear," said his mother, startling Chesney almost as much as her marriage had done. He'd never heard sympathy from her before. "Why don't you tell us about it?"

He pushed other thoughts firmly out of his mind. "Yes, mother," he said. "It's about the man I work for."

He told them about foiling the kidnapping of Poppy, of the ride in the limousine and the offer of assistance from her father and his entry into C Group. He told them about the kind of work he was doing as part of the group. When he began to report the conversation he had overheard, his mother interrupted.

"I've told you, Chesney: people who eavesdrop are liable to hear things said about themselves that they would rather–"

Now Chesney witnessed another incredible event: Hardacre was able to stop Letitia in mid-sentence with no more than a hand laid gently on her arm and another,

"Now, now," this one followed by, "sweetheart. Let the man finish."

Chesney swallowed his astonishment and went on. "They're going to have someone named Blowdell find out about me, about how to control me. And if I turn out to be a problem, this Blowdell is supposed to – his fingers made quotation marks in the air – "'take me off the table.'"

Hardacre said, "There's a Nat Blowdell. Lawyer turned political fixer. He's connected to the Twenty."

"These don't sound like very nice people," Chesney's mother said. "Why are you associating with them?"

Chesney didn't say his main interest was in Poppy Paxton. He had never discussed girls with his mother; early on he had gained a strong impression that the subject was another one of those that she did not wish him to bring up. "Mr Paxton is my boss, Mother – in my regular identity, at least. And C Group might develop some really useful intelligence to help me in my…" he could tell by her expression that she had had some thoughts about his new pastime; experience told him it would be best to skate on by that subject – "my other work."

He turned instead to Hardacre. "What concerns me," he said, "is that I may be being steered by…" – he glanced up at the top of the bookcase; Xaphan was lying on its back, blowing smoke rings at the ceiling, as if paying no attention – "certain interests." With the last two words, the young man pointed at the floor while giving Hardacre a look that said, *if you know what I mean*.

"Is it here?" Hardacre asked, looking around the room.

"Xaphan," Chesney said, "show yourself."

"Not suppose ta," said the demon.

"They already know about you."

"Well, in that case…" The demon disappeared from on

top of the bookcase and reappeared sitting on Hardacre's desk. A squeak escaped Chesney's mother, but again her beau patted her arm and she stood down.

"Whatta ya want?" the fiend said.

"Tell the reverend here what you said about Paxton and Baccala being 'covered.'"

The demon's already huge eyes widened in alarm. "I never said nuttin'."

"Reverend Hardacre is my lawyer," Chesney said, "you can discuss contracts with him."

"Oh," said Xaphan, eyebrows bobbling suggestively, "a shyster, eh? The boss says guys like you are already halfway home, if you catch my drift."

"I catch it and throw it back," Hardacre said. "Now what's all this about coverage?"

"Well, it's simple, see. Your boy here, he's got a contract with our organization. He fights crime and I gotta help him. But he don't get no help on nuttin' that's already covered by somebody else's contract."

"And vice-versa?" said Hardacre.

The demon shrugged. "Yeah. Any of my... associates tries to put the moves on the kid, I step in and warn them off."

"And not just two hours a day?" Hardacre said.

"No, that's full-time."

"So this Paxton, or his assistant, has a deal with the Devil?"

"I ain't saying, one way or the other," said Xaphan. "All I'm saying is, if I try doin' anything that throws a monkey wrench into what they're doin', *I'm* gonna get warned off."

"I see," said Hardacre. He interlaced his fingers then put the tips of both index fingers together and pressed them against the bottom of his lower lip. After a long pause he said, "Basically, Chesney here is safe from any direct action. He can't be killed or injured or held hostage by demonic forces."

"You got it."

"But against mortals acting on their own?"

"He's on his own."

Chesney said, "What about the costume? Does it protect me if, say, this Blowdell tries to shoot me?"

"The suit works alla time," Xaphan said. "There's a technical term; I think it's 'permanently imbued' – but don't quote me."

"All right," Hardacre said, "that's settled. Now what about this business of Chesney being 'steered' as part of somebody else's plan?"

The demon hopped off the table and ambled toward a drinks cabinet set into one corner. It pulled the stopper from a crystal decanter and sniffed the contents. "Is that rum?" it said.

"Bourbon," Hardacre said. "There's a bottle of rum in the cupboard underneath."

Xaphan rooted around and came up with a full bottle of amber liquid. The fiend looked inquiringly at the preacher.

"Help yourself," the man said.

The demon found a tumbler and filled it. The weasel nostrils widened as it inhaled the odor of rich overproof rum. Then it put the glass between the pair of yellow tusks that sprouted from its upper jaw and drained the contents in one gulp. "Oh, my," it said, a long, thin tongue appearing to lick the moisture from its lips, "that takes me back."

"Have another," said Hardacre, and as the demon refilled the tumbler, he added, "I guess that stuff's hard to come by where you hail from."

"You said it, mack," said the demon. It paused to throw back half of the glass's contents, then held the rest up to the light and appreciated the liquor's deep amber hue. "Besides, down there everything tastes like sulfur and burnt meat."

A side table near Hardacre's chair held a cylindrical box of polished wood. The preacher lifted its lid and Chesney smelled the scent of fine tobacco. So did Xaphan. Hardacre said, "I always find a good scotch goes best with an equally good cigar. A friend of mine brings them in from Canada. They're seven-inch *Romeo y Julieta* Havanas, Winston Churchill's favorite smoke."

The demon angled over. "Can I?"

"Be my guest," Hardacre said. As the fiend produced a flame from the end of one finger and sucked its heat into the end of the thick cigar, the preacher said, "You have to be invited, don't you?"

Xaphan pulled his legs up and sat on the empty air, as if it were a tall stool. He blew a perfect ring toward the ceiling then drained his glass. "We don't need to go into no technicalities," it said.

"Sure we do," said Hardacre. "If you want another refill."

The demon's huge eyes contracted. "Smart guy, eh?" it said.

"Yeah," said the preacher, "sometimes, when the wind's in the right direction."

The man and demon held each other's gazes. Neither looked away. Finally, Xaphan smiled and said, "Okay, yeah, I got to be invited or it's hands off."

Hardacre rose and fetched the bottle and a glass for himself. He took Xaphan's tumbler and poured another generous measure into it but then set it down on the table beside his chair. He made a silent inquiry of Chesney and his mother, both of whom signaled that they did not want any. But the young man was watching the interplay between Hardacre and his assistant with close attention.

Hardacre poured himself another couple of fingers then resumed his seat, bringing the bottle with him and placing it on the side table. "Now", he said, "about this business of Chesney being steered?"

"*I* ain't doin' it," Xaphan said, its eyes on the tumbler's gold-gleaming contents.

"But you set him up to meet the Paxtons outside the museum."

"He wanted to stop a big job. I looked around, that was the biggest one I saw."

Hardacre nudged the bottle toward the edge of the table. The demon reached for it, but the preacher placed his hand over the mouth of the bottle. "You didn't arrange any of it?"

"Gimme," said Xaphan, "and I'll tell you how it works."

"Full story?" Hardacre said.

The fiend leaned forward, arms on its thighs. "I don't know the full story, mack. I just know the parts I know. That's what I'll tell you. Deal?"

Hardacre looked inquiringly over at Chesney. "Yes, I'd like to hear this," the young man said. He was thinking, I should have asked this kind of thing, instead of just jumping in the deep end.

Hardacre uncovered the bottle. Xaphan poured more rum into his tumbler, drank a little, then held the glass on one knee. "I don't know what's gonna happen. Maybe the boss sees the future – he kinda gives that impression, know what I mean? But us front-line guys, we do what we do, then we see what happens."

"Like us?" Hardacre said.

Xaphan took another mouthful, let the liquor roll around on its tongue before swallowing. "I don't think so," it said.

Now Hardacre leaned forward. "What's the difference?"

The demon looked like a weasel thinking about something it had never thought about before. "You guys think about what's gonna happen, what you wanna make happen, cause you get to choose what you're gonna do. We're just here and now, and when something happens, we just get to react." It thought some more. "The way we're supposc ta."

Chesney came in on this point. "So when you came to my apartment when we went out that first time, you didn't know what I was going to ask you to do?"

"Nah." The demon drank another mouthful.

"You didn't wonder?"

"We don't wonder, kid. We just do our jobs."

Hardacre said, "So Chesney asked you to find him a crime you could foil and you looked around and saw a kidnapping that was about to happen."

"Yeah."

"So you were seeing into the future?"

Xaphan thought about that. "Yeah," it said, "I spose so. But that's cause my job was to do his bidding. I guess I kinda ride on his will."

Chcsney said, "So you can see my future?"

Xaphan drained the last of the rum and held out the tumbler for more. "Answer the question first," Hardacre said, holding the almost empty bottle poised to pour.

The demon shrugged. "I can't see nobody's future. I can see what I need to see to do my job. You say, 'Take me to this guy,' like you did, then I can see this house cause this is where he is."

"So," Chesney said, "when you put me in the park to save Melda McCann, you didn't know she was going to pepper-spray me?"

The weasel eyes slid sideways. "Well... I saw she had the stuff on her, and I could see she was a feisty little piece–"

"Who," said Chesney's mother, "is Melda McCann?"

"Nobody, Mother," Chesney said, "just a girl I saved from some muggers."

"What does she do? Who are her people?"

"I don't know, Mother. She might be a nurse's aide. Or maybe a beautician. But we're trying to talk to the demon. It's important."

Letitia sniffed, unconvinced that his priorities were superior to her own, but Hardacre made a mollifying gesture that – again to Chesney's surprise – actually settled his mother down.

"So you didn't set me up?" the young man said.

"Not me. Not allowed, under the contract."

"When you arranged for me to have the new apartment, you must've gone back in time to make the previous tenant win the lottery."

One of Xaphan's eyes squinted at Chesney. "This time thing, it worries you?"

Chesney and Hardacre exchanged glances. The preacher said, "Let's say it interests us."

"Then pour some more." Xaphan extended the tumbler glass and, when it was first refilled then half-emptied, said, "Youse guys are in time. Clocks tick, morning, afternoon, evening, all that. We're… not. When we got business with youse, we step into time whenever the business is. When we're done, we step out." It drank the rest of the rum. "Got it?"

"So if I ask you," Chesney said, "where I'll be at noon next Tuesday…"

"I dunno. But, if you tell me you wanna be at a certain place at that time, and if I don't get warned off cause it's horning in on some other lug's contract, then come Tuesday noon, I'll take you where you wanna go." It upended the glass and let the last few drops fall onto its pink tongue. "Provided it's got something to do with this crime-fightin' hoopdedoo."

"I think I get it," Hardacre said. "The demon is an extension of your will, within a narrow range of activities specified in the contract." He held up one hand and began ticking off fingers. "It won't set you up for a fall. It won't let you interfere with the carrying out of someone else's contract, and it won't allow another demon to interfere with you when you're in your crimefighting role. It can't tell you the future but it can alter the past to help you, under certain circumstances."

Hearing this, Chesney was thinking again that he should have nailed all of this down for himself, before he put on the costume and went out to be a hero. It had seemed to him that crimefighting was another pool of bright light, that he could act with certainty and conviction. Now he was seeing that he had actually been flailing around in the darkness. But one question still troubled him. "Why," he asked his assistant, "all the coincidences? Why, of all the people who might have been getting kidnapped at that time, was it Poppy Paxton?"

The demon drew in a cloud of cigar smoke and let it filter out through its small weasel nostrils – and through its small weasel ears. It held out the tumbler and Hardacre gave it the last of what was in the bottle. While the drink was being poured, it said, "You're asking the wrong guy. I didn't make it happen." It took a drink and gave Hardacre a considering look. "Maybe it's got something to do with this book that you-know-who is sposed to be writing?"

"You heard about that?" the preacher said.

"Hell is a small place," Xaphan said. "Word gets around. Anyways, I hear you book writers like to sprinkle a few coincidences around."

"If it helps the story," Hardacre said.

"Well, let me ask you something," the demon said. "You think this is all some big book?"

Hardacre glanced at the papers on his desk. "It's an idea I've been pursuing."

The demon drank the last of the rum. "So," it said, "seeing as it's your kind that thinks about the future, how do you think it's gonna end?"

Hardacre sipped a little from his own glass and said, "I don't know, but I'm working on it."

The time spent at Hardacre's had eaten up half of Chesney's two hours and they agreed that it was important for the young man to keep his appointment with W.T. Paxton. "You could use the back-up," the preacher had said, and Chesney had to agree. Paxton might be able to provide the pool of light he needed to operate as The Actionary without plunging into the murk and muddle that had marked his two outings so far.

But when they were back in the place of winds, Chesney said, "Take me to my apartment first." A second later, they were in his living room. The demon had retained his Havana cigar and hovered at head height, puffing blue clouds. Though Xaphan had been smoking it continually, only a half-inch had been consumed. The grimy stub that the Churchill had replaced was nowhere to be seen. "That was good rum," the fiend said.

"Xaphan," Chesney said, "do you know where my father is?"

"I do if he's a criminal and you want to fight him."

"Is he a criminal?" the young man said.

The demon consulted some internal source of information and said, "I got him leavin' the scene of an accident. Also for swipin' some stuff."

"So where is he?"

For answer, the fiend exhaled a blue cloud, disappeared, then reappeared a moment later, hovering in the air with its fingers hoisting the back of the collar of a balding, fifty-ish man whose eyes were almost as wide as the weasel's but who otherwise bore a slight resemblance to Chesney. A copy of the *Racing News* was in one trembling hand, and his pants and briefs were around his ankles. "Here," the demon said.

"Wagner Arnstruther?" Chesney said.

"W-w-where am I?" The man turned his head now and saw what was holding him. He opened his mouth but all that came out was a croak. The demon shook him and said, "Answer the question, mack."

"Y-y-yes, I'm Wagner Arnstruther. What do you w-w-want w-w-with me?"

"Where do you live?" the young man said.

"What?" The man looked around, shock giving way to rising fear.

Xaphan shook him harder. "Tell the kid your address."

The man stammered out a sequence of numbers and a street name.

"What city?"

"Fresno."

"Zip code?"

But Wagner Arnstruther's teeth had begun to chatter.

"Put him back," Chesney said.

The demon shrugged and disappeared with Chesney's father. In a moment he was back, pointing the Churchill at the young man. "You didn't fight him," it said.

"Maybe next time," the young man said. "I've had a hard day, and it's not over yet."

SEVEN

They were in the place of darkness, the winds rushing by from all directions. "Wait!" Chesney said. "Stop!"

"What's up?" said the demon.

Chesney looked around. They were on a stony plain, with just enough light for him to see the demon beside him. The sky seemed to be pressing down upon them, a layer of filthy cloud and fog that was barely overhead. The winds carried an acrid stink of ancient rot. Above the rush of air, Chesney thought he could hear moans and lamentations. "Where are we?" he said.

"Outer circle," Xaphan said.

"Of Hell?"

"Well, yeah."

"Why?"

The demon looked at him. "You really want to stand here and talk about this?"

Chesney noticed now that the winds were cold. Gusts of frigid air made his toes and fingers ache and blew stinging particles of grit into his face. "No," he said, "I wanted to make sure of something before we get to Paxton's."

"Okay, what?"

"Can you make me warm first?" The young man realized

that his feet were going numb. "And protect me from the wind."

"Sure." Immediately, they were surrounded by a head-high, circular stone wall, as if they stood in the world's shortest and narrowest silo. A fire kindled itself against the base of the wall opposite Chesney and the enclosed space grew warm.

"Now, what did you wanna get clear?" Xaphan said.

"How much time do I have left?"

The demon produced its pocket watch. "Thirty-two minutes, ten seconds."

"Okay. I can't afford to run over," Chesney said. "So when I'm down to my last two minutes, you tell me."

"Sure."

"In fact, anytime I'm about to run out of time, you give me a two-minute warning."

"Gotcha."

"And also a one-minute, and a thirty-seconds."

"Check."

"And also, I should be wearing my costume when I meet Paxton." Instantly, he was dressed as The Actionary. He remembered Lieutenant Denby's remark about his chin. "Make the mask cover my whole face." Now it did.

"You ready to go now?"

There was something about wearing the blue and gray outfit that centered Chesney. His mind grew clearer. "You didn't answer my question," he said. "Why are we here in the outer circle of Hell?"

"Short-cut," said the demon. "Also, the rules say I can go places with you, like room to room or across the street. But we're not allowed to go tooling around the world. We can only go back and forth from Hell."

"So whenever I want you to take me somewhere fast, we have to go through this Hell-hole?" Chesney gestured at the lowering sky above with its rags of wind-torn gray and black. "Isn't there a nicer neighborhood we could cut through?"

"No," said Xaphan, "this is about as good as it gets."

"Then how about we make this" – the young man gestured at the walls and fire – "a little more homey? Like, maybe a roof and a chair?"

The demon snorted. "So now you want a fortress of solitude after all."

"No, just a place I can go to and be out of the way, if I need to think."

"Oh, like a hideout, for when you got to take it on the lam?" the demon said. "That's been done."

"Well, sorta," Chesney said.

The demon stroked its weasel chin. "And I guess you'd want some of those, what you call your creature comforts?"

"Could be. What did you have in mind?"

"How's this?" said the fiend. The rough stone silo became a strong-walled chamber, with age-darkened oak beams supporting the ceiling and a blood-red carpet on the floor. A table and chair, of heavy wood and adorned with brass fittings, appeared in the center of the room and now one wall was pierced by a fireplace stacked with blazing logs. The sound of the wind died and the room grew comfortably warm. Finally, a drinks cabinet similar to the one in Billy Lee Hardacre's study appeared against one wall, boasting a row of filled decanters and a well-stocked humidor.

"I don't smoke," Chesney said, "and I don't drink much."

The demon looked like an unhappy fanged weasel. "I thought it was a nice touch."

"I don't need it."

"Maybe you'll develop a taste for the stuff."

"I doubt it," Chesney said. "The one time I tried a cigar

I threw up, and liquor makes me…" He trailed off, aware that something was bothering the demon. Chesney was not, his school counselors used to say, the most socially aware person they'd ever met; he often didn't know that he was getting on other people's nerves until they shouted at him or, back in his school days, punched him in the nose. But, once his mother had come to understand that he wasn't just a particularly hardheaded child, she had hired consultants and therapists to work with him. They had painstakingly taught him how to recognize and inter- pret body language and facial expressions, using his rational brain to accomplish what his more primitive cir- cuits should have, but couldn't. He studied the demon now, and the image that Xaphan now presented – cigar clamped between his fangs, hands thrust into pockets, head slung between his shoulders – was unmistakably that of barely contained annoyance. Once he focused on the matter, it took the young man only a few moments to de- duce the reason.

"*You*'d like it," he said.

"Who me?" said the fiend.

"Yes, you. You like liquor and cigars. Especially rum."

Xaphan puffed on the Churchill. "Well, so what? A hard-working demon's entitled to a little something, ain't he? I mean, now and then."

"But you can't have these 'little somethings' unless I in- vite you to," Chesney said. "Is that right?"

The demon shrugged. "Yeah, that's right."

"So this would be outside the terms of our contract?" He could tell by the way Xaphan looked down and away that he had touched upon a delicate point. "Well, is it?"

The fiend did not have the ability to look abashed. But it ground the toe of one spatted shoe into the carpet. "Okay," it said after a moment, "yeah."

"Then if I say it's okay for you to use the rum and cigars, I could make that conditional on…"

"On what?" Xaphan said.

Chesney stroked the side of his jaw. "I don't know yet," he said. "But let's just say you'll owe me."

The demon considered the proposition, then said, "Deal." It poured itself a tumblerful of dark rum, even darker than Billy Lee Hardacre's. "Does that include when you're not here?"

"I suppose."

Xaphan smiled and raised the glass.

"Hold it," Chesney said. "We're using up my time on your pleasures."

Xaphan tossed back half the tumbler's contents. "Nah. When we're here, we're outside of time. You've still got thirty-two minutes and ten seconds."

"Then let's go see what Mr Paxton wants."

"One more slug of this stuff." It drained the glass then exhaled a molasses-scented breath. "Oh, yeah. That takes me back."

With neither flash nor thunder, Chesney appeared in W.T. Paxton's library. He had the demon place him out of the line of sight of the two men, who were bent over a mahogany table, side by side, studying a spread of papers, and he enjoyed seeing both of them jump when he spoke from behind them, saying, "Here I am."

"How did you do that?" Seth Baccala said. "This place is supposed to be secure."

"I have my ways." Chesney saw the look of consternation on Baccala's face, but for The Actionary this situation constituted another pool of clear light. He felt confident and sure of himself.

For his part, Paxton – once he recovered from the

startlement – was delighted. "Told you," he said to his assistant, giving Baccala a mock punch to the shoulder. "This guy is something."

"The question is," Baccala said, looking Chesney over with a skeptical eye, "is it a 'something' we can use?"

"Yes," said Paxton. "I'm sure of it."

"Well, I'm not sure I want to be used," Chesney said. "So why don't you two tell me exactly what you have in mind, and I'll see if your plans fit into mine."

"See?" Paxton said to his factotum. "The guy's on the level. We can work together."

The skepticism still held the high ground on Baccala's face, but he said, "Let's sit down and talk about it."

"I can give you about twenty minutes," Chesney said. He looked around for a seat and settled himself in a comfortable chair that was one of five grouped in a semicircle near a fireplace in which a few lengths of wood burned.

"We've got a lot to talk about," the assistant said, positioning himself in a straight-backed chair opposite Chesney. He crossed his legs neatly, then tugged at the crease in his trousers.

"Maybe we do. Or maybe I'm out of here in five minutes."

"Good man," said Paxton, perching on the arm of an overstuffed armchair. "You know, one of the things that happen when you get somewhere in life, the way I have, is you're always surrounded by people who want to agree with whatever you say. I like the way you say what's on your mind."

"Well," said Baccala, "let's just discover exactly what *is* on the man's mind." He gestured at Chesney's costume. "What's this all about?"

"I'm a crimefighter," said Chesney.

"So you fight crime," Baccala said.

"That's what the word means."

The assistant cocked his head to one side. "What kind of crime? Embezzlement? Insider trading? Purloining office supplies?"

The man was trying to get a rise out of him, Chesney thought. But the actuary responded calmly. "Violent crime. Murder, armed robbery," – he looked pointedly at Paxton – "kidnapping."

"Why haven't we heard of you before?" Baccala said.

"I'm just getting started."

"But what did you do before this? Were you a policeman? A prosecutor?"

"My background, and my identity, are secret."

"But how did you get into this?"

"That's my business," Chesney said.

Baccala looked over at Paxton. "I don't like this." He looked at Chesney. "I don't think I like you."

"The feeling," Chesney said, "could be mutual."

Chesney heard a sharp report as W.T. clapped his hands. "Enough," he said. "You two are like a couple of hounds getting ready to tear it up. Let's look at the big picture."

"All right," Chesney said, swinging his gaze from Baccala to the older man, "what is the big picture? Politics, right?"

Paxton leaned toward the young man. "You bet, politics. You've heard the old saying: some people run for office because they want to do something; some because they want to be somebody."

"Yes."

"Well, I already am somebody," Paxton said. "I want to do something. I want to make the world a better place."

Chesney looked at Baccala as he said, "Better for who?"

"Never mind him," Paxton said. "Talk to the organ grinder. And the answer is, better for everybody. Sure, if crime rates go down, my company will do better. That doesn't mean squat to me. What am I going to do, buy another jet? Buy a football team?"

"People do," Chesney said.

"W.T. Paxton is not people," the older man said. "I got one life. I've spent a big chunk of it building a business. Now the business can run itself. I want to do something I can be proud of."

"You want to fight crime?" Chesney said. "By being a politician? By being a member of the Twenty?"

Paxton looked at Baccala again. "Told you," he said again, "no bullshit, this guy." He turned back to Chesney. "Straight out, I want to fight crime as a way of getting into politics. Once I'm in politics, I want to make a better world."

Chesney turned to Baccala. "Is he serious?"

The assistant met his gaze. "Yes."

"I'm not interested in politics," Chesney told Paxton.

"Good," said the older man. "I wouldn't want you for competition."

"What you do want is to use me to get where you want to go."

"Yes," said Paxton, "and in return for that, I will help you fulfill your dream." He leaned closer now, his voice lowering almost to a whisper. "It is your dream, isn't it? This is what you've always wanted to do, what you've always wanted to be."

The man's eyes were bright, his gaze piercing. Chesney involuntarily moved back. "I won't talk about my motivation," he said.

"You don't have to," said Paxton. "I can see it. This was your dream but it was always going to be just a dream, and then something happened and you had a chance to grab that dream, turn your life around. And you grabbed it."

Chesney cleared his throat. The man's intensity was making him uncomfortable. But before he could speak, Paxton pressed him.

"Well, now I'm offering you a chance to make that dream work. You can't just be a guy running around the streets, looking for the baddies. You need backup, information, intelligence, who's who and what they're planning. I can give you that!"

"What, from a bunch of actuaries on the tenth floor?" Chesney said.

"That's just part of it," Paxton said. "I've also got access to hard intelligence from the police department's anti-crime section."

"And how do you get that?"

"John Hanshaw's office."

Chesney stopped to think about it. The police commissioner was a powerful figure in the city's law enforcement apparatus. "Hanshaw is working for you?"

Baccala spoke. "With us."

"And what does he get out of it?" Chesney said.

The assistant smoothed his crease again. "He wants to move up," he said. "And playing a major role in a successful campaign against street crime could be his ticket to the big chair behind the big desk in the mayor's office."

"He's a man who wants to be somebody," Chesney quoted.

"Sometimes," Paxton said, "you need those kind of people if you want to get something done."

Chesney took a moment to get his next words straight in his mind, then he said, "You had another plan, didn't you?" Neither man said anything, but their silence seemed strained; they were both waiting for Chesney to drop the other shoe. He looked from Paxton to Baccala and back to the older man. "You staged the kidnapping of your daughter, didn't you? The one I interrupted.

That's why you weren't upset."

He waited for Paxton's eventual nod of confirmation. Chesney was still in a pool of light and he understood what he saw in the older man's expression. "You didn't want to, though. You were talked into it. Who by?" He gestured with a thumb toward Baccala. "Him."

Another nod from Paxton. "And somebody else."

"Nat Blowdell?" Chesney said. It was a guess but he knew it was a good one when he saw both men's faces open in surprise.

"How do you know about him?" Baccala said, his voice tight.

"Told you, I have my ways."

Xaphan's voice spoke in Chesney's ear. "Two minutes, boss."

The young man got up from his chair. "I want to think about this," he said.

"We're not finished," Baccala said.

"We are for now. I'll be in touch." Chesney moved toward the door.

"Wait," Paxton said. "Take this."

Chesney turned to see the older man scooping up the papers he and Baccala had been studying when he'd arrived. "What are they?"

"Read them," Paxton said, sliding the pages into a file folder and offering them to the young man, "and do what you think is right."

Chesney took the folder. "A test?" he said.

"One you won't have any trouble passing, if I'm any judge," said Paxton.

"No promises," Chesney said, "but I'll look at it." He opened the door, then turned back to them just as Xaphan's voice told him he had one minute left. "Don't open this door for a little while."

He stepped through and closed the door behind him. He was in a wide, carpeted hallway with closed doors to either side and niches between the doorways that held statues and ornate vases. "Xaphan," he said, "get me home."

Again he was in the winds and darkness, then back in his living room.

"I gotta go," the demon said.

"One question," Chesney said.

"Make it quick."

"When I disappear, what does anyone watching see?"

"They see you disappear."

"But do I fade, or wink out, or vanish in a puff of smoke?"

"You wink out," said the demon, "like this." And then he wasn't there.

He left Chesney with a file folder in his hand, a scent of sulfur in his nostrils and the memory of the last thing he had seen before the winds and darkness of his last brief transit through the outer circle of Hell: the door opposite W.T. Paxton's library opening a crack and one deep-blue eye peeking out at him as he vanished.

When Chesney showed up at C Group the following morning, Sitting Bull returned the meta-analysis to him. "Good work," the chief said, "but they want you to develop a key-nodes timeline for an archetypal situation. Can you do that?"

"Yes," said Chesney, "but it might take a while."

"Take as long as it takes to get it right."

The actuary booted up his computer and set to work. He had already assembled newspaper clippings and TV news clips on the thirty most recent kidnappings or disappearances that fit the template Denby had cynically described. And he had quantified the coverage in terms of column inches and seconds of airtime, as well as in the placement of those inches on front pages or inside pages, or of those seconds in the key minutes before a TV news broadcast broke for the first commercial.

Now he identified the key events in the typical sequence of events that occurred in the coverage: the initial report of a missing girl or woman; the first formal police statement; the release of a photograph or, even better, video; the initial search; the finding of evidence suggesting foul play; the gathering of reporters and cameras at the victim's home; interviews with neighbors, friends, workmates; reports, usually false, of sightings of the victim; the distraught family's first appeal; reports, sometimes false, of ransom demands; more police statements; a second appeal from the family; the identification of an alleged suspect, followed by an arrest then a subsequent release for lack of evidence or, sometimes, a prosecution for having made an opportunistic ransom demand although the arrestee had had no connection to the actual kidnap; the convergence of media on the suspects; more sightings; the finding of more evidence that, often, turned out to be as spurious as the sightings; the emergence of psychics with insights, some spurious, some possibly real.

And around and through all of these events, the spin-offs: "think pieces" in newspapers about why people go missing and why some are never seen again, along with recaps of notorious cases from bygone times; on television, interviews with former police and FBI agents, criminologists, psychologists, psychics and, most prized of all, former victims who survived their ordeal.

Chesney plunged into this welter of data, creating graphs and sequences, noting the timing of events and correlating them with peaks and valleys of newspaper circulation figures and television viewership statistics. He worked through the morning, ate lunch at his desk, then carried on through the afternoon. The work held his attention; he could feel the patterns emerging from the data, so that as the end of the day neared he was close to paring away the nonessentials. The shape of the archetypical blonde-goes-missing, weeks-long media event was there to be seen. A few refinements, and he'd be able to present his employer with a complete, step-by-step template for how such a story evolved and unfolded, almost hour by hour.

"Arnstruther," said a voice behind him, "I'll need your hard drive and any hard copies of your work."

Chesney came out of the crisp, clear world of numbers to find the sweating, always-worried face of Arthur Entwistle looming over him like an anxious full moon. "I beg your pardon?"

"We're closing up. Didn't you read the email?"

Chesney had read nothing all day but material related to the meta-analysis. He had turned off his email program because he did not like to be distracted by its successive attempts to let him know that something was waiting for him in its electronic mailbox.

Entwistle put a damp hand on the actuary's mouse and called up the email program, then clicked through to a message whose subject line read: *Urgent – read immediately*. He opened the email and Chesney quickly scanned the several points in the body of the message. It was from Seth Baccala and detailed a series of security measures that henceforth would apply to C Group.

At any time that a member of the group left his desk, his computer was to be put on standby, behind a double password lock. At the end of the day, all work was to be collected and locked away – Chesney looked up and discovered that a man-sized strongbox had been installed while he'd been immersed in his timeline analysis – and each computer's hard drive was to be removed from its deck and stored in the safe. Failure to comply with any of these measures would bring instant dismissal.

"What's up?" he asked the section chief.

"I don't know," Sitting Bull said, "but I spent an hour being grilled by Baccala and some security consultant this morning. They are way serious about keeping everything in-house." He looked around, even though they were the only ones left in the office. Chesney saw by his computer's clock that it was past five-thirty.

"Who's this security consultant?"

Entwistle lowered his voice. "He didn't give me his name. But he looked like the kind of guy who could take you for a helicopter ride and make sure you never came back." He looked around again. "You'll meet him tomorrow. They questioned Kevin and Neil after me today. You'll get your turn tomorrow."

"Why all the cloak-and-dagger?" Chesney said, although he had a good idea.

"They're not telling me," Sitting Bull said, "but my guess is there's already been some kind of leak." He leaned closer to the young man so that Chesney could tell that the chief's antiperspirant was waging an unequal battle against his sweat glands. "You haven't been shooting your mouth off, have you?"

"Me?" said Chesney. "Who would I talk to?"

Entwistle straightened and a sound came out of him that might have been a laugh. "Yeah," he said, "you're the last one I'd suspect."

Chesney wanted to ask him what he meant by that, but the chief was now urging him to get his material together, shut down his computer and extract the hard drive. Chesney complied, and five minutes later he was putting his coat on as the chief triple-locked the safe. The young man went back to his desk and retrieved a file folder from his desk then turned toward the door.

"What's that?" Sitting Bull said.

"Something I'm working on," Chesney said. "My hobby."

"Show me."

"It's nothing. It's about stolen cars."

"I said, show me." Entwistle held out a hand. Chesney handed him the file. "This is a company folder," the chief said.

Fortunately, the pages within were not recognizable as having anything to do with Paxton Life and Casualty. One sheet contained statistics on car theft, especially upmarket models. The other had a list of addresses scattered throughout the city. The third page was just a series of dates, including today's. Entwistle looked through them, puzzled. "What is this?" he said.

"Crime stats and correlations," Chesney said. "I told you, it's a hobby of mine. I brought it in to do some work on it at lunchtime, but instead I worked on the media meta-analysis."

"You're not doing something I should know about, are you?" The words sounded like tough managerese, but the tone behind them said, "Please don't tell me you're going to be a problem."

"No," said the young man, "I'm not."

Entwistle gave him back the folder and followed him out of the C Group office. Chesney saw that a touchpad lock had been installed on the door. Sitting Bull pressed his palm to it, and a red light on top of the lock began to blink. They went down together in the elevator, but the chief was descending to the parking garage while Chesney got out at the lobby. There was a pizza joint diagonally across the street. He went in, had two slices of pepperoni and pineapple, one of his favorites, then headed for the nearest alley. Deep in its darker recesses he called up Xaphan and said, "Get the costume on me. We've got work to do."

He had been thinking his way through it, over the pepperoni and pineapple and two classic Cokes. Now he told the demon, "Make sure no one can see or hear us."

"Gotcha."

He showed Xaphan the list of addresses. "Can you see what's going on at these places, right now?"

The demon didn't even glance at the list. "Sure thing."

"Can you make, like, a movie screen so I can see, too?"

"Uh huh."

"Okay, this one: 214 Bewley Street." A square screen thirty feet high appeared on the wall of the building across the alley. "Too big," said Chesney. The screen shrank to four feet. "Good." The Actionary peered at the image that appeared, with such clarity that it was like looking through a window: an auto repair and servicing shop, one car on a hoist, its transmission removed. The place was dark and deserted, its staff gone home, the lights out except for the winking red light of a motion sensor.

Chesney read another entry off the list of addresses, which said, "4415 Chester Avenue." This one looked to be a warehouse, also dark at the end of the day, except for a light in a second-story office at one end of the building, where a security guard was drinking coffee and watching a portable television.

"8700 Cooper Street." The screen lit up, showing another auto repair shop, this one with several service bays facing each other across a wide concrete-floored aisle. The lights were on and the place was busy. Every bay was occupied by a vehicle, as was the open space between, and every one of the vehicles was an up-market, late-model sedan, SUV or sports car costing at least sixty thousand dollars. Chesney was no aficionado of high-priced cars, but he would have bet that the red Lamborghini must have gone for upward of two hundred thousand.

"What are they doing?" he asked his assistant.

"Changing the vinnies."

"The what?"

"The vehicle identification numbers," the demon said.

"What about him?" Chesney pointed to where a man in a sharply tailored suit was sitting at a desk at the end of the open space, printing laboriously on a sheet of paper.

"He's entering the new numbers on a manifest."

"What for?"

"For the ship. These cars are going onto trucks, and the trucks are going to a ship."

"And where's the ship headed?"

"St Petersburg."

"Russia?"

"You got it."

Chesney smiled. "Those are stolen cars."

"Yep."

The young man restrained the urge to act prematurely. He had learned his lesson from Melda McCann. The gangsters – they had to be members of organized crime; the activity was plainly organized – were still readying the cars for shipment. "Show me the other places," he said.

There were three more addresses on the list. Two were empty. One was a parking area behind a derelict factory; men were loading cars into containers on the backs of three tractor-trailers lined up side by side. "We'll do that one first," he told Xaphan.

"Okay, ready?"

"Hold it." Chesney had been thinking that part through as well, over pizza and Coke. He gave detailed instructions to the demon. "I don't get hurt in any way. No innocent bystanders get hurt in any way. You don't do anything, or fail to do anything, that leads to the criminals getting away. No evidence gets lost or damaged. At all times, you act to assist me in arresting and restraining those men in a manner that leads to their trial and conviction." He looked the demon straight in its huge weasel eyes. "Got that?"

Xaphan did not blink. "You're the boss."

"Don't forget it. All right, I want to hit the truck-loading operation first. Let's come in with the flash-bang again, hyperspeed and the strength of ten. And as I knock them down, you tie their hands and ankles so they can't get away."

"I got ya."

"But they don't see you."

"Right."

"Right. On a count of three. One... two..." The next syllable was just departing from Chesney's lips when he entered his hide-out in Hell then emerged almost instantly in the yard behind the old factory. The first thing he saw was a startled face right in front of him; it belonged to a big-bellied man wearing a dark suit and a garish tie, his eyes blinking in slow motion from the bright flash that had preceded Chesney's arrival. The crimefighter closed his fist and planted it in the middle of the button-straining stomach, and saw the gangster's face form a comic mask around the whoosh of air from his open mouth.

The man was slowly sagging to his knees as Chesney pushed past him. The Actionary had entered the scene between two of the trucks; now he left the breathless man to be secured by Xaphan and ran toward the rear of the vehicles, where ramps led up to open containers and cars were being loaded. In his excitement, he forgot that he had told the demon to give him hyperspeed, so that the three running steps he took carried him past the cars and across the open space behind them and into a heavy sliding door on the back of the factory. He bounced off, unhurt and walked at what seemed to him to be a normal pace back to where the action was.

The hoods who had been loading the cars were still reacting to the flash and bang of his entrance and probably, Chesney thought, to the noise he must have made crashing into the heavy steel door hard enough to make it reverberate. The Actionary strode to a Mercedes-Benz that was idling at the foot of one of the ramps. Its driver, a thin-shouldered man in a fake-satin windbreaker, with a cigarette dangling from a corner of his mouth, was opening his door to step out.

Chesney assisted him, yanking hard on the edge of the door, but remembering to limit his effort lest he pull it off its hinges. Still, the man holding the inner handle was dragged clear out of the car, sprawling sideways onto the filthy asphalt. Chesney bent, lifted the man clear of the ground, and clipped him on his unshaven jaw. He saw the criminal's eyes glaze and moved on to the next target.

There were, altogether, eight of them, and Chesney dealt with each quickly and smoothly. The last one turned to run, but had made no more than a couple of steps before The Actionary seized his belt, hoisted the man off his feet, and rapped gauntleted knuckles on the back of his head. The thug sagged, unconscious, in Chesney's grip and the crimefighter hauled him back to the scene of the action.

"I want some big, thick rope," he told his assistant.

"Here," came the instant answer, as a coil of two-inch cable appeared on the ground.

"Help me yank them into a circle, out here in the open, then wind the rope around them," The Actionary said.

"Make it tight enough that they can't get loose but so they can still breathe." That didn't take long. The men were all unconscious, slumped over, their hands tied behind their backs. When the heavy line was wound around them, Chesney thought they made a good picture – it could have been an illustration straight from a Malc Turner episode.

"See if one of them has a phone," he said, and when the demon brought him a cell, he punched in his six-six-six prefix then dialed 9-1-1. He told the police operator that men with guns were shooting at each other and gave the factory's location. Then he left the phone on and placed it on the ground. He whispered to Xaphan, "Make some gun noises."

"Bang, bang," said the demon.

"Real gun noises."

Instantly the sounds of pistol shots reverberated off the back wall of the factory, then came the stutter of automatic fire. "Tommy gun," the demon said. "Always liked that sound."

"Let's go to the other place," Chesney said. "Same rules and restrictions. Count of three."

The roundup of the car-theft ring at the chop-shop went even more quickly and smoothly. Chesney remembered not to overshoot his targets. He also found that open-handed slaps, when delivered at almost supersonic speed and with the strength of ten men, were all that was needed to render an opponent unconscious. This time, instead of tying the criminals up, he threw open the big, segmented door, went out into the parking lot behind the garage and dragged in a half-empty dumpster. He then piled the five bound and senseless thugs into it. Then he called the police again, from the phone in the business office, and reported that an armed robbery was in progress.

"Statistics show that police respond more rapidly to reports of men with guns," he told his assistant.

"Well, I never," said the demon.

They went back into the service area. Chesney stood with arms folded and contemplated the dumpster full of hoodlums. Now he could hear distant sirens. "Are those headed for the first place?" he asked Xaphan.

"Yep. And that one" – Chesney heard a nearer wail rising in pitch – "is coming here."

"Home," he said. "I want to see the news."

"...this breaking story. Police responded to this shut-down factory after receiving a report of shots fired. When officers got there, expecting a gun battle in progress – that's deep gang territory – they found this..."

The image on Chesney's television cut away from the artfully coiffed cable-channel newsreader at her desk in the studio to the kind of jerky, jump-around shots that meant that the camera operator was running toward the scene, the camera jiggling on his shoulder with each step. The screen showed the loading area behind the old factory, several squad cars parked at odd angles, blue lights flashing, headlights illuminating the three big trucks lined up, the luxury cars waiting to load and the clump of gangsters sitting on the asphalt, the two-inch rope still wrapped around them.

The image now jump-cut to a close-up of the bound men. Some of them were still unconscious. One – Chesney recognized the big-bellied man he had hit first – was yelling at a cop standing over him, but almost every other word of what the gangster was saying had to be bleeped out of the soundtrack. The uniformed cop, in helmet and bullet-proof vest, an automatic weapon slung from one shoulder, was grinning at the hoodlum. Now he took out a cell phone and used its built-in lens to snap a picture. That sent the big-bellied man into a tirade, the only word of which that wasn't bleeped was "you."

"And if that wasn't enough," – the news reader was back, smiling into the camera – "at almost the same time, police were called to a garage on Cooper Street, where they found another seven unconscious men," – the image cut away to the scene at the chop-shop, the minicam shooting down into the dumpster – "tied up and left in a dumpster."

Now the screen showed the street outside the garage, and Chesney recognized lieutenant Denby with a thicket of microphones pointing at him from several directions. A female reporter to his left was asking him, "What do you make of this, lieutenant?"

The detective shrugged. "Too early to tell, Marcia," he said. "We've got what looks to be several gentlemen engaged in changing the vehicle identity numbers on what appear to be stolen cars. How they all ended up in a dumpster, we don't know yet. We're investigating."

A man to his right said, "Is this evidence of gang activity?"

Denby gave the reporter a look that could have been translated as "Well, duh," but he recovered his official police-talking-to-media expression before saying, "Well, Josh, there's seven of them in the dumpster, and I think it's safe to assume they all know each other."

"No, lieutenant," the reporter said, "I mean is this a case of one gang of car thieves being hit by another gang?"

Marcia chimed in, talking fast. "Lieutenant, are we seeing the outbreak of a gang war?"

"Gangsters don't usually knock each other out and tie each other up," Denby said. "When they have disagreements, they lean toward more permanent solutions."

A uniformed policeman leaned in, cupped his finger beside the detective's ear and whispered something the microphones did not pick up. Denby's eyes betrayed surprise for a second, then he said, "I've got to go. There'll be a statement tomorrow."

The image cut back to the studio. "Gang warfare?" said the newsreader, quirking one perfectly shaped eyebrow. "At this point, police aren't saying. We'll keep you updated on this fast-breaking story from the mean streets. Meanwhile, in Washington–"

Chesney changed the channel. There was no coverage on any other station yet. The other local stations had skimpy news departments and it would have taken a much bigger story to convince the station managers to break into prime-time programming. He'd see the local news reports at eleven.

He picked up the phone, entered his anti-trace numbers and dialed Paxton's private line. "So, did I pass?" he said, when the magnate picked up.

"Flying colors, my boy. Are you happy with the results?"

"Yes."

"Want to do it again?"

A pause, but Chesney didn't really need to think about it. "Yes."

"Then why don't you come by tomorrow night? We'll talk."

"All right."

He hung up and turned to Xaphan. "How much time do I have left tonight?"

Out came the demon's pocket watch. "Twenty-eight minutes."

"Why do you do that?" Chesney said. "You must know how much time is left without looking at that thing."

The fiend lifted its weasel eyebrows as it regarded Chesney's costume. "Why do you dress like a fruitcake?"

"How about I order you not to insult me?"

"Howzabout I remind you if it don't got to do with crimefighting, I don't got to do what you tell me." The demon puffed on its Churchill before adding, "Fruitcake."

"Howzabout I tell you to lose the cigar? And forget about the rum?"

The demon stuck out its lower lip. "No need to be a hard case," it said.

"We're wasting time," Chesney said. "Is there a mugging or a murder about to happen before I run out the clock?"

"Nah."

"Is there anything?"

"There's a guy gonna give his girlfriend a smack over in the park."

"We'll do that, then. No flash or bang, just put me behind him. Double speed and strength ten."

On a count of three, they jumped through Hell to the riverside park. The altercation was taking place beneath a tree that provided shade on sunny days and complete privacy for amorous couples at night. The couple occupying the spot may have used it for trysts before, but tonight it was the scene of conflict.

A man in his late twenties or early thirties stood with his back to Chesney. The Actionary had a quick impression: more than medium height, wide in the shoulders, wearing going-out-on-the-town clothes, his hair gelled into spikes. The man's attention was completely focused on someone in front of him who was masked from The Actionary's view, but was female. He heard her gasp as the man made a motion. Chesney thought at first that he had hit her, but he heard no sound of a blow and realized he had only seized her arm. But it must have been a hard and painful grip, because she followed the gasp with an, "Ow! Let go of–"

"You don't dump me, bitch!" the man was saying. And now his other hand was coming up and Chesney could see what would come next: a hard backhander across the woman's face. It would hurt her. The hand was big and there was a heavy ring on one finger, a dark faceted stone set in silver, glinting ominously in the thin light from a distant streetlight.

Chesney stepped forward, reached over the man's shoulder and took hold of the hand as if he were going to shake it. He applied pressure and felt the fingers squeeze together. Now it was the assailant's turn to gasp. Chesney pulled, and spun the man around to face him.

"You don't hit women," he said, using his best Malc Turner voice. He had planned to knock the wind out of the man with a punch to the solar plexus, but now that he had him turned around he saw, even in the dim light, that this was a fellow who set a lot of store by his clothing. The shirt was silk, the suit was probably from a designer's catalogue, and there was some kind of logo worked in metal glinting from the buckle on the thin leather belt.

Chesney changed his plan. He spun the man around again, took hold of the back of his collar and belt. The man began to splutter and squawk – it seemed he couldn't decide exactly which swear words to use – but Chesney paid no heed. The river was fifty feet away. He frogmarched the fellow down to the bank and threw him ten feet out into the cold water. The splash was satisfying.

He turned away, then looked back to make sure the man could swim – it would be just like Xaphan to trip him up like that – and saw that the water was only hip deep here. He left the bully stumbling and shivering in the river – the man had finally settled on a multisyllabic accusation of incest which he kept repeating in a steadily rising pitch, but he made no move to come anywhere nearer to The Actionary.

Chesney turned back to the woman beneath the tree,

meaning to say, "Are you all right?" and maybe advise her to take more care in selecting her next beau. She came out from under the shadow of the tree, and stopped with arms akimbo, fists planted on her hips.

"You again?" said Melda McCann.

"I brought him out to the park because I didn't want him busting up my things," she told Chesney as they walked back to her apartment. She slipped an arm into his, as if they were an old-fashioned courting couple out for a stroll. It felt good there, so good that he reached with his free hand to pat and squeeze hers. That made her clutch his arm a little tighter to her. He could feel the soft pressure of one breast against his bicep.

"If he broke things when he got mad," Chesney said, "that was a sign he would use violence." This was not an observation born of Chesney's own experience, but something he had read somewhere. Still, it seemed to be the correct thing to say at the moment; Melda squeezed his arm again.

"You're right," she said. "I always pick the losers, the mama's boys and overgrown spoiled brats. Until now." She looked up at him.

It was probably one of those moments, Chesney thought, when he should say something. Unfortunately, nothing he had read equipped him for the task. He settled for patting her hand again and was surprised to find that, incredibly, his instincts were right on the money again.

"Do you believe," she said, "in destiny?" When he didn't answer right away, she said, "You're the thoughtful type, aren't you? A deep thinker. Jeez, that's such a relief after all those guys with their cute little lines they got from some men's magazine." They walked another couple of steps. "So, do you?"

"Do I what?" Chesney had lost the thread of the conversation, thinking about all the cute-but-useless lines he had read in magazines and how-to books.

"Do you believe in destiny?"

He told her the simple truth. "For some people I do."

"I knew it. A thinker. And an action man." Another arm squeeze, and this time she was definitely pressing her breast against him.

They had reached her doorstep. All at once, Chesney remembered the kiss. She was relinquishing his arm and turning so that they were face to face. He felt her arms go around his waist and then she was pressed up against him. She looked up at him and he felt her breath warm against him lips.

"You didn't call," she said.

"I've… been busy."

"Oh, yeah?"

"Watch the news tonight," he said.

"When are you going to be not busy?" She shifted her weight in a way that somehow settled her closer against him. He realized that when he had had the demon create the costume, he had not stipulated that it should be able to disguise the unmistakable sign of sexual arousal. The Driver never had that problem. And now she noticed and pressed against him harder. "Do you want to come in?"

"Two minutes," Xaphan said.

"What?" Chesney said.

Melda moved against him. "I said, do you want to come in?" She said it in a way that told Chesney the double entendre was doubly intended.

"Two minutes," the demon said in his ear. "Less now."

"I have to go," Chesney told Melda.

She pulled back and looked down between them.

"You're kidding me," she said.

"No," said Chesney. "I don't want to go. But I really have to."

She brought her eyes up to his. "You haven't got another maiden to rescue?"

"No."

"Good," she said. She looked down again at the bulge in his costume. "Cause that's not good manners."

"One minute," said the voice in his ear.

"I've got to go."

"But you'll call me."

"Yes."

"When?"

"Soon."

"Tomorrow?"

"Yes."

"Promise?"

"Promise."

She loosened her grip on his waist, stepped back. "Cause it's nice, you rescuing me and all. I really appreciate it. But it's not a basis for a relationship."

"I've got to go. Please don't watch."

"You're not going to turn into a pumpkin?"

"Goodbye."

He would have liked to kiss her again, to be the kisser rather than the kissee, but there was no time. "Xaphan," he said, "make some fog or something, so it looks like I just fade out of sight."

A cloud of gray swallowed him, then he was in the fire-warmed room in Hell. A moment later he was in his apartment.

"This is getting complicated," he said to the demon, but found he was talking to a puff of ill-smelling vapor.

• • • •

By the next morning, the story of the car-theft ring had gone nationwide. Enough police officers who had either been on the scene or had heard the details from their buddies in the squad room had talked to their contacts in the media. And the video footage from the news crew that had managed to get to the scene outside the old factory on the heels of the first cops to respond to the shots-fired call had gone viral. The clip of the big-bellied thug swearing at the cop with the phone camera, without the bleeps, was number three on YouTube's most-viewed list.

Most of the initial coverage played the story for the humor content, but the follow-ups were now starting to ask the serious questions: who had knocked unconscious more than a dozen hardcase hoodlums, many of them armed, and left them tied in a bunch like cartoon characters, or piled on top of each other in a dumpster? The speculation had moved on from gang warfare to the possibility that a vigilante group, maybe consisting of off-duty cops, had pulled the stunt.

But while Chesney was drinking his morning coffee and packing a lunch, inbetween flipping among the channels, a cable news service broke the story open with an exclusive: some enterprising producer had canvassed local businesses around the chop-shop garage to find out if any of them had security cameras whose fields of view included the scene of the action. The on-air reporter solemnly assured the viewers that the tape had been turned over to the major crimes squad – but not, of course, before the producer had made a copy of it.

The security camera was mounted ten feet up on the rear wall of a plumbing supply outfit and covered its loading area and parking lot. But the property was separated by only a chain-link fence from the parking area at the rear of the chop-shop. The camera's field of view, as it swept constantly from side to side, included the big, segmented steel doors with unbreakable glass panes that could be rolled up to admit cars to the service bays.

Chesney's phone rang. He glanced at the caller ID display and saw that the call was from Billy Lee Hardacre's private line – which probably meant his mother was phoning to upbraid him for associating with criminal elements. With only a slight twinge of guilt he muted the ringer and kept on watching the TV.

The image was grainy and only in black and white. The big roll-up doors were down, but light was showing through the windows set into them at head height. Then there came a sudden bright flash that caused a halo afterglow to appear on the tape. When the image cleared again, moments later, the doors were being flung upward at high speed. There was a blur of movement, and now a dumpster that had been standing against a wall a few feet away suddenly sped into the lighted garage. More blurs of motion, and then a stillness. A wide-shouldered man wearing a one-piece, skin-tight garment was visible, standing with legs apart and arms folded, surveying the gangster-filled dumpster for a moment as if contemplating a job done to his satisfaction. And then he winked out of existence.

"Holy shit!" said someone in the studio, then someone else said, "Maury, your mike is open." And now the anchor, standing before a bank of monitors that were combined to show one floor-to-ceiling image of Chesney and the dumpster, said, "Let's take a look at that in slow motion. We've had our technical people improve the quality of the original image."

The tape picked up from just after the flash and halo effect finished. The focus moved in tightly on one of the windows in the garage doors, showing a man turning his head in slow motion. Then a blur of action appeared from the side, and the man's head snapped back. For just a second, the object that had come into view so quickly was still.

"That," said the anchor, "is an arm ending in a fist, apparently wearing some kind of glove or gauntlet. Let's see that again." The image repeated. "Pow!" said the anchor.

Now the image blinked as it jumped to a later part of the tape and the focus pulled back to show the doors just as they were thrown high. Chesney was still moving too rapidly to be seen in detail, but the man-shape was recognizable, and when he pushed the dumpster into the service area, his outline was even clearer.

"We've done some calculations," the anchor said, "and that man is moving at between two hundred and seventy and three hundred miles per hour." He paused. "If that is a man."

A panel of experts had been electronically assembled. The first one the anchor threw the discussion to turned out to be a designer of military and police robots. He was a thirtyish man with a vulnerable face – Chesney thought he had probably spent his high school years taking roundabout routes home to avoid having his books dumped in the gutter by less academically inclined classmates.

"...definitely not a robot," the man was saying. "He's bipedal, for a start."

The next talking head was a shaven-headed man who had coached an Olympic sprinter to a silver medal. "Can't be done," was his verdict. "No human being can move that fast."

They also had an ex-district attorney who had written a book on organized crime. "I don't know what to tell you," he said. "You ask me, you should be talking to somebody like Stan Lee."

● ● ● ●

At Paxton Life and Casualty, nobody was talking about the mysterious events of the previous evening. Sitting Bull had started his day with an early-morning call from Seth Baccala and was at work before any of the actuaries arrived. Although it was not yet nine o'clock when Chesney came through the door of the C Group office, the section chief's shirt was already showing dark circles under the armpits.

"Arnstruther," he said, "you're with me." He beckoned Chesney with the crook of his finger, then tapped on the door of Baccala's office.

Paxton's factotum was at his desk, studying a piece of paper that lay on top of an opened file folder. He did not look up, nor did he invite Chesney and Entwistle to sit. He continued to read as the two men came to stand before his desk, then he looked up abruptly, his face stern, and said, "Arnstruther, who've you been talking to about C Group?"

"Nobody," Chesney said, then corrected himself, "except for Miss Paxton."

Now Baccala's face showed surprise struggling with some other emotion – Chesney thought it was anger – and he said, "Poppy? What have you got to do with Poppy?"

"Nothing. We had a discussion about crime statistics the other day. I assumed that since she was in the C Group office and she's the daughter of–"

"Never mind, then," Baccala cut him off, then looked down at the file again before coming up with another accusatory glare. "What's your relationship with Billy Lee Hardacre?"

"He's my mother's... friend." The question took Chesney by surprise. How had they known? The answer came to him quickly: C Group was a Paxton company secret; every potential member of the staff would have been investigated;

all of their landline phones were probably tapped, their emails intercepted and scrutinized.

The man at the desk saw Chesney hesitate, and wanted to know why.

"I've only just found out about them," Chesney said. "She's never had a… boyfriend before."

"Have you talked to Hardacre about C Group?"

Chesney had been raised to tell the truth. Luckily for him at this moment, the same woman who had sought to impose that standard on him had, by her constant suspicion and frequent resort to psychological pressure, guaranteed he would grow up to be a very good dissembler. The actuary had survived many an adolescent grilling by his mother, who could have given masterclasses to the KGB. "No," he said, "I haven't."

"What about talking to the other members of C Group?"

"Only in the office. We don't socialize much."

"Are you aware of any of your colleagues talking to anyone outside the group?"

"I'm not aware of pretty much anything the other guys do. We play poker once in a while. But that's it."

"Heard any office gossip?"

"No. People tend not to tell me stuff." Chesney said. "I think it's because I'm not really interested."

Baccala looked him over. "What are you really interested in, Arnstruther?"

The young man's answer was immediate. "Numbers."

Now he saw skepticism in the other man's eyes. "Nothing else?"

Chesney realized this was probably not a good opportunity to admit to a deep involvement in comix about crimefighters. His long experience of being probed by Letitia Arnstruther had taught him that sometimes a completely tangential response could throw an interrogator off stride.

"Pornography," he said. "But not all the time."

Baccala threw a questioning look at Entwistle. "This boy is all work, not much play, Mr Baccala," the chief said.

Paxton's assistant appeared to have lost his train of thought. After a moment he closed the file and said, "You can go to work."

Entwistle stayed behind as Chesney left the office. But he didn't quite close the door and stood outside it for a moment pretending that his cuff had come unbuttoned. As he fiddled with it, he heard Sitting Bull saying something in a low voice that sounded like, "...almost at the level of high-functioning autism. It's not uncommon among math whiz-kids."

Baccala said something that Chesney couldn't catch. Then Entwistle said, "It's in the file. When he first applied here, Tom Bichon in HR, he checked his references with one of his professors. The prof said he's brilliant when it comes to math, and he zeroes in totally on anything that he's interested in. But everything else – I mean what you and I would call normal life – to him, it's just background noise. He's not talking to anybody; he doesn't *have* anybody to talk to – which, I think, is the way he wants it."

Baccala spoke again, and this time Chesney heard, "Miss Paxton?"

"He's harmless," said Sitting Bull. "When it comes to girls, he's like a perpetual twelve-year-old kid."

Chesney realized that some of the other actuaries were looking at him. He made a what-can-you-do? face and went to his desk. Sitting Bull had left Chesney's computer's hard drive waiting for him to install. In less than a minute he was back at work on the media meta-analysis, refining his archetypical sequence of events. Baccala and Hardacre and even The Actionary slipped to the back of his mind as he immersed himself in a world of complex integers and plot points on graphs.

Time passed. Chesney became aware of a scent of perfume and his heartbeat quickened even before he looked up from the monitor. Poppy Paxton was standing beside his desk. When she saw that he was aware of him, she leaned closer and whispered into his ear, "I want to talk to you."

The warmth of her breath on his ear made his throat close, even as he realized that The Actionary could have handled this situation with aplomb. He collected himself, swallowed, and whispered back, "What about?"

"I'll tell you at lunch time. Where do you go?"

"The park, usually."

"Alone?"

"Yes."

"Good. I'll meet you there."

And then she was gone, though her perfume remained, like a ghost hanging over Chesney's shoulder. He looked around. The other actuaries were looking at him as if he had acquired some new and unlikely anatomical feature. He shrugged, as if the whole thing was a mystery to him – which it was. He went back to his work, but it took him a while to get back into the zone. The lingering scent of Poppy Paxton was a distraction.

On his way to work that morning, Chesney had stopped in at a donut shop and bought himself two chocolate-topped Boston creams to augment his homemade sandwiches. He had felt he deserved a treat after busting up a million-dollar car-theft racket. So he was carrying two paper bags when he entered the park shortly after noon and made his way along the winding paths to the bench where he usually sat. Poppy Paxton was not waiting for him, but when he sat down and turned to look around, he saw her coming along the same route he had taken. She had waited and watched, then followed him.

She was wearing a belted half-length coat over dark slacks, shoes of some kind of shiny leather with high heels that clicked on the pavement, and a knitted cap perched on the side of her head. Chesney normally didn't notice what people wore unless it was more than a little out of the ordinary – Halloween costumes or a wedding dress – but he saw that Poppy was attired in the way models wore clothes in magazine ads or televised fashion shows: it all fit together and it expressed a common message to the world, a message that here was a young woman who meant to get what she wanted, because life had taught her that she just about always would.

He couldn't help comparing her to Melda McCann. Melda, in her own way, was a force to be reckoned with, but Chesney thought that life had taught her a different lesson. She hadn't been surprised to find herself in a park with a boyfriend who was about to give her a smack, as the demon had put it. He had a mental image of the two young women, each going along a long corridor interrupted by doors. As Poppy approached a barrier, it swung open before her and she breezed on through; Melda had to push her way through, every time, and sometimes she just bounced off.

"There you are," said Poppy. She sat beside him and Chesney had a sudden memory that the last time he had shared this bench, the seat Poppy was taking had been occupied by the Devil. He had put the two paper bags that held his lunch beside him when he sat down. Now Poppy opened each one in turn, and when she found the Boston creams she extracted one and, with a smile that said, "May I?" but without waiting for an answer, she bit into the sweet pastry.

"Mmm," she said, her pink and pointed tongue licking a dab of cream from her upper lip, "I haven't had one of those since I was a schoolgirl."

"Be my guest," Chesney said. His mother had taught him that when faced with a lack of manners, the good-mannered person carried on as if the burden of polite behavior was being equally shared. Poppy Paxton smiled and took another bite.

Chesney formed words in his mind while she chewed, examined them and decided that they were appropriate for the occasion. "What did you want to talk to me about?"

She swallowed, licked her lip again, then looked around as if she was playing a spy in a school play. Then she gave Chesney her full attention, both eyes at maximum strength, lips slightly parted. He had the sudden realization that she had practiced this very look in the mirror, even as he recognized that it was having the intended effect on him. He was involuntarily leaning toward her and he was holding his breath. And he could see that she was completely aware of the effect she was having.

She let the moment extend a little longer, then she spoke in just above a whisper. "I want you to do a little…" – she paused and looked around theatrically again – "investigating for me."

"I'm sorry?" Chesney's mother had always preferred to hear that phrase instead of "I beg your pardon," and the habit had stuck.

Poppy leaned in closer. He could smell the perfume again, and realized she had probably refreshed the application before following him into the park. "There's something going on," she said. "Something peculiar."

"To do with C Group?" he said.

"Yes."

"I can't talk about anything that goes on there," he said. "Mr Baccala has been very explicit."

She flapped a hand as if batting away a bothersome insect. "Never mind Seth," she said. "I can deal with him." She lowered her voice again. "This is not about numbers or charts and graphs. There's this man…"

Chesney waited. She seemed to be gathering her thoughts, but not doing a very good job of it. "A man?" he prompted.

"I met him a few nights ago. He… well, I think someone tried to kidnap me. And he prevented it. Daddy says I don't know what I'm talking about, but I do."

"You should talk to the police," Chesney said. "Lieutenant Denby."

"I don't want to get Daddy all stirred up. But back to the guy: he's very strong. Muscular. I don't usually like them… " She broke off, then restarted, "Anyway, he's been in touch with Seth and Daddy. They're working with him on some big project, and C Group is part of it." She frowned and bit her lower lip, and despite all the designer clothing and footwear, for a moment Chesney thought she looked like a little girl, a little girl who was used to getting her way but who wasn't getting her way just at the moment, and who was determined that she would. "He was at the house the other night and… well, you're not going to believe this…"

Chesney realized he was supposed to say something here. He channeled Malc Turner. "Try me," he said.

Now it all came out in a rush. "He came out of Daddy's study, and I was peeking through the door from the parlor, and I saw him just… disappear!"

It was Chesney's turn to look around theatrically. "Disappear?" he said.

"One second he was there, and then he was gone. Not even a puff of smoke."

Her expression invited a comment. Chesney was thinking that the smart thing to say was probably something like, "Oh, come on," but he opted for his second choice. "Amazing!" he said.

"Exactly what I thought!" She was leaning toward him again, the eyes drawing him into her world of wonder and conspiracy. "And then I saw him on TV this morning, and he was rounding up these car thieves and leaving them all tied up for the police."

"Amazing!" Chesney said again.

"I want to meet him," she said.

"Oh," was the best Chesney could do.

"And I want you to find out who he is and where he is."

"Me?"

Her hand was on the bench next to the donut bag. She slid it along the wooden slats until it encountered Chesney's. Her flesh was very warm. "I would be really grateful," she said.

Chesney knew his mouth was open, but he had no idea what ought to be coming out of it at this moment. "Um," he said.

She leaned in closer. Her hand squeezed his. "*Really* grateful," she said. Then she kissed him with lips that would have been sweet even without the touch of Boston cream.

EIGHT

For the first time in years, Chesney found it difficult to concentrate on his work. The monitor screen would disappear and be replaced by the sight of Poppy Paxton, eyes closed as she leaned in to kiss him. He had kept his open, not wanting to miss a moment of the experience. He could still smell a trace of her perfume and it seemed that the touch of her lips on his had left a permanent sensation, as if the two strips of flesh were almost imperceptibly humming.

He shook his shoulders and went back to the data. He was further refining the media meta-analysis to quantify the ways in which different media fed off each other as the story progressed, with print backgrounders amplifying and deepening the impact of TV coverage among key psychographic segments of the public, while talk radio raised the intensity of feeling among the print-averse elements of the population.

Tracking the emotional indicators, as recorded in public opinion polls during previous "blonde goes missing" incidents, Chesney thought it was no wonder reporters had long since stopped asking interviewees what they thought about this or that burning issue. Instead, they asked only how people *felt* about things. For many people, it seemed, the words *think* and *feel* were identical synonyms.

Though not for Chesney Arnstruther. He knew that making a distinction between thinking and feeling was one of the qualities that made him different from most people. But he was finding that when it came to Poppy Paxton, he couldn't keep his feelings out of his thoughts. He was thinking that if he told Poppy one or two things about The Actionary, things that nobody else knew, she might reward him with another kiss. And that would feel pretty darn good.

"Hey," said a voice behind him, "you don't hear me talking to you?"

In fact, Chesney had been hearing Poppy Paxton talking to him. He'd been replaying in his mind her voice saying, "*Really* grateful." He turned now to find Lieutenant Denby leaning over him, looking angry.

"Sorry," the actuary said. "I was... working something out in my head."

"Whatever," said the policeman. He beckoned with one hand in a get-up-and-come-with-me motion. "Let's us two take a walk. We need to liaise some more."

That meant that Chesney had to save his work, turn off his computer, remove the hard drive and gather his files together so he could give them to Sitting Bull. Entwistle fussed and muttered, apparently annoyed at the disruption of whatever he'd been doing, but one look at Denby's glowering face made him pull his head down between his shoulders. Even so, the delay caused Denby to grow increasingly impatient.

By the time he and the actuary were in the elevator heading down to the street, the detective was showing all the signs of a frustrated man who was ready to punch someone. Chesney recognized the signs from a childhood studded with punches, none of them his own. So he smiled when they got out on the sidewalk and said, "How can I help you, lieutenant?"

"Get in the car."

An unmarked police car was parked in the loading zone outside the Paxton building. Chesney got into the passenger seat and a few moments later, the lieutenant took them away from the curb and out into the mid-afternoon traffic. They turned right at the first corner, drove a block and turned right again.

"Where are we going?" Chesney said.

"Good question," said the policeman. "Did you know it's one of the three great questions posed by some ancient philosopher? 'Who are you? Where do you come from? Where are you going?' If you can answer them, you'll know the meaning of existence."

Chesney said, "I'm Chesney Arnstruther. I come from right here. And apparently, I'm going around and around the block. But I don't know what it all means."

"Good answers," said Denby. "So I've got another question. What the hell's going on at Paxton Life and Casualty?"

"Now *I* don't know what you mean."

They turned a corner. "I'm a good cop," Denby said.

"I believe it."

"I'm such a good cop that I not only have snitches and contacts in the underworld, I've even got one in Commissioner Hanshaw's office."

He looked over at Chesney for a response. The young man thought it was a good time to smile encouragingly. "Is that a good thing for a good cop to have?"

Denby appeared to consider the question as he prepared to turn another corner. "Sometimes," he said after a few seconds, "I have to wonder." He took a breath and let it all out. "My contact in the Commissioner's office told me an interesting story. Hanshaw got his hands on an intelligence file from the anti-crime section, about some stolen cars that were going to be shipped out of the country."

Again he looked at Chesney for a reaction. The actuary kept his face neutral. "Go on," he said.

"Anti-crime was working up some more detailed information on where and when these cars would be going out from," Denby said, "cause we don't have the manpower to stake out every possible location every night. Then, the next thing anybody knows, we're getting calls about shots fired here and an armed robbery there, and when we respond, what do you think we find?"

"I saw the news reports," Chesney said.

"You saw the video, the guy in the fancy-dress costume?"

"I thought he looked kind of… cool," Chesney said.

They turned another corner, the car's tires squealing a little. That meant they were going faster than was advisable, according to the driver's ed manual that Chesney had memorized in high school – though he had never actually acquired a driver's license. When taking the test he had been judged as too narrowly focused on certain details of the driving environment, like his habit of adding up the numbers and letters on license plates then factoring out the total for primes. He'd been heavily into primes that year. Now he told Denby, "We're going too fast."

The lieutenant was still processing Chesney's earlier remark. "'Cool?'" he said. "You think he looked cool?"

"Yes," Chesney said, "and now we're going even faster."

Denby eased up on the accelerator, but only a little. "You know, some of those hoods had guns. Suppose they'd started shooting? What if some citizen driving by had got one through the head?"

Chesney knew the answer to that: no bystanders could

get hurt. But he couldn't tell Denby that. He said, "I thought you said that shots *were* fired."

"No," the lieutenant said. "That seems to have been sound effects, just to get a quick roll from the squad cars. But what if it had been real?"

"But it wasn't."

"But what if?"

"Lieutenant," Chesney said, "I'm not good at what-ifs, except when it comes to calculating statistics. What do you want from me?"

The car slowed down for the next corner. "Yeah," the detective said, "sorry. Cops hate it when amateurs get in on the game. Vigilantes. Self-made heroes. Cause somebody always gets hurt. But I shouldn't be taking it out on you."

He drove on for a while, then said, "To answer your question – the Commissioner's office calls for intelligence from anti-crime. They get it. Here's the interesting part: a few minutes later, Hanshaw calls W.T. Paxton. Next thing we know, some yutz in a body suit is trussing up bad guys and calling 9-1-1. Couple of days before, this same Paxton sets up a crime stats group, with the blessings of the Commissioner and the Mayor. You see where this is going?"

"No," said Chesney.

They rounded another corner. "Well, yeah," said Denby. "Neither do I, really." He bounced the heel of one hand off the top of the steering wheel. "But there's a connection. Occam's razor." He looked over at Chesney. "You know what Occam's razor is?"

Anybody who did statistics for a living, or even for a hobby, knew about William of Ockham's thirteenth-century insight. "Entities," Chesney said, "must not be multiplied beyond necessity."

Denby looked at the young man and his eyebrows climbed in a way that meant he was impressed. "Well...

yeah. Or, to put it in cop terms, the simpler the solution to a problem, the more likely it's the right one. Like, when someone calls us and says he's found a body, the first thing we do is we take a really close look at the caller, because there's a good chance he's the one who did the deed."

"Yes," said Chesney, "you're much more likely to be murdered or assaulted by a relative, friend or co-worker than by a stranger."

"Good boy," said Denby. "So all in the same week we get Paxton's secret stats group, the Commissioner stirring up anti-crime, and Mr Superdude doing his thing. Chances are, there's a connection."

Chesney said nothing.

"Which brings me," said the detective, "to you." He looked over at Chesney and this time the actuary found the policeman's expression hard to decipher.

"What about me?" the young man said.

"You're a gifted amateur, aren't you?"

Chesney had learned that often when he didn't know the right answer to a question, the best thing was to say nothing. The person asking the question might supply more information that would clarify things. And for some questions, though he never knew why this was so, no answer was the best answer. He tried that approach now.

Denby saw that no response was to be forthcoming. "And a cagey one, too," he said.

"I'm not the guy," said Chesney. "We've already established that."

The policeman turned another corner, talking as he spun the wheel. "You're going to be my guy," he said. "My gifted amateur detective – inside Paxton Life and Casualty."

"Me?" said Chesney.

"You," said the lieutenant. "You're going to find out who this masked marvel is, and then you're going to tell me."

"How am I going to do that?" Chesney said.

"By being on the inside, by listening, by putting two and two together and getting four."

"But I'm sworn to secrecy," Chesney said.

Denby's response was an expression Chesney knew how to read. He'd seen it on the faces of classmates who'd demanded his lunch money and refused to accept his explanation that he needed it to buy lunch. "Kid," the policeman said, "I hate to do this to you, but you're the only in I've got."

"Suppose I say no?"

"You could do that. There's nothing I could do to you while you're close to Paxton, part of his special group."

"That's true," Chesney said.

"But guys like Paxton," the policeman went on, "they're only your friend when they need you. Once you've done what they need doing, the invitations to cocktails at the tennis club stop coming in the mail."

"I've never been invited to the tennis club," Chesney said. "I don't play tennis."

"What I'm saying is, Paxton is your friend now. He won't be forever. But a cop is like an elephant. He never forgets a friend." Denby gave Chesney a look the young man also recognized from the schoolyard. "Or an enemy."

"I may not be able to find anything out. They just have us crunching numbers."

"Give it your best shot. I've got feelers out here and there. But the right little tidbit from you could be the piece that makes the rest of the puzzle fit together. That's how detection works." He turned another corner and they were back on the street where Paxton Life and Casualty stood. "At least sometimes."

Chesney already knew what he was going to answer, but he thought it best to look as though he was thinking

about it. After a moment he said, "All right. If I hear anything, I'll tell you."

"Good boy," said the lieutenant, pulling the car into the
curb. They were back at the loading zone. As Chesney got
out, Denby said, "It's been a pleasure liaising with you."

Chesney had just got his hard drive reinstalled and his
work back on the monitor when Poppy Paxton came into
the C Group office again. "We need to talk," she said,
beckoning him to follow her out into the corridor. Chesney saw Arthur Entwistle's brows draw down and knew
that was not good, but he didn't expect Sitting Bull to give
him any real grief over doing what W.T.'s daughter told
him to do.

"I haven't had a chance to find out anything yet," he
said, when he joined her in the corridor and closed the C
Group door.

"New assignment," Poppy said. She took out a high-
end cell phone and worked its controls. "Look at this,"
she said.

Chesney looked at the phone's small rectangular screen.
It was acting as a browser, connected to the internet site
of a cable news network. He saw video footage of a street.
The picture quality was not good and the image jumped
around. The video must have been shot by a cellphone,
he thought. Then there was a blur as the camera was
swung to point at something, and from then on the image
held fairly still.

Chesney recognized the location right away. It was the
sidewalk outside Melda McCann's place, with the park
visible across the street. The streetlights were on so the
figure in blue and gray walking away from the camera
was clearly visible. Then a kind of fog filled the space
where the walker had been.

The next thing Chesney saw was the face of Melda Mc-Cann looking out of the screen. She was talking. Poppy touched a control and now Melda's voice came, with remarkably good sound quality for such a tiny speaker. Chesney could recognize the annoyance in her tone – and could see it in her face – as she told whoever held the microphone, "...twice he kissed me, and twice he said he'd call. But did he? So, this is for you, Mr Actionary!" She stuck out her tongue and vibrated air over it to make a rude noise.

The image showed a blonde young woman holding a hand mike with the station's logo on it and speaking excitedly. "So there we have it, Chuck," she said, "the mystery crimefighter apparently calls himself 'The Actionary.' Twice he allegedly saved Melda McCann from street crime, twice he allegedly kissed her and promised to call. But then he never did. Not the first man to make a promise to a young woman then vanish into the mist, but maybe the first to manufacture his own fog. Back to you, Chuck."

A square-jawed, gel-haired man appeared now. "And this just in," he said, shuffling pages on his desk. "We've tracked down Todd Milewski, the estranged boyfriend of Melda McCann, the man The Actionary is alleged to have tossed into the river. We go live to Modeen Williams on the east side."

A caramel-colored young woman with perfect make-up and fingernails in turquoise polish said into the camera, "That's right, Chuck," before turning to point her microphone at a man in his late twenties standing in the doorway of a house. "Todd," she said, "tell us what happened."

"Dude's an ass–" The rest of the expletive was inaudible as Modeen Williams swiftly clamped a manicured hand over the spongy ball on the end of the mike. "We talked about this, Todd," Chesney could hear her saying. Then she put the mike to the man's face again.

"Dude's a total jerk–" This time Milewski caught himself and did not add "off" to the insult. "Snuck up on me, threw me in the water. I'd like to see him try that face-to-face. I'll go all taekwando on his a–." He formed his hands into positions that looked as if he was playing charades and his lips into a sneer, but the reporter had again covered the microphone's pickup.

"Melda McCann alleges that you were about to assault her when The Actionary intervened."

"My ass!" said Milewski, and this time the reporter wasn't fast enough. The man pulled the mike from her and shouted into it, "Hey, Melda! I'm on TV, bitch! I'm a celebrity now, so you can go f–"

The sound went dead as Modeen Williams and Todd Milewski wrestled for possession of the microphone. Then Chuck reappeared. "More on that interview later," he said. "We apologize for the offensive language. Meanwhile, Police Commissioner John Hanshaw told reporters that although he does not support vigilante action, the rounding up of the city's most notorious car-theft ring has got to be seen as a significant blow to organized crime. Here's what he had to say–"

Poppy Paxton cut the sound and put the phone back in her purse. "You see that?" she said.

"Yes," said Chesney.

"Here's what I want you to do…"

"I don't think I can find The Actionary. It looks like he can just disappear at will."

She waved that argument away with a perfumed hand. "He's obviously got a thing for this McCann woman. Anytime she's in trouble, he shows up."

Chesney was not sure where this was going. "So…?" he said.

Poppy showed him a face he also remembered from the schoolyard, that of a mean little girl with a plan to get her own way. "So we get her in trouble."

"That doesn't sound like a good idea. This is a man who beats up armed gangsters and throws taekwando fighters into the river."

"You let me handle that," Poppy said.

Chesney shook his head. "I don't think so."

She put her fists on her hips and showed him a smile that had no friendliness in it at all. "What do you think would happen if I told my father you made improper advances to me?"

"He wouldn't believe it," Chesney said.

Her smile grew even colder. "He did last time." She cocked her head to one side and her hair fell perfectly onto one shoulder. "Do you like working here? Do you like working anywhere?"

Chesney tried the incompetence approach. It sometimes worked. "I'm not a detective," he said. "I don't know how to find people."

"Don't worry about that. I know where to find Ms Melda McCann," she said. "The bitch works at Sugar 'n Spice."

"Sugar 'n Spice?"

"It's where I get my nails done." She touched Chesney's arm, and this time her hand lacked all warmth. "Just be ready when I say go," she said.

Chesney was thinking about Occam's razor as he packed up for the day and handed in his materials so Sitting Bull could put them in the safe. He was reflecting on how although William of Ockham was right about the simplest solution usually being the right one, many of the situations Chesney had got into over the years had turned out to be more complicated than they first appeared to be.

Now his new role as the crimefighting Actionary looked to be replicating the pattern. As he had conceived the idea, it would have been just him and his not-so-faithful demonic sidekick, prowling the city streets for malefactors and delivering swift justice. But right away, the Paxtons had got into the game. Then, next time out, Chesney had met up with Melda McCann, who at first had seemed to be a clear-cut case of a victim needing to be rescued. Instead, she had pepper-sprayed him in the moment of his triumph, then kissed him and made him promise to call.

But then he hadn't called. He might have told himself he was too busy, what with all the work at the office and capturing car thieves, not to mention a side-trip out to discover his mother "married in the sight of God" to Billy Lee Hardacre. But the truth was, he had never been any good at calling girls. The two times he had tried it, back in high school, had been notable for their lack of conversational flow. There had been silences, long silences, as Chesney had struggled to think of something to say that could possibly be of interest to the person on the other end of the line. The scripts that he wrote in advance never seemed to survive past the first couple of exchanges. Finally, he concluded that he was never to master the art of social dialogue.

He saw no reason to assume that The Actionary, even given his alter ego's considerably greater self-confidence, would be any better at chit-chat. So neither of them had called Melda McCann, which had made her angry. And when she had seen the television news coverage, she had made her own call – to the channel's local news bureau. And she had presented them with a cell phone photograph that she must have snapped as he was walking away and telling Xaphan to cloak him in mystery.

And Melda's story had angered Poppy. Chesney was not an adept student of female psychology, but even he knew that when a girl who's used to having everything her own way loses a prize beau to a nobody – he envisioned it as a head cheerleader being dumped by the captain of the football team for some girl who couldn't even shake a pompom – trouble ensues.

And trouble was what Poppy had in mind for Melda, with the actuary as her accomplice, in order to make The Actionary show up. At which point, Poppy no doubt intended to have what Chesney's mother would have called "strong words" with the crimefighter. Hell was not supposed to have as much fury as a scorned woman, according to some old-time poet. Well, Chesney had seen Hell up close, and he had seen Melda McCann's noisily vibrating tongue on a cell phone screen. So far, Hell was ahead on points, but when Poppy Paxton weighed in and climbed into the ring, the odds might change.

These thoughts troubled the young man as he made his way home, stopping at the supermarket to pick up a frozen entree for one that he would microwave and eat before visiting W.T. Paxton again, as promised. That step, at least, he was resolved to take. The car-thief roundup may have had unexpected repercussions – he would have to instruct Xaphan to prevent any cameras from recording his image when he was in his Actionary mode – but it was nonetheless a resounding success. He had caught the bad guys in the act and turned them over to the police. He was willing to try another one of Paxton's leads.

He arrived home and put the meal – Szechuan beef with rice noodles – into the microwave and set the controls. It was only as he turned to hang up his coat that he saw the red light flashing on his portable phone. He checked the display and saw that the call had come from Hardacre's private line that afternoon and that the phone company's computer had recorded a voicemail.

A cold shiver climbed Chesney's spine and shook itself loose from his shoulders. He imagined his mother seated in her new boyfriend's study, the wide-screen television showing Melda McCann telling the world that she had been twice kissed by lips that only three people in the world knew belonged to the only son of Letitia Arnstruther. He had told his mother that she was just a girl he had saved from some muggers, then quickly moved the conversation on to safer ground. Now that ground had collapsed beneath him, plunging him straight down into the abyss of his mother's anger. In the fury stakes, Hell might prevail over a manicurist's Bronx cheer, but Letitia Arnstruther was a much more formidable contender.

The chime on the microwave rang five times, telling him that his dinner was ready. Chesney realized he had been staring at the telephone display and its flashing message of doom for the better part of two minutes. He retrieved the piping hot meal, but ate it standing in the kitchen, scarcely tasting the spicy flavor and not noticing when he burned his lips on the hot noodles.

But Chesney Arnstruther had been born with the capacity to chase unwanted thoughts from his mind and concentrate intensely on matters that inherently interested him. Being The Actionary was one of those matters, and so he put his plate and fork in the dishwasher, and summoned his demon. Xaphan immediately appeared, a fresh Churchill poking from between its sabertooth fangs. It removed the cigar, blew a perfect donut of smoke, and said, "What's up, boss?"

"Costume," said Chesney, and was instantly transformed into his alter ego. "Where is W.T. Paxton, and what is he doing?"

"In his study, waiting for you."

"Then let's go there, but no theatrics."

"Okay." The demon put the cigar back under its sabertooth.

"No, wait." Chesney had had a thought.

"What?"

"Is anybody else with him?"

"Baccala."

"What are they talking about?"

"You want to listen in?"

Chesney's mother had always told him that eavesdroppers never heard anything good about themselves. In truth, Chesney had long since lost interest in what other people thought of him, since his experience had shown him that most people of his acquaintance never gave him a second thought, and those few who did mostly thought he was peculiar. But it seemed to him that The Actionary had a legitimate interest in knowing the motivations of people who said they wanted to help him fight crime. This was well within the pool of light, so he answered the demon in the affirmative.

Immediately, W.T.'s voice sounded from the air: "...not calling the shots on this. I am. It's my career, it's my daughter, and I'm the one who found this Actionary fellow and brought him into the picture."

Now Seth Baccala spoke. "All I'm saying is he's not a man to cross lightly. There was a plan – more than a plan, we had advanced to the implementation stage, then all of a sudden it was full-stop and revise everything."

"In the words of a great philosopher," Paxton said, "'Stuff happens.' I said a moment ago that I'd brought The Actionary into the picture, but the fact is he brought himself in. At that point, the plan went to Hell."

"True," said Baccala, "but–" Paxton's assistant broke off.

Chesney heard the sound of a door opening, then another voice he recognized.

"Daddy, I have to talk to you about something."

"This is not a good time, Poppy," the older man said. "I'm in a meeting. And we're expecting someone."

"That's what I want to talk to you about. You're waiting for *him*, aren't you? The man we gave a ride to the other night, the one who was on TV?"

There was silence that began to stretch. Chesney said to Xaphan, "Have we lost audio?"

"Nah, the old man's trying to decide what to say."

Now Poppy's voice came again. "It's just that I saw him here the other night. And you've got those people studying crime. And then that man, The Actionary, he goes out and catches those crooks, and it's all on TV. But you don't say anything."

Paxton said, "It's really not something for you to worry about, sweetheart."

Baccala added, "It's all under control."

"But what's going on?"

"It's just politics," Paxton said. "We're going to clean up the city, and this man is helping us do it."

There was another silence, then Poppy said, "I'd like to meet him again."

Her father cleared his throat, then Baccala chimed in, "That's not a very good idea."

Chesney heard that same hard note in Poppy's voice that he'd heard during their last conversation. "Why not?"

"Sweetheart," W.T. said, "there are some big things tied up in this. Political things. I wouldn't want you to get," – he cleared his throat again, then once more, as if something had stuck in it – "involved," he finished.

"But I *want* to be involved." And now her voice turned even sharper. "In fact, I think I *am* involved."

Baccala said, "What are you saying?"

"The other night, at the museum," she said, "when The Actionary appeared in that big flash of light..."

"Go on," her father said.

"Well, he said he had stopped some men who were trying to kidnap me." Another silence lasted until Poppy said, in a way that meant she expected an answer, "Daddy?"

Chesney heard the older man sigh, then, "Sweetheart, this is not a good time."

"I want to know what's going on." Chesney could imagine her standing with arms folded, one designer shoe tapping peremptorily on the carpet.

"Poppy..." Her father's voice had a long-suffering tone.

She spoke over his objection. "And I want to be part of it."

"Miss Paxton–" Baccala began.

"You stay out of it! This is between my father and me!"

The assistant's voice was level. "Miss Paxton, you are putting your father in a difficult position." She tried to interrupt but Baccala spoke over her. "He has given commitments to people of standing in the community – has given his word – not to discuss this matter outside a very small circle–"

"Daddy!" Chesney heard her foot stamp the carpet, despite the depth of its pile.

Baccala bore on, regardless. "And it would be a very troublesome thing if he were to break his word. The repercussions would be serious – no, more than serious, they would be grave."

Now came another silence, broken after a few moments by Poppy, though now her tone was that of a girl who was used to wheedling what she wanted out of an indulgent parent. "Daddy..."

"No," said Paxton. "Seth's right, sweetheart. You can't know what's going on. For your own good, as well as for the success of our… project." Chesney heard a sound that must have been Paxton getting up out of his chair. "Now, out you go, and we'll talk about this later." Poppy was apparently going, though not without protest. Chesney could imagine the older man leading her by the arm to the door, saying, "When it's all done, you'll understand that we have to do it this way. It's all for the best, you'll see."

Chesney heard a door open and close, the latter abruptly muting the young woman's protests. Then came the sound of a key turning in a lock and some muffled thumps that he took to be one of Poppy Paxton's stylish patent leather pumps marring its finish and the paintwork of the door.

Paxton said, "She'll have to know at some point."

Baccala answered, "Better if it comes as a surprise. A lot will be riding on how she handles herself." The older man sighed, and the assistant said, "You've seen the numbers."

"True. And with this new factor the time can be shorter." Paxton sighed again and Chesney heard the soft sound of the older man lowering himself into his chair. "Still… but where is our masked hero?"

Chesney told the demon, "Enough. Let's go and see what they want."

A moment later, they were in the fire-lit room the demon had built for their transit through the outer circle of Hell. But instead of immediately moving them both on to Paxton's, the fiend went to the drinks cabinet and poured itself a glassful of dark rum, which it downed with lip-smacking gusto and a sigh of satisfaction.

"What are you doing?" Chesney said.

"Just one for the road," said the demon, filling another tumbler with brown fluid.

Chesney noticed now that beside the cabinet was a pile of wooden crates with faded labels that advertised their origin on a Caribbean island. "Where did these come from?" he said.

"A shipwreck," said Xaphan, between swallows. "A freighter called the *SS San Cristobal* went down carrying two hundred and forty thousand cases of rum. Some of it was salvaged, but the rest is still sitting there."

The Actionary frowned. "I didn't give any orders about stocking this place to be your private pantry."

The demon gave him a wide-eyed look, but no fanged weasel could ever hope to look innocent. "I took it as kind of implied," it said.

"You took it as an opportunity to get yourself a private stock. I don't even drink the stuff." Chesney now noticed that several boxes of Havana's finest were on the floor beside the rum cases. "And I don't smoke cigars. Where'd they come from?"

"Fire in the warehouse."

"Did you start the fire? I don't remember authorizing arson, even by implication."

"Nah. Watchman had a taste for rum. He passed out just after lighting up a Montecristo. But they got him out."

The young man recognized that the conversation had begun to meander. He decided to refocus on the central issue; Xaphan used the pause that followed to pour itself another glass.

"When I authorized you," Chesney said, "to make a more comfortable way station for my trips through Hell, I meant it to be more comfortable for me, not a place for you to indulge your appetites."

"Aw, come on," said the demon. Its fangs seemed to grow longer.

But Chesney was in Actionary mode, and not prepared to brook any arguments. "No," he said. "This is not part of our deal."

"Nobody's getting hurt," Xaphan said. "You know, Hell ain't no picnic. These little luxuries, you might take them for granted, but down here…" It drank off its glass and swiftly poured another, puffing furiously at the cigar as the rum gurgled and splashed into the crystal.

"Not part of the deal," Chesney said.

The demon looked up at him sideways and said, "Maybe it could be."

"We're not rewriting the contract," Chesney said. "I don't need to ask a lawyer to know that that's a bad idea."

The demon gestured with both stub-fingered hands. "Oh, no, no, no, no, no," it said. "It could be just a little arrangement between you and me."

"Can you do that?"

The fiend thought for a moment. "Somethin's changin'," it said. "It all started wid you and Yathak.

"Who's Yathak?"

"The one you called up, accidental-like? Looks like a big toad."

"I remember."

"After that, a lot of us got moved around, new jobs, new ways. And there's me, I'm up there fightin' crime, doin' good. It's kind of a strain, you know?"

Chesney wasn't good at empathy, even for demons. He said nothing.

"And now," Xaphan went on, "there's this talk about a book, and how it's gonna change things even more. Maybe even…"

"Maybe even what?"

The weasel head moved from side to side. "I dunno. Nobody knows. There's guys sayin' maybe it all comes to a end and we start somethin' new."

Chesney tried to imagine what that might mean. After a moment, he said, "I can't deal with that. I do numbers.

I fight crime. I don't do end-of-the-world." He refocused. "What about our deal?" He gestured to the rum and cigars. "You really like this stuff?"

Xaphan spoke around the cigar that had found its way back between the fangs. "Told ya, I got a taste for it that other time I was up your way."

"And you can't get it on your own."

"I told ya that, too. I can't do nothing up there unless it's your will."

"So if my will says no smokes or booze?" The demon didn't answer, but appeared to be genuinely downcast, peering into its glass and swirling the last inch of liquor. Chesney let the question hang between them a little longer, then said, "What's in it for me?"

Xaphan looked up. "Name it."

"Well, first thing," the young man said, "no more little tricks, like the pepper spray."

"Yeah, okay."

"More than that, you're on my side."

"Whatta ya mean?"

"What I say. You look out for me, don't let me get blindsided. I'm starting to see this whole business as more complicated than I thought it would be."

The weasel's face scrunched up in discomfort. "That could be tricky," it said.

"How so?"

"Well, you're the boss, these two hours a day. The rest of the time, I got to answer to you-know-who."

"Okay, always during the two hours, and anytime loyalty to me doesn't directly conflict with your standing obligations."

"I dunno. Like I say, it's tricky." Xaphan reinserted the Churchill for some thoughtful puffs.

Chesney decided The Actionary should not be getting

jerked around by his assistant. "Well," he said, "why don't we go and ask the big boss what he thinks?"

The cigar shot out of the demon's mouth and landed smoldering on the carpet. "Now, now, now," the fiend said, "let's don't be hasty."

"Make up your mind," the young man said, "either you got my back or my will sends all of this stuff back to where you got it."

The demon picked up the cigar. "You got it."

"There might be other things I want to cover under this side deal," Chesney said. "Like how you help me even when it doesn't strictly involve crimefighting."

"Hey, now–"

"If you don't like it, we can always call this extra arrangement off, go back to where we started."

Xaphan looked at him with what Chesney thought was, for the first time, respect. "You know," it said, "you ever end up here as a…" – it waggled its eyebrows – "permanent resident, you could do all right in the contracts division. Maybe I'll put in a word."

"Right now, just let me know if we have a deal."

"We have a deal," said the demon.

"Good. But we're wasting time. I should have been at Paxton's quite a while ago."

The demon poured itself another glass. "You're forgetting, time don't count down here."

"And you're forgetting who's the boss. Drink that and let's go."

The demon tossed back the rum, clamped its cigar between its teeth and twirled one finger. Instantly, Chesney found himself in Paxton's study. "I'm fading you in," the fiend said.

"Fine."

Paxton was sitting in one of the chairs near the fireplace, where a well-banked fire threw warmth into the room. He had been reading a document in a file folder and looked up, a little startled, as Chesney appeared in a chair opposite him. But the older man soon recovered. "How do you do that?" he said.

"I'm not telling," Chesney said.

Baccala had been straightening papers on the big mahogany table, but turned at the sound of Paxton's voice. He was surprised but recovered quickly. "Good evening. Shall we get right to business?"

"Suits me."

The assistant took a seat between the other two men. "Were you satisfied," he asked Chesney, "with how the car-theft operation went?"

"Yes."

"So were we. This time, the target is the traffic in illegal drugs. Are you interested?"

"Yes."

"May I?" Seth Baccala said to his employer, taking the folder from Paxton's hands. He took out a sheet of paper and handed it to Chesney.

The Actionary scanned the document. Again, it was a list of addresses. When he was finished, he looked inquiringly to Baccala.

"These are all known locations," the assistant said, "at which drugs are stored and prepared for distribution to wholesalers or to street dealers. Or where cash is collected before it's moved on to money launderers."

"Known to whom?" Chesney said.

"To the police, to the DEA."

"Then why don't they raid them?"

Baccala didn't answer right away.

"Tell him," Paxton said.

"Because," the assistant said, "it takes time to set up a raid. Judges, warrants, even just the time to schedule the police who will go out on the operation."

Paxton cut in. "And during that time, the drugs and money are always moved to somewhere else."

"Always?" Chesney said. "That seems statistically improbable."

"Not when there's a leak," Paxton said. "And there's always a leak."

Chesney felt an excitement building in him. "You want me to find out who the mole is?" The Driver had dealt with a situation that involved an informer. Chesney had learned from that episode some of the language of espionage and intelligence.

But Baccala said, "That won't do the job. Catch one, and there's another one right behind him, ready to take the money."

"There's just too much money in that business," Paxton said, "and there's always some clerk or some patrolman who needs it. The way to have an impact is to take the drugs and the money."

It made sense to Chesney. "All right," he said.

"Then we're done," Paxton said.

"Not quite." Chesney folded the paper and said, "Xaphan, hold this for me." The demon took the sheet, which meant that from Baccala's and Paxton's perspective, it suddenly disappeared. "What happens after?"

"What do you mean?" Baccala said.

"This has all got something to do with politics and the news media," Chesney said. He was looking at Paxton as he spoke and saw the man nod. But Baccala gave him a sharp look.

"Why do you mention the media?" the assistant said.

"Never mind," Chesney said. "I'm asking you, when do the politics come into it? And what's my part in that?"

"It's a fair question," Paxton said. "Tell him, Seth."

"We need three successful operations," Baccala said, "to build maximum interest in you and what you represent–"

"What do I represent?" Chesney interrupted.

Paxton answered him. "Law and order. Justice. Safe streets and schoolyards. Decency."

"That sounds like a political platform," Chesney said. "I'm not running for office."

"No," said Paxton, "I am." He sat back in his chair and regarded Chesney with a level gaze. "I'm going to run for governor. And your endorsement of me, our partnership, is going to make me unbeatable."

Chesney did not immediately respond. Politics, to him, was one of those dark and murky places where pools of clear light were few and far between. "I'd need to think about that," he said.

"Why?" Paxton pressed him. "Aren't we partners in fighting crime?"

"Yes, but not in politics. I'm not going to give speeches or call press conferences."

The older man laughed. "Nobody's going to ask you to give a speech. And *we'll* handle any press conferences. All we'd want you to do is to say something like, 'I know Warren Paxton. We've fought crime together. I think he'd be a good governor.'"

"Again," Chesney said, "I'd need to think about it."

"We need you on-side," Baccala said. "If you're not on side, then there's no point in our doing this."

"I said I would think about it."

"Well," Baccala looked to his boss for confirmation as he spoke, "we can't keep on feeding you information like this unless you're giving us what we need."

Paxton nodded, his eyes on Chesney. "It has to be a two-way street," he said. "The research is costing me money and causing me to call in favors downtown."

"Let me think about it," was all Chesney could say. He had no intention of giving them a commitment here and now. "I might want to talk to somebody about this first."

Baccala reacted quickly. "Who?"

The question came so fast that Chesney almost spoke the name that was in the front of his mind. But if he said, "Billy Lee Hardacre," there would be Hell to pay, so he swallowed and said, "I have a kind of... mentor."

"Who?" Baccala said.

"I'm not saying."

Baccala swore, but Paxton extended a hand in a calming gesture. "Tell me this much," the older man said, "is your mentor in any way involved in politics?"

"No," Chesney said.

"And he's not a reporter or anything like that?"

"No." Chesney knew he was stretching the truth a little, but not far enough to break it.

"A wise old counselor?" Paxton said, a small smile briefly occupying his lips.

"Something like that."

Baccala wanted to say something but Paxton waved him off. "Then that's good enough for now," he said. "You go and talk it over with your mentor, and in the meantime maybe you could do something about these drug operations. We'll get together again in the next few days and settle things."

"All right," Chesney said. He stood up. "This time, I won't let myself get photographed."

Paxton made the same don't-worry gesture he had used on his assistant. "Photos are good. They build interest. And the TV boys and girls can't live without them."

"And that's important?" Chesney said.

"It is," the older man said. "You're going to be a star, son."

"I'm still not giving any speeches." It was time to go. Chesney spoke to Xaphan and a moment later he was in the fire-lit room. The demon was already pouring himself a drink, talking as he tilted the bottle. "This time, I made it look like you was moving away into the distance, getting smaller and smaller. Then I made a little plink of light as you disappeared. Nice touch, huh?" The fiend threw back half a glassful and smacked its thin, black lips. "Oh, that's the real McCoy," it said and raised the glass again.

Chesney took the paper from his belt and showed it to his assistant. "Show me what's going on right now at these places," he said.

The demon gestured with one hand while the other poured rum down its throat. The screen appeared in the air, blank at first, then an image appeared: the dingy kitchen of an older house, but instead of a normal table where a family might have eaten breakfast together, there was a long utility table pressed against one wall. Three men and one woman were seated side by side along the table's length, all busy at tasks that reminded Chesney of a factory assembly line. At one end several brick-sized bags of heavy plastic were stacked up.

A thin-faced man with a scar on one cheek took one of the bags off the stack, laid it flat in front of him, then carefully sliced open its top. He took up a little plastic scoop and put it into the slit, lifting out a measure of white powder. This he placed on a small white tray with one curled-down edge. The bullet-headed man to his right used a butter knife to separate the heap of powder into smaller piles, then scraped one pile onto one of several metal discs stacked before him like poker chips; he placed the disc and its lightweight burden on top of a pharmacist's scale with a liquid crystal display screen. He read the figures that appeared then used the knife to lift a little of the powder off the disc and return it to the tray. Satisfied with the result, he passed the disc to the next person on the assembly line, a middle-aged woman whose lips were enclosed in a network of smoker's wrinkles. She carefully emptied the powder into a tiny plastic packet and sealed it, then slipped the disc back onto the stack in front of the second man, who was already weighing the next portion. She passed the packet to the man on her right, beetle-browed and prematurely balding, who put it with a line of identical plastic oblongs and ticked a tally mark on a sheet of paper in front of him. "Thirty-seven," he said.

Another man was in the room: a heavily-built specimen in his thirties, whose fashion sense ran strongly in the direction of black leather and heavy gold jewelry. He sat at another table, observing a bank of four video screens that showed the street outside and what appeared to be a high-fenced back yard that contained a pair of restless pit bulls. The man's eyes never left the screens and one hand rested on a dark, rectangular object on the tabletop that Chesney at first did not recognize as a machine-pistol. The Actionary also noticed that the door to the man's right dully reflected light; it was made of burnished steel.

The work went on in silence as Chesney watched. After a few seconds he said to the demon, "They're going to be there for a while. What else have we got?"

Together, they went through the list of addresses Paxton had provided. The next three were unoccupied, with no sign of drugs or money. The one after that was a warehouse. Five men sat at a table playing seven card stud. Chesney read their expressions as indicating boredom, and when he asked Xaphan his assistant confirmed that they were waiting for delivery of the stuff that was being weighed and packaged in the first house. They were middle-rank distributors, the fiend said, who would take the cocaine to sellers at the retail level – or, as the demon put it, "mugs on the corner and in the speaks."

Two more premises were not being used for nefarious purposes that evening, although in one of them a man and a woman were engaged in an activity that Chesney had seen only in a video. He was interested to note that the woman made a lot less noise than the actresses in porn movies, and that the whole business was over a lot sooner and without any pauses to change positions. He filed the information away for further consideration.

The last scene to appear on the screen showed a well-appointed modern living room with comfortable, stylish furniture, including a wall-to-ceiling entertainment center with a six-foot wide plasma TV and modular speakers. Three men were visible, dressed in tailored suits and expensive shoes. One was on the cream leather sofa in his shirtsleeves, jacket neatly folded on the cushion beside him, watching a football game on the TV; the others were positioned so they could watch the hallways that led to the front and rear doors, though their eyes would slide toward the screen whenever the crowd noise crested.

Chesney watched for a while, then said, "I don't see anything actionable here."

"Look closer," said the demon. The men's jackets became transparent and Chesney saw holstered pistols on the two watchers. Beneath the jacket on the couch was another boxy machine-pistol. "And get a load of this," Xaphan said. The entertainment center disappeared, showing the paneled wall behind. Then one of the panels also shimmered out of view and Chesney saw the steel door of a man-sized safe. "And presto!" said his assistant, as the safe door vanished to reveal shelves stacked with cardboard cartons the size of wine cases, with hand-holes cut into their ends. Now the sides of the boxes became invisible, and Chesney was looking at stacks and stacks of used paper currency.

"They're waiting for the armored truck," Xaphan said, pouring itself another glass of rum. "Then it goes to the airport and they fly it to Panama."

"Money laundering," Chesney said.

"That what they call it now?" the demon said. It was more interested in the contents of the glass.

"When does the truck come?"

"Nother hour."

"Good," said Chesney. The pictures that passed through his mind were bathed in pure, clear light. "So here's what we'll do."

"Lieutenant Denby, please," Chesney said into the cell phone. The phone wasn't his, but its owner wouldn't be allowed to use it once he got to jail. In the meantime, she was sitting, dazed, on the kitchen floor of the house where the cocaine sat in one- and two-gram bags on the long table. Her wrists and ankles were taped together, as were those of the four men who had been there when Chesney had appeared in another flash-and-thunder entrance.

"This is Denby," said the phone.

"Lieutenant, if you go to 1843 Meadow Drive, you'll find five people who, up until a minute ago, were in the process of preparing several pounds of cocaine for the street."

"Who is this?"

"The Actionary."

"The what?" The policeman's voice sounded different.

"The Actionary. Did you put me on a speaker phone?"

Denby ignored the question. "The guy in the spandex suit?"

"It's not spandex. It's–"

"I don't care if it's spun gossamer," said the detective. "What the Hell are you up to?"

"I'm fighting crime."

"Well, who asked you to?"

The pool of pure light in which Chesney saw himself standing dimmed and shrank a little, but only for a moment. He pushed back the darkness and said, "Somebody's got to do it."

"Yeah, and that's me and the rest of the trained and experienced men and women you hired for the job."

The darkness crept in around Chesney. "I'm just trying to help," he said. "And right now there are five members of a drug cartel and a lot of cocaine waiting for you at 1843 Meadow Drive. Do you want me to let them all go?"

He heard Denby sigh on the other end of the cell phone connection. "No," said the cop, "but don't be surprised if some judge does."

"Why would that happen?"

"Probable cause. Do we have sufficient grounds to enter those premises and arrest those people?"

"Oh," said Chesney. "Just a minute." He spoke to Xaphan privately. A moment later, he said into the phone, "Now they're all out of the front porch, and so is the cocaine."

Denby sighed again. "Well, I guess we can't ignore that."

Chesney heard sirens in the distance. While he'd been talking into the detective's speaker phone, someone had dispatched squad cars. "I have to go now, Lieutenant. But you might also want to visit," – he asked Xaphan for the address again and repeated it into the phone – "7708 Arthur Avenue. There's about five million dollars in used bank notes stacked up in a hidden safe and three gangsters tied up in the living room." He paused to think. "Although by the time you get there, they'll be sitting in the driveway."

He looked at Xaphan and the demon disappeared, only to return an instant later. "In the driveway," it said. "I turned on the spotlights over the garage door. Can't miss them."

"Better come quickly though," Chesney told Denby. "If the neighbors get there first, some of the money might go missing. It's not a very nice neighborhood." He closed up the phone and went out to the front porch that ran the width of the house and was overshadowed by the second story. Here the demon had rearranged the drug processors so that they were now sitting elbow-to-elbow on a sagging old sofa. The drugs were piled at their feet.

"Good work," Chesney said. "Have you got the tape?"

"Here," said his assistant, holding up a flat black cassette. Moments before Chesney had appeared in the kitchen, Xaphan had repositioned one of the surveillance cameras so that it could cover the subsequent events. The fiend assured the young man that only The Actionary would be seen, zipping around the enclosed space at blurring speed, trussing and disarming the occupants, then standing over them, hands on hips like a satisfied gardener looking down on a crop well raised.

"Make several copies," The Actionary said, "and distribute them to all the television and newspaper newsrooms."

A stack of cassettes appeared in the demon's hands. Xaphan disappeared for a moment, and when it returned its hands were empty.

"We're done," said Chesney.

"Great," said the demon, "I could use a—"

"So," said a deep voice behind them, "here you are."

Chesney turned at hyperspeed, but the tall man standing in shadow at one end of the porch was not startled. Chesney used his enhanced vision to take a good look at the stranger's face and saw a look of cool amusement as the man looked him over. "Good costume," he said.

"Xaphan," said Chesney, "let's—"

The man in the shadows put up a hand. A heavy gold ring set with diamonds sparkled as it came into the glow from a streetlight. "Not just yet," he said.

It took Chesney a moment to understand, then he said, "You heard me speak to—"

The stranger had a habit of interrupting. "To your demon? Yes."

"You're not supposed to—"

"I've built my career on doing what I'm not supposed to." The remark was followed by a chuckle.

Chesney found nothing about the situation amusing. "We have to go," he said. The sirens were no more than a couple of blocks away.

"All right. How about my place?"

"Who are you? What do you want?"

Red and blue lights were approaching. "Didn't you say we had to go?"

"Xaphan," Chesney said, "we'll go to this man's place but..." Immediately, they were in a great hall, hung with banners and old-style weapons, a fire roaring in a fireplace big enough to roast not just an ox, but its conjoined twin, too. Chesney had been going to say, " keep an eye on him," but there was no need to finish the instruction. The demon stood beside him on the polished marble floor, regarding not only their host but the abnormally tall, stick-thin shape that hovered behind him, its elongated arms and legs encased in black hose and tunic that looked vaguely medieval to Chesney. The other demon's face was a long, pale parody of a man's, a white triangle of bone, but where its nose would have been was a wriggle of worms. "Hello, Xaphan," it said.

"Melech," said Xaphan. Chesney's assistant looked around. "Any chance of a drink?"

"No," said the man. He was revealed now as a mature specimen in a business suit of conservative cut, square-faced and strong-jawed. "Now why don't you and Melech disappear for a while. Your master and I need to talk."

Xaphan looked to Chesney. "Hold it," the young man said, "I need Xaphan to get me home on time."

"Time," said the stranger, "is not an issue here."

Chesney understood. "This is Hell," he said. Over the fire's roar, he could hear the faint howl of the wind. "The outer circle."

"Well done," said the man, though he still appeared more amused than impressed. "Now shall we send them away?" He gestured toward the two fiends.

"I could take Melech to your place," Xaphan said.

Chesney read in the demon's eager expression its intention to further reduce the abandoned cargo of the *SS San Cristobal*. "All right," he said, "but come when I call."

Instantly, the two men were alone. The stranger gestured with one hand and a pair of comfortable chairs appeared. "Let's talk," he said.

Chesney sat. "You did not have to tell your demon to do that."

The man smiled, showing large, square incisors. "In this place, whatever I want, I get."

Chesney bristled. "I wouldn't make that assumption," he said.

The man chuckled again. "I cannot compel you," he said, "nor can Melech. It's a matter of–"

This time Chesney interrupted. "Of wills. I know how it works." He leaned back and crossed his legs to mirror the stranger's posture. When he'd studied body language, he'd learned that people unconsciously copied each other when they talked; it was supposed to ease tension. He never did it unconsciously, but he had learned to remember to do it on purpose – though not too much, because people also got angry when they were too closely mimicked.

"So," said the man, "you wanted to know who I am and what I want."

The man paused for emphasis. Chesney had read about that technique, too. This whole situation must be about power. The stranger was trying to be dominant. He decided not to appear submissive. "I've already figured out who you are," he said. "You're Nat Blowdell."

He saw a new expression flicker across the other man's face, too fast for Chesney to be able to read it. But he bet that, if he applied Occam's razor, the right answer would be that he had just scored a point that he hadn't been expected to score. "But I don't know what you want," he said.

"What I want," said Blowdell, "is to rule the world."

NINE

"Why?" Chesney said.

The question seemed to catch Blowdell off-guard. "What do you mean, why?" he said.

"Well ruling the world could be fun, for some people at least. But what's the point if you have to make a deal with the Devil so that when you die you get stuck in Hell, with something like Wormy Nose there doing awful things to you forever and ever?"

"Why don't you answer your own question?" the man said. "Obviously, you've made your own deal, all for the sake of running around in spandex busting crooks."

"It's not spandex," Chesney said.

"Stick to the point."

"Okay. I didn't sell my soul. I'm the exception to the rule."

Something like delight seized Blowdell's features for a moment, then he put on a poker face. "I heard something about a guy who caused Hell to go on strike, and then he got some kind of settlement..."

He was looking at Chesney as if he expected the young man to say something. Chesney said, "I can't talk about it."

"You just did. So it really happened?"

"I can't–" Chesney began but the man was already waving away his denial.

"I also heard," Blowdell said, "that the whole thing may be about to change."

"What 'whole thing?'"

The man made a breezy gesture. "Everything. Heaven, Hell, the order of the ages. Full-scale housecleaning. Fresh start. All made new."

He was looking at Chesney expectantly again. This time The Actionary remained silent. After a long moment, Blowdell said, "They say somebody's writing a book."

Chesney adapted a line he remembered from a Malc Turner episode. "Somebody, somewhere, is always writing a book," Chesney said.

"Yeah, but this is no ordinary book."

Chesney said nothing. The silence went on for quite a while, broken only by the crackling and popping of the fire. Finally, the young man started to rise, saying, "Well, if that's all…"

Blowdell shook his head, slowly as if for emphasis. "It's not all," he said.

Chesney sat down again. "What do you want from me?" he said.

The other man settled himself more comfortably in his chair. "I want to tell you a story," he said.

"I don't want to hear a story. I have things to do."

"You'll want to hear this one. It's a ghost story."

"I don't like ghost stories. They're not real."

"This one is," Blowdell said, "and you need to hear it."

It was a fairly long story. It began with Blowdell introducing himself. His full name was Nathaniel Aston Blowdell III. He said he was, by training, a lawyer but his profession was that of a public relations consultant specializing in political campaigning. He was a founding partner in the K Street firm of Harper Blowdell, which graciously accepted fees from political action committees representing candidates from both parties in Congress and had an enviable track record for getting its clients elected.

"For a long time, I was content," he said. "Business was good and after Bush came in, it got even better. The partnership worked fine.

"And then something unusual happened. While doing a little fishing, all alone in a boat out on Chesapeake Bay, my partner in the firm, Wilson Harper, choked to death on a liverwurst sandwich."

Chesney knew what to say in this circumstance. "I'm sorry for your loss."

"Don't be. Our partnership agreement allowed the surviving partner, in the event that one of us met with a sudden demise, to buy out the deceased's interest at a more than reasonable price. Wilson's widow was not pleased, but the contract was ironclad."

Again, this seemed like one of those moments when Chesney should say nothing.

"That," Blowdell said, "is when the unusual thing happened."

"The choking on a sandwich wasn't unusual?"

"The man ate like a starved hog," Blowdell said, and laughed. "He'd had the Heimlich maneuver twice, and it didn't teach him anything. Still, if the lump of liverwurst hadn't got him, his heart would have. He weighed more than four hundred pounds. The Coast Guard had to use a cargo crane to get him out of the boat."

Blowdell paused, as if to imagine the sight of his dead partner being hoisted onto the deck of the cutter. Chesney wondered if that was the unusual thing, but then it turned out it wasn't because Blowdell went on to say, "And then, in the evening after his funeral, he came to see me."

"Really?" said Chesney. He was pretty sure that was the thing he ought to say in response to Blowdell's expectant pause.

"Really and truly. And this is where it becomes a ghost story." Blowdell unlocked his hands and steepled his two sets of fingertips as a sign that he was putting his next words together carefully. "He appeared in my bedroom just after I'd turned in. At first I thought he was a hallucination brought on by fatigue and the stress of dealing with his wife and the extended family, who had threatened lawsuits and hinted at worse."

Apparently, the Harper family name was originally Arpa and they hailed from near a town called Serradifalco in Sicily. Blowdell's partner was the white sheep of a considerable clan of people who saw *The Godfather* not as a drama, but as a documentary.

"So when he came hovering over me like something out of Scrooge, I told him to go to Hell. He told me he'd already been there, and it wasn't as bad as he'd expected – at least not for senior public relations practitioners."

Again, Blowdell paused expectantly, but this time he read Chesney's discomfort. "And you know why," he said, "don't you?"

"I'm not allowed–"

Again, Blowdell waved away the young man's non-answer. "Yeah, yeah. So my dead partner tells me the situation down below is fluid, no one knows where it's going to end up, and maybe a couple of smart operators – one upstairs and one down – can turn it to their advantage. He's already got one of the Dukes of Hell eating out of his hand for setting up an operation to identify and enlist unnoticed opinion leaders in various communities.

"And then he tells me about this book…"

The book had been in the Arpa family for generations,

taken as collateral for a loan that could never be repaid. It had come to the New World when some ambitious cousins of the mainline Arpas came over to open the American branch operation; it soon grew to dwarf the traditional gambling, loansharking, extortion and prostitution rackets that had been left behind in the old country.

"And no wonder," Blowdell said. "They had infernal backing. Old Tancredo Arpa, Wilson's great-great-uncle, stole the book from his cousins, who'd never had the stones to do what it told how to do." He paused and looked pointedly at Chesney. "Of course, you know what kind of how-to that was."

"How to summon a demon."

"Exactly. Which old Tancredo – who was then young and devil-may-care Tancredo – used to call up a demon and they got to work building a criminal empire."

"And where's Tancredo now?" Chesney said.

"Fourth circle," said Blowdell. "Iron scorpions and burning sleet."

"Which is where you'll end up," said Chesney. He started to get up again. "I've already had this conversation. I'm not interested in your book or ruling the world or–"

"Neither was I," said the other man. "Short-term gain for long-term pain. And I do mean pain, and I do mean really long-term." He smiled at Chesney and it was one of the smiles that Chesney hadn't learned to read, except he was pretty sure it wasn't friendly.

"I'm going now," The Actionary said.

Blowdell's smile widened. "Then you'll miss the best part of the ghost story–"

"I don't care."

"–the part you're in."

Chesney did not sit down again, but neither did he summon Xaphan to take him away. Blowdell took his stillness for an encouragement to keep on talking. "Wilson told me about the book and where to find it. And he told me about this guy who'd summoned up a demon and made some kind of deal that did not put him in line for an eternity of red-hot pokers up the fundamental orifice."

He paused again. Chesney realized he was supposed to say something. He said, "My deal was different. An exception to the rule."

Blowdell clapped his hands. "Exactly!" he said again. "An exception to a rule that was not supposed to have any exceptions. A loophole in a contract that was not supposed to have any loopholes."

"Just because I got one," Chesney said, "doesn't mean–"

"I'm way ahead of you. I know I'm not going to get your deal. But that's okay. Your deal," – he gestured to indicate Chesney's costume – "is not what I'm after."

"What are you after?"

"I told you – I want to rule the world."

"And then?"

"And then…" Blowdell held his hands as if they cradled a bubble that then popped, and when it popped he said, "Nothing." He punctuated the final word with an audible *pop* from his lips.

"What nothing?"

"I figure to rule the world until it ends. In fact, I mean to make sure it ends."

"Judgment Day," Chesney said. "And down into the pit you will go." He could remember a preacher from his boyhood pronouncing exactly those words with great satisfaction while his mother nodded in affirmation.

But Blowdell was shaking his head again. "No. Because it's not going to end like that. That's just a leftover from a previous draft."

"Oh? And exactly how is it supposed to end?"

"Nobody knows. The line has not yet been written."

"How do you know?"

"Because," said Blowdell, "word got around Hell that all this" – he gestured in a way that was meant to take in Hell, Heaven and everything inbetween – "is just a draft of a book that…" – he briefly put a finger to his lips – "well, we can't say the name here, but you know who I mean. He's writing a book, and all this is just a draft, a work-in-progress."

Chesney tried to look as if he was hearing something ridiculous, but he had never been good at contriving misleading facial expressions.

"I'm surprised I never noticed before," Blowdell was saying. "The evidence is all around us."

"What do you mean?"

"You know what a bell curve is?"

Chesney was an actuary. The bell curve was as fundamental to his world as gravity. "It is how the distribution of natural variation appears in nature," he said. "Most samples clump up in the middle, then the statistically less likely ones tail off to either side so the graph has the shape of a bell."

"Well done," said Blowdell. "And do you know what fractals are?"

Chesney did. "Feedback and recursion."

That got him a different smile. "Neatly put. And have you noticed that things that look smooth and even, like the curve of a baby's cheek, turn out to be not smooth or even, once you get close enough? That there's not a pure shape, or a straight line, or a smooth curve anywhere in creation?"

Chesney nodded. "I hadn't thought about it, but you're right."

"And have you ever taken a close look at atoms?"

"That's hard to do," Chesney said. "They won't stay still."

"They're mostly empty space," Blowdell said. "Matter is not really *there*, is it? All matter, stars, planets, you, me, when you get down to the underlying structure, it's like some flimsy stage set made out of cheesecloth and cardboard."

"So?" Chesney said.

"So what kind of..." – Blowdell gestured toward the ceiling – "creates a universe that, when you really, really, look at it, turns out to be a slapped-together piece of gim-crack, trompe-l'oeil–"

"I don't know that word."

"Something that fools the eye on a casual glance," Blowdell said, "like a trick of perspective that makes a Hollywood starlet look like a fifty-foot-tall woman." He paused to gather his thoughts again. "But what kind of... you-know-what, produces such a tacked-together creation?"

"I don't know," Chesney said.

"I do. A you-know-what who's just bashing out a rough draft, that's who."

Chesney wanted out of this conversation. He sensed that it was not leading him anywhere he wanted to go. Specifically, it threatened to take him out of the pool of light in which he was a happy and successful crimefighter and plunge him into murk and darkness, where nothing could be relied upon. "I have to go," he said.

Blowdell paid no attention. He was caught up in his narrative. Chesney had seen villains get that way in comix. Apparently they couldn't resist showing off their brilliant schemes. "And there's this other thing that was getting whispered around Hell," he said, "not just that this is a book we're all in, but that it's the characters who are making it work."

Chesney said nothing. It didn't seem like a good idea to confirm the rumor. But Blowdell was watching him and his smile was broadening again.

"So I asked myself," the man said, "what kind of character am I? Am I a bit player? Am I a spear carrier, a background figure just there for atmosphere?"

Chesney said, "I'm going to guess that you answered that with a no."

"Bet your ass I did. I was always good at spotting an opportunity." Blowdell's eyes took on what Chesney thought writers meant when they described someone as having a distant look. "And, man, this is some kind of opportunity."

"So you're going to make yourself," Chesney said, "into a major character in a divine book, where you get to determine which way the story goes and how it all ends."

"You got it."

"Isn't that taking a huge risk?"

"It was," the other man said, "until I saw you flashing about that garage and piling gangsters into a dumpster."

Chesney opened his mouth but nothing came out.

"That's right," Blowdell said. "You were the clincher. You showed me the way it all really works. That's when I used the book and made my deal."

"Xaphan!" Chesney said. He stood up and the demon appeared beside him, a drink in one hand and a fresh Churchill in the other. Melech also popped into view, his nose-worms thrust into a tumbler of liquor. "We're going," Chesney said.

"Wait," said Blowdell. "I need to ask you a question."

"Make it fast."

"I'm getting to it." The older man rose from his chair and moved closer to Chesney, so that he could gently poke the young man in the chest for emphasis, "I made my deal because you showed me that eternity is not eternity. That forever is not forever."

"That doesn't make sense," Chesney said, but the young man had labored under the curse of logic all his brief life, and he could already see where Blowdell's rationale was taking him.

"Don't be disingenuous, kid," said the other man. "Sure it makes sense. All the sense in the world. And it means that all that guff about eternal suffering and nasty demons flaying your genitalia with broken glass is going to go the way of Noah and the Flood and the Tower of Babel."

"Not my genitalia," said Chesney. "Yours."

Blowdell moved his mouth in a way that conceded the point. "But not," he said, "if the whole show folds before the final act."

"And that's what you think is going to happen."

Again, the slow head-shaking. Chesney thought the man must really like doing that. "No, that's what I'm going to *make* happen."

"How?"

"Well, first, I'm going to help Warren Paxton become President of the United States. I'll be his Machiavelli, pulling the strings and working the levers behind the scenes. He'll be the face; I'll be the power. And that will be only my first stepping stone.

"As I think you know, I had a plan for Paxton that was already in motion, at least until you stepped in. Paxton thinks you're going to be a game changer, but I doubt it." He looked at Chesney sharply, but there was still amusement behind the gaze. "All you want is to be a comic-book hero, isn't it?"

"I want to be a crimefighter, that's true."

"Paxton's waiting for you to give him an answer. I figure that answer will be no." Blowdell spread his hands and smiled. "So we'll go back to Plan A."

"You're going to stage a fake kidnapping of Poppy Paxton and use the media attention to make her father an instant public figure."

"More or less."

"I've seen the meta-analysis."

Now Blowdell's smile faded and he leaned forward. "But there's one question I still need you to answer: are you going to interfere?"

"Kidnapping is a crime. I fight crime."

"It's that simple?"

"Yes. But if you want it complicated, I am also fond of Ms Paxton. She doesn't know about the plan and she'll be terrified."

"So you're going to be a complication?" As Blowdell asked the question, he looked sideways at his demon, Melech. The fiend's pale eyes slid over Chesney.

But the young man had faced down tougher infernal beings. He said, "I suggest you find another path to ruling the world – one that doesn't hurt people I care about." He signaled to Xaphan. "Now I've got something important to do."

"Hello," said the voice on the other end of the phone connection, "Melda McCann speaking."

"Um," said Chesney.

"Hello? Who is this?"

"Er," said Chesney. He had been in a pool of light when he had entered the six-six-six prefix into his phone at the apartment. The moment Melda picked up and said hello, he was metaphorically a teenager again, his sweat slicking the phone's plastic surface while his tongue seemed to have grown too large to navigate between his teeth and palate. "It's... it's me," he said.

"Me who?"

From reflex, he almost said "Chesney," but managed to choke off the second half of the first syllable. He swallowed again, his throat suddenly dry, and said, "From the other night. You said I should call."

Now there was silence from Melda's side of the conversational divide, then she said, "Mr Flash Bang? My knight in shining armor?"

"The Actionary," he said, with only a slight creak in his voice, "yes."

"So you changed your mind?"

"About what?"

"About calling."

"No, I–"

"Cause you shouldn't think I've got nothing better to do than sit around waiting for you to find a moment in your oh-so-busy schedule where you've got nothing on, so you figure you'll throw old Melda a bone–"

"It's not like that!" Chesney said.

"Oh, it's not? Oh, pardon me. Please, pardon me, Mr Actionfigure. And do explain it to me, how it really is, but make sure you use small, simple words, cause I'm–"

"Please!" Chesney managed to get out. "I really wanted to call you, bu…"

"But?"

"But… I'm not very good at…" He had to swallow again. "I get all…"

"You're not trying to tell me you're shy?" Melda said.

Chesney wished he could see her face at this moment, so he could study her expression and determine whether the right answer to the question was the truth or a fib. One of the reasons he had flunked adolescent telephone gab was that he had never mastered the art of understanding tone of voice. Sarcasm usually went right past him. Now the silence was extending and he knew he had to say something, so he opted for the truth. "Yes," he said.

"You're shy?" she said.

"Yes."

"You bust up drug gangs and car thieves, but you're too shy to call a girl on the phone?"

Chesney was sure her tone of voice was conveying a message he wasn't receiving, but he was committed now, so he said, "I'm not very good at–" And then what she said registered. "Wait a minute," he said, "you said drug gangs?"

"You haven't seen the news?"

"I've been in… somewhere where they don't get TV."

"Where the Hell would that be?" Melda said. "Never mind. It's all over the TV. Drugs, piles of cash, gangsters tied up. You're everybody's hero. You're a celebrity."

"Oh," said Chesney, "well, that's good. So, you see, I really have been kind of busy–"

She laughed, and he was pretty sure it was not one of those harsh, scorn-filled laughs, and then he was completely sure when she said, "I was just ragging you. A girl's got her pride, you know."

"Oh, okay. When I saw you on TV–"

"What? You mean when I went," – she made the rude tongue noise again – "Nah, I was just having a bad day, some rich bitch went off on me about she didn't like the color of her nails – the color she picked out – and then that reporter kind of egged me on, said it would be more likely to make the news if I hoked it up a little."

"Oh."

"You don't mind, do you, sweetie?" she said. "It was fun getting on TV. All the girls at the salon were totally stoked."

"No, I don't mind," Chesney said, and he really didn't. He was replaying in his head the word he'd just heard her call him: "sweetie." It was the first time anyone – including his mother – had ever called him by a pet name. He found that he liked it. After another couple of replayings he decided that he liked it a lot and wanted to hear it again.

Meanwhile, Melda had been saying something else and he had missed it. "Sorry," he said, "could you say that again?"

"I said, when are we going to get together?"

"You mean..." – he swallowed again – "like a date?"

"Exactly like a date," she said. "So much like a date you couldn't tell the difference."

"You mean, like dinner or a movie?"

"Or dancing, if you like the clubs. Not bowling, though. Todd always wanted to go bowling."

"Um," Chesney said.

"What?"

"There's a problem."

"What kind of problem?"

"A... limitation," he said.

"What kind of limitation?"

"I can only... I only have powers... I can only be The Actionary for a limited time."

Another silence, then she said, "How limited?"

"If I tell you," Chesney said, "it has to be a secret."

"Who'm I gonna tell?"

"Well, that reporter, if he interviews you again. Or, really, anybody. It wouldn't be good if bad guys knew about it."

"Ah. I get it. I won't tell. Just between us. Cross my heart."

"Okay," he said. "Two hours."

"Two hours? Two hours when? A day? A week?"

"Two hours out of every twenty-four. Although I could arrange to do them back-to-back, so that would make four hours."

Melda said, "So we could go out at ten at night and you'd be good until two in the morning?"

"Yes," said Chesney, "except I only have my powers when I'm crimefighting. Otherwise…"

"Otherwise, you're just a guy in a Halloween costume?"

Chesney couldn't think of a good answer. There was silence. "Are you still there?" he said.

"I'm just thinking," she said. "So, when you're not being a crimefighter – that's, like, twenty-two hours per day, right?"

"Right."

"Well, who are you then?"

"My regular identity."

Another silence, then, "Which is?"

"That's another secret."

"Okay, I'm crossing my heart again."

Chesney hesitated. In the comix, crimefighters and superheroes kept their identities secret to protect their friends and loved ones. If criminals could get their hands on those innocents, they might take revenge or try to pressure the hero into leaving them alone. "If I tell you, it might put you in danger."

"Two minutes," said Xaphan. The demon was lying on its back, floating at about the height of Chesney's waist, blowing complicated patterns of cigar smoke.

"I'm a big girl, sweetie," Melda was saying. "I can take care of myself."

That was twice she'd called him sweetie. Chesney stopped to replay the endearment in his head one more time. He wondered if he should call her something in return. But what?

Now it was her turn to say, "Are you there?"

"I have to think about it," he said. "It could be complicated."

"Well, we should talk about it."

"One minute," said the demon.

"I've got to go," Chesney said. "My two hours is almost up." He wondered if, once his Actionary time ran out, his name and phone number would appear on her phone's caller ID display.

"Call me again?" she said.

"I will."

"Promise? For sure?"

"Promise. For sure."

"Thirty seconds."

"Okay," Melda said. Good night."

"One thing."

"What?"

"Would you say, 'Good night, sweetie'?"

He heard her laugh again. "Good night, sweetie."

"Ten, nine, eight..." said Xaphan.

"Good night," Chesney said and hung up the phone.

The demon winked out, leaving an image made of cigar smoke dissipating in the air. It seemed to be a self-portrait of Xaphan's head and shoulders, the pose showing the weasel mouth open to receive a stream of liquor.

Sugar 'n Spice was only a couple of blocks from Chesney's office, on Chestnut Street, a boulevard that was lined with upmarket clothing and shoe stores, interspersed with restaurants and cafes in which people who shopped at those kinds of stores liked to get together and show each other their designer labels over expensive coffee. Chesney had not often walked down that block, but at lunchtime the next day he made an exception to his routine.

He had woken up thinking that maybe the best way to keep in touch with Melda McCann would be to introduce himself as The Actionary's best friend. That ruse had worked for crimefighters and superheroes ever since the days of Clark Kent and Superman. Even Malc Turner sometimes acted for The Driver when his alter ego couldn't put in an appearance.

Chesney hadn't made up his mind whether to approach Melda in his secret identity. He had tried imagining a conversation, where he would casually introduce himself as an emissary from The Actionary. But when he played his proposed opening remark in his head, he realized right away that "emissary" was the wrong word to use; it would work fine in a book but it would be sure to sound funny coming out of a real person's mouth.

"Messenger" also wasn't right; nor was "courier." Maybe he should just make it light and breezy and say something like, "The Actionary – he's a friend of mine – asked me to drop by and give you a message."

That might work, he thought as he turned a corner and found himself on the right block. He repeated the sentence to himself as he made his way toward Sugar 'n Spice; he'd found that the benefits of rehearsing opening lines to women he intended to speak to outweighed the looks he inevitably attracted when he walked along, mumbling to himself.

The street was busy at midday, the sidewalks crowded with women in impractical fashions and men without neckties but with three days of stubble along their jawlines. Chesney could remember when going tieless and unshaven was a mark of low socio-economic poverty. Now the affluent went around looking as if they were homeless. Chesney could also remember when the only place you could expect to see a tattooed lady was in the circus. He had long since decided that he would never respond to the lure of fashion.

Sugar 'n Spice was a storefront midway along the block on the opposite side of the street from Chesney. He waited for an ebb in the flow of traffic then crossed over and idled beside the edge of the big window, holding his paper lunch sack. His plan had been to peek through the window and scope out the premises, to see if, first, Melda was there, and, second, if the layout of the place made her easily approachable.

But that plan was made difficult by his discovery that the inside of the big window was coated in some bronze-colored substance that made it hard to see in. The name of the establishment was spread across the window in a circular cartouche done in the same dark coppery shade, but the spaces between the lettering and the edge of the big circle had been left as clear glass.

That meant there were only two ways to see inside: open the door – also bronzed glass, with the hours of business rendered in darker paint – and peek in; or look through the window's clear lacunae. After a moment's reflection, Chesney opted for the latter course. He sidled up to the glass and, cupping his hand to shield his eyes from the noontime glare, he peered through clear glass in the top curve of the large, ornate "S" at the left of the cartouche.

But he could see very little. The interior was not brightly lit; the designer had gone for indirect lighting on the upper walls, and tall floor lamps scattered about. With the light passing through the painted window, the effect was to create a golden glow to surround the women who sat in chairs before wall mirrors or reclined on chaise longues at the rear of the salon. The latter might have been getting their nails done, but if Melda McCann was one of the uniformed staff seated beside the reclining customers, Chesney could not tell.

"Ding-dabble," he said to himself in disappointment.

A voice beside him said, "Hey, what are you up to?"

It was a familiar voice. He turned and found himself the object of a frowning gaze that was also familiar. "Melda," he said, "there you are."

Melda McCann stepped back. She was carrying a cardboard tray full of paper cups of aromatic coffee from the cafe two doors down. "How do you know my–?" She broke off and peered closely at him. "Hey, I know you!" Her voice had gotten louder. "You're that creep who's always at the hot dog cart in the park, leering at women. I've seen you looking at me."

Chesney would have denied that he ever leered, but he was not given the chance. "What are you doing here?" she demanded, and then he saw her brows draw even closer together as she backtracked to her earlier question. "I want to know," she said, in a tone that indicated she wasn't going accept anything less than full disclosure, "how you come to know my name. Are you stalking me?"

"N-n-no," Chesney managed to get out. Then he remembered his opening line. "The, er, The Actionary, he's–"

Her eyes widened. "You saw me on TV, didn't you, you creep?" Her hands were occupied with coffee cups, but now she was stooping to place the tray on the sidewalk. Her purse was slung from her shoulder and as she rose from her crouch, one hand went into it and rummaged around.

"Oh, follyfluke," said Chesney. He knew what she was groping for. This was definitely not a good time to make an approach on behalf of his other identity. As the black cylinder came out of Melda's purse, he turned to run, but instead bounced off a well-fleshed, middle-aged matron who had stopped to witness the altercation. She fell backwards into the arms of a slim young person of indeterminate gender who was either not up to, or simply not interested in, the responsibility of assuming an unexpected burden. He let the woman complete her descent, and her ample fundament struck the sidewalk with a sound something like that of a prime Christmas ham landing on a butcher's counter, while the androgyne, back-pedaling out of harm's way, arms waving in elegant helplessness, stepped off the curb and into the street.

Horns blared, tires screeched, metal met metal, glass rattled and shattered. Chesney, though aware of the concatenation of sounds and events, paid them no mind. His mind was focused on the black cylinder, which he knew was close behind him because when he had bounced off the plump woman, he had fallen back against Melda McCann, who was pushing him off with both hands so that she could unleash another chemical Hell against him. And this time, Xaphan was not there to heal him.

He straightened, got his feet under him, but found no escape path. The way in front was blocked by the seated matron, who was making plenty of noise but no immediate effort to get back up. A balding man of rib-concealing girth now stooped to put his hands under her arms with the clear intent of lifting her up, disregarding the counsel of a woman in a plaid coat who kept shrieking into his ear, "Wesley, don't move her! Wesley, don't move her!"

Wesley, either stone deaf or philosophically disinclined to accept advice from the quarter whence it was issued, heaved the plump woman half-upright. But then he uttered a combination gasp and grunt, while an odd expression took over his face: a rictus of agony coupled with open astonishment at the discovery that some part of his body that had always given loyal service – probably a lumbar disc, Chesney would later think – had chosen that moment to desert and betray the until-now-happy commonwealth that had been Wesley.

Chesney later regretted that he had been forced to add to the man's troubles, especially since the fellow was only trying to help a fallen stranger. But events had reached the moment of crisis. Behind him, he heard Melda voice a triumphant "Hah!" that could have but one meaning:

she now had her can of pepper-spray deployed and ready for action. His way otherwise blocked, Chesney sprang forward, placed both hands on the top of Wesley's bowed head, and leapfrogged over the injured good Samaritan, drawing from him a fresh bleat of pain and disappointment.

Chesney landed surprisingly well, considering that acrobatics had never been one of his pools of light. But his escape routes were still limited. The sidewalk remained crowded and every pair of eyes was focused on him. A distinguished-looking man in an expensive overcoat was reaching out to bar the young man's way. Chesney could not go into the street because that direction was blocked by the person of uncertain gender, who seemed to be giving in to an impulse to swoon into the arms of another helpful bystander, not noticing that the latter's act of charity was compromised by his lifting of the former's wallet.

Even had he been able to get past the combination of faint and felony, Chesney could not have easily crossed the street. What had been a line of free-flowing traffic had now become a stationary wall of automobiles. There were no longer any spaces between the vehicles; indeed, some front and rear ends had connected so violently that it was difficult to see where the one ended and the other began. A variety of car alarms were combining to enliven the normal urban soundscape, and drivers were exiting their vehicles to examine the damage and point fingers of blame in various directions.

The distinguished-looking man's fingers now connected with Chesney's lapel and he said, "Hold it, you!" From behind, the young man heard Melda say, "Don't let him–" and did not stay to hear the completion of the sentence. He repeated the move he had applied against one of the thugs who had tried to kidnap Poppy Paxton, setting the heel of his hand against the man's chin and pushing up. But, since he was not in his Actionary garb, his strength was not as that of ten men, nor even of a single strong individual. The man in the overcoat pushed back with the muscles of his neck and shoulder, meanwhile renewing his attempt to grasp Chesney's jacket.

"I'll fix him!" Melda McCann's voice came from the background, along with a stream of dark liquid. And, for once, Chesney's luck turned bright. The pepper spray merely touched its intended target's ear before going on to strike the distinguished intervener on the nose and in the mouth that was opened to say, "Got you!" – words that were never uttered because the two affected body parts instead gave themselves over to sneezing and retching.

The grip on Chesney's lapel now failed and the young man forced himself past the knot of people on the sidewalk and turned to leap onto the hood of a stationary sedan, further denting its already rumpled surface and provoking its driver to call the young man names that his mother would never have countenanced. But Chesney did not stay to hear. He wanted distance between him and Melda McCann's cylinder of incapacitating spray and he now made every effort to create it. Within seconds he had crossed the street, rounded the corner and woven his way through shoppers and lunch-goers. If any of them were wondering what was causing all of the commotion on Chestnut Street, they would have to seek elsewhere for enlightenment.

After half a block, he slowed to a walk, breathing heavily. He was surprised to find that he still held the paper bag that contained his ham-and-cheese and bran muffin. These he thrust into the hands of a homeless man sitting on the sidewalk. Chesney had lost his appetite.

Back at the C Group office, Chesney dug a candy bar out of his desk drawer – he usually kept one or two to replenish his blood sugar if some interesting set of calculations kept him past quitting time. He chewed without tasting, his mind unwillingly replaying the sequence of events outside Sugar 'n Spice. That could have gone better, he told himself. He would have to reexamine the whole question of relations between the Actionary, his secret identity and the rest of the world. Clearly, it was another one of those complex knots that would have dulled William of Ockham's best-honed razor.

He turned to the fill-in assignment Sitting Bull had given him, while they waited for W.T.'s reaction to the meta-analysis. Chesney was building a mathematical model to correlate street crime, income and educational levels, unemployment trends, the fluctuating cost of street drugs, and police manpower statistics. He was not convinced that the work would have any practical value, but Entwistle had told him the main output would be a series of interesting graphs that could be used in town hall meetings and, perhaps, a series of television commercials. Whether or not the graphs would really be useful to Paxton's political ambitions, this afternoon Chesney found the interplay of numbers a comfort to his stressed nerves. He slid into the ratios and correlations like a harried man who slips into a warm and soothing bath, eyes closed and with only his nose poking metaphorically above the surface.

So it was a disconcerting experience, when the afternoon had more than half worn on, that Chesney's real-life nostrils again told him that Poppy Paxton had once again loomed into his vicinity. He redoubled his concentration on the monitor's screen, his hands moving from mouse to keyboard and back again, to assemble the raw mathematical data into a fitting architecture. But the scent did not diminish, and now it intensified as the young woman bent to place something between Chesney's eyes and the monitor.

It was her expensive, multifunctional phone, its screen turned toward him to show a still picture. As his gaze went to it, Poppy pressed the central button on the keypad and the picture became a moving video image. He saw a street scene: a stoop-shouldered young man peered through the opaqued window of Sugar 'n Spice. A young woman in a blue uniform approached him. There followed a brief exchange of unheard dialog, then a series of events that ensued at a rapid pace. The video froze on an image of the young man just after he had leaped over a car's hood and was running obliquely out of shot, leaving behind him a background of frozen chaos.

The phone remained between Chesney and his monitor. He said nothing, nor did he move, though he felt the muscles between his shoulder blades draw tightly together, as if they expected to receive an imminent pounding of a female fist, or perhaps the thrust of a poisoned stiletto. Chesney found that his views of Poppy Paxton, that had once been bathed in clear light, had decidedly darkened.

"Well?" she said, in a tone that could have frozen helium.

"Well... what?" he said.

"What's between you and the bimbo?"

Chesney did not look up. He did not wish to confirm what his imagination told him would be the expression on Poppy Paxton's perfect face. Even so, his instant response was to defend Melda McCann, despite her having accused him of creepery then tried to create a furnace-like environment in his eyes and nasal passages, and for the second time. "She's not a bimbo," he said. "It's just that she gets defensive when she feels threatened."

Poppy, however, wanted Chesney to get the full measure of her displeasure. She spun his chair around so that
he must either look into her face or stare at her bosom.
Reluctantly, he chose the former, and saw eyes like shards
of blue ice that dissected him while her exquisite lips said,
"I don't give a rat's heinie how she feels. I want to know
how you come to be connected to her." She poked a manicured fingernail into his chest, one poke for each word,
as she added, "And I want to know now."

Chesney looked around. The C Group office was fully
staffed this afternoon, but not a single eye was turned
their way. Every head was bent to a screen, keyboard or
hardcopy document. He realized that this must be how it
was for the unlucky gazelle taken down by the leopard,
singled out for a very bad end while its herd-mates looked
away and got on with their grazing.

"I, er," he said. He had no idea what was about to come
out of his mouth. And he never would, because at that
moment Lieutenant Denby stepped into the C Group office and arrested him.

TEN

"What's the charge?" Poppy wanted to know, after the detective had made Chesney stand up, turn around and be handcuffed.

"Are you his lawyer?" Denby asked her.

"No."

"Then it's none of your business." The policeman took Chesney by one arm and said, "Let's go."

But Poppy put her hand on Chesney's other arm – it was cold, the young man noticed – and tugged the other way. "Just a minute," she said, "I'm not done with him."

Chesney had seen a nature documentary once – or maybe it was one of those you-gotta-see-this video clip shows that YouTube had made possible – in which a half-grown water buffalo calf was set upon by a pride of lions at the edge of a river. Struggling to escape the cats, the calf stumbled hind-end first into the water. Immediately, a crocodile lunged from beneath the surface and seized the prey from behind. Seeing the video, Chesney had felt sympathy for the calf. Now, as Denby's and Poppy's grips tightened their respective holds, he could almost envy the creature.

"Let him go," said the cop.

"You let him go."

"No, now take your hand off him, or…"

Poppy struck a pose and adopted a tone that Chesney imagined had worked for her in many a previous confrontation. "Or what?"

Denby produced a second set of handcuffs. "Or I'll pop you for obstructing a police officer."

"You wouldn't dare. My father—"

"Yeah, I know," said Denby, "he's best buddies with the police commissioner. But you know what, missy? Right now, I don't give a flying…" – Denby paused to consider, then went with – "focaccia loaf about Commissioner Hanshaw, or your old man, or all the rest of the Twenty put together." He paused again, to let his words sink in, then continued. "I'm a cop who's been jerked around once too often this week, and I'm in no mood for spoiled princesses or" – he looked at Chesney – "gifted amateurs." He jangled the handcuffs. "So you can let him go or you can come with him."

She let Chesney go. "I'm calling my Daddy," she said. "And he'll be calling his lawyer."

"Fine," said Denby, "he'll know where to find us."

The detective led Chesney out into the hall and pressed the elevator button. They could hear the faint clack of machinery somewhere in the shaft. "What am I charged with?" Chesney said.

Denby didn't look at him. "How about incitement to riot? Or leaving the scene of an accident you caused? Or – and this is so much worse – pissing off a policeman?"

The elevator arrived and Denby put the young man inside and stepped in after him. He pushed the button for the lobby and waited for the doors to close. When the car began to descend, the detective turned his prisoner around and released the handcuffs.

"Does that mean I'm not under arrest?" Chesney said.

Denby leaned against the wall and crossed his arms. "For now, we'll call it a gray area," he said.

"I'm not good with gray areas," Chesney said.

"Too bad. You're in one." The detective studied the young man. The actuary read the policeman's expression as that of someone who is trying to make up his mind. He thought he ought to say something to tip the process in his favor, but he had no idea what the right words would be, so he remained silent.

They arrived at the lobby and Denby indicated that Chesney should follow him out the front doors. Another unmarked police car was in the loading zone, but this one had a wire grill between the front and rear seats. "Get in," said the detective.

"Front or back?" Chesney said.

"Front," said Denby. "For now."

When they were seated in the car, the policeman unlocked the glove compartment and took out a small video camera. He flipped out the screen built into one side and said, "Look at this."

Chesney looked. He saw the same dismally familiar scene that Poppy Paxton had shown him, though from a different angle. The camera's resolution was also better than her phone's. The video started at the point where Chesney had fled the confrontation. It had been shot with a telephoto lens, so Chesney had a close-up view of himself as he placed his hands on the stooped Samaritan's head and vaulted to freedom. Denby slowed the image so that he saw the pain on the bald man's face.

"That's assault," Denby said. "Aggravated, if the guy suffered serious injury."

"I was just trying to escape Melda's pepper spray."

"That could be a mitigating factor. You should tell your counsel. Or Paxton's." The detective paused to see if Chesney had anything further to say, and when nothing was forthcoming, he said, "But what interests me – no, let me correct myself – one of the things that interests me is that you refer to her as Melda."

Chesney started to say something, managed to say, "Er," then thought better of it.

"You've met her," Denby pressed him.

"I've seen her on TV."

Denby nodded, as if the young man had made a good point. "So you have. And you happened to remember her name." He appeared to consider this a moment, then said, "And what prompted you to pay her a visit this afternoon?"

"Er," said Chesney again.

"Were you struck by her display of pulchritude on the news? The part where she blew a Bronx cheer at," – Denby crooked his fingers to make quotation marks in the air – "The 'Actionary?' Did that stir your affections? Or were you just after her autograph?"

"Um," said Chesney.

"Before you answer that, though," said Denby, "there's one other little matter I'd like you to clear up for me. That's this." He adjusted a control on the camera and now Chesney was seeing himself coming down the block toward the Sugar 'n Spice salon. His lips were moving. The camera zoomed in until his face filled the little screen. "You probably don't know this," Denby said, "but your modern police department uses outside consultants. One of the experts I like to consult is Abie Klitchman. Do you know him?"

"No."

"He's the old guy who runs the shoe repair shop on South Buchanan, just by the library."

"I think I've seen it," Chesney said. He looked at his shoes. They were a little worn at the heel, but he had never had a pair resoled and reheeled. When his shoes wore out, he bought new ones. "What's that got to do with–?"

Denby waved a hand in an *oh, nothing* gesture. "The thing is, old Abie's been deaf from birth, but he reads lips like you wouldn't believe." He drew Chesney's attention back to the close-up of the young man walking toward the salon, his lips moving. "And he says that what you're saying here is, 'The Actionary – he's a friend of mine – asked me to drop by and give you a message.'"

Chesney stared at the video. It was a moment before he realized that he was mouthing the words along with his image on the screen.

The detective leaned back and smiled and said, "So, what's that all about?"

It occurred to Chesney that he could lie. He saw the entire architecture of the tale appear before his eyes like a mirage in the desert: he had seen Melda jogging in the park; he would like to get to know her, but was shy; then he saw her on TV saying that The Actionary had kissed her; all he had to do was present himself as the hero's nerdy friend – Superman's Jimmy Olsen, Malc Turner's Dwayne Urban – and the ice was broken. But she'd recognized him and tried to mace him and he'd run away in shame and disgrace.

It wasn't a pretty story, but it was a plausible one. Lieutenant Denby might buy it. But then again, he might not. And the chances seemed good, by Chesney's reckoning, that he only had to annoy the detective a little bit more before he found himself sharing a cell with a person or persons he would prefer not to meet at close quarters. When it came to lying, Chesney could only claim regular success in dealings with his mother, and he wasn't entirely sure that he got away with it even with her; sometimes, he suspected she had largely lost interest in the Chesney project.

"I'm waiting," said the policeman. "If it's taking this long, I'll bet it's going to be a good one." He took out his phone and pressed controls on it. "I hope you don't mind if I record it. I'll probably want to share it with the guys down at Police Central."

The complex architecture of the grand lie abruptly lost its cohesion and tumbled to the desert sands. But that left only the truth which, in this case, was not the kind of story to spring on a skeptical policeman. It was a brand of truth that, for most people, took some getting used to. Chesney was pretty sure that the lieutenant was in no mood for the thunderclap of theological revelation; he would need to ease his way into the idea of an actuary who accidentally called up demons, put Hell out on strike, and wound up as a costumed crusader against crime. On reflection, he decided it had not been a good idea to call Denby to come and collect the bad guys with all their drugs and money. The gesture had been better meant than it had been received.

"Kid," said the policeman, "I asked you a question." He took out his handcuffs and clinked them together.

Chesney opted for the middle ground. "The Actionary *is* a friend of mine," he said. "And he did ask me to give Melda McCann a message."

Denby regarded him as if he were a humdrum old family pet that, after years of mooching about the place and sleeping on the hearth rug, had unexpectedly demonstrated the capacity to do startling tricks. "Really?" he said, and shook his head. "Gosh, I don't know where to start. Let's see, how did you two become friends? Was it a shared interest in crime statistics? No, better yet, if it's not too personal, what was the message he wanted you to bring to Ms McCann?" Now, he put down the handcuffs and slapped his forehead. "No, wait, I've got it! *Who the Hell is this Actionary clown and where can I get my hands on him?"*

The last sentence came loudly. Even as he flinched, Chesney saw pedestrians turn to stare at the car. His mother had always warned him against causing scenes in public. Apparently, Lieutenant Denby had had the benefit of a different upbringing.

"I... I can't tell you," Chesney said.

The policeman spoke in a soft voice. Perhaps he was remembering his own mother's advice that he who raised his voice had already lost the argument. "Why not?" he said.

"I... promised."

"You promised?" said Denby.

"Yes."

"So you know who The Actionary is, and you know where to find him, but you won't tell me because you promised not to. Have I got this right?"

Chesney was fairly sure there was sarcasm behind the question, but sarcasm had always been, to him, like a shade of blue to the color-blind. Still, there could only be one answer. "Yes."

"Turn around and put your wrists together," said Denby. "You are under arrest, and you are going to stay under arrest until you tell me what I want to know." He finished pinioning Chesney then took him out of the car and put him in the rear seat. Then he got back behind the steering wheel and started up the engine. "And if you wait too long, you just might get charged with aggravated assault, and leaving the scene of an accident, and anything else I can think of."

He put the car in gear and pulled out into traffic. As they left the curb, Chesney saw Poppy come out of the front doors of the Paxton Building. She had her phone to her ear and was talking to someone while signaling for a cab.

"You notice," Denby was saying, "that we're not circling the block."

"Yes," said Chesney from the back. The tower atop Police Central was visible only a few blocks away. They were heading for it.

"That's because I'm disappointed in you, kid."

There didn't seem much that Chesney could say in reply, so he said nothing.

"You never called," the detective said.

"Sorry?"

"You were supposed to be my liaison with C Group. But I never heard from you."

"There was nothing to report. All we did was crunch numbers."

"A lot of police work is crunching numbers," Denby said. "I might've been interested."

"I'm sorry," Chesney said. "I'm not used to people being interested in what I do."

"Huh," said the policeman. "Well, get used to it. I'm very interested in what you get up to with your buddy in spandex."

"It's not–" Chesney began, then thought better of it.

Too late. Denby was watching him in the rear-view mirror. "Funny," he said, "somebody else said that to me, not that long ago."

Chesney swallowed. He had often read that, even if you had nothing to hide, it was best not to say too much when questioned by a policeman. Now he realized that when you did have something to hide, the only safe course was to say nothing at all. Then he realized that the fact that he was saying nothing at all at this moment, after the exchange he had just had with Denby, was probably telling the policeman all he needed to know.

Still, he said nothing more until they pulled into the

basement garage under Police Central. Denby took him out of the car and escorted him upstairs. Here, after handing Chesney over to a bored, gray-haired, uniformed sergeant, the detective walked away without a backwards glance. The sergeant asked him his name and address and other particulars, all of which the cop wrote down in neat capital letters on a blue form. Then Chesney was passed on to a pair of officers who arrived talking to each other about a football game in which TcShawn Bougaineville had performed prodigious feats of catching and running. Their conversation continued, unbroken, while they took the actuary to a brightly lit room where he was photographed from two angles, then to a cubicle where all of his fingerprints were taken, along with a scraping of skin from the inside of his cheek. He was then relieved of all that was in his pockets, plus his belt and shoelaces, and finally put into a cold, bare cell.

"I want to call someone," Chesney said at one point in the proceedings. The cops interrupted their dialog to look at him as if he had performed some social faux pas that they were too polite to mention. Then they went back to their discussion of Bougaineville's broken field running.

Chesney spent an uncomfortable time in the cell. He didn't know how long it was because they had taken his watch, but it seemed to be at least an hour before another uniformed policeman came and took him to a small room with a table and several chairs and a large mirror on one wall. Chesney had seen enough police shows to know that the mirror would be semi-transparent to anybody standing on the other side. He had also read somewhere that police watch suspects's body language for a while before they interrogate them. Supposedly, someone who is guilty will fall asleep while waiting; the innocent will stay awake. Chesney had no fear that, in these circumstances, he would drop off. He doubted he would sleep even once he got home tonight – *if* he got home at all.

The room was quiet. The chair was hard. They hadn't handcuffed him again after fingerprinting him. He fought the urge to get up and pace around the room. That wouldn't look good. Finally, after what seemed an even longer wait than his time in the cell, he heard voices in the corridor outside the closed door: two men, arguing, and a woman's voice providing counterpoint.

The door opened. Lieutenant Denby stepped halfway through the opening, using his body to prevent someone else from entering. He gave Chesney a sour look. "Kid," he said, "is this your lawyer?"

He stepped aside to let Chesney see a silver-haired, pink-skinned stranger in a dark topcoat over a tailored suit and silk tie. The man was nodding at Chesney over the lieutenant's shoulder, but stopped when the detective's head snapped around to see what was going on.

Chesney did not have a lawyer. His mother did, and that was whom he would have called if they'd let him. The stranger was not his mother's lawyer. He began to explain and saw Denby's face begin to light up. Then Poppy Paxton forced her way between the two men, showing Chesney her angry face. Denby put an arm out to block her, but he couldn't prevent her from saying, "Say yes, you idiot!"

"Yes," said Chesney, "he's my lawyer."

Denby's expression changed. He dropped his arm to allow the silver-haired man to come into the room, but restored the barrier when Poppy tried to follow. "Remember I said I would arrest you for obstructing a policeman?" he asked her, then spoke to the lawyer, "Tell her I can do that."

"He can, Miss Paxton." The lawyer's voice was well modulated. It reminded Chesney of the Devil's when they'd met in the park. "Please have a seat in the waiting area. This won't take long."

Poppy went, trailing small cyclones and thunderstorms.

The lawyer came into the room, unbuttoning his overcoat. Then he shook hands with Chesney and said his name was Robert Trelawney. He sat down next to Chesney while Denby took the seat opposite. The detective produced a card and read from it, the words exactly the same as the young man had heard on countless TV shows and in movies. When his recitation was finished, Denby asked Chesney if he understood his rights.

"Yes."

"What are the charges, Lieutenant?" Trelawney said.

"Common assault. The ADA is considering aggravated assault."

"Grounds?" the lawyer said. Denby showed him the image stored on his phone. Trelawney's face took on an expression that suggested the policeman had just told him a joke but muffed the punchline. "You won't get that past an arraignment," he said. "What else have you got?"

Denby seemed reluctant, but he showed the man the close-up of Chesney rehearsing his opening line. "I've got an expert lip-reader who says the suspect is saying that he's a friend of The Actionary and that he has a message for Ms McCann."

"What expert are we talking about? Koehler? That Gervais woman who testified at the Borgneous trial?"

The detective kept his face straight. "A reliable police source," he said.

Chesney thought it was time to speak. "He's a man who repairs shoes down by the library."

Trelawney stood and buttoned up the lowest button on his overcoat. "You've got nothing. Release my client." He gestured for Chesney to rise.

Denby also got to his feet. "He's a material witness," he said. "He knows the identity of this character who calls himself The Actionary, who is turning the town upside down playing vigilante."

Trelawney chewed the inside corner of his lip. He turned to Chesney. "Is that true?"

The lawyer gave a tiny shake of his head. Chesney knew the man wanted him to say no. But if he told the police he didn't know his other identity, he'd never be able to tell people that he was The Actionary's best friend. And he had come to understand that not being able to play Jimmy Olsen's role as well as Superman's could be a significant handicap as The Actionary's career developed.

The two men were waiting for his answer. He said, "I do know him. We're friends."

Trelawney said, "You can't hold people because you're after their friends. This isn't North Korea."

Denby's face wore the same look Chesney had seen across the poker table, when someone called one of his bluffs. "He's acting as a go-between. He's part of the setup."

Trelawney undid the lowest button again. They sat down. The lawyer said to Chesney, "Did you really have a message from this Actionary person to Ms McCann?"

"Yes."

"Did the message have anything to do with the Actionary's vigilante behavior?"

Chesney took a moment to think about it. "No," he said, "it was personal."

"Whisper the message to me," Trelawney said, cupping a hand to one ear.

Chesney leaned in and whispered, "He wanted me to tell Melda that they couldn't go on a date because he would attract a lot of attention."

"A date?" Trelawney said, straightening up.

Chesney understood that he didn't have to whisper now. "Yes. She wanted him to take her out."

The lawyer looked at Denby. "Have you any evidence that suggests my client is involved in The Actionary's vigilantism?"

Denby looked grim, but finally he said, "No."

"Well, then." Trelawney stood again and his fingers went to the button.

The lieutenant slammed his palm against the tabletop. "I need him!" he said. "He's the only connection we've got to this yo-yo! And if we don't get him under control, somebody's going to get killed."

"No," said Chesney, "they're not."

"Mr Arnstruther," Trelawney said, "I advise you not to say–"

But Denby seized the advantage. "Why not?" he said. "What do you know?" Chesney would have liked to call a time out. He wanted to ask the lawyer if they could do that, but Denby wasn't letting go of the only fingerhold he'd managed to lay on his material witness. "Come on, kid! What do you know?"

"It's a long story," Chesney said. He heard Trelawney sigh. The lawyer relinquished the overcoat button and sat down.

"Start at the beginning," Denby said.

"Well," said Chesney, "I like to play poker with some of the guys from work…"

The lieutenant's phone was on the table between them, where Trelawney had set it down after looking at Chesney silently mouthing his planned opening line. At that moment, the phone vibrated against the battered formica. Denby frowned at it, then scooped it up and glanced at the display, while saying to Chesney, "Don't stop." But then whatever was on the phone's screen registered with him and he pushed a control and said, "Denby. What is it, Frank?"

Chesney couldn't hear what Denby was hearing, but he saw the detective become very interested, even as he was trying to keep any expression off his face.

After a few moments, the lieutenant said, "No, don't interfere. The whole idea is that when that woman's in trouble, Mr Spandex shows up. As long as nobody pulls a knife or a gun, let 'em go at it. I'll be there as soon as I can." He broke the connection and stood up, saying, "This interview will have to be suspended, counselor."

Chesney had heard Denby say, "that woman." Now the young man said, "Is Melda McCann in trouble?"

Denby looked at him coolly. "Hard to say. My partner says she's being stalked."

Chesney got up. "Is someone going to attack her?"

"I wouldn't be surprised," the policeman said. He turned to the lawyer. "Is Poppy Paxton your client, too, counselor?"

"My firm acts for the family. Why?"

Denby blew out his cheeks and said, "Because right now, she is following Melda McCann through Riverside Park. And by the look on her face, my partner thinks when she catches up she's going to be a good candidate for an assault charge."

"I'd better come with you," said Trelawney.

"Sure," said Denby. "Why should the police have all the fun?"

"I want to come, too," said Chesney.

"Oh, no, no, no," said the detective, shaking his head. "The way I see it, Ms Paxton is experiencing an overpowering urge to connect with your best buddy – the one who doesn't wear spandex. And she figures that waling on Melda McCann is a sure-fire way to get him to show up." He looked up at the ceiling with a "maybe-so" expression, then said, "And since that's happened twice, she could be right. So we'll just let things develop. Cause I've got a pretty strong urge to connect with him, myself. And if Mr Action Hero shows, we'll scoop him up." He turned and opened the door, said, "After you, counselor," then paused in the doorway to address Chesney. "And if he doesn't show, we'll want to come back to you."

Trelawney poked his head in the doorway. "I'll be back," he told the young man. "Sit tight and say nothing."

And then they were gone. Chesney sat in the chair and looked at himself in the mirror. Although the room was brightly lit, he felt that he was as far from a pool of light as he had ever been. The habit of a lifetime, a habit almost as powerful as instinct, told him to turn away from the situation. He was not responsible for what Poppy or Melda did. And neither of the women was in serious peril, not with police officers watching. The worst that might happen was that Poppy would get on the wrong end of Melda's pepper-spray. And maybe she even deserved a dose of mace; she had probably been making life less enjoyable for people like Melda – plebeians whose livelihoods depended on pleasing princesses like Poppy – ever since she'd been old enough to stamp her foot and pout.

Nor was Melda completely blameless. Chesney had rescued her from a mugging and then from a beating by Todd, and she had repaid him by using their acquaintanceship to get herself fifteen minutes of fame and TV exposure. In her own way, she was as selfish as Poppy.

And yet... He could hear his mother's voice, from all those Sundays, all those years ago: *The rule is not, "Do as others do," but "do as you would be done by."*

He squirmed in the hard chair. He would have liked to ask his mother's advice – or even Billy Lee Hardacre's.

They seemed to have the benefit of basking in clear pools of light no matter what came their way. But they were both far from this bare room with the lock on the door, and probably occupied with each other and their own concerns. Chesney realized there was only one source of assistance he could turn to.

"Xaphan," he said.

The demon appeared across the table from him, a fresh Churchill glowing in its weasel mouth, its stubby fingers wrapped partway around a tumblerful of dark liquid. "What's up?" it said.

"I have a problem."

The furred brows executed a complex motion that let them go in two directions at once. "Does it have anything to do with fighting crime?"

"I'm not sure," Chesney said. "It may be personal."

"Can't help ya." The demon swigged from its tumbler. "That it? Cause I was in the middle of something."

Chesney noticed that one of the demon's hands was below the table. "What have you got there?" he said.

"Nuttin."

"Show me."

"It's none a ya bizness."

For Chesney, this situation was not confused. He said, "Show me, or my will sends back the liquor and the cigars. Permanently."

The demon's lower lip protruded in defiance.

Chesney said, "I mean it."

Xaphan lifted its concealed hand. It contained five playing cards, all of them clubs, the highest the ace.

"Ace-high flush," Chesney said. "Strong hand."

"I think I'm on a winner," said the demon.

Despite himself, Chesney was interested. "Who are the other players?"

"You wouldn't know 'em. Oh, no, come to think of it, you met Melech."

"You're using my place in the outer circle of Hell to play cards with your friends?"

"They're not friends," Xaphan said. "We don't have friends."

"Don't quibble. You're using my place."

The demon lowered it gaze. "Didn't think you'd mind. We ain't hurtin' nuttin'."

Chesney was not sure if he minded or not. "I thought you guys were always run off your feet," he said. "Where did you find the time?"

"It's eased up a lot lately," Xaphan said. "Plus..." But then it seemed to think better of finishing the thought.

"Plus what?"

"Nuttin' you need to know about."

Chesney was learning to translate demon-speak. "Or something you don't want me to know about," he said. The fiend looked at him in a way that made Chesney think he was being tested. The young man reminded himself that, in this relationship, he was the one who had the will. He met Xaphan's gaze and did not look away first. "So, we can talk about the rules of our relationship, and how that parlays into you having a place to play poker with your... associates." He paused to let that sink in. "Or we could talk about how you could help me with my problem."

The demon glanced at the five clubs, almost wistfully, Chesney thought. Then it said, "So what's this problem?"

"I'm locked in this room. I think someone's watching me through the mirror."

Xaphan didn't even glance at the glass. "They ain't."

"But somebody might come and check on me," the young man said, "and I have to be somewhere else. As The Actionary."

"Let me finish this hand," the demon said.

"I don't have much time."

His assistant disappeared then reappeared so quickly that the only thing Chesney noticed was a slight shimmer and the fact that the cards were gone from its hand. Also, it was smiling. "Awright, let's see what we can do here," it said. "Get outta the chair."

Chesney stood up. Xaphan gestured and suddenly Chesney saw a duplicate of himself sitting where he had been a moment before. His double sat with elbows on the table and chin resting on both fists. The face held no expression until the demon motioned again. Now the duplicate appeared to be deep in thought, with small movements of mouth and eyebrows indicative of important matters being weighed and considered.

"Long as nobody touches it," the fiend said, "you're fine."

"What if somebody does touch him?" Chesney said.

"It ain't a him. It's an it."

"Whatever."

Xaphan gestured again. "There," it said. "Now anybody comes inna room, it throws a fit and passes out. But then we'll have to switch ya back."

"All right," Chesney said, "here's what I need to do."

It was late afternoon in the park. Chesney reckoned that Melda must have booked off early from Sugar 'n Spice. She was walking the same path as the first time he'd rescued her, though this time she was not burdened with shopping bags. But, as before, she knew nothing of his presence because he had had his assistant render him invisible. About thirty paces behind her came Poppy Paxton, her hands jammed into the pockets of her stylish overcoat and her head jutting forward like the prow of one of those ancient ships that used to sink each other by ramming.

"Where are the cops?" Chesney asked Xaphan.

"The one who's shadowin' the redhead is over there, behind those bushes," the demon said. "Plus there's two in a squad car by the park gates."

Chesney looked toward the bushes. "I don't see anything."

"He's keepin' outta sight. This'll help." A large red arrow, like something from an old-fashioned newspaper ad, appeared in the air beyond the bushes, its point aimed at the hidden detective and moving in tandem with him.

"That's good," Chesney said. "Where's Denby and the lawyer?"

"Just about to arrive at the gates. Okay, they're there and now they're gettin' out of the car. The two uniforms are comin' with them." Xaphan pointed at another hedge. "They're keepin' behind those bushes, there."

"Put arrows over them, too," Chesney said. Four more red arrows appeared.

Melda was walking at a brisk pace. The young man saw her glance back the way she had come, but the only person in sight was Poppy. When they made eye contact, Poppy called out, "Hey!"

Melda reacted by slowing her pace for as long as it took her to recognize the other woman as one of her steady customers. "Hey, yourself!" she said, then resumed speed.

"I want to talk to you!" said Poppy. Her heels clicked more rapidly on the asphalt as she strove to catch up with Melda.

"I'm on my own time!" Melda spoke over her shoulder. "I don't want to talk to anybody."

"You'll talk to me!" said Poppy, then added, "bitch!"

The word brought Melda up short. She turned toward her blonde pursuer. "Excuse me?" she said. "What did you call me?"

"You heard me!" Poppy was closing fast. Melda was waiting for her, hands on hips, fingers spread and pointing down. Chesney was glad to see she wasn't reaching into her shoulder-slung purse.

"You got a problem with your nails?" Melda said.

"I got a problem with you!"

Chesney's mother had been shocked when, back in high school, he had come home and told her about two girls who had gone at each other behind the gym. They had punched and kicked like boys, and blood had flowed from one's nose and the other's split lip. The winner had ended up sitting on the loser's chest, holding a hank of her hair so she could smack her head against the concrete until a teacher had pulled her, kicking and swearing, off her dazed opponent. Chesney had seen other girl-fights that he had not told his mother about – she was never reluctant to blame the messenger who brought her unpleasant tidings – and he could see that this confrontation between Poppy and Melda was slipping into a familiar pattern.

He couldn't intervene as The Actionary. That would have made things worse between the combatants. Worse yet, it would have brought him into direct conflict with Lieutenant Denby, and he was pretty sure that a crime-fighter should not disobey a direct order from a police officer. But after a moment's thought, he conceived a plan.

His idea was for the demon to mount a distraction a little farther off in the park. Nothing dangerous, and no one was to get hurt, Chesney had made clear to his assistant. The demon was to borrow a car, then cause it to crash through the hedge that marked the park boundary on this side of the green space. The car would career across the lawn and the walkways, then plunge into the amphitheater – empty at the moment – and tip over. Smoke would emerge, portending a possible fiery, movie-type explosion.

Any police on the scene would have to render assistance. While that was going on, Chesney would approach

Melda and Poppy in disguise and tell them that they were under surveillance and that Denby wanted them to fight so he could arrest both of them and The Actionary. That ought to put an end to the lieutenant's operation and give Chesney time to come up with a long-term solution to the Poppy-Melda imbroglio.

"Let's do it," he said to Xaphan. The demon gestured and the young man looked down at himself to see the disguise. He had not been specific on that score. "Something that prevents them from recognizing me, but it has to make me look like someone they can trust immediately." He'd already had one learning experience concerning the dangers of approaching Melda McCann unexpectedly in the park.

His hands protruded from sleeves of some white material. He looked down and saw that he was wearing a robe that went all the way down to his ankles. Around his waist was a red satin sash from which braided tassels hung. Chesney felt weight when he pulled his head erect. He reached up and felt some kind of tall, stiff headgear; he lifted it from his head and recognized it as a gilded miter.

"No good," he told Xaphan. "They're not going to believe I'm sending the Pope with a message."

"They'd trust him," the demon said. "He's spose ta be completely kosher, ain't he?"

"Something a little less out of the ordinary. And hurry!"

The fiend gestured again. Chesney looked down and saw ordinary street clothes. "Who am I?" he started to say, but even as he spoke he looked over toward the two women and saw that there was no more time. Poppy was saying something in a voice too low to be heard at this distance, while shaking a manicured index finger very close under Melda's nose. Melda's hands had come off her waist and had formed themselves into fists.

"Bring in the car," the young man said to Xaphan, "and let them see me!" This last was called over his shoulder as he ran toward the imminent fistfight.

"You got it!" said the demon, flinging both of its short arms out with a showman's flamboyance. Immediately, the air was filled with the sound of an old-fashioned police siren, rising and falling in a nasal wail.

Chesney ran toward Poppy and Melda. Beyond them, across the park's open lawn, he saw the ten-foot-high hedge burst open. A speeding automobile crashed through it in a shower of leaves and branches. The vehicle had a narrow grill, with two huge round headlights mounted on swept-back fenders. Red lights flashed from behind the chromed radiator. In less than a second, the rest of the car was in view: a long, green hood held closed by black leather straps, a square windshield and a green, box-shaped passenger compartment, with front and rear fenders painted black – and connected by a wide running board.

The car emerged from the hedge, seemed to gather itself, then sped across the grass toward the concrete bowl of the amphitheater, its undulating siren rising in both pitch and volume.

"I always liked that old battlewagon of Alphonse's," Xaphan said.

Chesney could not afford the time to ask for a clarification. Poppy and Melda had broken off their fight to turn and watch the huge old car – a 1928 Cadillac V-16, armor-plated and painted in the Chicago police department's green and black by Al Capone's gang, Chesney would later learn – scream across the park and strike the low rim of the amphitheater. The impact threw the vehicle's nose upwards even as it roared on, and the car stayed airborne for a good two seconds, long enough for it to reach the middle tier of seats before its heavy front end tipped it down and it crashed with a great *whang* of crumpling metal, then flipped end-to-end to land upside-down on its roof. A moment later, smoke eddied up from the engine compartment and a voice from somewhere shouted, "Look out, boys! She's gonna blow!"

By that point in the proceedings, Chesney was standing beside the two women and saying, "Excuse me, ladies." They turned and he saw their eyes widen in surprise that immediately began to shift toward pleasure. Chesney briefly wondered what they were seeing, but he did not vary from the script. He said, "The Actionary – he's a friend of mine – asked me to give you a message." He told them that the police were watching and hoping they would get into a fight, which would draw The Actionary so Lieutenant Denby could arrest them all. "But he's not going to step into a trap, and he would like it very much if you two ladies would not give the police what they're looking for."

He had prepared further lines in response to their expected objections – expected, that is, to come mostly from Poppy; Chesney had come to the conclusion that the rich man's daughter was primed to reject out of hand any suggestion regarding her conduct that did not spring from the mind and will of Poppy Paxton. But now he was surprised to see that she was giving him an almost deferential nod while saying, "It was very kind of you to take the time to come by and tell us, Tom. I think we can–"

"Mr Hanks," Melda said, rummaging in her purse, "could I have your autograph? The girls at the salon will be just–"

"Excuse me," Poppy cut in. "Mr Hanks and I were talking. Why don't you run along?" She turned back to Chesney. "I'm having a little get-together this weekend, Tom. Just a few friends. I wonder if you–"

"Listen, Princess," said Melda, poking a finger into Poppy's shoulder, "you're talking to a friend of my boyfriend." Now she turned to Chesney. "Speaking of which, Actch and I were thinking of a little barbecue this weekend. Maybe you'd like to drop by?"

"I don't know," he said. "I may be busy." Now that he listened to it, he realized that he recognized the voice with which he had been speaking. He had last heard it only recently, when a cable movie channel had rerun *The Green Mile*. He supposed he would have to explain the deception to Melda and Poppy some day, though he doubted either of them would welcome the news that The Actionary didn't really hang out with Hollywood A-list celebrities.

"I've got to go," he said. Beyond the two women, Chesney saw uniformed police officers, along with Denby and a woman in plainclothes who he thought was probably the detective who'd been keeping Poppy under surveillance. They were all standing on the lip of the amphitheater, looking down into the bowl. Denby was shaking his head and his mouth was forming odd shapes, as if the words he wanted to say were too disjointed to get out through a normal vocal apparatus. The other detective had just taken a photograph with her cell phone and now was looking from the screen to the amphitheater in disbelief. The young man could no longer see smoke rising. Xaphan, true to his orders, must have returned the car to wherever he had found it – an automobile museum "in some hick burgh down south," the demon would later report. He had also repaired all the damage.

Denby's face was losing its confusion and rediscovering the anger Chesney had seen when the detective had arrested him. The lieutenant was coming towards them, with a speed and body language that indicated he was forming a new agenda and fully intended to see it carried through.

"I've really got to go," said Chesney. He turned and walked swiftly away, but immediately he heard Denby's voice behind him, loud and angry, calling, "Hey, you! Hold it right there! Police!"

"Xaphan!" Chesney whispered, even though the others couldn't hear him summon his assistant. The demon appeared instantly, floating in the air beside him so that they were at the same eye level. Chesney said, "Get me out of–"

From behind him came a noise he had heard before – a sighing, moaning, keening sound of chill despair – and a freezing wind made the hairs on the back of his neck rise up as if they meant to march over the top of his head and find themselves a warmer home. Chesney turned and saw that a dark, circular hole, almost twice his own height, had appeared in the air behind Poppy Paxton. Framed in the circle was a heavily muscled man covered from pate to toe in a form-fitting costume of solid black, except for the palms of his hands and two slanted, almond-shaped lozenges where his eyes should be, all of which were colored a deep crimson. And now another slash of red appeared as the figure opened its mouth to emit a cruel laugh, revealing lips and tongue the same shade as its eyes.

Poppy turned, already shivering in the frigid wind. Chesney saw her stiffen in shock. He heard her begin a scream that instead turned into a frightened squeak when two crimson-palmed hands took hold of her shoulders and lifted her bodily from the asphalt path. Her head drooped as if his touch had rendered her senseless.

The young man was already sprinting toward the kidnapping, calling, "Xaphan! Costume! Speed!" as he ran. He felt the Actionary suit envelop him, and his velocity suddenly increased so that he sped past Denby and Melda in a blur.

But the figure that had snatched Poppy Paxton matched Chesney's speed. It turned and, hoisting the young woman onto one broad shoulder as if he were a fireman rescuing a child from a burning building, raced away into the darkness beyond. It was a tunnel, Chesney now saw, and the cold, sour wind gave him a good idea where it led.

ELEVEN

Chesney leaped through the opening, his demon gliding beside him. The hole was closing, but he noticed that it was not doing so quickly. Why is that he wondered, even as he took a first step in pursuit?

The kidnapper and his victim were out of sight. Chesney couldn't tell if that was because of the darkness within the tunnel – which was becoming deeper the farther he went into it – or because it turned or twisted ahead of him. A few paces farther on, he discovered that the latter explanation was the correct one, and he was not surprised to learn that the conduit did not curve to left or right, but suddenly angled *down*. He went forward and felt his feet go out from under him and then he was sliding, then outright falling, into blackness, the freezing air stinging his eyes, bringing tears that froze on the cheeks of his mask.

"Xaphan!" he said, "protect my eyes."

"Okay," said the demon, which was dropping unconcernedly beside him, and the stinging instantly stopped. "What about the others?"

"Others?"

The demon gestured upwards with one spiky thumb. Chesney twisted his neck and looked where Xaphan was pointing. In the darkness above him he could make out two other hurtling shapes, their clothing flapping with the speed of their descent. "Yes," he said. "Innocent by-standers don't get hurt, remember?"

"They ain't so innocent," the fiend said. "And they weren't standin' by. They was runnin' and jumpin' to come after us."

"Protect them!" Chesney said.

The demon went on as if he hadn't heard. "Now the frail, maybe, she got mixed up in all this. You could call her a bystander. But that flatfoot, he's out to get you. I think we should just let him freeze."

"No!" said Chesney. "Don't argue! Or you've had your last glass of my rum!"

The fiend shrugged its weasel shoulders. "Your call," it said.

Chesney looked up again. Lieutenant Denby and Melda McCann continued to fall through the darkness with him, but he could see motion now. The young woman was pushing down the skirt of her beauty salon uniform, pushed up by air resistance, and their faces no longer appeared to be coated with frost. That was a relief, but he had no idea how he was going to explain what was happening to them. He decided he would just have to deal with the situation as it developed – his first obligation was to rescue Poppy – then worry about repercussions afterward.

Time passed and they continued to fall. For a while, Chesney could hear snatches of speech between Melda and the detective, but then there was nothing but the rush of air past his ears. He supposed they had run out of things to say.

The speed of his fall did not slacken, but it seemed to him that there was a change in the orientation of the shaft below him. A few moments later, it became more than a seeming, as the wall behind him gradually curved inward enough to rub against his heels. Then his shoulders and his buttocks were in contact and in a very short while he was no longer falling but sliding feet-first at great speed down an inclined tube. Gradually, the angle of the incline lessened, though the speed seemed to remain the same and he felt no sense of friction from his dorsal contact with what was now once again the floor of an inclined tunnel. His assistant kept formation a few feet above him.

Chesney bent forward and sat up, the sour wind rushing past his face. He peered down what he could see of the tunnel between his feet and thought that the darkness lessened ahead. A few more seconds and he was sure of it. He could see a gray circle, small but growing larger. He looked over his shoulder and saw Melda and Denby sitting upright too, and now there was light enough to see their faces: the young woman's full of fear and a determination not to show it, the policeman's grim with purpose. In Denby's hand was an automatic pistol.

The stinking wind grew stronger and over the rush of its passage along the tunnel, Chesney could hear it wuthering and moaning past the tunnel mouth. The circle of gray light, dim as winter twilight on a clouded day, now gaped wide; beyond, the young man could see the barren, stony plain of Hell's outer circle. And out on the emptiness stood the figure in black and crimson, arms akimbo, fists on hips, waiting. At its feet lay a crumpled heap that was Poppy Paxton.

"Is it a demon?" Chesney asked Xaphan.

"What, that?" said his assistant. "Nah! That's the mug Melech works for, the one that wants to rule the world."

"Blowdell?"

"That's the bird."

"All right," said Chesney, "then I'll need strength and speed."

The weasel face looked askance. "You gonna take him on?"

"If I have to. I have to rescue Poppy."

The demon made a noise of discomfort. "You don't get no help. Hell don't fight Hell, remember? Them's the rules."

The fiend's reminder came as Chesney reached the end of the tunnel. At the last moment, some imperceptible force decelerated his slide so that he exited out onto the plain at a gentle speed, and with the floor of the tube at about knee-height above the gritty surface he took a few steps forward then stopped to study the enemy.

Blowdell regarded him in turn. Chesney could not see the expression behind the mask, but the man's wide-legged stance and the cocked angle of his head suggested that his opponent believed he had an unbeatable hand and did not disdain to show it. That prompted a thought. The young man spoke quietly to his assistant. "Does he know the rules?"

Xaphan did his Cagney shoulder hitch. "Only if Melech told him."

"And would Melech have told him?"

"Only if he asked."

"Can you ask Melech if he did?"

The demon consulted some inner process then said, "Sure."

"Then do so," said Chesney.

"No."

"No, you won't ask Melech? Or, no, he didn't tell Blowdell?"

"That's the one," said Xaphan.

Chesney needed the situation to be clear. "So all he's got is what he'd normally have?"

"Yep."

"And me?"

"You've got whatever you'd normally bring to the party."

Despite the perpetual murk under Outer Hell's lowering, wind-torn sky, it seemed to Chesney that he now stood at the center of a pool of clear light. He remembered a line from an episode of *The Driver*: "Time to cut the cake," he said.

"There's cake?" said Xaphan, looking around.

"Maybe later," said The Actionary.

Behind Chesney, while they'd been speaking, Lieutenant Denby and Melda McCann had emerged from the tunnel. The policeman stepped past him, saying, "Stay right there. You're under arrest."

"Lieutenant–" Chesney began.

But the detective raised the hand that was unencumbered by a pistol and said, over his shoulder, "I'll deal with you later." A bitter gust of wind tried to peel his suit jacket off, and he paused to button it and pull up his collar. He looked around at the barren land and up at the sky, then shook his head as if these were matters to be dealt with later. Then he took a few more steps toward the villain and brought up the gun in both hands, saying, "You in the funny outfit. You are under arrest for kidnapping. You have the right to remain silent, but anything you say may be–"

Blowdell had been watching him come. Now he threw back his head and laughed. It was an artificially augmented sound, a booming peal of derision that overpowered the howling wind. "You're a little out of your jurisdiction, Lieutenant," he said.

At Blowdell's feet, Poppy stirred, recovering consciousness. She pushed herself up on straightened arms, looked about her, dazed and shivering, and saw Chesney in his Actionary guise and the policeman with the leveled gun. She followed the direction of Denby's aim, looking up to see Blowdell looming over her, and she screamed. This time, the villain did not cut her off, and when she had finished her first shriek, she went on to top it with another.

"Let her go!" said Denby.

"Where?" said Blowdell, gesturing to the emptiness around them.

Denby spoke firmly, although his teeth were chattering. "Put your hands in the air and kneel down!"

Blowdell made a small noise with his teeth and tongue and lazily lifted one hand to point at the policeman's pistol. A crackling bolt of black energy shot out of the villain's extended finger. When it struck the gun in Denby's hand, the weapon shattered like ice, the pieces flying in all directions. One struck the detective's face, the impact causing him to spin around and gasp in pain. Chesney saw blood fly from a gash on the man's cheek.

Chesney stepped up beside the policeman. "Lieutenant," he said, "you can't do anything here. Better leave this to me."

The detective looked at the blood on his hand, then his gaze took in the emptiness around them as if he were seeing it for the first time. "Where in Hell are we?" he said.

"The outer circle," Chesney said.

"Exactly," Blowdell's enhanced voice boomed, and he indulged in another exaggerated laugh. At his feet, Poppy tried to crawl away, but her captor flicked one hand in a casual gesture toward her and she sprawled as if a weight had landed on her back.

The villain laughed again. "Wish I'd known about this years ago," he said. "Ah, well, plenty of opportunity to make up for lost time. The question now is," – and here he turned his crimson eyes on Chesney – "are you going to be with me?"

"Shouldn't that be followed by 'or against me?'" said Chesney.

"No," said Blowdell. "You're either with me, or you're simply... not."

The young man knew that when people were pondering momentous issues they often cupped their chins with thumb and forefinger. He did this now and half turned, so that he could say to Melda and the detective, "Come and stand behind me." He saw them look at each other then they both came forward. Out of the corner of his mouth, he said, "Have you got your pepper spray?"

Her voice was a whisper but he heard it. "Yes."

"Keep it ready."

"What good can that do?" said Denby. "You saw what he did to my weapon."

"I know something he doesn't know," said Chesney. In his boyhood encounters with bullies and lunch money thieves, he had often known things his oppressors hadn't, but on those occasions knowledge hadn't been power. This time, Chesney's mind was bathed in clear light. Now he broke off his pretense of contemplation and said to Blowdell, "I don't think I can do that."

The villain shook his head. "Ever hear the expression 'irresistible force?'" Without waiting for an answer, he said, "They actually have that here. And when I say, 'they,' I mean, 'I.' Here's a taste of it."

With that, Blowdell raised one of his oversized arms and threw out one hand toward Chesney. Nothing happened. He repeated the action, then looked at his palm in puzzlement. He thrust his hand toward the stony ground to one side; again, the black energy struck from his fingertip and solid rock cracked and exploded, fragments spinning away in all directions, while a fountain of dust and stone chips flew into the air.

A jagged chunk of gray rock about the size of an egg landed at Chesney's feet. He bent and picked it up then went forward, saying to Denby and Melda, "Keep me between you and him."

He didn't wait for an answer, but kept moving forward until he was only a few feet from Blowdell. He looked at Poppy, saw that she was not injured, just held in place by some invisible force. He looked up at his opponent and had a brief flash of memory from childhood: the many times he had been confronted by bigger boys – and, one time, a particularly aggressive neighbor girl – and the stages through which those encounters had inevitably proceeded, until little Chesney was bruised, scraped, sometimes bleeding, and always stained by his own tears. This time it will be different, he thought.

He spoke privately to his assistant. "Xaphan, if I hit him in the head with this rock, will he feel it?"

"Sure."

"And Melech won't interfere?"

"Not allowed to."

Chesney hefted the rock in his hand, saw Blowdell's red eye spots follow the motion. "Do you know the story of David and Goliath?" the young man said.

Blowdell studied the gloved index finger that had spewed black force before. He flexed it and pulled at it with his other hand. Then he pointed it dramatically at Chesney. Again, nothing happened. The villain looked at the finger again, shook it, and tried once more. Nothing.

"Hey," said Chesney, and when he had Blowdell's attention, he flung the rock.

Chesney's childhood had included a long history of the throwing of objects, starting with beanbags in kindergarten and moving up through softballs, snowballs, dodgeballs, basketballs and regulation baseballs. At summer camp, he'd tried his hand with lawn darts, horseshoes, quoits and – memorably for the counselor in charge – he had once even discharged an arrow from a bow.

His success rate was minimal. Any correlation between the throwing of the object and its arrival at its intended destination was entirely random. Chesney had been reliably informed by a physical education teacher who held an advanced degree in human kinesiology that the sides of barns need fear nothing from anything flung at them from the hand of Chesney Arnstruther.

But all of those previous attempts had been conducted out in the regions of darkness, never from within pools of pure, cool light. Chesney was conscious of the irony of the present situation – he actually was standing on a darkling plain – as he threw the jagged rock in the recommended overhand style he had been shown time and again by the kinesiologist, but had never before been able to master. It flew straight and true and he saw it strike Blowdell's forehead. He even heard the sound of its impact, despite the constant wail and whuffle of the wind. He also heard the "Ow!" that came from the villain as Blowdell raised a hand to the wound, felt the torn cloth of his mask and brought away gloved fingers whose tips were smeared with blood.

Chesney said, "You can't hurt me, Blowdell, but I can hurt you!" It wasn't true but Chesney had no qualms about lying in a good cause.

Blowdell touched his glove to the wound again, then saw even more blood this time. "That's not fair!" he cried.

"Well," said Chesney, stooping to pick up another rock, "that's why they call it Hell."

He saw Blowdell pull himself back together. "But I can hurt her!" he said. He gestured toward the young woman at his feet. "How about I splatter your girlfriend all over Hell's half acre?"

"I don't have a girlfriend," said Chesney. Behind him, he heard a one-syllable sound from Melda McCann but ignored it and continued, "Besides, don't you need her for the campaign?"

"That plan's no longer operative," said Blowdell. "I've seen the numbers. People lose interest in a recovered kidnap victim. A dead one has much deeper impact and far more longevity. The idiots come and pile teddy bears and bouquets against her front gate."

Poppy moaned and tried to crawl again, but the invisible weight held her down.

Chesney knew the man was right. He had crunched the numbers himself. But he said, "W.T. Paxton would never have agreed to that."

"True," said Blowdell. "But he'll be a much more motivated anti-crime candidate when he's striving to avenge the murder of his blonde, blue-eyed daughter." He laughed again, the pain in his forehead apparently forgotten. "She had so much to live for, cruelly cut down in her prime. Now her grieving father vows never to let another parent suffer as he has suffered. The copy writes itself."

"Except," said Chesney, "if you kill her, I'll keep throwing rocks at you until you're dead. Which, by the way, means you'll have to pay up your side of the deal you made with the guy who runs this place."

"Boss," said Xaphan quietly in Chesney's ear, "that ain't strictly true. Youse guys can only die in your world."

"You mean I can't kill him here? And he can't kill Poppy?"

"Nope."

"But I can really hurt him?"

"You can make him wish he was dead," the demon said. "I mean, that's the whole point of this place."

"But he can really hurt Poppy."

"I can fix that," said Xaphan, "so fast she won't even feel it."

The pool of light remained strong in Chesney's mind.

Then a thought occurred. "Xaphan, you are being more helpful than you used to be."

"I been thinkin' about what he's been sayin', how things are changin'," the demon said. "But I kinda like our setup. I wouldn't wanna see it all go west on me."

"But aren't you breaking some rule?"

The demon looked as thoughtful as a fanged weasel could contrive. "Bending. Anybody asks, I'm gonna say you're a special case."

"Thank you," said Chesney.

"Don't mention it," said the demon. "And I mean, really, don't gab it around."

Blowdell interrupted. "I suppose you've been consulting with your demon," he said. "So have I."

"Then you'll know you can't kill anybody here," said Chesney.

"I know I'm not supposed to," the villain corrected him. "But you should remember, the whole reason I'm here is because I know the old rules are changing. You taught me that, and I suppose I ought to be grateful. Though, somehow, I'm... not."

"That doesn't surprise me," said Chesney.

"The way I see it, he who first takes hold of the new regime takes home the prize. And I'm a taker."

The rock in Chesney's had felt reassuringly solid. "Okay," he said, "take this." He flung the stone and again it went unerringly toward Blowdell's head. But this time, the villain moved the target to one side and the missile flew harmlessly by.

Blowdell stood with hands on hips again. "You want me," he said, "you come and get me."

Chesney knew how to throw a punch. He'd seen it done countless times. He'd never been able to translate that knowledge into actual achievement – at least not without

demonic assistance, which in this case would be against
the rules – but he felt the cool light surround him as he
stepped forward.

When he neared where the opponent stood, waiting,
he realized that having Poppy Paxton between them
would be a hindrance. So instead of going directly at
Blowdell, he circled around him. He'd seen that done in a
lot of movies and TV shows, and he was not surprised to
see that it worked here in Hell. As he moved to his right,
the villain turned with him. In not too many steps, he was
facing the other man and the young woman was lying to
one side. Time to do it, he thought.

Chesney had no real plan for the fight; he would hit
Blowdell as hard and as often as he could until he won.
But there was a simple trick he'd once seen used in a
schoolyard tussle and he employed it now. He cocked his
right fist back and went straight at the opponent. Blowdell
balled his own gloved hands and crouched to meet the attack. As he came within striking range, Chesney drew the
right fist even farther back and, as Blowdell's eyes were
drawn to the motion, the young man brought up his left
and drove it straight into the villain's mask-covered nose.

The shock went up his arm. Blowdell's head snapped
back just like the kid's had in that long-ago schoolyard.
Chesney did what he had seen the other boy do, and
brought his already-cocked right fist around in a looping
roundhouse that connected exactly where the left had.

The villain had been rocked by the first punch. The second caught him when he was already back on his heels
and he took an involuntary step backward. Chesney
stepped in and used the right again, although his knuckles
were stinging from the first impact. This time he tried a
straightforward punch, putting his shoulder and all the
momentum of his forward motion into it. The shock of

impact went right up to his shoulder, but he heard a *crack* and felt something give in Blowdell's nose.

The other man brought up both hands to cover the injury, then reached to the back of his neck and pulled off the mask that covered his head. He let it drop and put one hand to his nose, which was pouring out blood and looked to be half again the size it had been the last time Chesney had seen Blowdell.

"You broke my nose!" the villain said.

"You still feel like a taker?" Chesney said. "Because we could see how much of that you want to take." It sounded to the young man like just the kind of thing Malc Turner would say under the circumstances.

"You bastard!" Blowdell blubbered through a stream of blood and mucus. Chesney thought the whine in the man's voice meant that the fight was over, but as he began to lower his fists, Blowdell charged at him, swinging both arms in an uncoordinated fluster of wild punches.

Chesney did not have time to consider the irony of his situation: the many times he had been the bleeding-nosed combatant, rushing at some more able fistfighter in just such a useless, rage-filled frenzy, only to be peppered and popped until he lay sobbing on the ground.

Except that, in this case, he didn't get to pepper and pop Blowdell. The man's sudden rush caught him by surprise, one of the unaimed blows striking his temple hard enough to make his head ring, then the villain's bulk collided with him and knocked him flying.

His back and shoulders skidded over grit and sharp stones, his Actionary costume protecting his flesh. But the suit conferred no invulnerability from the effects, a moment later, of Blowdell's leaping on him. The bigger man's weight knocked the air from Chesney' lungs. The young man was lucky that he had windmilled his arms as he'd fallen backwards, so that his arms were outstretched when Blowdell landed on him; if the villain's considerable mass had pinned his limbs to his chest, Chesney would have been in real trouble. He had seen bigger kids pin smaller ones beneath them in just that way, and things always went poorly for the underdog.

He was lucky, too, that Blowdell was no more handy at fisticuffs than Chesney – and that his bulk was mostly flab and untoned muscle. So when the bigger man got himself up onto his knees, his hams compressing Chesney's midriff, and raised a fist to bring it down in a hammer blow on Chesney's forehead, the young man found he had options. This was the first fistfight of his life that had not begun with disaster and then gone downhill; so far he had landed three telling blows, all on the same target; he opted to reinforce success – he gave Blowdell's battered nose its fourth thumping.

The villain emitted a scream that was mostly squawk. His eyes filled with tears, and he flinched backwards. That allowed Chesney to sit up, put both hands flat against his opponent's chest and push Blowdell off him. The bigger man fell back and rolled to one side, then got to what would have been his hands and knees if one of those hands hadn't been cupping his nose.

Chesney stood up. This would have been the time to kick Blowdell hard in his well-padded ribs, but that wasn't a hero's move. So he said, in the voice he always gave Malc Turner when he was reading a Driver adventure, "Had enough?"

He could see Blowdell's lips moving, though he couldn't hear anything. "I said, have you had enough?"

A hard hand closed on the back of Chesney's neck, clawed fingertips met over his larynx. The Actionary costume protected him, but could not prevent his being lifted bodily from the ground and shaken like a puppet in the hands of an angry child. Then Chesney was flying through the filthy air, fast and far, turning over and over, rising almost to the base of the scudding clouds. Now he was falling, the rock-strewn surface coming up at him with unforgiving speed. He wondered if the suit could cushion the impact, then he was softly descending, and being rotated so that when he touched down he landed lightly on the balls of his feet.

"You all right, boss?" Xaphan said, releasing him from a stubby-fingered grasp.

"Yes. What happened?"

"Melech," said the demon, in a tone of disbelief, "...broke the rules!"

"Have I still got speed?" Chesney said, looking at the tiny, distant figures across the plain.

"Yeah, but you don't need it," said Xaphan, and even as the fiend spoke Chesney ceased to be where he had been flung and was standing confronting Blowdell. The villain had got to his feet, his nose completely healed. His demon stood beside him, its facial worms wriggling and twining themselves around each other in a show of agitation.

"Now we'll see," said the man in the crimson suit. "Get him!"

Melech fixed its pale eyes on Chesney and flexed its long, root-like fingers as it raised both arms above its head.

"Hold it!" said Xaphan.

"Stay out of this!" said the villain's demon.

"You don't touch my boss!"

Now the two fiends faced each other, Melech's arms poised. Xaphan threw down its cigar. Chesney heard a low sound; it was a moment before he realized that his demon was growling.

Melech said, "My guy has got to win. There's a lot riding on him!"

"Touch my guy and you're breaking the rules," Xaphan said. "You forget what happens when you break those rules?"

Melech made a sound like an old man clearing his throat. "Don't talk to me about rules. There are no rules any more!" it said. "All of this is winding up! We're getting a whole new deal!"

"Yeah, well I already got my deal!" said Xaphan. "It's a sweet deal and you ain't screwin' it up! Lay a finger on my guy and I'll fragmentize ya!"

For a long moment the two fiends faced each other. Chesney sensed that something was poised on a knife-edge balance. Then he saw Blowdell's lips moving. The villain was whispering something in his demon's ear, a direct reversal of the usual relationship. And now Melech let out a shriek that outdid the wind. The demon swung both its arms down in a motion that brought its hands together like a diver's, the pointed, black-nailed fingertips aimed at Chesney. He saw a crackling of dark energy form around the end of the digits, then his view was blocked as Xaphan leapt into the air to interpose itself between him and Melech.

The energy that came from Melech's hands was like the stygian force that Blowdell had flung against Denby's pistol, but far stronger. To Chesney, sheltered by his assistant, it seemed that a dark aura blossomed between the two demons. Xaphan was driven back against him. The young man stumbled and backstepped, but Xaphan still hung in the air, shielding him against the continuous blast. Yet it seemed to the young man that his assistant had lost some of its substance, as if Melech's blast had thinned whatever nonmatter Chesney's demon was made of. He saw the weasel head droop, the short arms drop to Xaphan's sides as if the demon had suddenly become exhausted.

But then his assistant's head came up. Xaphan did an exaggerated version of the Cagney shoulder hitch, as if shaking off the effects of a punch. Then it flung wide its short arms and clapped its stub-fingered hands together. The impact of palm meeting palm rang like thunder. A burst of invisible force sprang from Xaphan's hands and struck Melech, sending the other demon skidding backwards on the heels of its long-toed feet, leaving two parallel tracks in the rock. Now it was Melech's turn to shake itself, but Chesney saw that holes had appeared in its form, as if it had been shot by a cartoon scattergun.

From Melech came a sound like large angry bees. The worms at the center of its face stuck straight out, their tiny mouths open as if in silent screams. It brushed with long-fingered hands at its front, fretfully, as if dislodging errant sparks thrown from a bonfire. Some of the holes in its body shrank and closed themselves, though others gaped wide so that Chesney could see through Melech's torso the dim and barren plain beyond. And now Blowdell's demon looked at Xaphan with eyes like blue coals.

"Get down, boss," Chesney's demon said. "Flatten out." The young man dropped to the ground as Melech wove its arms in a complex series of gestures. The young man sensed energy flowing into the demon, and the bone-pale face seemed to glow with a ghastly light.

"No, you don't," said Xaphan. Its two palms were still pressed together from the thunderclap. Now the weasel-headed demon ripped its hands apart while at the same time shouting out a multi-syllabic word that Chesney forgot even as he heard it. A roiling torrent of force, the color of a dead star, erupted from between Xaphan's palms and struck Melech square in the midriff. The effect was like turning a jet of boiling oil against an ice sculpture: the worm-nosed demon's substance shredded and melted, dissolving upward toward its neck and downward to its ankles, until in a moment, all that was left of its corporeality was head and feet, the latter resting on the former.

A side-eddy of the blast struck Blowdell, throwing him to the ground, where he lay on his back, inert, for several heartbeats. Then he rolled over and began shakily to rise. Chesney looked to the side and saw that Denby had crawled to where Poppy still lay and had protected her with his body. Melda was on her knees, looking dazed, but the young man saw that she had gotten her can of pepper spray from her purse and was holding it down by her side, a finger ready on the button.

Xaphan flew over to where Melech's remains lay. The blasted demon's long toes were wriggling, as if trying to get a grip on the air. The head sat upright, its stump of a neck resting on the insteps, and the eyes glared up at Xaphan.

"What were you thinking?" Chesney's demon said.

But the answer came from another voice. And from another direction. "More to the point," the voice said, "what is going on here?"

Xaphan looked up, startled, then its head hunched down into its shoulders and its eyes looked everywhere but up.

Chesney lifted his head. Suspended in the air, on a throne of writhing, intertwined snakes that looked to be fashioned of living black iron, their eyes and tongues the color of rubies, the Devil looked down on the scene. Chesney had thought he had seen Satan angry before. Now he knew that he had never seen him more than irritated.

"Um," said Xaphan.

"Wrong answer," said the Devil, raising a black-nailed finger.

"Wait!" said Chesney. The finger remained poised, but the eyes that the ruler of Hell turned on the young man sent a chill through him, as if his bones had turned to marble that had seasoned a thousand years in an underground tomb. But he swallowed and kept his voice calm as he said, "I can explain everything."

TWELVE

They retired to Chesney's comfortable room. He had Xaphan raise a fire in the fireplace to warm the three visitors who lacked the protection his Actionary costume gave him. His demon also unobtrusively expanded the size of the premises, adding a raised dais on which the Devil naturally parked his dark throne. Satan sat with one elbow on an arm of the great chair – the armrest was formed by the slowly undulating body of a huge black mamba – then rested his bearded chin on a closed fist. His lightless eyes passed over the two demons, then paused to regard Blowdell, who did not meet his gaze. Now the Devil looked at each of the three shivering humans, Melda met his gaze, albeit with difficulty, and put her arms protectively around Poppy. Lieutenant Denby stepped in front of the two women.

"How chivalrous," said Satan, though his tone made it clear that chivalry was not a code he honored.

"I am a–" Denby began, but had to break off when a dry throat put a crack in his voice. He swallowed and tried again, pointing at Blowdell, "I am a policeman, and that man is under arrest for kidnapping, resisting arrest and assault on a police officer."

"No," said the Devil, "he isn't."

"There's no extradition from Hell," Blowdell said. He laughed and looked toward Satan as if expecting the joke to be shared. The look he got in return could have frozen lava. The villain took a step backward.

The entity on the throne pointed a finger at the detective. "You will not speak again in my presence without my leave." Denby opened his mouth to protest, but no sound came out. The Devil was already ignoring him, speaking to the other humans. To Chesney he said, "I do not care about your picayune squabbles, except when they foment discord among my subjects. You said you could explain. You will do so, now."

Chesney felt himself far from a pool of light. He said, "I would like to bring in the man who advised me the last time we had a... problem to resolve."

"Hardacre?" said the Devil, shaking his head. "I don't want him here. He smells of Throne."

"He understands it all better than I do," the young man said.

"Do the best you can," said Satan, "and do so quickly. I am not known for my patience. Why are my subjects fighting each other?"

Chesney did not really know the answer. If it had been a question of numbers, of describing a complex algorithm, he could have laid it all out in precise detail. But this was a matter of behavior: human behavior, about which he knew little; and demon behavior, about which he knew even less. Again, he wished that Billy Lee Hardacre were there.

"I'm waiting," said the Devil, in a tone that said he wouldn't be waiting much longer.

Chesney's eyes cast about the room, as if the answer might pop out of the walls or furniture. His gaze met

Melda's, and he saw her nod her head to encourage him. "Go, Actionary," she said, softly.

But this was not the kind of problem The Actionary could solve with a display of fisticuffs. I'm not the one to explain this, Chesney thought. It should be the Reverend Billy Lee.

Then another voice spoke in his head. *It has to be you, because you're the one who's standing here. So get on with it.*

The Devil tapped a finger on the head of a black cobra. "Speak!" he said.

"All right," Chesney said, but before he began, he reached up and pulled the mask and cowl from his head. For some reason, he felt that he should do this as himself. When his face appeared, Denby scowled and tried to say something; Poppy came far enough out of her funk to look offended; but Melda's eyes opened wide, as if he were a magician who'd just pulled off a snappy little trick. She gave a short laugh, and the sound of it put courage into the young man.

"It's all changing," he said. "I don't know why or how, but there's a new book being written, though nobody knows what it's going to say."

The Devil made a gesture of angry dismissal. "Don't start that again. I am real. I am not some character in a book."

Chesney was going to argue the point, but the Devil raised an admonitory finger and the young man changed his mind. "All right, fine," he said, "you don't believe you're a character in a book, but" – he pointed at Blowdell – "*he* does. He believes that everything is winding up, and that he'll never have to make good on the deal he made with you. More to the point, he's convinced that demon you assigned to him that he's right."

Melech's head still rested on its feet on the floor before the dais. The Devil's eyes narrowed as he turned his attention to the demon's remnants. "Is that so?" he asked. Melech's reply was inaudible, but Satan apparently understood the gist of it. He leaned forward in the throne and flicked a hand as if batting away a fly. What was left of Blowdell's demon exploded soundlessly into an expanding cloud of dust that disappeared almost as soon as it had formed. Chesney saw Blowdell relax and realized the man had been holding his breath.

Now Satan turned his face toward Xaphan. "What of you?"

Chesney spoke up. "He told Melech to abide by the rules. 'Hell doesn't fight Hell,' he said. Then he defended me when Melech tried to destroy me."

"That's what happened," Chesney's demon said.

"To whom are you loyal?" Satan said.

"To you, boss. All the way."

"And how far is 'all the way?'"

Xaphan shook its head. "That one's outta my league. I just do my job."

The Devil looked at the drinks cabinet. "And enjoy the perks," he said.

Xaphan thought this was a good moment to study its spatted shoes.

The figure on the throne turned to Blowdell. "You," he said, "what do you have to say?"

With a motion of his chin, Blowdell indicated Chesney. "He's lying," he said. "I made a deal and I intend to stick with it."

Satan stroked one finger along the line of his jaw and studied the costumed villain. "Contract," he said, to no one in particular. He held up one hand and a parchment scroll appeared in it. He opened it and studied the words written on the stiff, dry skin. After a moment he placed a finger at a point on the page and read, "'The parties swear to honor in full faith the provisions sworn hereto. Failure to do so renders this agreement null and void.'" He looked at Blowdell. "Have you honored this contract in full faith?" he said.

Blowdell drew himself up. "I have."

"Hmm," said the Devil. He sketched a complex figure in the air, and glowing lines followed his fingertip then faded. When the last mote of light dimmed away, a ghostly wraith hung in the air before the throne. Chesney saw that it was a transparent version of Melech, as flimsy as gossamer.

The demon's reappearance caused Blowdell to flinch. The Devil noticed. "You thought the witness was gone?" he said.

"I…"

Satan turned back to the rippling apparition. "Melech," he said, "if you wish to shorten your period of reconstitution, speak now: did this man suborn you?"

Melech's voice was the faintest whisper. "He did."

"What did he offer you?"

"Kingdoms, pleasures." The wraith paused as if needing to gather strength, then it said, "Liberty."

At that, the Devil's face grew very dark indeed though his eyes blazed with a fearsome energy. "Whom else did he coax to perfidy?"

"Azraïl," whispered Melech, "Tammaz, Broche, and Urian."

"Is that all?"

"Yes."

Chesney had seen the ruler of Hell irritated. He had seen him angry. Now he saw him furious. The air in the room crackled with energy. Every hair on every human's head stood on end. Even the flames in the fireplace drew back as if in fear. It seemed to the young man that they were trying to climb the flue and escape.

Blowdell had edged away. He cast about for an exit, but the room was doorless and without windows. The entity on the throne sought him out and pointed a finger. "Our agreement is void," he said.

"Does that mean," the villain said, "that I can go?"

The Devil's smile was even less pleasant than that of the dagger-fanged toad that had been his first glimpse of Hell. "No," Satan said. "But your having entered into a pact with me means that your insignificance is mine upon the moment of your demise."

"My insignificance?" said Blowdell. "What is that?"

"You'll find out," said the Devil, "but first..." He pointed a finger again, but this time the extended digit became the source of a narrow lance of sickly green light. Then finger moved and the thin line of energy moved with it. It passed though Blowdell's right wrist and his hand fell off, leaving a smoking stump. The man screamed and reached with his other hand to hold the injured wrist. But the green light moved again, and his left hand joined the right on the carpet.

Blowdell raised the two stumps before him. His face was contorted by a rictus of agony and disbelief. The finger moved once more, and Blowdell's right foot was cut from under him. This time, his scream faded to a moan as he toppled over onto one side, bringing up his legs in a fetal curl. He sobbed then screamed again as his left foot was severed. There was no blood, the green light cauterizing even as it cut.

Chesney was surprised to feel sympathy for Blowdell. The man was a bully, after all, and was only getting what he deserved. He stepped forward, but it was Melda who said, "That's enough!"

She had been kneeling with an arm around Poppy. Now she stood up, and said, "Leave him alone!" Chesney saw the pepper spray in her hand and realized she meant to use it.

The Devil turned his eyes on her and she flinched but stood her ground. "There's no need to be cruel," she said. "You've beaten him."

"Cruelty," said Satan, "is my... idiom. You'll see what I mean when I come to deal with you."

"You'll leave her alone," Chesney said. "She's not beholden to you."

"Think you so?" said the Devil. He gestured to the air and an image appeared: a young girl stealing a bottle of mascara from a variety store; the same girl, older now, whispering to another girl behind a concealing hand, then both turning to regard a third girl in an ugly dress and laughing while tears welled in their victim's eyes; a young woman, recognizable now as Melda, naked on a bed in a shadowed room, while a man Chesney recognized as Todd Milewski shed his last item of clothing and showed her his arousal. As the image of Melda reached for him, Chesney said, "Stop it!"

The Devil threw him a glance, and the young man realized that the display had been for his sake. "She'll be mine," Satan said. "Most of you come to me."

"No," said Chesney.

"As I told you once," the Devil said, "I did not make the rules. If you have a problem with them, you should complain to another quarter." He returned his attention to Blowdell, curled on the carpet, from whom came a continuing keening whine. The Devil rotated a finger in a small circle, and the green light lanced out to cut a dollar-sized piece of flesh from the villain's shoulder. The man screamed again and tried to crawl away. The Devil's green lance followed him, pricking and slicing.

Chesney saw the despair in Melda's face begin to change to hopeless determination. The hand that held the pepper spray began to rise. His own hands still tingled with augmented strength. Now he stepped to Blowdell and took hold of the villain's head, a palm to each temple. "I'm sorry," he said, then he twisted. He heard a sharp *crack*. The moaning stopped and the ravaged body hung limp in his grasp. He let it fall.

"Oh," said Melda, "poor man." Chesney did not know if her pity was for Blowdell or for him.

"Ah, the hero acts at last," said the Devil, as the green light winked out. "And do you think that ends it?" He indicated the screen that had been showing Melda's sins. It cleared then showed a new image: a naked and trembling Blowdell stood before a great brass gate that pierced a wall made of huge blocks of black stone. A winged and tailed demon stepped out of the gate, seized Blowdell's soul by the nape of his neck and thrust him inside.

The Devil chuckled and sat back on his throne. "You were explaining it all to me," he said.

"I'm finished explaining," Chesney said. "We're leaving."

Another cruel smile. "How?"

Chesney looked at Xaphan. The demon's head had remained down but now it cast a sideways glance of inquiry at Hell's ruler. "I think I need someone to tell me what's what," it said.

The Devil stroked his jaw again. "You serve him," he said, indicating Chesney. Then he looked at Melda, Poppy and the policeman. "Not them." To Chesney, he said, "I have committed myself not to harm you. To these," – he languidly waved a hand toward the three humans – "I have made no promises at all."

"You can't keep us in Hell," Melda said. "We're not dead."

"There are precedents," Satan said, "governing those who enter my realm voluntarily."

"What precedents?" she said.

"I am not required to tell you."

"Poppy didn't come voluntarily," Melda said. "She was snatched."

"Then she can launch an appeal," the Devil said.

"Where? To who?"

"Whom," said Satan, "and again, I am not required to tell you."

As they spoke, Chesney could see this was not going to resolve well. Again he wished he had Billy Lee to advise him. Or his mother. She was an expert on deducing the motivations of evil people so she could probably have sussed out where Satan was steering this situation.

Oh, for a pool of light, he thought. Then that other voice spoke in his head again, saying, "No use wishing. Remember what the angel said when last you negotiated with Satan. And Chesney did remember: "Your damnable pride," the Throne had said. And when he followed that thought, groping in the murk of his odd mind, he found an answer.

"You don't want them," he told the ruler of Hell. "You want me."

The Devil widened his eyes, as if the concept was novel. "Why would I want you?"

"Because I've caused you a lot of trouble. And you've decided that the apology wasn't enough."

Satan smiled almost indulgently. "You are right. All this trouble began with you, and it continues to grow. But we have an agreement. You may not be harmed, you may not be tempted, you may not be turned."

"Not by you," said Chesney. He saw it now. "But I can choose to put myself outside our agreement. I have free will."

"Indeed you do. And what might you want to do with that will?"

The idea broke suddenly into Chesney's mind, like a light switched on in a dim room. He remembered what Billy Lee had said about characters in books: they were what they did, and they were never surer than when they were doing what their natures demanded they do, putting it all on the line. He looked into the hard, shadowed face before him and said, "I believe I'd like to play you a few hands of poker," Chesney said.

"For what stakes?"

"If I win, they go free."

The Devil's eyes were bright. "And if you lose?"

"They still go free. But I don't. I will relieve you of the agreement that rankles you so."

"No more coming and going as you like?" the Devil said. "No more asinine crimefighting? No more forcing one of my subjects to do good?"

"That's right," said Chesney.

Satan regarded him for a long moment, when there was no sound in the room but the crackle and pop of the fire. "And your insignificance?"

"On the table."

The Devil said, "Get the cards."

The room had expanded once more, making the dais wider. Satan still sat on his writhing throne, but now a felt-covered table had appeared before him. Chesney recognized it. The Devil had dispatched Xaphan to bring them something to play on, and the demon had brought the five-sided poker table the young man had designed and built himself. As his demon positioned one of the Ikea chairs for Chesney to sit on, he gave the fiend an inquiring glance. But the weasel face remained impassive.

A pack of cards appeared on the table, the same cards that Chesney had bought for the times his fellow actuaries came over to play. He opened the deck, removed the jokers, and began to shuffle them. "Dealer's choice?" he said.

"Fine," said the Devil. "Cut for first deal?"

Chesney divided the deck into two stacks, riffled them together and placed the reunited cards on the table. "First," he said, "we need to agree on some ground rules." Satan raised one eyebrow, but Chesney pressed on: "You don't look at my cards; you don't rig the deck; you play the cards you're dealt – no substitutions."

"You call me a cheat?" The Devil's eyes narrowed.

"I call you the one who invented cheating."

The entity on the throne shrugged. "Fair enough."

"You agree to the rules I've stipulated?"

"Why not?" Again the knowing smile. "I've just reviewed every hand of poker you've ever played. I can't lose."

He's trying to psych me, Chesney thought, and it's working. But he shook off the chill that had settled between his shoulders. "We'll play seven hands, and we'll each start out with the same number of chips. The winner is the one who has the most after the last hand."

"Agreed." The Devil gestured to Xaphan, hovering nearby. Instantly, two blocks of pale colored poker chips, each consisting of ten stacks of ten, appeared on the table, one at each player's elbow.

Chesney pushed the cards into the middle of the table. "High card deals."

The Devil split the deck halfway down. The turn-up was the jack of spades. Chesney cut the cards a few below where Satan's fingers had reached. "Eight of hearts," he said.

Lucifer drew the cards toward him and shuffled them. "The classic game," he said. "Seven card stud, nothing wild. Ante up."

Chesney pushed a single chip to the middle of the green felt. The little disc was hard and smooth, with a fine grain visible beneath the polished surface. "Is that ivory?" he said.

Satan smiled. "Dead men's bones." He flicked a chip to place it next to Chesney's then dealt two down cards to himself and the young man. The next cards were dealt face up: the ace of diamonds for Chesney; the Devil drew the four of clubs.

"Ace to bet," said Lucifer.

Chesney looked at his hole cards: a deuce and the ace of spades. He pushed five chips out to join the antes. Satan checked his own hole cards, and saw the bet. Then he picked up the deck and dealt two more cards face up. Chesney got a deuce of hearts, Satan the king of hearts.

Chesney pushed ten chips forward. The Devil turned over his two face cards. "Fold," he said.

Chesney raked the chips toward him. He now had one hundred and six to the Devil's ninety-four. He gathered the cards and shuffled them. "Five-card draw," he said. "One draw, nothing wild."

They anteed again and Chesney dealt the cards. He fanned his hand and saw a five, six, seven and eight of mixed suits, and a jack. "Your bet," he said.

"Five," said Satan, pushing the chips to the middle of the table.

Chesney saw the bet and said, "Cards?"

The Devil discarded one card; a moment later, so did Chesney. He looked at the new recruit: a nine. "Bet?" he said.

"Ten."

Chesney looked at his straight. He pushed twenty chips forward. "See you and raise you ten."

The Devil matched Chesney's stack. "Call," he said.

Chesney laid out his straight. Lucifer showed a club flush, the highest card a seven. He raked in the pot and now he had one hundred and twenty chips to Chesney's eighty.

"Let's do that again," he said, threw an ante into the middle of the table, and dealt five cards each. Chesney anteed and looked at his cards. He had been dealt nothing he could use – not even a low pair, and his highest card was a nine.

"Fold," he said.

The Devil collared the two lonely chips and passed the deck to Chesney. "One hundred and twenty-one to seventy-nine," he said.

"I know," said Chesney, throwing another chip out to the middle of the table. "Let's play your game." He dealt two cards down to each of them then waited for his opponent to ante. When the Devil's chip joined his, he dealt two cards face up. His was a king; so was Satan's. "Your bet," he said, lifting the edges of his hole cards for a peek. He had drawn two queens.

The Devil's impassive face revealed nothing as he checked his own down cards then pushed five chips forward. Chesney saw the bet and dealt two more cards: a four for himself, a six for Satan. "Still to you," he said.

Lucifer set down five more chips in the middle of the felt. Chesney matched him and dealt two more cards, and now each of them had a pair of kings showing. The Devil lifted his hole cards, as if he might have forgotten what was there, and smiled at Chesney – not a winning smile, but a winner's. "Ten," he said.

"See your ten and raise you ten," said the young man.

"I'll see that," said Lucifer and the game continued.

Chesney's next card was a queen; the Devil's was a ten. "My bet," said the young man. "Twenty." He was counting out the chips when the Devil folded. And now it was Chesney's turn to hold a hundred and twenty chips to the Devil's eighty.

Satan gathered up the cards, threw a chip out to ante, and said, "Five-card draw, deuces wild," but did not deal the cards. Instead, he sat back and shuffled the deck slowly, his head cocked to one side to study Chesney.

"Tell me," he said, "How did you feel when you killed that man?"

Chesney thought about it. He could recapture the moment exactly. "Sad."

"He was your enemy."

"Before. He was my enemy before. Then he was just a human being who was being tortured."

"You triumphed over him, yet you felt sad?"

Again, Chesney recaptured the moment. "I felt right about exposing his lies. The truth had to come out."

"But the truth led to his being killed and consigned to my punishers."

"That was the fate he had lined up for himself," the young man said. "He gambled and lost." He saw the Devil watching him and said, "Why are you bringing this up now? Are you trying to distract me from the game? When I'm winning?"

Lucifer kept on shuffling the cards and looked away. "Do you think you're winning?"

"Yes."

The Devil's response was a short laugh and a fast deal of the cards. Chesney picked his up and spread them to see what he had. A pair of sixes, a jack, a nine – and a deuce.

"Your bet," said Satan.

"You didn't answer my question. Why the questions?"

The Devil examined his cards. "You interest me," he said.

"I annoy you. You would like to hurt me."

Satan pulled a card from the middle of his hand and tucked it into one end of the fan. "I am capable of mixed emotions. You have caused me a lot of trouble. You have brought... uncertainty into what had seemed... settled."

Chesney said, "I have only tried to do what is right."

"As you saw it."

"Yes."

"That is one of the things that interest me about you. Given the opportunity to gratify yourself, you choose to pursue an ideal. That, in itself, is not rare. But it is usually accompanied by a surrender to the sin of pride – a perverse self-gratification from self-denial. You don't fall into that trap. It makes you... uncommon."

Chesney put ten chips in the middle of the table. "The people who studied me when I was young said that I had a simple mentality."

"The simple are as susceptible to sin as the complex," Satan said, putting ten chips beside Chesney's then adding ten more. "Their sins are just less... elaborate. You are different."

Chesney saw the Devil's raise and discarded the jack and the nine. He noticed that his opponent held on to all of his cards. "Standing pat?" he said.

"I think I will."

Lucifer dealt Chesney two cards: a seven, and another six. "Still your bet," the Devil said.

Chesney calculated the odds. Four sixes was not a terribly strong hand when there were still three wild cards unaccounted for and when the other player was playing the cards he was originally dealt. The Devil might be bluffing, or he might be sitting there with four of a kind.

Chesney felt the urge to push, that wild feeling that came over him only when he was playing poker, the sense that anything was possible, that he should draw his saber and charge.

But from the corner of his eye, he could see Denby and Poppy and Melda. He turned and looked at them. The policeman's face was a composite of anger and fear, with an undertone of shame; Chesney thought it probably bothered the man deeply that he could not resolve this situation, but had to rely on an actuary. Poppy's face was a blank; she seemed to have succumbed to shock and despair.

But Melda was looking directly at the young man and when their eyes met she gave three little nods that said, *You can do it. I believe in you.*

What he saw in Melda McCann's face should have strengthened his urge to push his luck. If he bet high and won this hand, Lucifer would find it hard to recover enough chips to win the over-all contest. If he folded now, their chip counts would be about even; they would play one more hand, and he only had to beat the Devil by one chip to win the chance to leave with the three people he had just freed from eternal torment.

Melda clenched a fist and brandished it in a "go-for-it" gesture. But Chesney could not ignore Poppy's hopeless stare. He threw his cards onto the table and said, "I fold."

The Devil had a good poker face. But he also had pride. And when he raked in the chips and tossed the cards across the table to Chesney, the young man saw a flash of something cross the darkly handsome face. That some-thing, he realized, was the same expression he'd seen on Ron's face when he played Chesney for a healthy pot.

And them it struck him. All that talk about me being "different" and "interesting" – that was meant to make me feel unsure of myself, to remind me of how many times I'd lost a pot by not playing the odds. And with that real-ization came that other voice he'd been hearing in his head: he wants you not to trust your instincts. He knows that if you trust in yourself, you will win.

"Oh, doh-re-mi," Chesney said to himself. He'd been played and suckered. But he was still in the game. He had ninety-nine chips to the Devil's one hundred and one. And there were still two more hands to play. "Back to seven-card stud," he said.

They anteed and he dealt them two down cards each and one face up. Chesney had a pair of fours in the hole and a nine showing. The Devil showed a five. Chesney bet five chips. Lucifer folded, without even looking at his hole cards. "We're back where we started," he said, as Chesney took the two lonely chips from the middle of the green felt.

"You didn't even look at your cards," Chesney said.

"Didn't I?" Satan assembled the cards and shuffled the deck. "Perhaps I'm overconfident. After all, I really have nothing to lose."

He's trying to rattle me, Chesney thought. He's smarter than I am, and a lot slicker when it comes to knowing what makes people tick. Aloud, he said, "Let's play the last hand."

"Five-card stud," Satan said. He tossed in a chip and dealt them each a down card. Chesney peeked at his: the ace of hearts.

"Bet," said Lucifer, after he'd checked his own hole card.

"Five," said Chesney.

"I'll see you." Satan dealt the first face-up cards, a jack for Chesney, a king for himself. "My bet," said the Devil. He added ten chips to the pot.

Chesney saw the bet and watched Lucifer deal two more cards. A queen for Chesney, a second king for the Devil. "We might as well both just go all in," said Satan, pushing his chips across the felt. "Neither of us will fold this time."

The young man pushed the discs of bone into the middle of the table. "Let's see the cards," he said.

Lucifer tossed a card to Chesney. It was a king. Then he dealt the last king to himself. The Devil had three kings showing; Chesney had a jack, queen and king of mixed suits, and an ace in the hole. If Chesney's next and last card was a ten, he would have a king-high straight. Satan could beat that if his last card matched the hole card, giving him a full house of three kings over some other pair.

The Devil flicked a card across the table. Chesney saw it as it came toward him and his heart sank. "Nine of spades," said Lucifer. "Was that what you were looking for?"

Lucifer dealt himself a deuce. "No help," he said, "but then I suspect I don't need it." He flipped over his hole card. It was a five. "Beat three kings," he said.

Chesney hands were cold. His fingers felt numb. He reached to turn over his hole card, the useless ace that topped a busted straight, a losing hand that would send him to Hell. As his thumb and finger almost touched the card, he heard Melda McCann give a surprised yelp followed by a bark of anger. She spun around and squirted a stream of pepper spray at Xaphan, saying, "Keep your hands to yourself!"

The demon wiped the chemical off his muzzle with one stub-fingered hand then licked its palm. "Not bad," it said, "but I prefer rum."

The Devil looked around, scowling. But his eyes came back to the table as Chesney turned over his hole card. "I guess that's that," he said. He flipped the pasteboard oblong and blinked. The last time he had looked at it, it had been an ace; now it was a ten. And his losing hand was a king-high straight, good enough to roust Lucifer's three kings and chase them from the winner's circle.

A sudden chill filled the little room. Though the air remained still, the cards on the table were caught as if by a blast of wind and sent flying. The bone chips rattled in their stacks. Lucifer sat motionless on his throne, gripping the serpentine armrests so tightly that thick veins throbbed in the backs of his hands, moving like snakes trapped in quicksand. His dark eyes bored into Chesney with a fathomless malice but behind the animosity, Chesney thought he saw something else: call it uncertainty, even self-doubt; whatever it was, it was an unfamiliar feeling for the ruler of Hell, and a troubling one.

Xaphan appeared at Chesney's elbow. "Boss," it said, "we should get these people out of here. They don't belong."

Chesney came back from wherever he had been. "Yes," he said, "let's do that." To Lucifer, he said, "Goodbye," and thought about bowing his head – the Devil was the monarch of this place, after all – but something told him that would not be a welcomed gesture. He let Xaphan do it for him.

A moment later, they were in the park. "Get me out of this costume," Chesney said. Instantly, he was dressed in chinos, loafers and a checked shirt. Xaphan spoke quietly in Chesney's ear. The young man turned to the others and said, "If you want, we can make it so that you forget all of this."

Denby's face lost its rigor, but only for a moment. "No," he said, "and you're still under arrest." He reached for the young man but the demon growled and the policeman stepped back. His hands were trembling.

Chesney said, "Why don't I come in to the station voluntarily and we'll talk about it tomorrow?" To Xaphan he said, "Give the Lieutenant back his pistol."

"Ya kiddin me? That flatfoot?"

"Do it."

"It's in his holster." The demon rolled its eyes.

Denby looked from one to the other. "Nine o'clock tomorrow morning."

"I'll be there," Chesney said.

"Not him," the policeman said.

"Just me."

"One thing I can tell ya," Xaphan said, "if ya try to tell

people about it, they'll think ya got a screw loose and they'll send ya to the laughin' academy. I seen it all before."

"He's probably right," Chesney told the detective. Denby made a face but nodded in agreement.

Poppy spoke up, though in a small voice. "I'd like to forget it. I wish it had never happened."

"Done," the demon said.

Poppy looked about her. "What happened?"

"You fainted, Ms Paxton," Chesney said. "Lieutenant Denby is going to take you home."

The policeman took the hint and laid a gentle hand on the young woman's arm. She seemed a little vague but went with him when he guided her toward where he had left his unmarked car.

Melda watched them go. Then when Chesney turned to her with a questioning look, she said, "Not me."

"You might have bad dreams," the young man said.

"I've had worse."

"Shall I walk you home?"

"Why not?" She looked around, one hand rubbing her rump. "Where's that half pint weasel? I'll bet he left a bruise on me?"

The demon was visible to Chesney, hovering at head height to one side. "Xaphan, fix that," he said.

"Hey," said Melda, "the pain's gone."

"He apologizes," Chesney said. He took her arm and they walked toward the park gates.

"No, I don't," said his assistant. "I hadda do it."

"Why?"

"Distraction," the demon said, "while I fixed the cards."

"You what?"

"You was gonna lose. I turned the ace into a ten."

"Are you having a conversation with that thing?" Melda said, "cause I see your lips move but I don't hear anything."

"Xaphan was telling me," the young man said, "that he pinched your behind to create a distraction while he fixed it so that I won the game." To the demon, he said, "But Satan and I agreed there'd be no cheating."

"Uh-uh," said Xaphan. "The ground rules were that *he* couldn't cheat. Nobody said nothing about you 'n me."

"Surely, that was implied?"

The demon looked like a large weasel that had just heard a good joke.

Chesney relayed this to Melda. "Huh," she said, then after a moment's reflection, "you should keep that little weasel dude around. He's got some smarts."

"Long-term," Chesney said, "cheating the Devil out of something he wants can't be a good strategy."

Xaphan said, "I kinda got the feelin' he didn't really want you down there with all them other mugs. I think maybe he wants you up here, stirrin' the pot."

"Why?"

The fiend shrugged. "With the boss, you don't ask why. Sides, with this business, I don't think even he knows why. But I figure he figures he'll let you run and see where it all goes, get me?"

They were out of the park and crossing the street. Melda said, "I guess I'd better hear about this thing you got me into."

"It's a long story," Chesney said.

"That's all right. You can tell me while I fix us some supper." She looked Chesney over closely and appeared to come to a decision. "And if that's not enough time, you can finish telling me over breakfast."

"Ulp," Chesney said.

"Meantime, send the demon home."

They had reached her door. She found her key and unlocked it. Chesney turned to Xaphan and said, "I'll call you."

• • • •

Chesney did not get back to his apartment until almost noon the next day. His phone was blinking to tell him that he had a message. The number on the caller ID was Billy Lee Hardacre's, but the recorded voice that spoke in his ear was his mother's.

"Where are you on a Sunday morning?" she asked rhetorically. "I need to see you out here at Bill's as soon as you can get here."

"Xaphan," Chesney said.

Immediately, the demon was hovering beside him. "What?"

"I need to go to Hardacre's."

"Now? Sure."

They stayed at his room in Hell only long enough for his assistant to pour and drink a healthy tot of rum, then they were on the doorstep of the preacher's palatial house. Chesney went to knock then thought of something. "You didn't ask me," he said to Xaphan, "whether this has anything to do with crimefighting."

"Yeah, I know."

"How come? Have I just let myself in for some kind of infernal bill?"

"Nah," said the demon, "The boss says from now on you get service whenever you call, whatever you need, no extra charge."

"Why?"

"I told ya, ya don't ask why."

"I'll accept an educated guess."

The demon shrugged its shoulders. "Y'ask me," it said, "the boss is worried, count of all the things that's changin'. And a lot of those things kinda rub elbows with you. So when he keeps an eye on you, he's keepin' an eye on the general situation, see?"

"So he's watching me right now?"

"Maybe. Can't tell. You're out here talkin' to that preacher, I'd say it's a good bet."

"Hmm," Chesney said and gave the old-style bell-pull a tug. Chimes sounded from inside the house. A moment later the door was flung open.

"There you are," said his mother. "I phoned you three times yesterday evening and twice this morning. Where were you?"

"I… I was out."

"Well, I didn't think you were sitting there ignoring my calls. Where were you, and what were you doing?" She placed her hands on her hips, a stance that her son knew meant that she would not settle for less than a full and comprehensive explanation.

"I was with," he said, "a young lady."

A succession of expressions crossed Letitia Arnstruther's face: disbelief gave way to outrage then slid toward calculation. "Was it Miss Paxton?" she said, with a tone that said the situation might be bearable after all.

For a moment, Chesney was tempted to lie. He had, after all, spent part of yesterday with Poppy Paxton, not that she would remember any of it. But after what had transpired between him and Melda McCann in the past few hours, he felt that he had added a new pool of light to his existence and that he was standing in it now. "No," he said, "I was with Melda McCann," and knowing he might as well go for broke, he added, "my girlfriend."

There was a phrase Chesney had come across in old-time novels: "high dudgeon." He realized that he had until this moment had only a vague idea of what it meant, but that he was now seeing the exact definition, as his mother's eyes widened, her precisely arched brows rose to previously unscaled heights, and she said, "Now, you listen to me, young man–"

Then a broad masculine hand came from behind her, covering one of the fists planted on her hips, and an arm encircled her waist. Billy Lee Hardacre filled the rest of the doorway. "Now, now, Letty," he said, "we've got bigger fish to fry."

Chesney's mother's face went from high dudgeon to meek compliance – My goodness, the young man thought, she almost simpered – with a speed that outdid anything he could have achieved in his Actionary suit. "If you say so, Bill," she said.

The preacher drew her back to make way for Chesney. "Come on in, son," he said. "Might as well bring your little buddy with you. He's part of this, too."

The four of them crossed the broad foyer toward Hardacre's study, his arm still around Chesney's mother. "Part of what?" Chesney said.

"You remember," said the older man, "the angel who came to the negotiation?"

Chesney was not likely to have forgotten. "The Throne."

"Well, we've kept in touch. We've been working on something."

"What?"

"A new book."

"Another novel?"

"I'll show you," Hardacre said.

They neared the study. The door was closed, but a light shone from beneath it, from around the jamb, and through the keyhole. It was a pure serene light, much like the one Chesney imagined surrounded the parts of his life in which he felt clear-minded and competent.

"You're writing a sequel to the Bible?" he said.

Hardacre formed his mouth into a "sort-of" expression. "Call it a new chapter," he said.

Hardacre opened the door. A creamy light, sourceless

yet almost tangible, filled the study. It was brightest over the big, old desk, in the middle of which rested a stack of manuscript pages.

Xaphan said, "Wow, that stings!" and drew back into the foyer.

Hardacre used his free arm to guide Chesney toward the source of the glow. "I need you to look at the draft."

"Why?" said Chesney, "I'm no critic."

"No," said the preacher, "because of this." His finger touched the words centered at the top of the glowing page: *The Book of Chesney*.

Chesney squinted his eyes against the light then began to read the text. He finished the first page and began to read the second. After a few lines, he broke off and flipped through the pages at random, reading a sentence here, a paragraph there.

"You see," said Hardacre, "it's about you."

Chesney put the pages back in order. "No," he said, "it's not." He walked out into the foyer. "Xaphan! We're going."

ABOUT THE AUTHOR

Matt was born sixty years ago in Liverpool, England, but his family moved to Canada when he was five. He has made a living as a writer all of his adult life, first as a journalist, then as a staff speechwriter to the Canadian Ministers of Justice and Environment, and – from 1979 until a few years back – as a freelance corporate and political speechwriter in British Columbia. He is a former director of the Federation of British Columbia Writers and used to belong to Mensa Canada, but these days he's conserving his energies to write fiction.

He's been married to a very patient woman since the late 1960s, and he has three grown sons.

Of late, Matt has taken up the secondary occupation of housesitter, so that he can afford to keep on writing fiction yet still eat every day. He's always interested to hear from people who've read his work.

Matt's website:
www.archonate.com

AFTERWORD

The minority of readers who aspire to see their own names appear on the covers of novels and the tables of contents of anthologies may be interested in the genesis of this one. Even those who have no such ambitions may summon up a mild interest in how such things come to be.

It is a convoluted story, and I will ask the reader's kindness in following the twists and turns until we reach the heart of the labyrinth. Let us begin back in 2001, when the Aspect imprint of Time Warner Books released two Jack Vance-influenced science-fantasy novels of mine in paperback, just in time for the events of September 11 to turn the American mood rather sharply away from light and frothy satirical fantasy.

Warner Aspect did not ask for a third book, but a senior editor at Tor, the biggest SF publisher in the world, said he would be interested in seeing one in the same far-future setting. I duly wrote it and turned it in, and began to count down the eighteen months or so before it would appear. While doing so, it occurred to me that the new book was less likely to sink without trace if I raised my profile among prospective readers by writing stories for the SF magazines.

I wrote a short story about a far-future private detective, living in a city of Old Earth one age before Vance's Dying Earth. Gordon Van Gelder, editor of the *Magazine of Fantasy & Science Fiction*, bought it and intimated that he would not mind seeing another in the same vein.

Now, the story had begun as one of those what-if concepts, specifically "what if you came to realize that you were living in a world that was the result of some unknown someone's three wishes having gone bad?" I hadn't expected to take it any further, but the central character, the brilliant but egotistical discriminator Henghis Hapthorn, seemed to have potential so I wrote another story about him. It, too, sold.

I then wrote four more, and rather than make them self-contained episodes, I set them within a framing story: that from time to time and for no known reason, the operating principle of the universe switches from rational cause-and-effect to what we might call sympathetic association – or to use the vulgar term, magic.

The stories sold and Henghis Hapthorn became a beloved figure among at least some of the *F&SF* readers. My profile did rise, but not sufficiently to provide buoyancy to the Tor book when it came out in late 2004. By late 2005, I was casting about for a publisher again. This was during one of my having-an-agent periods, and the agent suggested that if I drafted up some novel outlines for Hapthorn, she would try to sell them.

I drafted them, out she went, and as always when I have an agent pitching for me, nothing came of it. One editor at a highly reputable small imprint, whom I will not name, wanted to buy the series. But he was overruled by his publisher and had to decline, an act that he said made him feel, for the first time, "evil."

The agent and I parted company, fairly amicably, and

I went on to sell the Hapthorn trilogy to Night Shade Books, who published the first in 2006 and the third in 2009.

So, let us recap: an idea that started out as the basis for one short story grew into six related stories (and a couple of one-offs besides) and then blossomed into three sequential novels. In modern publishing, that's not unusual: readers like series because they know what they're getting, and publishers like them because they can more reliably predict sales. So what started out as a concept for a few thousand words had to expand to fill a need for about three hundred thousand.

Now let us move on. The editor who was made to feel evil by his publisher also felt guilty. When we ran into each other in the queue waiting to go into the awards banquet at the 2007 World Fantasy Convention, he did me the favour of introducing me to Marc Gascoigne, who was then the publisher at Solaris books.

Later on, in the spring of 2008, I pitched Marc a concept for a fat-spined, two-volume, heroic fantasy about a war in Heaven, on Earth and in Hell, between archetypal figures who didn't know that all of them were the remnants of a god who had fragmented himself before dissolving himself into his Creation. Marc and his editorial team took it under consideration.

Then, for reasons that baffle the logical mind, Solaris decided to let Marc go. Naturally, that ended my attempt to interest him in my two-volume epic. But then, a few weeks later, I read in the trades that HarperCollins had snatched up Marc and asked him to launch the Angry Robot imprint. I immediately got back in touch and repitched the Heaven and Hell concept.

My idea was mulled, weighed, sifted – whatever it is that publishers and their helpers do – and ultimately found not suitable for the tone of Angry Robot. In the final days of 2008, Marc sent me an email to that effect.

Now, the reader may have gathered from the preceding paragraphs that I am not one to be crushed by rejection. As it happened, when I received the email, I was midway through writing another story intended for *F&SF*, about a nerdish fellow who accidentally causes Hell to go on strike and emerges from the resulting confusion as a costumed crimefighter with a Jazz Age demon as his reluctant helper.

Having read Marc's kindly "not right for us" email, I replied by attaching the half-finished rough draft of the Hell-goes-on-strike story and said, "Fair enough, how about this instead?" I received a reply in only a few days, in which Marc said he admired my get-back-on-the-horse attitude and would like to see the story when it was completed.

A week or so later, I sent the finished story to Gordon Van Gelder and to Marc. The former bought it for *F&SF* and the latter asked me where I saw the crimefighter going from the point at which I'd left him. I roughed out a few directions, sent them in, and, in not too long a while, received an expression of definite interest. After numbers had been crunched, somewhere around mid-2009, I had an actual offer – for three books and an option on a fourth.

Now all I had to do was take a character and situation I'd created to fill about twenty thousand words and evolve and extrapolate them to fill some three hundred and sixty.

Again.

In such a circumstance, some authors ask for divine help. I decided to dragoon it, and arranged for Jesus – the historical one at least – to become a character in the second book, which I finished a few weeks before this afterword was written.

Where it all goes from there, God only knows.

Matthew Hughes

ANGRY ROBOT

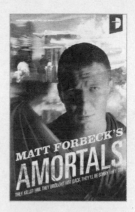